MAISEY YATES

Smooth-Talking Cowboy

A Gold Valley Novel

Praise for *New York Times* bestselling author Maisey Yates

"Fans of Robyn Carr and RaeAnne Thayne will enjoy [Yates's] small-town romance."
—*Booklist* on *Part Time Cowboy*

"Passionate, energetic and jam-packed with personality."
—USATODAY.com's *Happy Ever After* blog on *Part Time Cowboy*

"Yates writes a story with emotional depth, intense heartache and love that is hard fought for and eventually won in the second Copper Ridge installment.... This is a book readers will be telling their friends about."
—*RT Book Reviews* on *Brokedown Cowboy*

"The setting is vivid, the secondary characters charming, and the plot has depth and interesting twists. But it is the hero and heroine who truly drive this story."
—*BookPage* on *Bad News Cowboy*

"Yates's thrilling seventh Copper Ridge contemporary proves that friendship can evolve into scintillating romance.... This is a surefire winner not to be missed."
—*Publishers Weekly* on *Slow Burn Cowboy* (starred review)

"This fast-paced, sensual novel will leave readers believing in the healing power of love."
—*Publishers Weekly* on *Down Home Cowboy*

**Welcome to Gold Valley, Oregon,
where the cowboys are tough to tame, until they
meet the women who can lasso their hearts:**

Cowboy Christmas Blues (ebook novella)
Smooth-Talking Cowboy

**In Copper Ridge, Oregon, lasting love
with a cowboy is only a happily-ever-after away.
Don't miss any of Maisey Yates's
Copper Ridge tales, available now!**

From HQN Books

Shoulda Been a Cowboy (prequel novella)
Part Time Cowboy
Brokedown Cowboy
Bad News Cowboy
A Copper Ridge Christmas (ebook novella)
The Cowboy Way
Hometown Heartbreaker (ebook novella)
One Night Charmer
Tough Luck Hero
Last Chance Rebel
Slow Burn Cowboy
Down Home Cowboy
Wild Ride Cowboy
Christmastime Cowboy

From Harlequin Desire

Take Me, Cowboy
Hold Me, Cowboy
Seduce Me, Cowboy

Look for more Gold Valley books coming soon!

For more books by Maisey Yates,
visit www.maiseyyates.com.

MAISEY YATES

Smooth-Talking Cowboy

ISBN-13: 978-1-335-00698-1

Smooth-Talking Cowboy

Recycling programs
for this product may
not exist in your area.

Copyright © 2018 by Maisey Yates

The publisher acknowledges the copyright holder
of the individual work as follows:

Seduce Me, Cowboy
Copyright © 2017 by Maisey Yates

Printed in U.S.A.

CONTENTS

Dear Reader,

I'm so excited to welcome you to Gold Valley, Oregon, a small Gold Rush town nestled in the mountains, surrounded by ranch land. Where the cowboys are tough and hardworking - and they just need the right women to tame them.

In Smooth-Talking Cowboy, Olivia Logan is having a rough few months.

After a break-up she didn't really want, she's looking for a way to win her perfect boyfriend back - by enlisting the help of the most imperfect man she knows.

Luke Hollister is all wrong for the Princess of Gold Valley, but the two of them together somehow feels so right. And inconvenient lust might just turn into true love.

Happy Readings

Smooth-Talking Cowboy

CHAPTER ONE

OLIVIA LOGAN SUPPOSED it could be argued that she wasn't heartbroken, so much as she had broken her own heart. But it could not be argued that she had flattened her own tire.

Someone had left *something* sharp in the road for her to drive over with her little, unsuspecting car. Because people were eternally irresponsible, and Olivia never was. She never was, and still, she often got caught up in the consequences of said irresponsibility. Because such was life. That the idiot who left something treacherous in the road wasn't the one with the flat tire was another painful reality check.

Olivia had had quite enough of life being a pain in the rear. If there was a reward for being well behaved, she hadn't yet found it.

She got out of her car to look at the flattened tire in the back on the passenger side, bracing herself against the frigid wind that whipped up right as she did so. The typical chilly Oregon January weather did nothing to improve her mood.

And there it was. Silver and flat, sticking into her tire. A nail.

Of course. She was running late to work down at Grassroots Winery and she had a flat tire as well as a broken heart. So, all things considered, she wasn't sure it could get much worse.

She scowled, then looked down at her phone, trying to figure out who she should text. Normally, it would have been her boyfriend, Bennett, but he was now her *ex*-boyfriend because she had broken up with him last month at Christmas.

She had her reasons. Very good ones.

She couldn't text him now, obviously. And she probably shouldn't text his older brother Wyatt, or his *other* older brother Grant, because their loyalty to Bennett made them off-limits. Even for pitiful Olivia and her flat tire.

She was pondering her quandary, sitting on the outer edges of Gold Valley with her car halfway in the ditch when a beat-up red truck came barreling down from the same direction she had just come. Her stomach did a somersault and she closed her eyes, beseeching the heavens for an answer as to why she was being punished this way.

There was no answer. There was only a flat tire. And that red truck that she knew well.

Oh well. She needed rescuing. Even if it was by Luke Hollister. She moved closer to the road, crossing her arms and standing there, looking pathetic. At least, she had a feeling she looked somewhat pathetic. She *felt* pathetic.

Luke would stop, because despite being a scoundrel, a womanizer, he had that innate sense of chivalry that cowboys tended to possess. All *yes ma'am* and opening doors and saving damsels from the railroad tracks.

Or the side of the road, in this case.

The truck came closer, and she registered the exact moment Luke saw her. Felt it, somehow. She took a step back, making room for him to pull off and up next to her car.

His truck kept going.

She stared after him. "He didn't stop!"

She had been incredibly peeved that Luke Hollister had been the salvation she hadn't wanted, but she was even more peeved that he had declined his opportunity to be said salvation.

Then she saw brake lights, followed by reverse lights.

Slowly, the truck backed up, easing its way up beside her.

Luke leaned across the seat, working the crank window so that it was partway down. He had a black cowboy hat on, covering most of his dark blond hair, his green eyes glittering with humor beneath the wide brim. And then he smiled. That slow, lazy smile of his that always made her feel like he had spoken an obscenity.

"Olivia Logan, as I live and breathe. You seem to have gotten yourself in a bit of trouble."

"I didn't *get myself* into any *trouble*," she said crisply. "There was a nail in the road, and I now seem to have a flat tire." He just looked at her, maddeningly calm. "You weren't going to stop," she added, knowing she sounded accusing.

"I thought better of it. I'd hate it if you were eaten by wolves."

"There are no wolves here," she said, feeling impatient.

"They recently tracked one that came down from Washington. Just one though, so probably the worst that would happen is you'd get gnawed on, rather than eaten in your entirety."

"Well. I'm glad you decided to help me avoid a vicious gnawing," she said grumpily.

"I could change the tire for you," he said.

"Do you want to pull off the road before we have this discussion?" she asked.

He looked in his rearview mirror, then glanced back at her. "There's no one coming. It's not exactly rush hour."

"There is no rush hour in Gold Valley."

But that didn't mean someone wouldn't be pulling up behind him on the narrow two-lane road soon enough.

He still didn't move his truck, though.

"Luke," she said, "I need to go to work."

"Well, why didn't you say so? Do you have a spare tire?"

"Yes," she said impatiently.

"I'll tell you what. I'll drive you down to work, and then when I head back this way I'll fix your tire."

She frowned, suspicious at the friendliness. "Why would you do that?"

"Because I'm going that way anyway," he said. "You still work at the winery?"

She nodded. Grassroots Winery sat in between the towns of Copper Ridge and Gold Valley, and Olivia worked predominantly in the dining room at the winery itself. It wasn't, she supposed, the most ambitious job, which usually didn't bother her. She liked the ambience of the place, and she enjoyed the work itself. But she had always assumed that she would marry a rancher and help him work his land. Make a home for them. The way her parents had done. That seemed silly now that she was single, and there was no rancher in her future.

She had been sure that by now Bennett would have come back to her. Was sure that breaking up with him would make him realize that he had to commit or he could lose her.

Except he seemed all right with losing her. And that

was terrible, because she was not all right with losing him.

With losing that vision of her future that she had held on to for so long.

"How will I get home?" she asked.

"I could help you out with that, too, but I'll have your car in working order by then."

She narrowed her eyes. "Why are you being nice to me?"

That wicked grin of his broadened. "I'm always nice."

She let out an exasperated sound and clicked the lock button on her key fob before climbing into the passenger side of his truck. She struggled to get in because of her skirt and nylons, but finally shut the massive, heavy door behind her.

"Thank you," she said, knowing she sounded ridiculously prim and not really able to do anything about it. She *was* prim.

She grabbed hold of the seat belt, then pulled it forward, having to wiggle it slightly to get it to click. His truck was a hazard. She straightened, held tightly to her handbag and stared straight ahead.

"You're welcome," he said, stretching his arm over the back of the bench seat. His other forearm rested casually over the steering wheel. His cowboy hat was pushed back on his head, shirtsleeves pushed up past his elbows, forearms streaked with dirt as if he had already been working today. Which meant that he had likely been out at Get Out of Dodge before driving down toward town. She wondered if he had seen Bennett.

"Were you out at the Dodge place today?" She tried to ask casually.

"You want to know if I saw your boyfriend," Luke said. Not a question. A statement. Like he knew her.

And this, in a nutshell, was why she didn't really like Luke. He had a nasty habit of saying the *one* thing that she wished he wouldn't. With a kind of unerring consistency that made her suspect he did it on purpose.

"He's *not* my boyfriend. Not anymore."

"Still. You're wondering about him."

"Of course I wonder about him. I dated Bennett for a year. I'm not going to just…not wonder about him suddenly."

"I expect, Olivia, that you could go down to Get Out of Dodge on your own pretty feet and find out how he's doing for yourself if you had half a mind to."

Olivia cleared her throat and looked at Luke meaningfully. Which he seemed to miss entirely. "I don't know that I would be welcome," she said, finally.

"Come on. It's been at least…six months since Wyatt has run anyone off the property with a shotgun."

Olivia sighed. "You're a pain—do you know that?"

"Now, is that any way to talk to your roadside savior?"

"Normally, I would agree, but I suspect that you're trying to irritate me on purpose. Otherwise, you would have just answered my question." She settled back into the bench seat, looking down at the floor mats that were encrusted in mud. She had no idea why Luke had mats on the floor of his truck at all. It seemed ridiculous when the whole thing was covered in a fine layer of dust and small bits of hay.

She felt woeful on behalf of her black pencil skirt.

"You caught me," he said, sounding not at all contrite. "I am absolutely trying to irritate you. I would say that I'm succeeding, too. You do know how to make a man feel accomplished, Olivia."

"And you know how to make a woman feel feral, Luke."

"You and I both know you've never felt feral a day in your life, honey."

She wanted to argue with him. Except he had a point. But she was not going to give him the satisfaction of knowing that. Instead, she sniffed and looked out the window as they crossed into the town's city limits and drove down Main Street.

The redbrick gold rush era buildings that lined the streets were picturesque, and whenever her friends from college came in from out of town they commented on them. To her they were simply buildings, rather than charming relics that looked as though they could have come out of an Old West movie. To her, having lived in Gold Valley her entire life, it was home.

Sometimes she wondered what it would be like to see the town for the first time. With fresh eyes. To see it as something unique, rather than something that simply *was*.

The Logan family, founders of Logan County, had been the first settlers in the area, after coming from the East Coast on the Oregon Trail.

As they paused at the four-way stop she took a moment to look at the faded, painted advertisement on the side of Gold Valley Saloon. She couldn't quite make out what it said, and it was one of those things she had never really bothered to try to do, because it was something else that was simply there.

It was early in the day so the saloon sign—the only lighted sign allowed on Main Street, and only because it was a classic neon sign that had first been put up in the 1950s—wasn't turned on at such an early hour, and there was a large Closed sign propped up in the window. In fact, most of the businesses on Main were closed at this hour.

The coffeehouses were open already—three of them all within walking distance of each other—because if there was one thing Oregonians liked more than craft beer or wine, it was definitely coffee. The little greasy spoon café that had been there since the middle of the last century was probably packed full of people getting their daily hash browns and bacon.

They started driving again and that cut off her ruminations as they headed out of town and down the highway toward the winery.

"What business do you have down this far?" she asked.

"I was headed down to Tolowa to hit up the Fred Meyer. Got to grab a few things."

That was Luke. A man of few words until he wasn't, and then they were annoying ones.

"I see," she said.

"I didn't see Bennett this morning," he added. "Since you were wondering."

"Right. Well." And that made her wonder if he had been there. Or if he had spent the night somewhere else—which made her stomach feel like acid. All things considered, Bennett was probably happy that she had cut him loose. She of the self-inflicted metaphorical chastity belt, who had been making him wait to be intimate until he had proposed to her.

But now he was free.

She sniffed again.

She and Luke lapsed into silence as they continued down the winding road. Finally, Luke turned off the main road and onto the long, dirt drive that led up to the winery.

"This parking lot," she said, gesturing to the paved lot on the left.

The road forked there, and the right turn would have taken them up to Lindy Parker's house. Lindy owned the winery and lived on the grounds. The unintentional parting gift of her cheating husband after their divorce.

She hopped out of the red truck as quickly and delicately as possible, but even so, her skirt hiked itself up a few inches above her knees. She hurriedly pulled it down, and when she chanced a look back at Luke, she saw that he was looking at her a bit avidly. He smiled, and that same flipping sensation she had felt in her stomach when she had first spotted his truck made an irritating return.

"I still have your number from the beach trip," he said, referencing a time over the summer when a group of them had driven in a caravan over to the coast for a beach barbecue that she had ultimately found a bit too sandy to enjoy. "I'll text you. Let you know how things go with your car."

"Thank you," she said, trying to avoid sounding wooden and uptight, both things she had been accused of being several times over.

He was actually being nice, even if he was mixing some annoyance with it.

"You are very welcome." He reached up, grabbed the brim of his hat and tipped it slightly, and she felt something inside of her tip in response.

"I'll look for that text." She gripped her bag tightly and walked quickly toward the refurbished barn that was now a rustic but elegant dining room.

When she walked in, both Lindy Parker and her ex-sister-in-law, Sabrina Leighton, were standing at the window, staring out of it, and then turned to look at her with curious expressions on their faces.

"What?" Olivia asked, blinking.

"Who was that?"

"No one," Olivia said, and then suddenly realized how all of it looked. Her denial hadn't helped. "I got a flat tire."

Lindy only stared, and Sabrina's mouth quirked upward at the corner. "And you hitchhiked here?"

"No. I know him. I mean, he did pick me up on the side of the road. But, he's…a family friend." Of Bennett's family, but she didn't add that last part. Because it only underscored just how tangled up her life was with Bennett Dodge, and the whole rest of the Dodge family. That Luke was embroiled in her life simply because she had spent so much time at the dude ranch growing up.

Because her father and Bennett's father had always been so close, and because Olivia had carried a torch for Bennett for her entire childhood, all through high school, and then finally, that torch had become something real after college.

Her memories, her connections… She had so few that weren't involved in the Dodge family in some way. And now she wasn't really involved with them anymore.

Her thoughts had gone off track, and she had a feeling that Lindy and Sabrina were interpreting her silence to mean something different.

Lindy's follow-up question confirmed that. "A family friend?"

"Yes. He rescued me and is going to fix my car. Which seems really nice, but since he was on his way to Tolowa, it was actually just logical."

"Okay," Lindy said, clearly disbelieving.

Olivia sighed, and then her eye caught sight of something glittering on Sabrina's finger. "Sabrina. What is that?"

Sabrina curled her hands into fists. "We don't have to talk about it, not if you don't want."

Olivia didn't have to answer, because she knew exactly what it was. An engagement ring. Which meant that Sabrina's boyfriend of almost *no time at all* had already proposed to her.

Because apparently Olivia Logan was the only person in the entire county who was commitment proof.

"Congratulations," Olivia said, forcing a smile for as long as she could before turning away to keep from crying. She shed her long coat and hung her purse up on the peg, then took a deep breath, closing her eyes. She was not going to be a baby about this. She was going to be happy for her friend.

The whole world didn't stop just because she was going through a heartbreak, and she knew that. She still had to go to work, people still had to get engaged, her tire was still going to go flat, and Luke Hollister was still going to be a pain. Life went on. The world still turned.

"Thank you," Sabrina said, smiling. "It's hard to believe. Especially since until a couple of months ago I was mostly convinced that I hated Liam. And now I'm marrying him."

Those words hit Olivia in a funny way. Because she had never been confused about her feelings, not like that. She had always known that she loved Bennett Dodge. The same way that she'd always known she had to work to make her parents proud. To make sure she didn't cause them worry. The same way she had known since high school she wanted—needed—to be different than her sister. Better.

Olivia was, and always had been, confident in her feelings.

When she felt something it was set in stone. Just like she had always known that she didn't like whiskey, shellfish or Luke Hollister. And that was just how it was.

CHAPTER TWO

By THE TIME Luke Hollister pulled his truck into the driveway of Get Out of Dodge, it was lunchtime, and he had been paying closer attention to his texts than he would like to admit.

Just in case Olivia needed a ride.

He shook his head as he took a left in the long driveway and pulled around to the back of the property to the heavy equipment barn.

It was an involuntary reaction that he had to her. One he'd had for the past seven years or so. She always caught his attention when she was in the room. Like a shiny lure dangling in front of a fish.

He made her mad. She didn't like him, and that fascinated him. *Everybody* liked him. He could charm the panties off any woman and stay friends with her afterward. It was his gift.

But not Olivia Logan.

He got out of his truck and rounded to the back, opening the tailgate, a loud, rusted sound filling the air as it lowered. A smile curved his lips, imagining Olivia's prissy little self sitting in the cab of his truck earlier today.

She'd looked like she was terrified she was going to get his uncouthness on her, and she'd seemed particularly horrified by the thought.

And for some damned reason that thought made his

gut tight, made his blood run a little bit hotter and a little bit faster.

Hell no. That woman was off-limits for a host of reasons. Starting with *he didn't get involved with women who wanted more than a night of fun* and ending somewhere around *her being Bennett Dodge's ex-girlfriend.*

Bennett was like a brother to him and there was no way in hell he was stepping in the middle of that.

He let out a long, slow breath, visible in the frigid cold air, and started to unload the bed of the truck. Wyatt had insisted they had to start making a little bit more of a show out of the place, so he'd been sent to pick up curtains, bed sets and rugs.

It was Wyatt's show, after all.

The Dodge family might feel like his own in some ways, but he wasn't part of them, not really. Still, if a man could become blood brother to a place, he had certainly become family with Get Out of Dodge. Enough of his own blood had soaked into the dirt, and he had absorbed a hell of a lot of its dust into his lungs.

Not that he and Wyatt were at odds when it came to what to do with the ranch. But sometimes Luke felt nostalgic for how it had been ten years ago. When he'd first arrived with no knowledge of how to work a ranch, no money in his pocket and no one on earth who cared if he was dead or alive. Back then, Quinn Dodge had run the place. The patriarch of the Dodge family was a gruff, no-frills kind of man, and Luke had appreciated his method of doing things.

Wyatt Dodge wasn't a frilly guy himself. The oldest of the Dodge children was just pragmatic. He had recognized that with the influx of tourism coming into the neighboring coastal town of Copper Ridge, they could certainly capture some of that for Gold Valley. Luke agreed. But he also resented the fact that the back of his truck was filled with doilies.

"You got the stuff," Wyatt said, walking into the shed and wiping his forehead with his forearm.

"I did," Luke said. "And, I think we should make Jamie get all of the rooms decorated. Tell her it's women's work."

"Right. I'm not in the mood to die at the hands of my little sister, thanks. She would probably hit me in the face with a shovel and ask me if that's women's work, too." Wyatt leaned back, stretching and then grunting, putting his hand down on his lower back. "You know what else is a stupid idea?" he asked.

"What?"

"Riding bulls into your midthirties. My back was ready to quit way before I was."

There was a lot of money to be had in the rodeo as long as a man was good at what he did, and as long as he was smart with the money he made. Wyatt Dodge was smart. "Good thing you gave it all up to become an interior designer at your dude ranch," he said.

Wyatt snorted. "You hungry?"

"Starving."

"If you want to head on over to the mess hall there's some leftover chili in there."

The food situation was another issue they were actively working to sort out. Wyatt had been searching for a cook that could provide an authentic dude-ranch-type experience, but could do it in an elevated kind of way. At least, those were the words that he had used. That was another thing that Luke was fine with as it was.

Luke didn't particularly like change.

He didn't think the place needed to change. He'd spent his childhood entertaining himself. Riding his bike outside alone for hours, and when the weather was bad, inside watching old Westerns on the classic movie channel.

He'd always wanted to be a cowboy. A man who lived for the land. Who lived for honor and riding off into sunsets.

Then he'd moved to Gold Valley and found that dream at Get Out of Dodge. Now he felt like it was slipping away, along with his place in it.

Silently, he followed Wyatt into the kitchen, got down a bowl and filled it up with a good measure of chili, then piled a bunch of cheese and sour cream on top. Then, the two of them walked back out into the empty dining room and took seats at one of the long tables.

The benches weren't the most comfortable seats, it had to be said, but it was familiar. Home, as far back as he liked to remember.

The doors opened again, and in came Bennett, followed by Grant, Wyatt's younger brothers who had decided to go all in on the ranch when Wyatt had started this reinvigoration process.

"I'm starving," Grant said. "Chili?"

"What does it look like?" Wyatt asked.

"Like you got up on the wrong side of the bed," he returned.

"Don't ask stupid questions of a man who has been up since before dawn."

Bennett snorted. "You're always like this. Don't go blaming a lack of sleep. Anyway, this is your venture, jackass. The rest of us are just along for the ride."

"No one made you come. You got on the ride." Wyatt spread his arms wide. "Get off at any time."

"Right," Grant said, "because there were a field full of options available to me."

All of the Dodge brothers had spent their lives working the ranch in some capacity or another while supplementing their incomes with other work over the years. Grant had gotten married at eighteen and had taken a job working at the power company, where he had worked his way up over the years, needing a place that provided benefits because his wife had been sick.

He had carried on working there even after Lindsay had died. But when Quinn Dodge had remarried and retired abruptly a year ago, and Wyatt had decided that it was his time to try and give the ranch new life, Grant and Jamie had both decided to go all in with him.

Bennett, on the other hand, had a thriving veterinary practice working on ranch animals. But still, because he was his own boss, working with his friend Kaylee Capshaw, he did get to determine his own hours, and that meant he was able to invest time and a decent amount of money into the ranch.

Also, the fact that they had their own vet was damned helpful.

As for Luke, for him it had always been Get out of Dodge. But the more it changed, the more the Dodge children took control, the more he realized it had never really been his.

"Hey," Wyatt said to Grant, "you had a desk job. A lot of men would like a desk job."

"Yeah, those men have never had one," Grant said drily, moving to the dining room and heading toward the kitchen. Bennett followed close behind.

"You keep giving them a hard time and they are going to mutiny," Luke commented.

Wyatt lifted a shoulder. "They won't."

That was Wyatt all over. Sure of his place in the world. Sure of his authority.

Bennett and Grant returned and took their seats at the table with their bowls of chili.

"I've got vaccinations in a couple of hours," Bennett said. "So, if you have anything you need me to get done, now's the time to ask."

"What's that for?" Grant asked, "Rabies?"

"Scabies," Wyatt said, "probably."

"I'm not going to dignify that with a response," Bennett said.

"Why?" Luke asked, figuring it was time to join in the harassment of the youngest Dodge brother. "Is it something worse? A below-the-belt issue?"

"Vaccinating a litter of puppies," he said.

"You coming out drinking tonight?" Wyatt asked. The question was directed at Bennett. "Because you really should. Considering you're a free agent now."

"You never harass Grant about being a free agent."

Grant let out a harsh breath. "Because I'm not really."

"You should," Luke said to Bennett. Eager to smooth over that momentary rough patch. That was what he did. It was why people liked him around. "You can come, too, Grant. At least just because there's alcohol."

"Not my thing," Grant responded.

Luke wasn't going to press it. In his opinion, it was time for Grant to move on. Lindsay had died eight years ago. Of course, that was an easy conclusion for him to draw, since he had never been in love before. He didn't know what it was like to lose someone he felt that way about.

He had lost his mother, but that was different.

"Since when is beer not your thing?" Bennett asked.

"I like to do my drinking alone," Grant answered.

"That's concerning," Wyatt said.

Grant lifted a shoulder. "I'm concerning. That's not a newsflash. Anyway, you guys go out. Drink. I'm going to go home like an old person and sit in front of the TV."

Luke didn't see the appeal in that at all. But then, he wasn't a huge fan of solitude in general. He found that the louder it was, the less he had time to think. And he liked that. In general, he preferred to drink or fuck until he fell asleep. Because the alternative was to lie there and let memories chase around in his head like rabid foxes.

He really didn't see the appeal in that.

"I gave Olivia a ride to work this morning," Luke said, addressing the eight-hundred-pound breakup that seemed to be sitting in the middle of the table at the moment. "She had a flat tire."

Bennett looked up. "Really?"

"Yep."

He lifted a brow. "I bet she didn't like that."

"No. She did not. But then, you know she's eternally surprised when the world dares go against her express wishes."

"Yes," Bennett said. "I do know that about her."

Luke always had a hard time getting a read on Bennett's feelings for Olivia. The relationship had been a funny one. Intense, on Olivia's part. Which was why it was odd that she was the one who had done the breaking up. At least, from Luke's point of view.

"She'll come around," Luke said. "I mean, if you want her to. She asked about you."

Bennett took a bite of his chili. "Hey, she broke up with me."

"Lindsay broke up with me once," Grant said. They all looked at him, because Grant rarely mentioned Lindsay at least not by name. There was a lot of alluding to the past, to his marriage. But he didn't say her name very much. "Seriously. We were seventeen."

"Why?" Wyatt asked.

"It was when she got sick again. She was in recovery when we started dating. It came back and she wanted to let me go."

"How'd you change her mind?" Luke asked.

"I proposed," Grant said. "Told her I was in it for real, and it wasn't up to her to tell me how to live my life. That I wanted one with her."

They were silent for a moment.

"Proposing would have worked with Olivia," Bennett said. "That is why she broke up with me. I didn't propose to her on Christmas Eve."

"What are you waiting for?" Luke asked. "I thought that was the plan. To marry her."

It had seemed inevitable from the time the two of them had started dating a year ago. The obvious conclusion to something that they'd been circling for years. They were the two most respected families in town. Everybody knew that Bennett Dodge and Olivia Logan were destined to be together.

"Yeah," Bennett said. "It was. But I don't know. She broke up with me. So I'm taking the time to think about that. I care about her. She's a sweet girl. I mean, maybe *sweet* is the wrong word. But she's... She's something."

Luke chuckled. Yeah, Olivia Logan sure as hell was something. He finished up his lunch, then stood, going into the kitchen and rinsing out his bowl before passing back through the dining room. "I've got work to do," he said. "Hey—" he directed that at Bennett "—you can work on decorating the cabins."

"What?" Bennett asked, frowning. "How did I get nominated for that?"

"I'm your boss, little brother," Wyatt said. "And I say you need to hang some curtains."

Bennett laughed. "I'm the only one with a thriving business independent of this place. I'll pay to have someone else come and do it before I go hang any damned curtains."

"Save your money for some G-strings down at The Frisky Mermaid," Wyatt said, referring to the strip club down in Tolowa. "Since that's about all the skin you're seeing these days."

That forced Luke to think about the skin that Bennett had been seeing. Olivia's skin. Pale and pretty, and easy to turn pink with indignation. He wondered if she turned pink all over when she got like that. If her anger heated her cheeks, and other parts of her body, too.

He cleared his throat. "Yeah," he added. Feeling like it was a pointless addition, but needing to reorient.

Yeah, Olivia was hot. And there was something about that prim little attitude, that stuck-up manner of hers that got under his skin. Didn't mean he should be thinking about hers.

"See you tonight," Wyatt said.

"Yep," Luke responded, already heading out of the mess hall and back toward the machine shed.

He had work to do. And if there was one thing that had always provided him with some measure of sanity, it was work.

CHAPTER THREE

OLIVIA FELT LIKE there was a spotlight shining down on her as she walked into the Gold Valley saloon. Because she was alone, and she was certain that everybody in the room had taken note of that.

Happily, her boss, Lindy, had agreed to drive her back to her car, so she hadn't had to call Luke to come and pick her up from work. And also happily, he had made good on his promise to fix her car.

She frowned slightly thinking of that. That had been… Well, it had been awfully nice of him. It had saved her the cost of a tow truck. And the cost of getting the tire fixed. It wasn't like her dad wouldn't have paid for it. But she didn't want to inconvenience him. And he wasn't very happy with the way everything had gone down with Bennett. Ultimately, he probably would have badgered her into calling Bennett to try and patch things up with him.

She wanted things patched up with Bennett. She did. Which was why she was here in the bar, alone.

She frowned and edged up to the bar, sitting gingerly on one of the tall stools. For somebody who really wasn't a big bar person she sure did end up spending a lot of time in them. She didn't do much drinking, and she didn't especially like loud environments. But all of her friends seemed to. So when everyone went out after work they inevitably ended up either at Ace's in Copper Ridge or here.

Laz Jenkins, the owner of the bar, sidled down to her end, a broad smile on his face. "Good evening, Olivia. Your usual?"

Her usual was a Diet Coke. She sighed. "Yes." She looked down at the scarred bar top, at the contrast between her perfectly manicured hands and the rough-hewn wood. Then she looked up at Laz's broad back. "Thank you," she added, because she realized she had forgotten her manners. And Olivia Logan never forgot her manners.

It was early, and the bar was mostly empty, but she knew that they would be here. If she had wanted to avoid them, she would have gone down into Copper Ridge. Actually, if she had wanted to avoid them she would have gone home.

Her phone buzzed and she looked down.

Are you home yet?

It was from her mother. She lived in a little house on her parents' property, so her mother probably had a fairly good idea that she wasn't home.

No.

Will you be late?

Olivia sighed and brought up the little phone icon next to her mother's name. "I'm at the saloon," she said crisply when her mother picked up.

"Okay," her mom responded.

"Is everything all right?" She always defaulted to

worry. Which was funny, because Tamara Logan also defaulted to worry automatically. Olivia knew why. It was Vanessa's fault. But Vanessa wasn't within reach, which meant that Olivia was the focus of all her parents' concern.

In high school, one slip in her GPA and her parents had been terrified she was on the same dark path as her sister. They were twins, after all. And if Vanessa was susceptible, why wouldn't Olivia be, too?

She'd been treated like a rebellious teenager when she'd never once set a foot out of line.

"Everything's fine," her mom answered. "I was just curious if you were sitting at home or if you had gone out."

"I'm not with Bennett," she said.

Then, as if on cue, the door opened and there he was. Bennett and his brother Wyatt. Followed closely by Luke Hollister.

Her throat tightened, her stomach squeezing as if somebody had wrapped their fingers around it and made a fist.

"Have fun," her mom said, clearly sounding concerned.

"I will."

"Don't drink unless you have a ride."

In spite of her general physical distress Olivia laughed. "Mom, I never drink."

"I know. You always were a good girl."

That made her feel guilty. Guilty for being annoyed with her mom when her feelings were borne of concern. And not concern that came out of nowhere.

Olivia hung up and put the phone down with shaking fingers, just as Laz set her drink down on a block of wood that functioned as a coaster.

"Thank you," she said.

He treated her to another dazzling smile, his dark eyes twinkling. He was a lot older than she was, in his forties, maybe. It was difficult to guess his age. But she could definitely see why women came to the bar to stare at him.

Everything in her tensed as she turned away from the bar and back toward the door, lifting her Diet Coke. Bennett would have to come over eventually. Because he would have to order a drink.

The door opened again, and in came Jamie Dodge and Kaylee Capshaw. Jamie was the youngest of the Dodge siblings, a year younger than Olivia, and hadn't spoken to her since Bennett and Olivia had broken up.

And then there was Kaylee. Kaylee, Bennett's best friend. Who was only a friend, and Olivia had always believed that. She had always liked Kaylee. She truly had.

But for some reason the sight of the tall redhead made her stomach go from tight to curdled. It could be because Kaylee had been there the night she and Bennett had broken up. Because Bennett had brought her along when Olivia had been certain he was going to propose to her at the opening of the tasting room for Grassroots Winery in Copper Ridge over Christmas.

It had made perfect sense to her. Absolutely perfect sense.

They had been together for over a year and known each other almost their whole lives. It had been Christmas. Romantic. And he had brought her, which had made it clear he hadn't seen that night as momentous or romantic at all. Then when she'd told him how upset she was, he'd said he wasn't going to propose yet.

Just thinking about the entire situation made her face

hot. Made her feel like she was going to break into thousands of little pieces.

Of course, it wasn't Bennett whose eyes she caught. It was Jamie. Who looked at her like she was a particularly regrettable beetle that had wandered into her path. Kaylee, in contrast, smiled. The redhead conferred with Jamie for a moment, who frowned and went to sit at the table with her brothers and Luke.

It was Kaylee who made her way over to the bar. "Hi, Olivia," Kaylee said.

Kaylee was nice. That was the problem. It made Olivia feel mean having bad feelings about her.

"Hi," Olivia said.

"Are you meeting someone here?"

"I…"

She wasn't. That answer was sad. That answer revealed that she was very clearly stalking Bennett. She couldn't deny that. Not even to herself. She was. She was full on stalking her ex-boyfriend. Her ex-boyfriend who was her ex because she had gotten angry and broken up with him because he hadn't been doing things according to her timeline. She had been so certain that by ending things she would make him see that his life was empty without her.

But he was in the Gold Valley Saloon with his family and friends. She was sitting at the bar by herself drinking a Diet Coke.

Getting chatted up with *pity* by his best friend.

"I was actually hoping to see Luke," she said.

The lie rolled off her tongue easily. Which was strange, because she was not a liar. In fact, she was a terrible liar. She was well known for that in her family because her sister, Vanessa, had been such an accomplished deceiver, while Olivia had always turned bright red and been unable to make eye contact with the person she was attempting to fool.

She had stopped trying by the time she was eight years old.

"Luke?" Kaylee asked, her eyebrows shooting upward.

"Yes," Olivia responded. "He rescued me this morning." That at least was the truth. "I mean, my car got a flat tire and he happened to be driving by just at the right time. He gave me a ride to work. And then he fixed the car. I owe him a drink." As if she and Luke had discussed this.

"Oh," Kaylee said again, regarding her with a thoughtful expression.

Olivia smiled, attempting to look enigmatic, which no one had ever accused her of being a day in her life, and took another sip of her Diet Coke.

"Can I get you something, Kaylee?" Laz asked. He remembered everyone.

"A few shots of whiskey would be great. Whatever's cheap and still good."

He nodded. "How many rounds?"

"Four," she said, "I guess. Because I hear that Luke Hollister's is on Olivia."

Laz raised his brows, and then went about pouring Kaylee's shots. Olivia tried to appear engrossed in drinking her soda. Kaylee looked at her a couple of times, smiling awkwardly, and Olivia attempted to seem serene.

Then Kaylee collected the shots and went to the table everyone was sitting at. She said something to Luke, who cast a glance back at Olivia. Her stomach tightened. If he kept doing that she wasn't going to be able to take another drink of her soda. There would be nowhere to fit it.

She was afraid he was going to make her look like an idiot. That he was going to say she was crazy and he was of course not meeting her here. Because he had not planned to meet her here. She actually hadn't spoken to him at all since she'd collected her car. Which was rude, she realized.

But she just didn't like making overtures to Luke. He was a pain. And he always made her feel like she had an itch beneath her skin.

When he stood, saying something to the Dodge siblings with a big smile on his face, she felt like she'd been kicked in the chest by a horse. And then he was walking over to her. She crossed her legs, then wobbled, because she was up on a stool and it was an impractical position. She braced herself on the counter and blinked, then took a quick drink of her soda. Then set it down. She wasn't exactly sure what she wanted to be doing by the time he got to the counter. And then he was there, so the entire performance was moot.

"I hear we're meeting? And that you're buying me a drink?"

She pursed her lips and nodded. Then took another drink of her Diet Coke. "As a thank-you," she said finally after she swallowed her sip.

"Oh. A thank-you. Funny how I didn't get one earlier."

"I thanked you," she said. "You know. After you picked me up off the side of the road."

"But not for fixing your tire. And you didn't text me. I thought you were going to let me know if you had a ride."

"I thought I was going to let you know if I needed a

ride. And my boss gave me one. So I didn't." She cleared her throat. "Thank you. For fixing the car. I really do appreciate it. And I do owe you a drink."

"Is it possible that you were covering your ass, though? Because you didn't want to tell Kaylee that you were here to stare at Bennett all evening?"

Her face got hot and she had a feeling she was lit up like the damned neon sign that hung outside the saloon. "No… I don't…"

Her gaze drifted over to the table, to where Kaylee and Bennett sat next to each other. That stomach tightening turned into a twist. A mean, painful twist that sent a metallic taste flooding through her mouth.

"You don't care." Luke leveled his gaze on her. "Laz," he called out. "Can I get a shot? Something really good, because Olivia Logan is paying. And you know she's good for it."

Laz nodded and set about to pouring another measure of amber liquid into Luke's glass.

"Excuse me?" Olivia asked.

"I changed your tire, Olivia," Luke said. "Don't go getting me cheap alcohol."

"No. What do you mean *I don't care*?"

Luke sat next to her, his broad shoulder nearly brushing hers as he took his position on the stool. "You don't care about Bennett."

"Yes," she said. "I *do*. I care about Bennett… A lot. I love him."

"Why did you break up with him then?"

"It's complicated," she said.

"It's not that complicated. You want to be with him or you don't."

Great. She was getting lectured about love and relationships by a man whose longest relationship had been with his pickup truck. "I needed to be sure that he wanted to be with me," she said stiffly.

"Okay," he said, arching a brow. "By breaking up with him?"

"Well," she returned, "it's informative. I mean... I guess at this point not so informative in the way that I wanted it to be."

"You wanted him to see what he was missing?" Luke asked.

For all that he pretended not to understand her feelings, he seemed to understand pretty well. Better than she would like, actually. She didn't like that he could see through her quite so easily because if Luke could, surely everyone could. "Yes," she answered reluctantly.

He lifted a shoulder. "I still don't think you care."

She picked up her soda, and then redirected, brought it down hard on the bar. "I do care." Her heart was pounding and she was breathing fast. "Stop acting like you know what I want. Or you know what I think. You don't actually know me."

"Olivia Logan, I have known you since you were a stuck-up little girl. And I know you now that you're a stuck-up woman." Laz slid the tumbler of whiskey down in front of Luke and Luke tipped it up to his lips, downing it in one go.

Luke leveled his gaze at Olivia. "Don't tell me I don't know you."

"I'm not stuck-up," she said, bristling.

He shifted in his seat and her eyes were drawn to where his hand was wrapped around his glass. He had strong hands. A working man's hands. Callused and rough, vaguely dirty around the fingernails even when they were clean.

She imagined that they'd be rough to the touch. That they would scrape against her skin.

If she were to shake hands with him, or something. Because there were no circumstances otherwise under which they would ever touch.

She looked away.

"Okay, Olivia." His tone was so maddeningly placating it made her want to punch him.

"I'm *not*. Why do you think I'm stuck-up?"

"Because right now you're looking at me like I'm something you stepped in out in the cow pasture. In fact, you look at a lot of the world that way."

"I'm in a bar." She waved her hands around. "Which is not my natural habitat. I don't think I'm *better* than the bar, I just don't feel like I know my place in it. And anyway, you're not nice to me."

"Honey, I fixed your flat tire earlier and gave you a ride to work. What do you mean I'm not nice to you?"

She trawled back through her memory, trying to come up with the example of a time when Luke had been mean to her. Well, not mean, but maybe unkind. All she knew was that she felt upset after being with him often enough that she was certain he had to be.

"You know. You are… Provocative." He was. He provoked her. That was the word. Not mean, maybe, but she always left interactions with him feeling like she'd been poked with a stick.

He lifted one brow. "Provocative? Well. That has several connotations to it, sweet thing."

There he was. Provoking. "Do *not* call me that."

"Don't call you what?" He lifted his glass and indicated the empty state to Laz. "Honey or sweet thing?"

"Both. Neither. I am nothing remotely sugar-based to you."

"Well. My mistake."

Laz refilled Luke's glass and Olivia shot him the evil eye. "I'm not paying for two drinks."

"You're a peach, Olivia," Luke said. "I'm real sorry about that stuck-up comment."

She looked out of the corner of her eye and saw that Bennett was watching her closely. That Bennett was watching Luke and herself. She turned back quickly, focusing her attention on Luke.

"I'm not your peach, either." She sniffed.

For some reason she couldn't quite pin down, she settled into her seat a little more firmly and listed a bit to the side, her shoulder brushing up against Luke's.

He paused with his glass up against his lips, his green eyes turning sharp enough to cut straight through her. Her eyes lowered, resting on those lips, still pressed against the whiskey tumbler. He had just a bit of gold scruff right there around his mouth, spreading over his square jaw, the beginnings of a beard or just the end of a long workday. For some reason, she found herself captivated by it. And by the shape of his mouth.

Quickly, she raised her gaze back to his, and found it wasn't any more comforting.

Then his eyes narrowed and he tilted his head slightly to the side, looking quickly over his shoulder and back at the table of Dodges behind them.

"Don't play games with me, Olivia," he said, his voice low, rough. "You're not going to win any of them."

She swiveled her head to look at him, keeping her face blank. Keeping her mind blank. "What do you mean?"

"You leaning in like that. Because he's watching. You think you're gonna make him jealous?"

She reeled back, moving herself away from Luke. As far away as possible. "No. I wasn't doing anything."

He chuckled. "Yes, you were."

She hated him. She really did. He seemed to put the pieces of her motivation together faster than she did and it wasn't fair.

"No one would believe it," she said. "Nobody would believe that I..."

The words froze in her throat. Not just because she could hear how bitchy they sounded, but because suddenly she couldn't remember what she had been about to say anyway. Because he was looking at her with that steady green gaze, that glass still poised just below his lips and the overhead lights of the bar were highlighting that scruff on his face. Suddenly, she was thinking about the texture of that, too. She wondered if it would be rough, like she imagined his hands would be. He was a very rough sort of creature.

She was not a rough sort of creature.

"Oh, they'd believe it," he said, his lips tipping upward into a cocky smile. "Even good girls do something stupid every now and again." He took a swallow of his whiskey. "Might as well be me."

There was that itch, the one that bloomed beneath her skin whenever he was close. That felt like a cross between having a match struck against her flesh and stepping on a star thistle.

"I don't do stupid things," she said.

"Except for maybe break up with the boyfriend you claim you don't want to be broken up with?"

"I *don't* want to be broken up with him." She tapped the side of her glass. "I want to get back together with him."

"So you say. I don't buy it."

"I didn't ask you to buy it. I'm not trying to sell it to you."

"True enough. But, maybe we can try to sell something to him." He reached out and that hand she had just been pondering made contact with her skin. He squeezed her chin between his thumb and the curve of the knuckle on his forefinger. And it was rough. Just like she had thought it might be. Then he winked. "I'll see you around, kiddo."

Then he knocked back the rest of his whiskey and reached into his wallet, putting a twenty on the counter and walking back to where the Dodges were sitting.

She just sat there, staring at him like she had been clubbed in the head.

He had touched her.

And he had winked at her.

And he had called her *kiddo*, which for some reason felt a million times more offensive and slightly more disconcerting than *honey* or *sweet thing* had.

He was an annoyance. A constant annoyance.

She looked back into her Diet Coke, feeling flushed and prickly and isolated. Because nobody was sitting at the bar with her. She wasn't welcome at the table over there. Or anywhere the Dodges were. That hurt in a variety of strange and sharp ways. She had been friends with that family for most of her life and now she just wasn't welcome.

She had to believe it was because the breakup had hurt Bennett. And as much as she didn't want him hurt, she did want to know that he cared.

She sneaked another glance back toward the table, and saw that Bennett was looking at her again. Then she looked at Luke. At his broad back. Broad shoulders.

He was not looking at her. And she could still feel the impression of his touch against her chin.

Her gaze darted back to Bennett and she noticed that his expression was speculative. So she offered him that enigmatic smile she had been practicing earlier. Because she was working on being an enigma rather than a broadcast system.

Then she finished the rest of her Diet Coke and started to fish in her purse for some money.

Laz walked over to the bar and picked up the twenty Luke had left behind. "That actually covers everything, Olivia," he said.

And all she could do was stand there and stare, feeling light-headed. Because somehow, Luke Hollister had ended up buying her a drink, and that had not been the plan.

Olivia didn't like it when things didn't go to plan. But unfortunately, that seemed to be the story of her life at the moment.

She got up off the stool and walked slowly across the scarred-up wooden floor, looking down and shoving her hands in her coat pockets, careful not to look at anyone in the saloon. She edged the door open with her shoulder and walked out onto the street. It was dark out, and chilly.

The kind of cold that efficiently sliced through nice, sleek wool coats and penetrated down beneath the skin. But apparently not the kind of cold that could eradicate the heat left behind by Luke Hollister's hand.

She focused on putting one foot in front of the other as she walked down the uneven sidewalk, her each and every step bathed by the golden glow of the old-fashioned streetlights that lined the street.

Today had been weird. And it had contained far too much Luke for her liking.

Tomorrow would be different. It would be better. It would not begin with a flat tire. And it would not end with Luke Hollister's thumb pressed against her chin.

At this point in her life she was certain of very few things. But that was one of them.

CHAPTER FOUR

LUKE HAD NO clue what the hell he'd been thinking. But then, that was the theme with Olivia. She brought out the devil in him, and he had no interest in holding it back.

Still, touching her like that to get a rise out of Bennett was not the smartest. He tightened his grip on the steering wheel, tension crawling over his shoulders and down his back. Damn. He was wound tighter than he could remember being in a long time. It was because last night he'd ended up talking to Olivia instead of hooking up with someone, counter to his plan.

He let out a long slow breath as he watched the scenery fly by. It was clear out, sunny, though he knew that the air was as cold as—if not colder than—it would've been if it had been cloudy. Those crystal clear mornings had a way of cutting straight through you with no mercy. Maybe they were just worse because you could see the sun, and you expected that it might offer some warmth. But no.

Still, it looked nice. And if he pushed thoughts of Olivia Logan aside, it was almost soothing.

A shaft of golden light cut through the dense trees as he rounded the bend in the two-lane road, right at the spot where the property was. The property that was currently for sale by owner.

For sale by Cole Logan.

The Logans owned a fair amount of land in town. After all, they had been the first family to settle the area and large swathes of the countryside still belonged to them. And this one had famously been for sale for a very long time. Cole Logan had no need to sell it to just anyone, and he was particularly choosy about who he wanted settling, and what he wanted settled there.

Clearly, the man was much like his daughter. A control freak.

Without thinking, Luke pulled off to the side of the road, his truck idling. And he stared at the sign. That sign that he looked at every morning on his way to the Dodge ranch.

He was happy with his life working on the ranch. Although, with the changes, the focus returning to taking in guests and all of that, he questioned his place. And he hadn't done that since he was sixteen years old.

At the same time, sometimes that money felt like it was eating its way through his bank account like acid. Just sitting there. Sitting there for nearly twenty years useless and dead.

He knew why she'd taken out that life insurance policy. Because if anything happened to her, she had wanted to make sure he had a future. He could make something of himself.

But with the way it had happened...

It had to be the right thing. It had to be the right moment.

He stared at the sign, red and white and sticking up out of the ground, with a damn sunbeam shining on it.

He shook his head, putting the truck back in Drive and pulling back out onto the highway.

He turned the radio up, blaring a country song about being back roads legit, which turned his thoughts to things he liked. To drinking. Ranching. Women. Everything that made life worthwhile.

That carried him the rest of the way down the road and all the way to the Dodge ranch.

He parked his truck in the gravel lot that Wyatt was considering having paved over, and looked around. It was bare now, but he knew that Wyatt had landscape plans. Knew that Wyatt had a whole host of modernization schemes up his sleeve. He supported them. He did. He just wasn't sure anymore if he wanted to be an active part of it.

He frowned, killing the engine on the truck and getting out, walking slowly down the path toward the house, where he had a feeling he would find Wyatt sitting at the table in the dining area, his makeshift office, even though he had a real office. He claimed he preferred the one by the coffeemaker.

He opened up the front door without knocking, as was his habit. He had lived on the property for so many years, the entire place had eventually been opened up to him like a home. Quinn Dodge had been more of a father to him than anyone else ever had been. Surely more than the man who had been responsible for knocking his mom up and leaving her depressed and fragile, never to fully recover.

"Morning," he said, knocking his boots against the welcome mat and stepping inside, calling out the greeting to whichever of the Dodge brothers—or sister—might currently be in residence.

He found Bennett and Wyatt at the small kitchen table that sat in the corner of the modest room. A large thermos of coffee sitting at the middle of the table, both of them with full mugs in front of them.

"Good morning," Wyatt said, not looking up from the paperwork in front of him.

"What do you have there?" he asked.

"Looking over some different opportunities. Gabe Dalton has been doing some work with retired rodeo horses. And as crazy as it sounds, he swears that they would be perfect for the trail rides here. He has a few animals for us to look at."

The Daltons were another big ranching family in the area, and Luke knew that Gabe and Wyatt were pretty tight from their days riding on the rodeo circuit. Gabe had spent a fair amount of time hanging around the ranch too, and as far as Luke could see he was a stand-up guy, honest and definitely trustworthy when it came to his opinion on animals.

"Sounds good," Luke said.

"I'll definitely want to take a close look at them," Bennett said.

"Look under the hood?" Luke asked, moving through the kitchen and grabbing a mug out of one of the cabinets. "Kick the tires."

"Hey," Bennett said, "you wouldn't buy a used car without a mechanic having a look. Might as well have the resident vet take a look at your used horses."

Wyatt chuckled. "Fair enough."

"What else are you looking into?" Luke asked.

"Well, I had a talk with Dane Parker about the potential of doing some joint venture stuff with Grassroots Winery. I'm not sure. It might all be a little bit fussy."

Bennett shrugged a shoulder. "People like to drink."

"I'm not sure this is a wine place."

"People staying here might want to go on wine-tasting tours," Luke pointed out, even though he agreed that wine was a hell of a lot fussier than anything he wanted to deal in. He preferred beer for casual drinking and hard stuff for serious drinking.

Wine didn't fall anywhere on that spectrum.

"I don't know," Wyatt said. "I like Dane. But might be a lot of drama to step in the middle of. You know, seeing as Damien Leighton's ex-wife now owns the winery. I was pretty good buddies with him when we used to ride bulls."

"Sounds like you have a lot of options," Luke said.

And frankly, he wasn't really all that interested in any of them. He had liked the place the way that it was. Simple. Rustic. Appealing to the kind of people who wanted simple and rustic. At the same time, he also understood that you were going to catch a much broader base of people if you expanded the amenities.

But he wanted to get back to ranch work. Real ranch work. He wanted to dig postholes for fences. Wanted to wrangle cattle and ride horses.

He wanted a place of his own. His own land to work as he saw fit.

"How was Olivia?" Bennett's question jerked Luke out of his thoughts. "You talked to her at the bar."

"Yeah. I helped her out with her car, remember?"

Bennett nodded slowly. "Right. So you said."

"If you want to talk to her, go talk to her. She asked me about you, too. But I'm not a carrier pigeon for the lovelorn. So, if you guys have something to work out, go work it out."

Bennett's jaw firmed, a stubborn expression crossing over his face. "She's frustrating the hell out of me, because she's manipulating me. I don't understand why she doesn't get that I just want to wait until I have some things in order before I marry her. I didn't say I wouldn't marry her. I said not yet."

"Not a carrier pigeon," Luke said. "I'm not giving this information back to her."

Luke couldn't understand why the hell either of them were being so stubborn. If they wanted to be together, they should just be together. He didn't understand why Olivia felt like she needed a ring so badly, or why Bennett felt like he needed to wait. But, he wasn't going to get into the discussion. Because it wasn't his fucking problem.

He poured himself a measure of coffee, left it black and decided that he was going to get to work. "See you both later," he said.

"You just came in here to steal coffee and pass judgment?" Bennett asked.

"Yep."

He walked back out of the kitchen, across the stone floor that led to the front door of the large ranch house. He heard Bennett's footsteps behind him. Luke kept on walking and shut the front door behind him just to be difficult. He heard it open just a couple of seconds later.

"Something going on between you two?"

Luke turned around. "Me and this coffee? Yeah. Seriously red-hot love affair. I crave it. It's all I think about. I need it to survive."

"You and Olivia," Bennett said, his tone stiff. "I don't know how…"

"No," Luke said. "But, she's a grown-ass woman and apparently single."

"She wants a commitment," Bennett said. "And we both know you're not the guy to give that to her."

Luke's stomach tightened, and he chuckled past it. "Yes. We do both know that. I'm not giving a commitment to anyone. But you're apparently not giving one to her, either."

"It's complicated," Bennett said.

"How is it complicated? Either you love her or you don't."

"None of it's about love."

Luke stared at him. "Then what's it about?"

"I care about her. But sometimes she looks at me like..." Bennett shook his head. "I told her father that I would take care of her. After he had his heart attack, I promised I'd look out for her."

"Does Olivia know that?"

"She knows that her father wants us together. Hell, the whole town wants us together."

Luke couldn't deny that. They were definitely the golden couple of Gold Valley. The entire town took great delight in the idea that they would someday get married.

Like they were watching a favorite soap opera, using real people as characters.

"True enough," Luke said. "So why aren't you with her?"

"She wants things I don't think I can give. I'm not sure I can put her through any of that."

"Bennett Dodge, I've known you since you were ten years old. I don't know why the hell you wouldn't be able to give Olivia exactly what she wants. Exactly what she needs. You're perfect for her." For some reason the words burned a little bit on their way out. But they were true.

"You don't know everything about me, Luke," Bennett said, shaking his head and walking past him.

"You want to talk about it?" Which was the world's most ironic question since nobody knew everything about Luke, and he aimed to keep it that way. But Bennett was truly like a brother to him.

"No. If I talk to anybody about it, it has to be Olivia."

"Then talk to her, bonehead."

Bennett gave him a strange look. "Stay out of our relationship, Luke."

"You asked me into it, Bennett. You asked me what I knew, I gave you my opinion."

The expression on Bennett's face turned hard. "I asked you if there was anything going on with her."

"You did. That doesn't mean I owe you an answer."

He shook his head and turned and walked away from Bennett. He wasn't going to get in a fistfight with the guy over a girl he had barely ever touched.

He figured he would go muck some stalls. At least that would clear his head. Shovel shit to clear the shit and all that.

He walked into the barn and grabbed a pitchfork from the hook on the wall.

As he started on the first stall, he kept thinking of the comment Bennett had made about Olivia's father. About how Cole Logan was the one who wanted them together. Not exactly a declaration of passionate love, but Olivia said she loved Bennett, though as far as Luke could tell they didn't have enough chemistry to light a birthday candle.

But if Cole Logan wanted them together...

He shook his head, and shoveled another pile of manure up out of the stall, chucking it into a wheelbarrow.

He had some decision making to do.

He really hated change.

But it was starting to look like it was time to make one.

IT WAS LATE and Olivia was tired and cranky, feeling more than a little burned out after a long day at Grassroots. She missed having Bennett come pick her up. It had made her feel important, that she had a boyfriend who would come get her after work. That he was so solicitous and protective of her.

She missed it a lot.

She had missed it especially today when she had gotten into the car feeling exhausted and put upon, with the drive back to Gold Valley ahead of her. And now she had to make a stop at Get Out of Dodge.

Lindy had checked that it was okay. But Olivia hadn't seen the point in being difficult about it. It was late, and Bennett probably wouldn't be at the ranch anyway. He would either be at home or off on some veterinary emergency. Or, out at the bar. But it was very likely that the only person at the ranch would be Jamie. Even though things with Jamie were a little bit awkward, they weren't insurmountable.

Lindy wanted pamphlets dropped off, and for Olivia to nudge Wyatt about what he was thinking about the partnership with Grassroots. Once Lindy got something in her mind, she was headstrong. She was incredibly independent. In Olivia's opinion, the way that Lindy had left her husband and taken control of the winery, started from scratch, was admirable.

Not something that Olivia was certain she would have been able to do. She valued security and the opinions of other people too much.

She knew that Lindy's divorce had impacted how people thought of her. Which wasn't fair. Her ex-husband, Damien, had been cheating on her with one of the winery employees; it was hardly Lindy's fault.

But people were hard on women. Exceptionally hard.

Olivia took a deep breath as she turned into the familiar drive that led up to the ranch. She had been up here countless times. As a family friend, and then as Bennett's girlfriend. And it felt different now. Because it didn't feel like it was part of her anymore. Didn't feel like it belonged to her in any way.

It *had*. Like she was going to be part of this family. Part of this ranch that they had here. This legacy.

She felt sad about that.

There was a light on in the barn, and she stopped there. Jamie was probably putting the horses away.

She grabbed the pamphlets that Lindy had sent with her, clutching them in her hand as she headed into the red building.

When she saw who it was inside, she froze. It was not Jamie. Instead of her feminine, wiry frame, it was a masculine, broad-shouldered body. He was wearing a long-sleeved shirt, dark blue, and those sleeves were pushed up, which was providing her with quite an interesting show. He was bent down, the muscles in his forearms flexing with each pass of the push broom over the cement floor.

There was a black cowboy hat hanging on a hook, over the top of a bridle and lead rope.

She knew exactly who she was looking at. Because she had been fixated on those hands last night.

Her throat was dry. She couldn't remember why she had come in here in the first place.

She looked down. Right. The pamphlets.

"Luke," she said, his name coming out scratchy.

He stopped, midsweep, and then looked up at her, his green eyes hitting her with the force of a punch to the stomach. At least she assumed it was a similar sensation, though she had never been punched in the stomach before. But then, she had never felt anything quite like this before. Not since the last time he had looked at her, anyway.

"Are you looking for Bennett?"

"No," she said. "I was looking for Wyatt."

"I think he went out. Trying to drag Grant out of his hermitage, or something."

Olivia nodded. She worried about Grant. But she also wasn't surprised that he was still alone, even after all this time. She couldn't imagine him with anyone other than Lindsay. They had been together for so long. She had been the love of his life. She didn't know how you moved on from something like that.

She frowned. Was Bennett the love of her life? What if she didn't get him back? Was she also never going to be able to move on? Well, it wasn't like Bennett was dead. He was just not her boyfriend. That wasn't the same thing.

"What did you need?"

Luke's question dragged her out of her swampy thoughts. "Oh. I just… Lindy asked if I could bring these by." She thrust the pamphlets out toward him.

He just looked at them. "Okay."

She took a couple of steps toward him, with the pamphlets still held out. "Because she thought Wyatt might want to see these. You know, because I know that Lindy's brother had mentioned to him that Lindy was interested in doing some kind of a… You know, mutual promotion thing…"

"Wyatt mentioned as much," Luke said, propping the broom up and leaning against the handle. "He also said he wasn't sure about working with the ex-wife of a friend."

"Is he still friends with Damien? Because Damien is a cheating louse."

"Bros—"

"If you say bros before hos, so help me God, Luke, I will give you a paper cut with one of these pamphlets."

His green eyes glittered with wicked humor. "I wasn't going to say that."

"You were."

"I will take your pamphlets," he said, reaching his hand out, but not making a move toward her. She swore he was trying to be agitating.

She closed the distance between them and placed the pamphlets in his outstretched palm, her fingertips brushing against his bare skin.

She ignored the little zip that raced down to her stomach. "Thank you. Just make sure Wyatt gets them. For the record, I'm not sure that Lindy is thrilled at the idea of working with a bull rider."

"Why is that?" Luke asked.

"Pretty sure she hates everything associated with the rodeo, given her husband works PR for them, and also, bull riders specifically since he used to hang out with them. And, more specifically, Wyatt."

"Fair enough. Now, I don't know that I'm the best person to judge, considering I don't know that I'm a candidate for fidelity myself. But I've also never tried. And never promised it."

"Great. Congratulations on being slightly less disgusting than my friend's cheating husband."

He looked around as if he were searching for something. "Is there a badge for that?"

In spite of herself, Olivia laughed. "I'll have one made."

"I'll hold you to it."

"See you later, Luke," she said, turning on her heel and taking a deep breath as she started to walk back toward the barn door, trying to get a handle on her electrified nerves.

"Hey," he said.

She gritted her teeth. "Hey?"

"Yeah."

She turned around again. "What?"

"Your dad is still selling that plot of land out of town?"

"I guess. He turns down offers all the time. He has some very particular idea about who should have it."

"I've heard that," Luke said. "I want to buy it."

Olivia blinked. "How are you going to buy land?"

As long as she had known Luke, he'd lived modestly. Until he had been in his midtwenties he'd lived at Get Out of Dodge. Now he lived in some ramshackle cabin way out of town in the middle of the woods. He didn't scream financially sound.

"Don't worry about the how, kiddo," he said. "From a financial standpoint I'm not concerned at all. It's that purity testing he seems to be so fond of that worries me."

"My dad is rich enough that he doesn't need money. And that makes him a little bit eccentric."

"So it seems." Luke looked down at the pamphlets for a second, then back at her. "He really wants you and Bennett together."

"Why do you say that?" His assessment made her feel uncomfortable. She didn't even know why it bothered her, just that it did.

"Just saying. I doubt you would have been with Bennett if your dad didn't approve. You don't seem like the type."

Those words, so unerring, so accurate, sent icy little pinpricks down the back of her neck, all the way down her spine. She had no idea how a man who really didn't know her seemed to know her so well.

"Okay. So, say that my dad does want me to be with Bennett. What does that have to do with anything?"

"You want to be with Bennett, too," Luke pointed out.

"Obviously. I told you that. I told you that I loved him."

"And I told you that you didn't care, but you're sticking with your story. I respect that."

She gritted her teeth. "Because I know my feelings better than you do." Given her observation from a moment earlier she felt a little bit like she was lying, which was ridiculous. But it also made her feel guilty.

"What if I help you with Bennett? And you put in a good word with your dad. How about that?"

"How are you going to help me with Bennett?"

"He didn't like us talking last night. He didn't like me touching you. I have a feeling it'll only take a couple things like that to force him into making a decision. The problem is he's too certain of your feelings. Not certain enough of his own."

"Did you talk to him?" she asked, her stomach sinking. The last thing she wanted to hear was that Bennett had made it plain that he didn't know how he felt about her.

"Yes," Luke responded, giving absolutely no quarter to her fragile feelings.

"Oh," she said.

"He was asking about you. You and me. And he wasn't happy."

Heat streaked through her. "How could he possibly…" It didn't make sense. Bennett knew her. In the year they had been together they hadn't done… Anything. They had kissed, of course, but she had been holding out for a ring before they took things any further. He thought there was something going on with Luke? As if a guy like Luke would have any patience for her wanting a commitment before sex.

And that derailed her thoughts. Absolutely. Completely. Because thinking about Luke and sex in the same sentence turned her brain inside out and backward.

"Because he's jealous," Luke said. "Jealousy doesn't require logic."

"I don't…" She cleared her throat, blinking. "He really thinks you and I might be…"

"He's worried." Luke took a step toward her and her pulse sped up. "I think it's in your best interest to keep him worried."

The idea of tricking Bennett—tricking everyone—felt wrong. It made butterflies take flight in her stomach. Made her feel a strange, dull ache down low. Adrenaline. Excitement.

She didn't like it. She didn't like it at all.

Mostly because part of her kind of *did* like it. And that wasn't right. It wasn't who she wanted to be. It wasn't who her parents needed her to be.

Bennett was her goal, had been for a long time. And maybe, just maybe, if her end goal was good, the method to getting there didn't exactly have to be. Maybe.

"What do you have in mind?" she asked.

A smile curved his lips. "I hear you're damn good at playing darts."

CHAPTER FIVE

SHE DIDN'T NEED the reminder text that morning from Luke, letting her know that they were supposed to go to the saloon that night. That they weren't meeting there. That he was going to pick her up and drive her to create more of a spectacle. She remembered.

It was all she'd been able to think about all day.

It had been a slow day, which hadn't helped. They didn't have the farm-to-table dinners during the colder months, and weddings weren't particularly popular through January. They'd done a gorgeous Christmas wedding in one of the old barns, with white lights and holly boughs, a magnificent tree at the center of the massive room. Not that Olivia had enjoyed it since it had come on the heels of her breakup with Bennett and she'd been feeling more than a little Scroogey.

Right now the vast dining area was empty. She had a feeling that people would start to filter in sometime around lunch. There were always groups of friends who lived in between the towns who found it the perfect central meeting location for afternoon luncheons, fruit and cheese plates and a bit of wine with their conversation.

There was always something to do. There just wasn't enough. In fact, in order to fill her time Olivia had resorted to picking at her manicure, and she never did that. She had a date tonight; she really needed her manicure in good condition.

Her stomach felt like it dropped a couple of inches. She did not have a date tonight. It wasn't a real date. Nope.

"You seem distracted today."

Olivia looked up to see that her boss, Lindy, was staring at her speculatively.

"I'm not distracted," she said, the back of her mind blaring Luke's name like a neon sign. Calling her a liar.

"Did you give Wyatt the pamphlets?"

"He wasn't there. But I left them with Luke Hollister. I'm not sure if you know him."

"Is he the guy that brought you in the other morning?" Lindy asked, her tone suggestive.

Olivia didn't understand why just being with Luke would make Lindy think something was going on with him. Olivia didn't understand the rules to casual relationships and hookups.

She hoped Luke did. He seemed confident enough. In absolutely everything.

Except his ability to convince her father to sell him that property without her input. She had been turning that bit of information over for the past fourteen hours. It was difficult to imagine Luke being uncertain. It was easy to imagine him walking up to her father and sticking out his hand, shaking it. Giving him that cocky grin and saying, *Cole Logan, I want to buy that plot of land you have for sale there.*

Yes, that was startlingly easy for her to imagine.

She cleared her throat. "I've known him for a long time. He's very good friends with Bennett's family. You know, the Dodge family. The family that we were just talking about." She was rambling. And she did not ramble.

"Yes," Lindy said. "I *do* know the Dodge family."

"You don't like Wyatt very much, do you?" she asked.

Lindy frowned. "I don't know Wyatt that well. It isn't that I don't like him. It's that I have a strong suspicion of bull riders as a species. Cocky, arrogant assholes. Every last one of them. And the only man worse than a bull rider is the man who sells them as decent human beings. Damien did a lot of work with Wyatt in particular when he did ad campaigns and things. And, since you figure jackasses of a feather flock together, and Wyatt used to flock with Damien…"

"Didn't Dane used to hang out with them, too?" Olivia asked, referring to Lindy's brother.

"I suppose so," Lindy said. "I don't know. Wyatt is just one of those guys. He's too… A lot of things."

Olivia could relate to that assessment. That was kind of how she felt about Luke. He was too much. Too many things. How could one man contain so much? Self-assurance, attitude, a smile that seemed to light up the room and everyone in it. But lit up parts of her that made her flush to think about.

That thought stunned her. And for a full second she couldn't think of anything to say.

"Are you okay?" Lindy pressed her. She wasn't doing a good job of convincing Lindy that everything was okay. Mostly because she wasn't entirely sure that it was.

"I have a date tonight," she said. "With *not* Bennett."

Lindy's face relaxed, one corner of her lips turning upward. "Oh. And that's hard? Weird?"

She felt guilty, because of course her boss was associating it with her divorce. With moving on after a long-term relationship. And Olivia hadn't actually moved on.

"I guess. I just… It's not really a date. I want Bennett to see that I've moved on. And for him to not like that."

"Okay," Lindy said. "Are you sure that's a good idea?"

"No," Olivia said, feeling miserable. "I don't. But I don't know what else to do. And when he suggested it…"

"When who suggested it?"

"Luke. When I went to talk to Luke last night, he suggested it."

Lindy's eyebrows shot upward. "I see."

"Do you? Can you help me figure out if I'm crazy or not?"

"You might be," Lindy said. "But I hear love does that to you."

The dining room was empty, no customers in sight, so Olivia slumped at the nearest bistro table, propping her chin up on her elbows. "Were you miserable after your divorce?"

Lindy sighed and walked around to the other side of the table. She sat down, putting her hand over Olivia's. "I was a lot more miserable leading up to it. It's hard to find out that someone you love isn't who you thought they were. Or I guess that someone you love is exactly who you were afraid they might be, but you ignored all the signs."

"Bennett *is* who I think he is. He's a good man. I was impatient. I broke up with him because I wanted to have him make a commitment. And now…"

"You regret it."

"Yes."

"Olivia, I'm not an expert on love. Obviously. I think everyone knew that my husband was a bad bet. Everyone except me. But what I can tell you about loving

someone is that it doesn't make sense. And sometimes
you do the wrong thing hoping that the right thing will
come out of it. And sometimes you hurt each other even
when you don't mean to. Because loving someone is
scary. So, sometimes you act scared."

"*Bennett* is acting scared," Olivia said.

She wasn't scared. Commitment didn't scare her at
all. It was what she wanted. It was that end goal. That
bright, shining beacon she had been working toward for
so many years. She would have that life, that perfect life.
A little house all her own, a husband. It was what she
had always wanted. There was nothing to be scared of
when it came to marriage as far as she was concerned.
Her parents had a wonderful marriage. She aspired to
that. To that good life that they led.

To being that kind of person.

Scary was the unknown. Scary was having your
future tossed high up into the air. It was having no
plan. Being aimless. It was how Vanessa lived her entire life, as far as Olivia could see. Her twin sister, the
person she had been closest to from birth, was a vir-
tual stranger now.

Her partying, her drug use, had taken everything
from them that they used to share. Even their looks.
Nobody would think they were sisters now, much less
identical twins.

Her sister was so thin. Wasted down to nothing, her
skin ravaged, her eyes dull, her hair lank.

That was where aimlessness got you. It was where
living for the moment got you. And Olivia had never
been that person. No, plans didn't scare her. Permanence
didn't scare her. It was all those other things in between.

"Well," Lindy said, "men get gun-shy when commitment is on the table."

"I'm not scared of getting married. Or having a relationship."

"But apparently you're scared of having an honest conversation with the man that you claim you're ready to marry?"

Olivia placed her hand on her chest, where it felt like Lindy's words had literally stuck into her like a sword. "I just… I have some pride. I'm not going to beg him. I need him to try and get a better understanding of his feelings. Through… Seeing what his life might be like without me. I want him to understand that he needs me by saying that maybe I don't need him."

"But don't you need him?"

Olivia frowned. "Yes. But I have to have some pride."

"Okay. So, your version of having pride is trying to trick the man that you say you're in love with, by pretending to date a different man, so that he'll feel bad and ask you to marry him?"

Olivia did not like this line of conversation at all. Because when Lindy said it like that, it just sounded sad. And it didn't sound at all like it did when she thought about it. When it came from inside of her it all seemed logical. Repeated back at her it sounded manipulative and that wasn't what she felt.

"I'm just saying," Lindy said. "At a certain point in your relationship you're going to have been together for a long time. That's what marriage is. It's forever. It's supposed to be. And you're going to reach a point there where you realize you didn't practice telling each other the truth. You didn't practice sharing what was in your heart, what you were feeling, what you had for breakfast. And you're going to realize that you live with a stranger. And so does he."

"I don't think you can compare what happened with

you and Damien to me and Bennett," Olivia said. "And I don't think it's fair for you to try and take blame for anything. For you to say that he didn't know you as if somehow you could have told him what kind of cereal you had that day and he wouldn't have cheated on you."

"That's the thing," Lindy said. "He did the wrong thing. And he took us to a place where for me... We couldn't come back from it. But he didn't take us there by himself. He didn't get started on the road on his own. As much as it pains me to say it, our divorce isn't *only* his fault."

"I don't understand how that could be. You do the right thing, and you keep going forward on the right path, and things like that don't happen. He's the one that strayed."

"Yes," Lindy said. "He did. But why? It's the answer to that question that sits uncomfortably with me. Just... As I told you, I'm not an expert. I'm thirty-four years old and divorced with absolutely no prospects on the horizon. But I was married for ten years and I do know a little something about that. And about all the things that can go wrong. So just... Consider having a conversation with him? You don't have to cry or make a fool out of yourself. But... It might not be the worst idea."

Olivia frowned. "I don't know what I would say to him." To tell him that she was unhappy because she couldn't see where her life was going anymore? To tell him that she loved him and was miserable without him? That settled uncomfortably in her chest, too. Because it felt... Wrong. Like it might not even be true.

"I don't know," Lindy said. "Maybe I don't know what I'm talking about with you and Bennett."

"It's not like I didn't tell him," Olivia said. "I told him I wanted to marry him. And he said he didn't want to do that yet. I haven't been lying to him. I told him exactly what I wanted. I just want him to make a decision. A final decision. I'm the one that broke up with him. And I feel like he's the one who has to either close the door on it forever or come back. I would prefer that he came back."

Lindy sighed heavily. "I get that. I'm sorry. I'm sorry that I accused you of not asking for what you wanted. I know that you did. And you know… My marriage didn't work. So, you probably really shouldn't listen to me because I'm bitter and cynical, and I feel like I don't much believe in the power of love right now. So go on, make him jealous. I hope that he sees you with Luke and is overcome by the desire to pick you up and carry you back to his bed."

Olivia shifted uncomfortably. "I'd settle for an engagement ring."

A subtle crease appeared between Lindy's brows. "Right. Good luck tonight."

Olivia forced a smile. "Thank you." She had a feeling she was going to need to find a rabbit holding a four-leaf clover between its toes before she had the proper amount of luck she would need tonight, but she was just going to stick with a simple thank you.

A group of three women walked in after that, and Olivia was saved from her thoughts. She hoped that she could find a way to stay busy enough to avoid thinking for the rest of the afternoon. But she had a feeling that was a tad optimistic.

Still, considering that tonight she had a date with Luke Hollister, optimism was necessary.

CHAPTER SIX

LUKE WASN'T SURE what to expect when he went to pick Olivia up that evening after work. He had spent a good portion of the day imagining what Olivia Logan considered to be make-your-ex-jealous clothes.

He was slightly disappointed by the answer to the question.

It was a floral dress and a pair of leggings, accompanied by a tall pair of boots. Fair enough, he supposed, since it was cold as hell frozen over out there. But as far as he was concerned a little bit of skin wouldn't have gone amiss. Of course, he had never actually seen Olivia showing any skin, and he imagined it had been a little optimistic to expect she would start now.

Not that he needed her to expose any skin for him.

But he was a man, same as any other. Which meant that whatever type of creature he found sexually appealing he enjoyed seeing more of when at all possible.

He put the truck in Park and got out as Olivia whipped down the front steps of her little cottage, her brown hair a tangle around her face, her skirt blowing up around the top of her legging-clad thighs. All right, even though her legs were covered by that textured, gray wool, he could see the shape of them, and he definitely liked what he saw.

"You didn't have to get out of the truck," she said, clutching her purse and a cranberry-colored sweater to her chest, tucking a strand of dark hair behind her ear as the wind blew around them, sharp like a knife's edge.

"Sure I did, ma'am," he said, sweeping his black hat off his head and treating her to his most charming smile. "We are on a date, after all, and a gentleman always comes to the door to pick up his date, same as he walks to the door to drop her off."

"But this isn't a real date," she said, treating him to a very suspicious glare.

"I have to get into character, kiddo. If you're going to use me, you need to allow me to be used on my terms. That's the only way this works."

"You're using me, too," she pointed out. "So that you can offer on that land. Don't think I haven't forgotten."

"I like it when you play ruthless, Liv."

She sniffed. "Nobody calls me that."

"Good. Then it will be my pet name for you. I bet it will drive Bennett crazy." He grinned, and he couldn't help but notice that he was driving Olivia a little bit crazy, too. At the moment, she had the appearance of a ruffled wren. If she'd had feathers they most certainly would have been standing on end.

"Let's just go," she said. "I bet everybody's at the bar already."

"Now, here's a chance for you to learn a little something. Sometimes it's better to show up late."

She blinked, her brown eyes almost comically bland. "Why?"

He chuckled. "Because it gives space for the imagination. For Bennett's imagination. For him to imagine all the things we might have been doing in that time we weren't in the saloon."

Her eyes remained blank for a split second, and then suddenly her face turned scarlet. "Oh."

"Sometimes taking it slow is the best way to take it."

She swallowed visibly, her fingers curling more tightly around her purse. "Right." She lifted her chin, attempting to look imperious now, which was especially funny with that blush still lingering on her cheeks. "Oh, I suppose we've taken it slow enough. And if not, you can drive slow."

"No one tells me how to drive my truck," he said.

"You're exasperating," she said.

"Sure. But, if I didn't exasperate you, who would?" He moved along beside her and pressed his palm against her lower back. She stiffened beneath his touch, her shoulders going rigid. "Relax," he said, leaning in, ignoring the sparks beneath his fingertips. "You have to look like you like it, remember?"

She nodded wordlessly, and he guided her to the passenger side of his truck, opening the door for her.

"Another thing a gentleman does," he said, keeping his voice low.

He offered her his arm, but she braced herself on the rest inside the passenger door, hauling herself up into the large vehicle and settling into the seat. Primly. As she had done the first time. If someone had told him a couple of days ago that he would have Olivia Logan sitting in his truck two times in one week he would have said they were crazy. But, here she was. Looking no more comfortable today than she had the other day.

He shook his head and put his hat back on as he took his position in the driver seat, slamming the door hard behind him.

"Bennett always opens the door for me," she said as he pulled the truck out onto the main highway.

"Well, good for him. I would expect nothing different. In fact, if he didn't I'd have to have a serious talking-to with him. You know, kind of like an older brother thing."

"You're not his brother," she pointed out.

"No," Luke said. "But I'm older. Full of wisdom."

"Ancient," she said drily.

He took his eyes off the road for a moment, to look at that imperious little profile of hers. Her cheeks were still pink.

He heard a phone notification, and saw Olivia lift her phone up and text quickly.

"Who's that?"

"Do I owe you an explanation for all of my actions now?" she asked, her tone snippy.

"I'm making conversation, Liv," he said. "You know, since you're in my truck and making conversation with someone else instead of with me."

"It's my mother," she said.

"Checking in on you?"

"Yes. She does that. She just wants to know what I'm up to."

"And what did you tell her?" He was genuinely curious how she was going to spin this story to her parents. He was also fascinated by the fact that her mother checked in.

He'd been an orphan for all intents and purposes by the time he was sixteen, and before that, he had done a lot of the caregiving in his household. His only other real experience with a parent-type relationship was with Quinn Dodge, and while Quinn was definitely an involved father, he didn't hover.

"I told her I was going out with a friend," she said.

"That feels like an upgrade," he said. "Though, you might have told her you had a date."

"No," she said, "I mightn't have. Because then she

would want details, and she would want to know what time I was coming home, and she would want to make sure that I didn't have anything put in my drink."

He laughed. "A little overprotective?"

"Maybe. But we are close. She just wants to know what's going on in my life." He could tell that wasn't the whole story, but he could also tell that she wasn't going to give him much more right now. If she'd wanted to, she would have just come out and told him.

And he didn't do female excavation. He liked easy conversation; he didn't like to dig. Because that meant getting down to the bits of people they didn't want to share, which meant that they might want him to do the same in turn. He preferred stripping off layers of clothes to any other kind of stripping off of layers, thank you very much.

And since Olivia wasn't going to be stripping off any clothes for him—and he wouldn't ask her to anyway—there wasn't any point in courting any other type of stripping.

"Well, that's nice." Except to him it sounded stifling more than it sounded nice.

"It is. I have great parents. I'm lucky." Her tone sounded distracted. Distant.

"Sure," he said.

"You're very difficult," she said.

"Yes," he remarked, making his tone as contrite as possible. "It's been said. Frequently. Mostly by you."

She sniffed loudly, and he imagined that there was a very haughty face accompanying that sniff. "It's just… As far as I can tell you aren't accountable to anyone or anything. I don't understand that. I have my parents… I have goals… I have… Bennett."

"Technically," Luke pointed out, feeling like an ass

even as he said it, "you don't have Bennett at the moment."

"You're mean," she said.

"Am I wrong?"

"No. But… I feel like a gentleman wouldn't say that. And you're so into pointing out what a gentleman does."

"That's the trouble," he said. "I'm playing the part of a gentleman. But don't for one second confuse me with an actual gentleman."

At that exact moment, they drove down onto the town's main street, and Luke spotted an open parking space against the curb across from the Gold Valley Saloon.

He put the truck in Park, then looked at Olivia's resolute profile. "Ready?"

"Now who's impatient," she said, hands pinned firmly to the center of her lap, her eyes fixed straight ahead.

"Not impatient," he said. Except he felt something. A kind of restlessness rolling through him that left him feeling edgy. And he didn't do edgy.

He liked irritating Olivia—it was one of his great joys in life. He didn't so much like it when she managed to poke her own little stick back at him and make contact.

He got out of the truck, and he noticed that she stayed put. Waiting for him to open the door. In spite of himself, his lips curved up into a smile.

He opened it for her, then offered her his hand, which this time she took. The skin-to-skin contact hit him like a knockout punch. She was soft. So damn soft. That didn't shock him; he had expected her to be soft. What shocked him was the fact that such innocuous contact had him hot and hard in seconds. And maybe that was the reason, in and of itself. The fact that he hadn't been expecting the impact. Maybe that was why it landed with such accuracy, with such force.

Whatever it was, he'd felt less pleasure from a hand wrapped around more intimate parts of him than from her delicate fingers wrapped around his own.

"Let's go," he said, his voice gruffer than he intended. But dammit, he was affected. He wasn't used to being affected. He was used to doing the affecting. He was used to being the one causing a reaction, not contending with one. Particularly one he didn't want.

He didn't have a lot of practice in restraint. Life was pretty easy for him. Everything he had he'd worked for honestly. Everything except that money in the bank from the insurance settlement. And that was why it still sat there, because it occupied a place that was uncomfortable for him. A place he didn't know what to do with.

He didn't like things like that. He liked his life simple.

He wanted something, he worked for it. He wanted a woman, he slept with her. He wanted to be done with a woman, he cut things off.

He didn't do longing. He didn't do unrequited lust and unquenched desire. He didn't want things he couldn't have. Hell, usually he didn't even want things he had to *wait* for.

But there was money he'd received from a loss, from a moment in time he resented, and if he did nothing with it, it would be worse than benefiting from it.

And there was Olivia Logan. About to make him lose his mind because her hand had touched his. Like he was a green horse that had never been ridden.

In rebellion to those feelings, he held on to her more

tightly, shifted so that his fingers were laced through hers as the two of them walked across the street and toward the saloon. When he looked down at her, he almost laughed. Except that his throat was too tight, and his chest felt like there was a ten-ton weight on it.

Yeah, except for those things, he was tempted to laugh at Olivia, who looked like she was carved out of a particularly lifeless bar of Ivory soap. She'd gone waxen and pale, her expression frozen, her petite little shoulders stiff as they made their way to the front door of the bar.

"You're going to have to look a little bit less like you want to throw up on my boots, kiddo," he said.

"I don't… I don't know if I can do this," she said, extricating herself from his hold.

"It's too late, honey," he said. "We're already doing this. People have already seen us out the window. And they're wondering what the hell you're doing with the likes of me. But you know who's going to wonder that most of all? Bennett. Bennett Dodge is going to wonder what the hell you're doing with me."

"Is it going to cause trouble?" she asked, her dark brows knitting together, a little crease appearing between them. "Is it going to cause trouble between you and the Dodge family, because I know you're close…"

"You don't care," he said.

"Will you *stop* telling me I don't care about things?" she said, frowning deeply.

"When you stop lying about it, sure. You're worried about what people will think. Because you're worried that they'll think you're slumming it with a guy like me, right? Because I'm a no-account from nowhere and you're Olivia Logan. But that's the point, isn't it?"

"My mother is going to get phone calls." She

scrubbed her hand over her forehead, as if that could remove the worry lines that had appeared there at the mention of her mother.

He shrugged. "So what? Let her get phone calls. There are worse things. You can explain it to her. You can tell her the truth, or you can tell her our lie. Either way. But you're a grown-up, Olivia. And nobody gets to tell you what to do."

"Right." She sighed. "That's not how life works when you care about people, Luke. You don't just…do whatever you want and leave someone to worry."

"Why not?" he asked. "You can't control what someone else feels."

She made a frustrated noise. "That's not…you're missing the point. And I don't care if you miss the point. You and I just don't see eye to eye."

"We don't *need* to see eye to eye. We just need to work together for a bit. Now, do you trust me, or not?"

Her brown eyes narrowed into suspicious slits. "Not as far as I could throw you."

"Good. You shouldn't trust me. I'm not a gentleman." Right now he felt like a particularly hungry fox sniffing around the henhouse. "But, I do have the best idea running for how you can get Bennett's attention."

Olivia took a deep breath, shaking those stiff shoulders out, then looking up at him. "Okay."

"Okay." He took a step ahead of her and grabbed the handle on the door, pulling it open. "After you."

She walked in ahead of him, and he was struck by just how small and delicate she was. The top of her head wouldn't graze the underside of his chin if she walked under it. It made him want to pick her up, carry her over a threshold or some shit. And that was a weird impulse. Except, he supposed not really all that weird.

Since what he really wanted was to throw her down on a big bed and spend the rest of the night exploring every inch of her.

Damn. Things were escalating. She had always been an itch to him. From the minute that girl had turned eighteen she'd been a problem.

Pretty. Remote. She'd been far too young. So far off-limits that he'd never allowed his fantasies to get this graphic.

But he'd touched her now. Untouchable Olivia Logan. He'd felt her skin beneath his fingertips and it was like those chains he'd put around himself had dissolved. Now all that resolute control was getting strained.

Which wasn't a difficult thing to do considering he didn't have a whole lot of practice with control. Except for with her. With her, he had certainly tried over the years.

This was making it damn difficult.

He walked in behind her, pressing his fingertips against her lower back, again in defiance of that need rocketing through him. He clenched his teeth, wondering silently if he was a masochist and didn't know it.

"Why don't you go get us a table?" he asked, scanning the room to see if Bennett, Wyatt and Grant were already in residence.

Bennett and Wyatt were. Grant was unsurprisingly absent.

He wished the guy would get his ass in gear and get out more, he really did. But Grant was like a difficult burrowing animal. Certain times of the year, particularly in the winter, it was tough to get him out to do anything. He seemed to do better later in the year. Some people might attribute that to seasons on sunshine and whatever. Luke figured it had to do with the fact that his wife had died in February. The lead-up to the month was always tough.

He wasn't the most emotionally enlightened guy, that much was for sure, but he knew a little bit about loss.

About the way dates burned themselves into your brain. The way they seemed to exist in the back of your mind, eternally in your consciousness even when you weren't trying to be aware of them.

"Hey." Luke sidled up to the bar and signaled Laz as Olivia looked around the room, bewildered, clearly trying to decide which table to select. She was not good at subterfuge, that much was certain. It was kind of charming to watch her try. "I need a couple shots of whiskey."

"Olivia doesn't drink whiskey," Laz said, picking up a shot glass.

"All right. What does she drink?"

"Diet Coke."

"I'll still take the extra shot of whiskey. But, add the Diet Coke to it. In case she wants to mix the two."

"She won't," Laz said.

"She might before the evening is up," Luke said, confident. "You can just put that on my tab."

Olivia had finally made a decision, and was sitting at a table near the dartboard, looking lost. Luke acquired their drinks and went to join her. He slid the Diet Coke in front of her as he took his seat, then placed both shots of whiskey in front of him.

"Am I *that* trying to hang out with?" she asked, looking pointedly at the two glasses of alcohol. There was a hint of humor in her eyes and he found that more surprising than anything.

"The other shot is for you. In case you're feeling crazy."

"No. On a very rare day sometimes I feel regular soda crazy, but not so much hard liquor crazy."

"Do you not drink at all?"

"No, I do. I mean, I *have*. I just don't usually."

"Any particular reason?" he asked.

"I like control," she said simply.

"Well," he said, lifting the shot glass to his lips and knocking it back. He grimaced. "That's a shame. Because so do I."

She looked at him and blinked slowly, her expression comically bland. "Good thing this isn't a real date, then."

"Good thing." He stood up. "Because then you would be obligated to let me win at darts."

She huffed out a laugh. "I would do no such thing."

"Really?"

"Really," she returned. "Any man who needs to beat a woman at darts to feel good about himself is no kind of man in my book. I would rather see how my date fared in the face of defeat."

"So confident."

"With good reason."

"Okay," he said, "show me how it's done."

OLIVIA FELT LIKE she'd had alcohol, and she absolutely had not. But she felt bubbly, fizzy, and her blood felt slightly overheated. It was a strange turnaround from a few moments before when she had been certain that she was going to pass out. It was just that when Luke had held her hand like that...

She'd held hands with two men in her life. Which was lame and silly, and probably completely ridiculous to get worked up over, but her level of experience was what it was.

She had very briefly dated one guy before Bennett, and it could hardly even be called dating. They had gone out a couple of times. They hadn't even kissed.

But she had held his hand. And then she had held Bennett's. *Often*, obviously, as they had dated for more than a year.

Holding hands with Luke... It had been unexpected. It had been one thing for him to help her out of the car, although, even that small bit of skin on skin had felt significant. But once he had woven his fingers through hers her entire body had gone tight, like fencing wire, and she had found it almost impossible to breathe.

And it wasn't like when he shocked her, when he said things that made her blush. No, this was different. It had made her hot, then cold; it had set off a chain re-action that she could hardly figure out even now. It was just... Such intimate contact to make with a man she had known for so long, but never like that.

She had known Luke since she was a kid. Since *he* had been a kid, too, honestly. Even though he had al-ways seemed like a grown man to her, because that was a child's perspective on teenage boys. And that had always put him in this other realm, as this other thing, separate to her. But she wasn't a child anymore; she was a woman. And he was a man. And that was very... Alarming to fully realize. That there was no longer this invisible wall between them, something that kept them on separate sides of that divide. It made this game they were playing feel far too stark. Far too dan-gerous and real.

It felt like something different all of a sudden than what it had felt like when they had conceived it a bit earlier. Far different than that vague itch that usually rested beneath her skin when she dealt with Luke.

But now they were in the bar trading barbs, and getting ready to play darts, and that felt familiar somehow. And she was ready to jump into it with both feet. To do something to get herself back on balance, because she could not go back to that place she'd been in when his hand had touched hers. No, that, she did not want to contend with. Not at all.

So darts and good-natured banter it would be.

She was far better at darts than she was at banter, but you couldn't have it all, she supposed.

"Are you really that good, Liv?" he asked, his voice huskier than normal, and strange, the roughness abrading places inside of her she would rather it didn't.

She was back to feeling slightly dry of throat and out of her comfort zone.

"I'm better," she said. "Haven't you seen me play before?"

"Sure," he said, "but I've never played you. For all I know Bennett let you win. Usually, you just play Bennett."

"Bennett never *let* me win," she said. "He didn't have to."

"I wonder what he'll think of another man getting to play with you," he said.

Okay, this Luke she could deal with. Cocky and arrogant, throwing out innuendo expecting that it would make her blush. And yes, it often did. But at least that was a comfortable pattern. "That's what we're here to find out," she said.

She went over to the dartboard and collected the darts from where they were stuck into the cork, and then she carried them back to the line, steeling herself for her first shot.

"You're really not a bar girl," Luke said. "So how is

it exactly that you are the most notorious dart player
in Gold Valley?"

"I like to have a bit of mystery about me, Luke."

"Fine. You have to get a bull's-eye on this next shot,
or you have to tell me how you learned to play darts."

She laughed, then she straightened her posture,
cocked her arm back and let the first dart fly, effortlessly sticking it in the center of the bull's-eye.

"No shit," he said, slightly annoyed, slightly in awe.

"I told you I was that good," she said.

She liked darts. She had ever since she'd outgrown
the little wooden dollhouse she'd played with when she
was young. If there was one thing Olivia had done a lot
of, it was playing by herself. Because Vanessa always
wanted to push the boundaries, and Olivia never had.
So she'd played with dolls. And then when she was a
teenager, it had been darts.

She had spent hours fiddling with them down in
her dad's man cave in their house. Countless times
when Vanessa had decided that she was too cool for
Olivia and all of her rule following, when she had gone
out with her other friends. When she had decided that
drinking and sex were far more important than having
a bond with her sister.

When Olivia had ended up grounded because she'd
come home a few minutes too late, or her grades had
slipped and it had caused her parents to tighten their
restrictions on her, while Vanessa ran absolutely wild,
uncaring if she was grounded or not.

Olivia had thrown any kind of silent frustration she
had felt into sticking that sharp pin into the corkboard.
Into watching that dart fly straight and true and land
exactly where she wanted it. Control. Even in all those
muddled, mixed-up feelings, she had found control.

Had found a way to channel them. And God knew that had to be better. Better than simply exploding and getting messy emotion all over the people that you were supposed to love and care about. Better than going off and doing whatever you wanted.

Her parents had been hard on her. Harder, in the end, than they were on Vanessa. But hadn't she turned out better for it?

Olivia hadn't disregarded their parents' warnings.

Olivia had played darts.

"Okay," he said. "Now you have to tell me where you learned."

She tossed her hair, shooting him a smile. "I don't have to tell you anything, cowboy. Because I hit the bull's-eye. And I'm going to keep hitting the bull's-eye. All night long."

A strange crackle of tension arced between them and she felt as though she was electrocuted by her next breath.

She looked away from him, and her eyes automatically went to Bennett's table. He was looking at them. He really was. He was looking at her and Luke and he was not happy.

Their eyes caught for a moment and her breath hitched. It wasn't the same kind of tension that she felt standing there with Luke, but it was a strange adrenaline rush. That she was accomplishing this. That she, Olivia Logan, who was quite possibly the polar opposite of a femme fatale, was somehow managing to draw attention. To cause friction. Make a man jealous.

She noticed then that Kaylee was looking at Bennett, and then that she looked up at Olivia. The look was filled with so much anger that it made Olivia's breath catch in an entirely different way.

She flicked her attention back to Luke. "I'd say that we're drawing the focus of the crowd," she said softly.

"Good," he said, not looking over at Bennett's table at all. "That's what you wanted." He leaned back against their table, resting his forearms there, his hands dangling loosely over the sides. His green eyes were fixed on her. "You going to go again?"

"Of course," she said. She whirled around and faced the dartboard and brought her arm back one more time, zeroing in on that bull's-eye. Letting go of everything except for the target. She threw the dart and it landed satisfyingly right where she wanted it.

If only life were like darts.

"Good," he said, "one more, and then it's my turn."

"Yes, I do know how it works, Luke. Thank you."

"Bull's-eye," he said, "or you have to tell me how you learned to play."

She snorted. "I'm not even worried."

She turned away from him, facing the dartboard. And suddenly, she felt heat at her back. And then a large hand resting on her hip. He leaned over her shoulder, his lips near her ear. "I just want to see how it's done. How exactly you're standing. You know, I'm not anywhere near as good at this as you are. So, it would help if I could observe. If you could teach me."

She froze completely, her whole body going rigid like a board. The place he was touching her, on her hip, felt like it was on fire. So hot, the press of his palm against her so heavy that she could hardly breathe. That was reasonable, right? That it was the weight of it on her hip… Affecting her ability to breathe?

Her heart was thundering erratically, and when she lifted her hand again, it was unsteady. Her pulse was fluttering hard at the base of her throat, and more disturbingly there was an answering pulse between her thighs.

"I'm not distracting you, am I?" His breath was warm on her neck, and that was a very strange sort of intimacy. His breath against her skin. She could honestly say there was only one man whose breath she had ever felt. And it was not Luke Hollister.

"I'm fine," she said, not willing to admit that he was affecting her at all. She didn't want to give him that satisfaction. But then, she wasn't sure how she was supposed to throw a dart when her entire person was trembling like she was an overly excited rat terrier.

Olivia had never been accused of being overly excited in her life. She was hardly going to start behaving in such a way now.

She took a deep breath, her stomach twisting sharply. Then she lifted her arm, raising the dart back. She tried to zero her focus in on that little red dot at the center. To block out everything around her. But there was his heat. His lips so very close to her ear, his hand resting all proprietary and possessive on her hip.

Possessive.

What an odd word, except it was the one that fit. That's what it felt as though he had done. As though he had walked up and claimed possession of her in some way. And she should be okay with that. It should be what she wanted. The kind of display she was after.

But it felt terrifying and somehow outside the bounds of the game she knew they were playing. Somehow different than what they were trying to accomplish. She didn't like it at all.

And if she showed him that he was affecting her, if she missed the shot, there was going to be a lot more of it and she knew it. He might be claiming to help her out, but somewhere underneath all of that, she had a feeling that it was more of Luke messing with her. Why, she didn't know. She only knew that he seemed to take joy in it. And if nothing else she wanted to deprive him of a little bit of joy.

She let out a long, slow breath and ignored the fact that it was a bit shuddery. A bit shaky.

Then she drew the dart back and let it fly. She gave out a whoop of triumph when it hit the bull's-eye, even though it was resting just on the edge of that red, it was definitely there.

She whirled around without thinking, and brought herself nearly nose to nose with Luke.

"I hit it," she said, all the breath leaving her body as she stared into those green eyes. As the nerves in her face lit up like a power grid, every part of herself feeling electric and bright with him right there. She was conscious again of those whiskers that covered his face, just evidence of a long day spent working, a shave that had happened some twelve hours before.

And the shape of his lips.

The way the top lip dipped sharply in the middle, and the lower was fuller.

"I played darts in my father's basement," she said in a rush, taking a step backward from him.

If she didn't tell him he was just going to keep pestering her. She didn't know how much more of it she could take.

"Really?" he asked, his eyebrows shooting upward. "By yourself?"

"Yes."

"Not with friends?"

She frowned. "I didn't have a lot of friends growing up, if you must know."

"Why?"

"Because nobody likes a tattletale, Luke," she said, not meaning to echo her sister's words. Not meaning to reveal so much about herself. But echo them she did.

Her stomach sank, her hands getting a little bit clammy.

"Were you a tattletale, Olivia?" he asked, humor in his voice. Clearly, he didn't understand that they were treading on very bad memories for her.

When everything she had wanted had been at odds with everything she had been. When she had tried so hard to be both good and accepted, and found that she could only be one.

"Yes," she said, her teeth locked together. "I was. And so I played alone a lot, so I spent time at my parents' house in the basement playing darts. And I threw them and threw them and threw them until I could hit a bull's-eye every time. So you're never going to beat me. You're never going to throw me off my game, Luke Hollister. It's going to take more than invading my personal space to throw me."

"You were pretty thrown, darlin'. I just think you're that good at darts."

"I wasn't," she insisted, "not at all."

"You sure about that?"

Ugh. That cocky smile of his. It made her want to… It made her want to *something*, and she didn't know what. That was Luke in a nutshell for her. He made her feel restless and strange. Made her feel like her skin was too tight. And she had no idea what she was supposed to do with any of it.

Worse, she had no idea how to ignore it.

"Yes. I'm completely sure."

"Want to place a wager?" he asked, his grin getting that wicked bent to it that never failed to make her stomach a bit tighter, never failed to send a little shot of adrenaline through her.

She couldn't predict him, that was the problem. Because as they'd discussed earlier, he didn't answer to anyone.

This was dangerous, and she knew it. He was playing games with her, and she felt as though they were the kinds of games she might not actually know the rules to. But she was also angry that he had affected her, and angry that he had stepped on vulnerable places inside of her.

That anger propelled her forward.

"Sure." She tried to sound casual. Unconcerned, even.

"All right," he said. "We are going to do a little experiment. And then you're going to throw the dart, and try to hit the bull's-eye."

"Fine."

He held up the shot of whiskey, extending it to her. "You want me to throw the dart after I take a shot?" She laughed. "First of all, are we in high school? Are you peer pressuring me to *drink*? And second of all, that's not even a challenge."

"Oh, kiddo." He lifted his glass and pressed it to his lips, tilting it back, taking the whiskey down in one swallow.

She gaped at him, confused.

His mouth turned up at the sides in a smile she was sure was meant to be an answer, but only raised more questions inside of her.

"You're a lightweight, I assume," he continued, "since you claim you don't drink often. It wouldn't be very sporting of me to expect you to throw a dart after you take a whole big bad shot of whiskey. But I do think you should have a taste."

And before she could protest, before she knew what was happening, Luke had wrapped his arm around her waist and pulled her up against his body, where she was staring at those lips again. And then, he was closing the distance between them.

CHAPTER SEVEN

LUKE HOLLISTER WAS kissing her.

He was only the second man to kiss her. The second man to ever put his mouth against hers. But at the moment, she couldn't even compare the two experiences. She was frozen, and Luke was still, too, but he was… *Him*.

He tasted like Luke. Like sunshine and hard work. Like whiskey that lingered on his lips. And like a whole lot of trouble.

It was more than just taste, more than just the strange sensation of a mouth that was an unfamiliar shape pressed against hers. It transcended those physical things.

And it went somewhere deeper.

She was on fire. Melting. Her legs were weak, her stomach trembling. It was as if she had never been kissed before at all. That's how different it was.

His hand was so big, and it was pressed against her lower back, like he owned her. His other hand came up to cup her face—rough, callused—skimming over her cheekbone. He didn't take the kiss deeper. Didn't part her lips.

It was over in less than a second.

A chaste kiss. A simple kiss.

That left nothing chaste or simple remaining in her entire body.

There was a pulse pounding insistently between her legs, a slick wetness that had built up in defiance of everything she knew about herself. Her heart was pounding, her breasts heavy, her nipples tightened into painful points.

It was over. Over long before she was able to move or think or react at all. Over long before she realized they were still standing in the middle of the Gold Valley saloon, rather than in some moment that existed outside of space and time.

Luke Hollister had just kissed her in front of everyone.

Bennett was there. She remembered that too late. She remembered everything too late. Including why they were doing this. Of course. He was making a show, as he had promised he would do. And he was definitely trying to get a rise out of her, which she expected, because he was Luke.

All of that made sense. Except none of it made sense. Not inside of her anyway.

"Throw the dart," he said, his mouth so close to hers it would take nothing for her lips to touch his again. Nothing at all.

Then he withdrew, taking a step back and leaning against the table again, all cocky arrogance and that kind of masculine swagger she hated. She did. She hated it. And right now she was pretty sure she might hate him, too.

She turned away from him, drew her arm back and threw the dart. And it missed.

She hadn't missed a bull's-eye without meaning to in more than ten years.

Hot, angry tears pricked her eyes but she refused to let them fall. Because that was just stupid. This was a game. That was all. It was supposed to be a game where they made Bennett jealous. Where they made him think that he was in danger of losing her.

It was supposed to make Bennett feel wild and unpleasant things; it was not supposed to make *her* feel wild and unpleasant things.

Too late she remembered to look over at Bennett. And when she did, she had to force herself. He was facing away from them. For all she knew, he hadn't even seen the kiss.

"He saw."

She blinked, feeling numb. "What?"

Luke was looking at her, his expression grave. "Bennett saw the kiss," he said.

And just like that, she felt about two feet tall. Because not only had he read her mind just now, it confirmed to her that Bennett was all he had been thinking about during the kiss. She hadn't thought of Bennett until after. Much, much after. But Luke had been aware the entire time. And then, when she had been standing there feeling vulnerable and reduced, desperately trying to remember the purpose behind this entire interaction, he had read her. Unerringly.

Meanwhile, she couldn't read him or Bennett or anything. She couldn't even read herself.

"Good," she said, as if it was all she cared about. As if there was nothing more conflicting inside of her than whether or not they had managed to affect Bennett.

To say nothing about how she had been affected.

Except, she had missed the target. And there was no pretending that hadn't happened. She bit the inside of her cheek. "He's never seen me miss a bull's-eye," she said. "At least, kissing him certainly never made me miss a bull's-eye. That will give him something to think about."

She could tell by the particular curve of his smile that Luke didn't believe her. But he didn't say that. This, quite possibly, was the first time he had ever been a gentleman to her in any way that counted.

"You sure you don't want another drink?" he asked, taking a step backward, toward the bar.

She sniffed. "I don't like whiskey."

His smile widened. Why was his confidence so impenetrable? Why was he so... So much? "Really?"

"Really," she confirmed.

"I'll get you a refill on that Coke," he said, turning away from her and heading back toward the bar, leaving her to ruminate by the dartboard.

She chanced another look at Bennett's table. And he still wasn't looking at her. But she caught Kaylee's eye again. The other woman was clearly unamused with Olivia. Well, at the moment, that made two of them. Olivia felt like she had taken a step into a river, only to find that there was a drop-off sooner than she had anticipated. And that she had scrambled to find her footing, finding instead only algae. Now she was being swept downstream. As analogies went, it was both unpleasant and apt.

She wanted to run. She wanted to run right out the door of the saloon, down the main street, all the way back home. She wanted to abandon this mission, wave a little white flag of defeat, start over tomorrow morning and pretend that nothing had happened.

The only thing that kept her there was that sheer goal-oriented, stubborn nature of hers. She had started down this path, and she had to see it through.

Well, more accurately at the moment, she had started

swimming in this river, and at this point she just needed to see where the current would carry her. She couldn't undo what everyone had just seen. Couldn't pretend she hadn't just kissed Luke in front of God and everybody in the bar.

There was no taking that back. Sure, she could offer up handwritten notes to everyone in attendance explaining what she had tried to do, that she was very sorry and that it wouldn't happen again. Sure, she could stand up on a chair and make an announcement, that she and Luke had been engaged in a little bit of improv, and hadn't that been a great scene? But it definitely hadn't been real.

But that would be silly, and she wasn't going to do that.

Which meant she had no other choice but to allow the current to continue to sweep her along. And hope there wasn't a waterfall waiting for her at the end.

She beat Luke soundly at darts, which was the only expected thing to come out of the evening. Thankfully, she managed to get herself solid again, and didn't miss another shot for the rest of the night. Luke, on the other hand, was actually fairly terrible.

"Don't you know how to shoot a gun?" she asked when they had finished tallying the score, which had been more of a formality than anything else, because she had so obviously beaten him.

"Yes. With a scope. That's a little bit different."

"Pretty pitiful, Hollister," she said, feeling bolstered by the win and momentarily forgetting what had happened a half hour earlier.

"I know my talents. I'm okay with the fact that they don't lie at the dartboard."

"Really. Where do they lie exactly?"

"The back of a horse, out on the ranch and in the bedroom.

Heat flared through her body, bleeding out toward her cheeks, down her neck, lower. To all those places that had been affected by the kiss.

"If a man has to boast," she said, knowing her tone sounded clipped and stiff, "then it sounds a little like just that. Boastfulness with nothing behind it."

"I don't boast," he said. "I'm terrible at darts, and I never claimed any different. One thing you should know about me, Liv. What you see is what you get. I don't lie."

"Except now. What Bennett's seeing isn't real. Don't go claiming perfect honesty when you're in the middle of treachery."

"I'm being honest where it counts," he said. "You know what I want."

Something about the way the heat shimmered in his green eyes when he said that made her stomach tighten. Made her question if she actually did know what he wanted. If this really was all about Bennett and some property her father owned, or if there might be something else. But that was ridiculous. A man like Luke wouldn't want anything from a woman like her. A woman who barely knew how to kiss, much less anything else.

And if he did, it wouldn't be about her specifically, but about the fact that he was a man, and they had needs, and all of that. Particularly men like him, who didn't practice any kind of restraint.

At least, she had never witnessed him practicing restraint of any kind. He was about as different from Bennett as a man could be.

"I have to get up early," she said. "We should probably go."

But first, she really needed to use the restroom, because ultimately she had ended up having three Diet Cokes to keep her focus on something—anything—other than Luke.

"All right," he said, grabbing his jacket off the back of the chair.

"Just a second," she said.

She scurried across the bar, the sound of her footsteps swallowed up by the noise of the people around them and the music playing over the speakers.

She grimaced when she saw that there was a line outside the little single-use room. Strangely, she didn't want to talk to anyone. Strange, since what she and Luke had been doing had definitely been designed to draw attention. But she didn't want to actually contend with that attention in real time. She wanted to deal with it on her terms. When she was good and ready to deal with it. And that would be when she had been given a lot more time to process everything herself.

She looked up at the scarred, wooden wall and frowned when she saw a list of names carved into it.

Second to last was Luke Hollister. She put her fingertips against his name, a strange kind of energy zipping through her as she did.

"Found me," he said.

She looked up, startled. Luke was standing right next to her, his hands shoved into his pockets, his black cowboy hat positioned firmly on his head.

She jerked her hand back as though the wall was on fire and in danger of scalding her skin. "What is it?"

They were all men's names. She recognized a couple of them, but no one she knew very well. And she couldn't figure out what they might have in common.

Luke lifted a shoulder. "Dumb shit."

"What dumb… Stuff?" Now her curiosity was getting the best of her.

"They don't do it much anymore. This," he said, tapping his hand against his own name, "is from a long time ago."

"What? Did you… Drink the most beers or something?"

"When a guy hooked up in the bathroom they used to carve his name on the wall."

Her stomach plummeted down to her toes. "What?"

"Yeah, Laz put a stop to that. He didn't much care for people carving into the side of his wall when he bought the place."

"You… You…"

Just then, the bathroom door opened and a woman walked out, barely glancing at her and Luke as she breezed past.

"Looks like it's vacant." He gestured toward the bathroom.

"You're not going to wait outside for me, are you?" That was all she needed. Luke timing her bathroom break. While she was in there it would also probably be unavoidable to imagine him in there with that woman…

"Yes," he said. "Because I'm waiting for you."

"You're awful," she said, rushing into the bathroom and shutting the door firmly, locking it behind her. She pressed her palms against her face and realized that it was hot.

She looked around the small room and tried to imagine how on earth a person would… Do that. With everybody outside fully aware of what was going on.

She took care of her necessities, her heart thundering hard the entire time. Then, when she washed her hands, she went ahead and splashed some cool water on her face and her neck.

When she exited the bathroom, he was standing there, leaning against the wall, his head down, his black hat concealing his face. Then he looked up, revealing all that stunning masculine glory. Strong chin, square jaw, those lips that she had kissed. Lips that had kissed another woman and more in the bathroom she had just exited.

That thought was even more effective than the cold water she had literally just splashed on herself.

She walked past him without saying anything and he followed behind her.

"Hang on," he said when they got to the bar. "I have to settle my tab."

"You couldn't have done that instead of loitering outside the bathroom door like a pervert?" she muttered.

"I waited for you," he said. "You can wait for me."

She realized, dimly, somewhere in the back of her mind, that this all served the purpose that they had come here for in the first place. She wasn't here with him as a date. She wasn't. They were here so that they looked like a burgeoning couple. Which made him waiting for her, and them walking across the bar together, look romantic or something.

Of course, had she actually been here on a date with him, finding his name carved into the wall like that would have been even more upsetting. No. It would have been upsetting. It wasn't upsetting at all as it was. She didn't care how much of a whore he was. That was his business—and the woman's. Whatever woman was crazy enough to try and get involved with him with any actual sincerity.

He paid Laz, and then put his hand on her lower back

as they headed toward the door. She gritted her teeth, trying her best to keep her expression neutral until that first blast of night air hit her in the face as they walked out onto the street.

Then, she pulled away from him. She shoved her hands in her pockets and walked down the sidewalk, looking for the first crosswalk before making her way across toward the truck. He was already there. Because he had just gone directly across the street.

"That's jaywalking," she said.

"Do I look like I care?" he asked, rounding to the passenger side of the truck and jerking the door open for her.

"It doesn't seem to me like you care about much," she said, getting in and grabbing hold of the door handle, slamming it shut before he could do the honors.

He got in and started the engine, pulling away from the curb quickly, before she managed to get herself buckled.

"For the record," she said, once they were on the road, "it's illegal to start driving before the passenger is buckled, too. Like jaywalking."

She didn't know if that was actually true. But it sounded legitimate enough.

"Again," he said, "I don't care."

Now he was starting to sound snippy, and he had no right to sound snippy. *He* wasn't the one who had been kissed in the middle of the bar in front of everyone. Okay, so he had been. But it was different for him. Different for him because he was Luke Hollister, and he had kissed any number of women, and his kissing her wouldn't reflect badly on him. *She* was the one who had kissed only the second man she had ever kissed in her entire life, and then seen his name carved on the wall because he had…

They headed out of town, the glow of the streetlights fading in the distance behind them, the evergreen trees that lined the side of the road absorbing any light that was coming from the moon or the stars, making them feel ensconced in darkness, only the narrow glow of the headlights illuminating a very tight path in front of them.

She kept her eyes on the double yellow line on the road, something comforting about having that familiar sight to rest her eyes on while the rest of the world felt wild, untamed and unknowable.

And she couldn't even pretend it was because of the darkness. It was because of Luke. And the way it had felt when his lips had touched hers.

There was a certain point where she'd stopped worrying about unknown things in the darkness, because she had been convinced that she knew herself well enough she could find her way through anything. That she had decided firmly who she was, and who she would be, and had been at peace with that choice. But all of that assurance had crumbled around her in a bar tonight, and she didn't know quite what to do with that.

So she stared at the yellow line and hoped that it would guide her home, because God knew she didn't trust herself to do it. She certainly didn't trust Luke.

"What exactly are you mad about, Olivia?"

"Nothing," she said.

"You're a terrible liar," he said. "Things were going okay, and now you're mad at me."

"What does it matter? Nothing that happened tonight is real."

"Something made you mad. I want to know what."

"Like you care when I'm mad. You like making me mad."

"Sure," he said. "I like making you mad on purpose. Just a little bit mad. A bit of annoyance here and there. But when I do that, you can bet I do it for fun, and you can bet I don't do it on accident. This is different."

"Did you honestly have… Did you do…" She stumbled over the words, too embarrassed to talk about it in front of him. Which made her feel silly, and childish. She had no idea how to combat it. She cleared her throat. "With a woman. In that bathroom?"

He chuckled, the sound somehow absent of humor, flat in the cab of the truck, the only other sound the engine and the tires on the road. "You're mad about that?"

"You kissed me," she said. "I think I have a right to know where you've been."

"I'm well traveled, kiddo, and I think you already know that."

"In the *bathroom*?" she asked, incredulous. "And everybody in the bar knew what you were doing?"

"We didn't have sex *technically* speaking." He paused for a moment. "At least, not in the bathroom."

"Then why is your name on the wall?" she pressed.

"*Something* happened in there, not going to lie to you about that. And Wyatt Dodge is a dick when he's drunk."

She could hardly imagine Wyatt, who was like a steady older brother to her in many ways, behaving like such a… Such a juvenile frat boy. "Wyatt carved your name onto the sex wall?"

Luke huffed out a laugh. "Yes. But seriously, Olivia, I was like twenty-four years old, and so was he."

"*I'm* twenty-five," she said. "And I think it's immature."

"You're eighty down to your soul," he said.

"Still," she snapped, feeling particularly annoyed by that last comment. Mostly because it skimmed a little bit too close to the truth. "That doesn't make you less gross, and it doesn't mean that I want you to kiss me to prove points, unless we talk about it beforehand."

Suddenly, Luke slammed on the brakes and the truck lurched forward. "That does it." He steered the car off the road onto the shoulder, throwing it into Park, and then turned toward her.

Olivia shrank back, her heart thundering hard from the adrenaline of the abrupt stop, and from the sudden realization of just how small the interior of the truck was. How close he was to her.

"Not everything that happened tonight was fake," he said.

Her stomach lurched, so hard, so far up that she was afraid it might come out of her mouth. "Yes, it was," she insisted.

"No," he said, his voice as rough as the road they'd just been driving on. "It wasn't."

Before she could protest, he reached out, wrapping his large hand around the back of her head, drawing her forward. And then Luke was kissing her again. but this wasn't like *The* kiss in the bar. There was no audience; there was no excuse for it.

And this time, he wasn't still. He wasn't chaste or simple or careful.

He angled his head, forcing her lips apart with his tongue, and her world exploded behind her eyes.

This was *Luke*. Even in the dark there was no pretending any different.

She lifted her hand, with every intention of pushing him away, but then her fingertips made contact with the scruff on his face, those whiskers that had caught her attention on all those close examinations of him that she caught herself engaged in over the past week. She was touching it. Touching him.

There was only one word that echoed inside of her. A word that didn't make any sense, but one that shouted loudly nonetheless.

Finally.

She squeezed her eyes shut, so tight that a tear leaked out from one corner. Only because of how tightly she had closed them, not because of emotion. Of course not because of that. This was Luke and she didn't feel emotions for Luke.

Luke.

Instead of pushing him, she dragged her fingertips along that sharp edge of his jaw, tracing the line of his face down to his chin, brushing her thumb beneath his lower lip as he widened his mouth to taste her even deeper.

She could feel the motion of the kiss under her hand, and somehow, that added to the intensity of the moment.

Which seemed impossible, really. Because the kiss itself was so slick, so hot, so all consuming in a way that she had never imagined a kiss could be.

It eradicated her sense of responsibility, her sense of self. The reason that she was here in this truck with Luke in the first place. The fact that they were on the side of the road—a public road just outside of town where anyone might spot the vehicle and be able to identify it.

None of that seemed as important as what he might do next. As the way he might angle his head, the way the tip of his tongue might trace her lip, might slide against hers.

She was hot all over, her breasts heavy, the ache between her legs a fierce and unrelenting thing that made her feel hollow all the way through.

Luke shifted, pressing both of his hands between her shoulder blades before moving them down her back, coming to rest on her hips. He gripped her hard, his fingertips digging into her skin, through the thin fabric of her dress and her leggings.

Then, suddenly she found herself being hauled across the cab of the truck, as Luke quickly undid her seat belt and drew her up onto his lap, positioning them both at the center of the bench seat, her back to the dashboard.

He pulled her hard against him, until she could feel that telltale, uncompromising ridge between her legs. There was one moment where she thought about protesting. Where she had a spare brain cell in her head that told her she needed to put an end to this.

But it was only a moment. And when he flexed his hips forward, meeting that place at the apex of her thighs that was so desperate, so needy for some satisfaction, it burst into blinding brilliant light, lost completely in the heat and intensity of the moment.

He kept one hand placed at her hip, raised the other one and cupped her face, his hand sliding around behind her head, sifting through her hair as he continued to kiss her, deep and slick.

Then he abandoned her lips, and she groaned, her sound of regret quickly replaced by one of pleasure when that hot mouth of his made contact with the vulnerable skin on the side of her neck, down farther, down all the way to the neckline of her dress. And back up again.

She didn't know what was happening to her. Didn't know what had possessed her. She felt like a stranger inside of her skin, one who had no control over the reactions happening inside of her. One who had no understanding of them.

Of course she had been kissed. She had been kissed quite passionately before. But she had been so very aware of herself, so very aware of what was happening, of what might happen next and what she would allow.

Here, now, all of that had been blown apart. Reduced to such tiny fragments that she would never be able to piece them back together. In the moment, she didn't want to.

In the moment, all she wanted to do was feel.

There was no sound apart from their breath, hard and heavy, mingling together. A sign that the two of them were completely lost in this. Together. It was so intimate. Yes, of course, her tongue against his was intimate, her most sensitive place pressed against his was intimate. But their breath, their heartbeats, that evidence of what this did to them... Somehow that was even more. Even deeper. Even more impactful.

Something dark, delicious and unfamiliar was building inside of her. Dimly, she thought she should fight it. That it was something she had fought against before. But his hands were so warm, so large and masculine and wonderful holding her head, holding her hip. The whiskers on his face burning delicate skin on her cheek, her neck, her collarbone, too wonderful to pull away from. She rocked her hips against his, the rhythm natural, seeming to blend with the rhythm of their kiss as he licked a path down to the very edge of her dress, then lifted a hand and flicked open the top button, then the second.

Until he revealed the edge of her bra and licked around the edge of that, his tongue tantalizing the sensitive, aroused skin there.

She rolled her hips forward, the tension low in her midsection drawing up even tighter, that place between her legs slick and sensitive. He moved the hand on her hip lower, around to grip her butt, pulling her hard against him. And then the world burst into brilliant color behind her eyelids. She pressed her hips forward, rubbing herself against that hard ridge in his jeans as wave after wave of pleasure rolled over her, as internal muscles she hadn't been aware of before clenched tight.

She buried her face into the curve of his neck, a hoarse cry on her lips as she shivered through the on-slaught of release that seemed to be unraveling her, pulling at some previously unseen thread deep inside of her, undoing everything that had been Olivia Logan before. Leaving behind a worn, threadbare stranger that was sweating and panting in a man's arms.

In a truck. On the side of the road.

And then it hit her. Fully hit her.

She had been making out with Luke Hollister on the side of the road.

She'd...

She scrambled out of his hold, pinning herself against the passenger door, her heart pounding so hard she was afraid it was going to break into a million pieces as it slammed itself against her breastbone. As if it were try-ing to escape, or trying to destroy itself, to release her from this moment. From this humiliation.

She grabbed hold of the door handle and opened the door. And before she could fully think her next action through, she jumped out of the truck and started to walk back toward her house. Away from Luke.

Away from the kind of insanity she knew had the power to ruin her carefully laid plans.

CHAPTER EIGHT

LUKE WAS OUT of the truck and heading after Olivia before he had time to process what had just happened.

They had been kissing, of that much he was certain. An explosion of restraint that had reached its breaking point. At least on his end.

He was pretty sure he wasn't the only one, though. Judging by her response to the kiss. If he wasn't mistaken, she'd had an orgasm. And then she had tumbled out of his truck like he was an ax murderer chasing her down, and not the man who had just made her come.

"Olivia," he called after her retreating figure. He could just barely make out the shape of her, fluttery and small in the darkness.

She didn't stop moving away from him.

"Olivia Logan," he called again, taking three steps and catching up with her, grabbing hold of her arm and stopping her progress. "What the hell do you think you're doing?"

"I'm walking home," she said, jerking out of his grasp and starting down the road again.

"You are not," he said. "Get your ass back in the truck."

"Don't tell me what to do," she said. "I'd rather take my chances out here than get back into that truck with you."

"Don't do that," he said. "Don't act like I did something to you that you didn't like. Don't hide behind all your prickles and indignation. We both know you wanted that."

She laughed, a kind of hysterical hoot, her brown eyes glittering in the pale light. Her hair was a wreck, and he'd place a bet her cheeks were flushed from the pleasure he'd just given her. She looked like a woman who'd been ravished. He imagined she wouldn't like that one bit. "I *did not want that*. I have actively avoided things like that my entire life. *Nothing* in me wanted that."

"Then why did you respond the way you did?"

"Good night, Luke," she said, whirling away from him again and stalking down the road.

"It's dangerous out here. You can't see, any car driving on the road isn't going to be able to see and you're basically cougar bait."

"The way I see it, it's one predator or another, Luke, and I'm happy to take my chances on the ones with claws."

"Olivia, I would never do anything you didn't want," he called after her.

She turned toward him. "I'm just going to go home," she said, her voice tremulous.

"Let me take you home, Liv," he said through gritted teeth. "The last thing I want is for something to happen to you because I let you run off having a tantrum."

"I am not having a tantrum," she said, stomping her foot in the dirt.

"Honey," he said, "this is a tantrum. And I'm about over it. So either you get back into the truck, or I'm going to throw you over my shoulder and carry you back."

"You wouldn't dare."

"Try me, kiddo. Ask yourself if there's one threat I haven't made good on. I might be a jerk, Olivia, but I'm an honest one. And I swear to you if you don't get that pretty ass of yours back in my truck I will put it there myself."

He wasn't bluffing. There was no way in hell he was letting her wander around in the forest without a flashlight, with her purse back in his truck… Hell, he doubted she even had her cell phone.

She stood for a moment, and there was no making out her facial expression in the darkness. But he could sense her rage. Had a pretty good idea she was staring daggers through him, even though she probably couldn't see him very well, either.

"Don't touch me," she said, walking back toward the truck, careful not to brush him as she went past.

"I'd rather stick my hand in a badger den," he commented, walking behind her.

"I'd happily watch."

She climbed back into the truck and shut the door behind her. And he waited until she was buckled up before he got in and started the engine up again. He checked for headlights, and then pulled back out onto the highway.

His pulse was pounding, and only once they were back on the road did he realize that he was still hard and aching from that kiss. Olivia had come, but he had not. And he wanted to.

He gritted his teeth. He needed to get himself under control. Needed to get his libido reined in. Because he didn't do things like this. He didn't go after women who didn't want him; he didn't work this hard for a simple orgasm.

And he sure as hell wasn't going to try and coerce

Olivia into his bed. He could have most any woman back at the bar that he wanted. Why was he going to get embroiled in something this complicated? Sure. He wanted her. But he wanted a lot of things he didn't have.

Life was tricky enough at the moment. He was not going to add her to the mix. Her and her uptight demeanor. Why the hell would he want to take a woman like her to bed anyway? He could have a woman who was enthusiastically on board with everything, rather than little miss prim and prissy.

Thankfully, they weren't actually that far from her little house.

He saw the little half stone wall with the reflective address number on it and turned in. He followed the main drive for a while, then took a right, where he knew the road led to Olivia's cottage, rather than to her parents' house.

He pulled up in front of the little white-and-yellow cottage, illuminated by the small light on the porch, and didn't even bother to put his truck in Park. Just pressed his foot down on the brake.

"See you later," he said.

"Sure," she said, opening up the passenger door, the overhead light casting a glow on her face.

She was pale. More than that, she looked terrified. Not just angry. But honest to God scared.

He groaned, putting the truck in Park. Then he reached out, brushing his thumb over her cheekbone. "Olivia…"

For a moment she froze. For a moment she just stared at him, and he could see a small war being waged behind those pretty brown eyes. Then she jerked away from him, away from his touch. "Don't."

She shook her head, climbing down from the truck and slamming the door, clutching her purse and her sweater to her chest as she walked up to her front door. He watched until she was safely inside, and then shook his head, throwing the truck in Reverse and pulling out of the driveway too damned fast. But if he didn't leave now, he was going to be tempted to go after her, and he knew that would be a bad idea.

His heart was raging like he had just run a marathon, his whole body so on edge he had a feeling a strong breeze could push him over.

No. Only Olivia.

He gritted his teeth against that thought. That regrettably true thought.

There was no point wanting her. There never had been. She was Olivia Logan, of the Logans of Logan County. As close to royalty as you could find in rural Oregon.

He did not have an inferiority complex. That wasn't the issue. He was sure on her end those would be on her list of issues. As far as his went... She wanted love. She wanted marriage. She had made that abundantly clear. She was twenty-five years old and he was thirty-six. He had a hunch that she was inexperienced, and he sure as hell was not.

He was wrong for her in a thousand different ways, and his damned body couldn't seem to hold on to that reality.

No, he wasn't going after her. He was going home. He was getting in a cold shower.

And then he was getting blind-ass drunk so that he could forget he had ever put his hands on Olivia Logan.

Because he sure as hell wasn't going to do it again.

OLIVIA STUMBLED INTO the house on shaking legs. A great, gasping sob escaping as she shut the door be-

hind her and locked it. She didn't know if she was locking it against Luke, to keep him outside, or locking it
to keep herself inside.

Apparently, she didn't know anything. Not about herself, not about a man who had been in her life in some
capacity for close to twenty years.

She hadn't known she could want like that. She
hadn't known she wanted *him* like that.

But that word had played itself over and over in her
mind. *Finally. Finally. Finally.*

She couldn't scrub it out of her brain even now.

Even now, as she walked through the living room
and dumped her purse and her sweater on the couch,
unbearably conscious of the fact that her stomach felt
nauseous and that she was wet between her legs.

She heard her phone vibrate and she scrambled to
grab hold of it. She had three texts from her mother.
Asking if she was home yet.

And then another one rolled in.

Why were you with Luke Hollister at Gold Valley Saloon tonight?

She threw her phone on the couch like it was a rabid
varmint and took a step away from it, scrubbing her
face with her hands. She couldn't have this conversation. Not now. She couldn't answer these questions she
didn't have an answer to.

*There's a very simple answer. It's to get Bennett
back.*

She was a liar. Even her head was a liar. She certainly
hadn't made out with Luke in his truck to get Bennett
back. She hadn't...

She pressed a hand to her stomach. She had kissed him and had an orgasm.

She'd never had an orgasm before in her life.

She was a good girl. She had worked so hard to be a good girl. And to be everything that Vanessa wasn't.

To justify her existence. To justify the fact that Olivia the tattletale had ruined Vanessa the rebel's life. Hadn't it been essential to be good after that? To show it was possible to live the kind of life their parents wanted them to have? That it led to better places?

Or she was a hypocrite. She had to keep everything locked down so tight. She couldn't even let go of it in private.

But a few minutes in private with Luke, a few minutes in his arms, with his hands on her body, and she had let go of everything she had worked so hard for. Everything that she had trained herself to be.

Without thinking, she stumbled back toward the bathroom, flicking on the switch, flooding the room with light that was far too bright. Far too revealing of everything that had happened over the space of the last half hour. Her cheeks were flushed, her lips were swollen. Her eyes were bright and fevered.

She was suddenly aware of the fact that her neck burned, and she angled her head to the side, looking at her reflection, looking at the trail of red that ran down her skin.

Whisker burn, she realized.

Those whiskers that had been captivating her for all this time had left their mark, that was sure.

Who *was* she? She didn't have an answer to that. Or at least, not one she liked.

She pulled her dress up over her head, whirling around and turning on the hot water knob in her shower.

Then she wrestled with her bra, extricating herself clumsily before shoving her leggings and her underwear down her thighs.

She stepped beneath the spray of water before it was warm, shivering as it slowly grew hotter and hotter, sluicing over her bare shoulders.

She was determined to stand there until she felt normal again. Until she could no longer feel the impression of his lips on hers, his stubble against her neck, his hands on her hips.

She stood there until the water got cold again, and she could still feel his touch. She stood there until she was too miserable and exhausted to do anything but turn the water off, wrap herself in a towel and sit on the edge of her bed.

Slowly, she became aware of her body. Of the fact that her breasts still felt sensitive, of the fact that she felt achy and restless between her thighs still. That got her moving. Spurred her to dry herself off and get herself covered up in sensible, cozy pajamas.

She hoped that would make her feel more like herself.

But as she slipped beneath the covers and curled up into a tight ball, she still felt wrong. Still felt like somebody new. Somebody she didn't want to be.

And she was afraid that good girl Olivia, the Olivia that was so essential, wasn't someone she could simply get back to. Because she was afraid she had shattered that Olivia irrevocably in the cab of Luke Hollister's truck.

As she finally drifted off to sleep, all she could think was that nothing was right. She didn't know how it ever would be again.

CHAPTER NINE

WHEN OLIVIA WOKE up the next morning her phone was glowing on the couch. She had a raft of texts from her mother. And before she could bend down to pick the phone up, there was a knock at the door.

"Darn it," she whispered, picking up the phone and holding it to her chest.

She walked to the front door, the white carpet plush beneath her feet. Usually a comfort in trying times, but nothing was comforting to her now.

"Coming," she muttered as the knocking became more insistent. She had absolutely no illusions as to who it was.

She opened the door and came face-to-face with her mother.

Tamara Logan closely resembled Olivia, only older and more elegant. She was an inch or so shorter than her daughter, still as trim and petite as she had always been. There were fine lines next to her eyes, and not even one strand of gray in her brown hair. If that was accomplished by a hair salon, she would never say, and no one would be brave enough to ask.

"Thank God you're here," her mother said, breezing past her and walking into the room. She looked around her, as if she expected to see something out of place. Olivia had a feeling she was expecting, *dreading*, the possibility that she might find Luke Hollister in the house somewhere, enjoying a morning after.

"I'm *alone*," Olivia said.

"Good," Tamara answered, looking visibly relieved. "I can't tell you how many texts and phone calls I got about you and Luke. Kissing."

"I went on a date with him," Olivia said, wrapping her arms around herself. "It wasn't a big deal. It wasn't even a very serious kiss." The one in the bar that anyone had seen. She left out any mention of the kiss that had happened after.

She wasn't even going to think about that kiss, much less talk to her mom about it. She suddenly felt like she was thirteen again and staring down her very disappointed mother after the skinny-dipping fiasco.

Whose fault was this, Olivia? I can hardly believe it was yours.

Olivia swallowed hard.

"I'm not sure he's a very good man for you to be going on dates with," her mom said, frowning. "And I thought you wanted to try and patch things up with Bennett. I'm sure that by now he's regretting breaking up with you."

"*I* broke up with Bennett," Olivia said, realizing that she hadn't exactly explained the whole story to her parents. "He didn't break up with me."

Shock flitted over her mother's face. "But you were so devastated…"

"I know," she said, shifting in place, feeling about two inches tall. "I just… I don't want to be broken up with him. I didn't want to be. But, you know, I wanted to get married and…"

"He didn't?"

"Not as quickly as I did. I don't know. I'm questioning my decision making now." She was questioning a lot of things. And it was way too early in the morning for her to be trying to explain any of it to her mother, when she could hardly process what had happened the night before, much less what all had happened in the past month.

"I don't like not knowing where you are," her mom said. "I texted you so many times last night."

"I came home early," Olivia said, lying only a little bit, "and I went to sleep. Sorry."

Her mother looked so genuinely concerned that Olivia felt guilty. It was one thing to feel indignant in the moment, like her leash was too short. It was another to fully face the reasons she consented to that leash.

Her parents never knew where Vanessa was. They heard from her maybe twice a year, and it was rarely comforting. They deserved to have one child they didn't have to worry about constantly. She also knew that her parents worried about her even more because of Vanessa. Because they already had one child that was lost to them for all intents and purposes.

They had enough sleepless nights without adding Olivia to their list of worries, and for her part, she had done everything in her power to make sure that she wasn't doing that.

But last night she had. In a few different ways. And now guilt sat heavily on her chest like a rock, joining all of the other muddled feelings she was contending with.

"Nothing is happening with Luke," Olivia said. "It's not. I went out with him because I wanted to prove to Bennett, and to myself a little bit—" she said a small prayer asking for forgiveness for the lie "—that I could go out with someone else if I wanted to. But I promise I'm not blind to anything about Luke. I know him too well."

Tamara sighed heavily, that burst of energy she'd come in with clearly beginning to run out of steam. Her mother reacted with fear first. It was fear, Olivia knew that. She understood it. "It's all right if you want to go on dates."

"I know," Olivia said, feeling a little bit silly that she was twenty-five years old, standing there in a house on her parents' property offering justifications for a date she had gone on. Now she felt silly *and* guilty. So that was fun.

"But, I am relieved to hear that it wasn't serious. I'm sure that Luke is a nice enough man," Tamara conceded, "but I wouldn't say he was suited to you."

"No," Olivia said, agreeing with that wholeheartedly. And tried not to think about the way his hands on her body had seemed to suit certain purposes.

"Bennett is a much better choice. He's from such a good family. And he's such a good man. He'll take care of you."

Her mother's eyes shone with conviction. The absolute certainty that Olivia needed to be cared for. But then, her mom and dad took care of her now. So of course they thought she might need someone to take care of her later. Bennett had been an ideal *someone* to them.

To Olivia, too.

But she was starting to be concerned she had blown that potential future up, and that there would be no getting back to it. That felt hopeless. It felt scary. Like the future in front of her was blank, and the past behind her was slipping out of reach.

She'd had a plan. But in that space between the bar

and her house, something had happened. Something had happened with Luke. And it had done something to her.

"We'll see what happens with Bennett," Olivia said. "I know what I want. I don't know what he wants."

Those words tasted like a lie, too.

"You can always talk to me about these things," Tamara said. "I broke up with your father more than once before we ended up getting married. He was dragging his feet."

"Dad dragged his feet?"

"Terribly. And sometimes the breakup really is what you need to get some perspective. So, hopefully that won't be a long time coming for him."

"Hopefully," Olivia said.

Tamara leaned forward, pulling Olivia into a hug. Olivia suddenly felt very small, and young. Rumpled. Nothing made her feel more fragile than hugging her mother. She took a shaky breath, her shoulders shuddering, and tried to hold back the tears that were building. She was tired. She really needed coffee. Or she was going to fall apart.

"If he doesn't, then he's not the right one," Tamara said, taking a step back and patting Olivia on the shoulder.

"I guess so," Olivia said, taking a deep breath.

Words like *right* and *wrong* felt all jumbled and confused inside of her. Along with everything else.

"Everything will work out right for you, Olivia," her mom said. "You've done everything right. You don't have anything to worry about."

"Thanks, Mom," Olivia mumbled. "I need coffee."

"Okay. I'll leave you to that. I'm going out for breakfast with some of the ladies. Though, that new cook at Sugar Cup doesn't have the best customer service."

Olivia knew that her mother was referring to the very unpersonable Frederick Holt, who made a habit of serving up scrambles with a scowl.

"I'm sure if anyone can make him smile, it's you." Not necessarily because her mother was the friendliest, but because she was more formidable than most anyone. Hell on high heels. Always tactful, but never a pushover.

"We'll see," her mother responded. She gave Olivia's hand one last squeeze before breezing back out the door and getting in her little red sports car, the perk of turning fifty, she had called it.

Olivia closed her white front door, then stood there for a moment looking at her entryway. It was perfect, undisturbed as ever. Her mother had decorated the little cottage that Olivia now called home. And it was as perfect now as it had been the day she moved in five years ago.

There was a little rose garland with a ribbon on it above the door, framing it in a very charming fashion. Shabby chic furniture and country details were spread throughout the room. Cute little roosters and splashes of red amidst pale yellow and white.

Olivia loved it. But she was suddenly very aware that she had moved into a life created for her by her parents.

Neat, pristine, contained.

For some reason she thought of the dollhouse she'd played with when she was little. It had been an antique even then, an old wooden ranch house with two floors. A gift from her grandma. For her and for Vanessa, although Vanessa had never played with it.

When she'd been a little girl that was the life she'd · imagined. A simple house. On a ranch.

Nothing quite like this artfully staged cottage she called home.

That was silly. She had a good life. A good house. And there was no point having an issue with all of the wonderful things she'd been given. Not when she benefited from it so much. If it weren't for them, her job at Grassroots wouldn't be enough to pay her bills. She loved her job. She loved the people that she interacted with; she loved the people she worked with.

Her mother was right. She had always done the right thing. A momentary lapse in her judgment was hardly going to undo all of that.

She would make sure of it.

LUKE KNEW THERE was no way he was going to make it through the day without an interrogation from someone in the Dodge family.

What surprised him most was that it ended up being Bennett.

He had expected to get a lecture from Wyatt. Or to maybe get punched by Jamie, with her tiny fists and the fury of a younger sister whose older brother had been hurt.

The Dodges looked out for each other—that was a fact.

But Bennett was apparently in the mood to handle it himself.

Luke was working on digging a trench to deal with some of the drainage issues down by the cabins that sat closer to the river when Bennett approached, looking hard and stoic.

It was the first time that Luke was aware—in a practical sense—that Bennett Dodge was no longer a boy. But a man. A man who was none too happy with him and looked about ready to start a fight.

Luke wasn't the kind of guy to start a fight. Now,

he'd joined his fair share of bar scuffles in his day. But he didn't usually do much to rate someone coming after him. And when he did, he was pretty good at smoothing things over. He usually ended up having a drink with the person instead of punching anyone.

Bennett didn't look like he wanted to have a drink.

"You said that there was nothing going on between you and Olivia."

"When last we talked there wasn't."

"You're an asshole, Luke," Bennett said. "You can wander around with that don't-give-a-damn smile, thinking that nobody's going to see that, but I do. You're selfish. You don't do a thing but what you want. Olivia's not like that. If you hurt her, I swear to God…"

"*You* hurt her," Luke said, his temper going from zero to a hundred a hell of a lot quicker than he expected it to. "She felt like you promised her things you didn't deliver. So if I were you, I wouldn't be up in my face about *hurting Olivia*."

"She's not the kind of girl you mess around with," Bennett said. "She doesn't know the rules to that kind of thing. And you don't know the rules to having a relationship with a woman like her. There's not another outcome." Bennett continued on as though he hadn't heard the warning note in Luke's voice. As though he didn't hear him at all. "You could trick her far too easily."

"Look," Luke said, "first of all, Olivia's not a girl. She's a woman." A woman who had come apart in his arms last night. He might have known Olivia for more than half of her life, but he didn't see her as a kid. Not anymore. "And if there's one thing I am, it's honest. I've never promised Olivia Logan a damn thing. Not one thing. If she wants to spend time with me, that's her business. But I'm not the one that pretended I was in love with her. I'm not the one that pretended I might marry her someday when I never had the intention of doing that. Don't you dare lie to me and say that you did, Bennett. Because we both know that if you wanted to marry that woman I wouldn't have been at the bar with her last night. You're the one who lied to her. Not me."

"I never lied to her," Bennett said.

"Neither did I," Luke said, letting the shovel fall to the ground, crossing his arms over his chest. "I offered her a drink and a good time. If she wants to take me up on those things, that's her business. And you know whose business it isn't? Yours. Because you gave that right up."

"I didn't give up the right to care about her," Bennett said. "To be worried about her. She deserves a man that's going to take care of her. Not one that's going to play with her. She's been through enough."

Luke frowned. "What does that mean?"

"Everything with her sister. You know Vanessa went off and got herself in all kinds of trouble. She and Olivia used to be close. Olivia doesn't need to be hurt or abandoned by anyone else."

Luke only vaguely knew Vanessa Logan. She had never hung around the ranch as much as Olivia, and definitely not when she would have been the right age for him to pay any attention. He knew, of course, that she was involved in crappy stuff. Because it was a small town and it was impossible not to hear bits and pieces of everyone's life from time to time. Particularly when that person was tied to a family that had as much local fame as the Logans had.

Still, Olivia never brought her up, and Luke hadn't spared her any thought.

"What's happening with Olivia and me has nothing

to do with that. It has nothing to do with permanence, so abandonment certainly isn't going to figure in."

Bennett looked like he was holding himself back from punching him. And Luke had had about enough. "If you want to have a fight, Bennett, then go ahead and hit me. I'm not going to take it lying down. But I'm not going to be the first one to throw a punch, either. So make up your damned mind. And then maybe make up your damned mind about what you want with Olivia."

"I want to keep her safe," Bennett said. "That's what I want. You're not going to do that."

"Safety isn't any fun," Luke said, knowing he was really tempting Bennett's temper at this point. But Luke was in the mood to see it.

Somewhere in all of this, he realized that what he was doing might or might not help what he had promised Olivia he would help with. But he didn't care.

Because last night he was the one who had tasted Olivia. He was the one who had pulled her up onto his lap and let her ride him until she found satisfaction. Yeah. That was him. And that hadn't had anything to do with Bennett, either.

"Yeah, you say that because none of your shit has ever stuck to you," Bennett said. "Because you don't know anything about how hard it is to care for somebody and not be able to protect them."

Bile rose in Luke's throat. He was tempted to laugh, except Bennett was so damn full of bull that he could hardly stand it. Of course, he wasn't going to break a lifetime commitment to keeping his own stuff to himself just because Bennett had poked at his temper.

Luke curled his hands into fists, resting them at his sides. Right about now, he wouldn't mind throwing a punch at that Hollywood-square jaw of Bennett's.

Maybe he could get himself fired and he wouldn't have to go to the trouble of quitting. Wouldn't have to figure out that middle ground between being at Get Out of Dodge and being gone. He could just burn it all down. Except he wasn't that man. He didn't do things he couldn't take back. He knew too well how those decisions destroyed people caught in their wake.

"You're right," Luke said. "I wouldn't know anything about that. Are you going to throw that punch or not?"

Bennett shook his head. "It's not worth it."

"Why? Because you know I'll kick your ass?" Apparently he was more interested in goading someone into a fight today than he usually was.

"Because I'm trying to appeal to your better nature, and I'm not sure that you have one."

He wasn't going to punch Bennett. He wasn't. So instead, he smiled. A fight would only satisfy Bennett. A smile… That would piss him off.

"It'll be interesting to find out, won't it?" Luke asked.

He watched as Bennett grappled with his rage. And for a moment he really hoped the other man would haul off and hit him, because a fight would make him feel better, too.

But then Bennett took a step back and shook his head. "Sometimes you're like a brother to me, Luke. And other times I'm very much reminded that you're not one of us."

Much like the smile Luke had treated Bennett to, that comment landed a hell of a lot harder than a punch.

Luke watched Bennett walk away, and no matter how much he wanted to, he couldn't even be mad. Because it was true. He might have spent the past twenty years working on the Dodge ranch, but he wasn't a Dodge, and he never would be. He was the son of a woman whose name he hadn't spoken out loud since that dark day when he'd found her unresponsive in her room.

The son of a woman who had imagined that he—and the rest of the world—would be better off without her, and had taken her own life, leaving nothing but money in her place.

Money he hadn't touched.

Money it was starting to look like it was time to use.

The only thing worse than suspecting that his mother might have killed herself in order for him to have that, to have those opportunities, was not taking them.

He grabbed hold of his shovel again and punched the sharp tip through the ground, the force a satisfying release.

Bennett didn't think he understood loss. He didn't think he understood taking care of someone.

Luke understood worse than taking care of someone. He knew what it was like to try to take care of someone, to try and hold somebody to a world, to a life they didn't want to be a part of, and to lose that battle.

There was nothing on earth that could fix it. Nothing that could change the way it had gone. Not recriminations, not confessions. Certainly not confessions made out back behind a dude ranch between the river and the cabins, digging trenches. Made to the ex-boyfriend of the woman he had just about made love to last night in spite of every bit of better judgment saying it was wrong.

Yeah, there was no point to any of it. He was just going to keep digging trenches. Until everything with the land and Quinn Logan was settled. Until he had talked Olivia into giving her father a recommendation for him.

Because if there was one thing he knew, it was when to move on.

This place had been a comfortable one for two decades, but it wasn't a good fit anymore. For a few different reasons.

Olivia Logan was only one of them.

RARELY WAS OLIVIA cranky over having a day off, but today she certainly was. It all came back to wishing she had something to keep her mind occupied, when she categorically didn't.

She was sick of her own company and her house by the time she got dressed in a pair of leggings and an oversize sweater and plodded into town to grab some coffee.

She walked quickly down the sidewalk and pushed open the door to Sugar Cup, which was heavy and wooden, black paint worn down to reveal the natural grain beneath. She peeked cautiously inside, hoping that her mother and her mother's friends weren't in residence, and was gratified to see that they weren't.

She really didn't want to face that level of rumor mill in her current state. Though, she was well aware that by leaving her house she had opened herself up to the possibility of having to talk about Luke and what had transpired at the bar last night.

It was a tacit agreement that one made between themselves and their small town after controversy was stirred. And while she knew that, she was also willing to chance it today. She just couldn't spend another minute cooped up and in her own head.

She was confused, and she didn't know what she wanted to do. Whether or not she wanted to keep hammering at this thing with Bennett, or just hide in her bedroom for the rest of her life and get a cat or twelve and try to find some kind of work that allowed her to never have to put on pants with challenging waistbands ever again.

Yes, that was another option.

It wasn't like her plan to make Bennett jealous was going to work very well if she told everyone that nothing was happening with Luke and herself, but for some reason the subterfuge didn't feel easy when there was something real to it.

That thought stunned her, standing there in the middle of the coffee shop. She looked up at the large, wrought iron chandelier that hung down at the center of the rustic room. Then she looked back down at the distressed barn wood floor, revelation all but slapping her in the face.

That was the problem.

That saying there was something going on between herself and Luke had *truth* to it.

If it had been a lie, if all of it had been made up, it would have been much easier.

But it wasn't.

It was clear as the cold January day all of a sudden, and just as biting. *That* was the itch beneath her skin. The restlessness she felt whenever he was around. The restlessness she had felt whenever he was around for the past several years.

She was *attracted* to him.

A stupid revelation to have standing there dumbly in front of the extremely unamused-looking cashier, but a revelation she was having nonetheless.

She thought back to that day they'd all gone down to the beach, bringing several trucks and coolers and barbecues. They had spent the whole day down there, and she had spent all that time artfully avoiding contact with Luke, who had seemed bound and determined to harass her on some level or another every time she turned around.

He hadn't been wearing a shirt, and she had found it obnoxious, in spite of the fact that most of the men there had been without shirts, since they were swimming.

But there was something about Luke's partial nudity that had seemed gratuitous. By virtue of the fact that he was Luke.

She had tried to tell herself it was because he was annoying, and therefore his shirtlessness was also annoying.

But the fact that she remembered his body in great detail even now, a couple of years later, told her something else entirely.

She hadn't been dating Bennett then, but she had been fully committed to the idea of being with him someday.

Luke, and his broad shoulders, muscular chest, well-defined abs and general self, had been an obnoxious blight on the whole afternoon.

Which seemed ridiculous, because Bennett had a fantastic body. In fact, there was not a single muscle that Luke possessed that Bennett didn't.

So why were Luke's muscles emblazoned in her memory?

"Are you ready?" The blonde behind the counter with her high, messy bun, overly lined eyes and dour expression looked out of patience with Olivia.

That made two of them.

"What's the special?" Olivia asked, desperately seeking a sign.

"A Big Hunk Mocha. It's—"

"Is it sweet?" Olivia asked.

"Yes. It will make your teeth fall out." Her expression didn't lighten at all when she said it.

"Perfect." She needed sugar. Indulgence. Something to make her feel good in the midst of all the *uncomfortable* she was having.

If there was one thing she'd learned over the past few weeks it was that you couldn't eat healthy *and* also be sad. You had to pick one. And since happiness had been thin on the ground, sugar had been thick on it. So to speak.

"Olivia Logan." That hot voice, rough as a back road, washed through her. "As I live and breathe."

Luke. Of course it was Luke.

It was exactly what he had said to her when he had found her broken down on the side of the road. She wondered if that made it their thing. She wasn't sure how she felt about having a thing with Luke Hollister.

But then, given her thoughts of the past few minutes, she supposed it was undeniable that to an extent she did, whether she wanted to or not.

She really wished *not*.

She turned slightly, suddenly feeling a bit dumpy and far too casual in her sweater and leggings. Like the overabundance of knit and stretch she was currently swimming in announced the fact that she was feeling low, and that she had needed clothing that was kind and unchallenging in order to grapple with the rest of life. Which, she currently found unkind and far too challenging.

He was bound to know it was because of him.

"I didn't know you frequented coffeehouses," she said, sounding much more clipped and snippy than she intended. Then she looked up, her eyes colliding with his, her senses fully taking in all that was Luke. He was everything she wished he wasn't. Everything she *wished* that she built up to extremes in her imagination. Because surely no man could be so extravagantly handsome. Couldn't reach past every barrier, so carefully erected and tended over the past ten years, and get to *her* quite so effectively. But he was.

And he did.

"I didn't exactly want to hang around the ranch today," he said. "Figured I would take my break in town."

"Why is that?" she asked, wandering over to the other side of the counter, where she knew her drink would appear in a few moments. She clasped her hands in front of her, then lifted them slightly, then lowered them again. She felt restless. She didn't know what to do with her extremities, which was ridiculous. It wasn't like they were a new discovery.

She knew that she *must* stand and make conversation without feeling so incredibly conscious of her elbows and her wrists and where she was supposed to rest them. She must do it all the time. But she couldn't exactly remember how she accomplished that.

Luke placed an order that she couldn't quite hear, and the sullen cashier smiled at him, treated him to quite a bit more warmth than she had treated Olivia to. Then Luke walked over to wait where she was waiting for her coffee.

She felt tiny standing next to him, her head resting a couple of inches beneath the top of his shoulders. Typically, she wore shoes that added at least two inches to her diminutive height. But this morning she had gone for a pair of easy ballet flats, keeping with the theme of clothing that would nurture her wrung-out little body.

Sadly, what it accomplished with Luke in residence was making her feel fragile. Making her feel so much more aware of the fact that he was masculine to her feminine. Large and strong where she was soft and small.

And then she remembered what it was like to be folded up into all that strength, held close against that well-muscled chest, her thighs spread on either side of his...

Heat crept up her neck, into her face, and she knew that he could see the evidence of her train of thought written there across her pale skin.

"I got you a treat," he said.

"You didn't have to do that." She looked determinedly ahead, fixing her eyes on the scarred, wooden counter, gritting her teeth.

"I wanted to."

"Well, I didn't want you to."

"Too late."

Just then, her drink appeared on the counter in a mug that was meant to stay in the coffee shop, rather than beat a hasty exit. She found herself rooted to the spot anyway, because as much as she wanted to run away from Luke, she also wanted to stand there and talk to him. And she had no idea what that was about.

Don't you?

"Why are you trying to escape the ranch?" she asked, reaching out and grabbing hold of her mug.

"Bennett's not too happy with me," Luke said.

Images of the night before flashed before her eyes and she felt her mouth dropping open in horror. "He doesn't... He doesn't know..."

"He saw us together in the bar," Luke said, his tone maddeningly calm. "Remember?"

"Oh," she said.

Luke's coffee arrived—in a to-go cup, which just irritated her—and then a plate with a large cinnamon roll appeared.

"That's for me?"

"Yes, ma'am," he said, grabbing both the cup and the cinnamon roll and leading the way to one of the empty tables at the far end of the room.

Olivia followed him, and she felt a little bit like an obedient terrier, following after Luke's every move. It was the cinnamon roll. She was following the cinnamon roll.

"He doesn't like me associating with you," Luke said, taking a seat and placing the cinnamon roll at the center of the table. She noticed that there was only one fork.

Olivia sat across from Luke, clutching the mug, the warmth from the drink seeping through into her fingers. "Well, good," she said. "That's kind of the idea."

Luke shrugged. "Yeah."

She took a sip of her Big Hunk Mocha. It was indeed very sweet. "Did he say anything about…wanting me back?"

"I doubt that was a conversation he was ever going to have with me, kiddo. He told me to keep my hands off you." A smile touched Luke's wicked mouth. And she could confirm for a fact the mouth was wicked—it was no longer supposition.

"Well," Olivia said, feeling marginally pleased by that. "That's something."

Except, it also forced her to remember when Luke had put his hands on her in the truck. When it had had nothing to do with Bennett. She felt flushed again.

"We definitely caused trouble," she said. "My mother was filled with questions this morning."

Luke leaned back in his chair, lifting his hand and

pushing the brim of his cowboy hat upward with his knuckle. "Was she?"

Olivia looked down into her drink. "She said you're not good for me."

Luke frowned. "That's true enough. Of course, I don't want your parents being angry at me, considering I want to buy that land from your father."

"I don't think he'll stay angry with you when all is said and done. And anyway, he'll care more about what I have to say about you than he'll care about any kind of town gossip. My mother, too. She was worried, but…"

"What must that be like?"

"What?"

His lips quirked into a half smile, his large hands moving around his coffee cup, sending a strange shiver through her body. "To be the hen."

She let out a long, slow breath. "I don't know what you're talking about."

"I'm the fox," he said. "No two ways about it, Liv. The predator. The one that everyone knows they need to protect their daughters from. Protect their virtue from. I've always been that. Nobody knew who my people were, nobody knew where I came from. And even though I had Quinn Dodge to vouch for me, people have always been a little bit wary of me. I know what that's like. I don't mind it. I've found a lot of ways around it."

His words sat uncomfortably with her. With her image of him as that good ole boy who got along with everyone and everything. "Everybody likes you," she pointed out.

"Sure," Luke said. "Everybody likes me, but when push comes to shove they don't want me anywhere near their daughter, right?"

She blinked. "I suppose that's true."

"So I just wonder... I wonder what it's like to be the one everybody's worried about." He looked at her, long enough that it made her feel uncomfortable. Long enough that she had to look away. "Does it irritate you, kiddo?"

She frowned. "I don't know any other way. People worry about me because... I'm me..."

"Does it have something to do with your sister?"

She looked up, startled, her eyes crashing into his. "Vanessa? What made you think about Vanessa?"

"Bennett brought her up when he raked my ass over the coals this morning."

"He shouldn't have," Olivia said, looking down into her coffee again, her heart thundering sickly in her throat. "She doesn't have anything to do with this." She sighed heavily. "Or maybe she does. Vanessa is sad. And, I feel like underneath all of her rebellion she was obviously fragile. Because the world got to her. Addiction. Drugs. She just couldn't find a way out once she got in. Like when you put your foot in the river and it's moving a lot faster than you think. That's what I always think happened."

"Sorry," he said. "Do you think that makes other people worry you might be fragile, too?"

He was treading on such a tender place inside of her, and he didn't even realize it. Didn't realize that she probably worried about her susceptibility to the weights that had dragged her sister down more often than anyone else ever did.

For some reason though, she wanted to tell him. Because his words—his honesty—were echoing in her head. *What's it like to be the hen?*

There was something painful in that question. An acknowledgment that no one had ever worried *for* him.

She couldn't deny his question. The man had had his tongue in her mouth after all. So this wasn't more intimate than that, surely.

"My parents worry about me, because she's not even around for them to worry about. She rarely makes contact. She's impossible to find. For them, it's about protecting the child they can protect," she said slowly. "For the town? I don't know. It's like being the star of their favorite soap opera."

"Everybody thinks you and Bennett are perfect for each other. It's like watching your favorite couple on TV get destroyed by a very obvious interloper. A villain." He flashed her a smile that looked not villainous in the least, and somehow the fact that it lacked malice made it all the more dangerous.

That was the thing about Luke. Like he'd said, everybody liked him, but nobody wanted him to get too close. He was easy, and he was a nice guy, a helpful and accommodating guy. But he *was* a predator. She could sense that. Could sense that one wrong move and she could find herself being hunted.

"That's probably it," she said, trying to speak around her tightened throat.

"We're sure giving people something to talk about."

Olivia looked around the room and noticed that half the people in it were looking at Luke and herself quite avidly.

She put her head down. "I should have stayed home today."

"But then we wouldn't have run into each other."

Exactly. But she didn't say that out loud.

Suddenly, his green eyes turned serious, and that

sent her stomach into a free fall. She could handle Luke when he was being an ass. She could handle him when he was teasing her. It was a lot harder to handle him when he looked at her like this. Like he might say something grave. Or lean forward and kiss her again.

When it quit being a joke, quit being a show and became something much more real.

"You don't have to be afraid of me," he said.

Her stomach hollowed out, her fingers feeling restless. She wiggled them, tapping them against the mug. "You don't think I should be afraid of you?" she whispered.

"I didn't say that." She chanced a glance at him again, caught his eyes, and then held them. "I said you don't have to be afraid of me. You maybe *should* be. But you could push it aside for a little while, too."

Her heart skidded to a halt, then began to beat rapidly, flinging itself against her chest as if it was on a desperate mission to get itself out of here. To get away from him.

Her body was smart. At least, parts of it were. The parts that housed emotions, fear. Other parts…

Her breasts felt heavy, and that thick ache had started up between her thighs again. Those parts of her wanted more of what Luke had given her last night.

Because, of course, only Luke had ever made her feel that way. She had actively avoided ever making herself feel that way, and she had put such a careful distance between herself and Bennett physically. And it had been easy.

Bennett, who was such a beautiful man, had been easy for her to resist.

Bennett, with his broad shoulders and physique comprised of all lean, well-honed muscle. Bennett, with his dark hair, brown eyes and square jaw. She had been able to resist him. Had been able to put up that wall and stay firmly on the right side of it.

She wanted desperately to be able to do that with Luke and couldn't seem to.

That was galling.

"I think fear might be for the best," she said, her lips numb.

He lifted a shoulder. "Possibly."

She looked down at the cinnamon roll, at the melted icing pooling at the center. She wanted to lick it. But that was better than wanting to lick Luke again. "I'm not sure I'm hungry."

"Do you *have* to be hungry to eat a cinnamon roll?" he asked.

"You should be. That's the point of food, Luke. You're hungry, and you eat it."

"But sometimes you just eat it because you want to. Because it tastes good."

Suddenly, she had a feeling that the food in question was becoming a metaphor. She would rather it didn't. But then, as with all things related, it didn't seem to matter what she wanted and what she didn't.

"I don't," she said, sniffing loudly. "I don't believe in indulgence for the sake of it."

He reached out and grabbed hold of the fork, taking a large slice off the cinnamon roll and putting the bite in his mouth slowly. So very slowly. It was gratuitous. It forced her to watch the motion of his lips, the play of his throat as he swallowed.

"I do," he said finally. "Whiskey and cinnamon rolls. I do it because it feels good."

"Not me," she whispered. She wouldn't have been able to make her voice louder now if she wanted to.

"Try it," he said, his voice holding more temptation than all the butter in the cinnamon roll ever could. "You might find it's not as scary as you think."

She looked down at her hands, which were curled into fists on the table, her nails digging into her palms. Her heart was pounding, her throat dry. And she felt... She felt like she was being asked to make a choice she didn't think she could make. To jump over a hurdle she wasn't sure she wanted to clear. "That's what scares me most."

He swept his fork through the roll again, getting another bit and holding it out toward her.

In spite of herself, her mouth watered. "I'm really not hungry."

"But do you want it?" he pressed.

Yes, *yes* she wanted it. The cinnamon roll. And, worse, the metaphor attached to it.

He held the fork out and she parted her lips wordlessly. And allowed him to give her the bite. Flavor exploded over her tongue and she couldn't keep herself from groaning. Luke smiled. And suddenly the fox-and-hen comparison seemed all too apt.

She felt like a little cornered hen, shivering in the back of her coop, facing down a gleaming-eyed fox who most definitely wanted to eat her.

What a strange thing that was. That feeling. Being wanted. Hunted. Pursued. And for it to be something other than unpleasant.

But the worst part was, part of her wanted to rush out of her corner and offer herself to him, even knowing how it would end.

This was the kind of thing she'd avoided. Because she knew there was no good end to this, and she had to do what was right, not what was indulgent.

*You're in charge here. You know what you want.
You want Bennett. Luke and his hotness are just a distraction.*

He leaned back in his chair, looking as self-satis-
fied as if he'd just beaten her at a game of darts. "That
wasn't so bad, was it?"

"That's the problem," she said once she had swallowed. "It's not bad tasting. That doesn't mean it isn't
bad for you."

"Then you go work outside a little bit. The physical
equivalent of Hail Marys."

"That doesn't work with everything," she pointed
out.

He reached out, and her heart stopped as he pressed
his thumb against her lower lip, dragging it along the
edge. "You have a little frosting there."

Then he pulled his hand back and stuck his thumb
in his mouth, licking the frosting that had just been on
her lips off his skin.

An intimate shiver went through her.

"Maybe not," he said. "I still think it might be worth
it."

Olivia pulled the cinnamon roll toward her and took
the fork from his side of the table. Then she proceeded
to eat it far more quickly than anyone should eat a giant
cinnamon roll. But she couldn't sit there and have Luke
watch her like that. Couldn't sit there and allow him to
feed her. It was too much. She needed the cinnamon
roll to just be a cinnamon roll.

She needed her body to go back to being her own.

She needed some sanity, and she was worried that
she might not get it.

"Are you done with your coffee?" She was afraid
that if she finished the coffee she might die of glucose

trauma. Between the drink and the cinnamon roll it was all a bit more sugar than she had anticipated.

She was prosugar, but she had a feeling any more and she wouldn't be able to pass a sobriety test. Walking in a straight line would be above her pay grade.

"Yes," she said.

"Great," he said, standing. "Why don't you drive out to that property with me."

"What?"

"I figure," he said, "that since you're a Logan and it's Logan property, you're free to show me around."

Olivia felt like she'd been bulldozed. Seeing as she was typically the bulldozer in such scenarios, it was a bit shocking. She hesitated. "I suppose so."

"Are you busy?"

She was not. It was why she was tramping around in leggings in the middle of the day. "Well, I had some things I thought I might do," she said. Lying, obviously.

He smiled. "What things are you doing?"

"You know. I was thinking I might go get…a manicure. Or maybe have coffee with a friend."

"You already had coffee with a friend," he said, that smile widening.

"Not what I meant."

Actually, she kind of would like to have coffee with a friend. Maybe with Lindy, or with Lindy's sister-in-law Sabrina. Somebody who might be able to talk to her about all of the things that were going on right now. Except, then she would have to admit them. She would have to verbalize them, put them into words. She wasn't sure she could do that. She was having enough trouble thinking about them as it was.

"Well, you're done with your coffee. And, I don't actually think you need a manicure."

"And you're an expert on things like that?"

"I'm an expert on women's hands," he said pointedly. "Hands I think I might want on my body. And let me tell you, yours would do just fine."

Her eyes caught his and her stomach tightened. Because while she had expected to see that smart-ass glint in his eye, it wasn't there. It was that grave, serious face again. The way he'd looked before he'd kissed her in the bar last night.

And again in his truck before he'd pulled her onto his lap.

"Luke..."

He put his hands up in a gesture of surrender. "I promise I'll behave."

"You never behave."

He lifted a shoulder. "Fine. I promise I won't touch you." He paused for a moment. "Unless you ask me to."

"That's not going to happen."

"Okay."

Then, he headed out of the coffee shop and she stood, scrambling after him. What was it about him that compelled her to follow him? She could just let him walk out, and yet, there she was, following his lead, walking with him to his truck.

"Thank you," he said, opening up the passenger side door for her, just like he had done last night. She rolled her eyes and got in, allowing him to close it for her.

Luke started the engine and they went down the highway, in the direction of Get Out of Dodge, headed out to the old family property that Olivia hadn't been to in years.

"It's strange," she said as Luke turned his truck down the dusty road that badly needed to be regraveled. "My family owns so much land here in the county and I never

go to much of any of it. I just go into town, go home, go
to my job. I'm not really that conscious of it."

"Have you ever thought of moving to one of the bigger properties? Setting a place up for yourself?"

No, she hadn't. Because her entire goal had been to
marry Bennett. Which meant that she would be moving to Dodge land. And that meant that Logan land
didn't factor in.

"Okay," he said, adding no further commentary.

"What does that mean?"

"Nothing. I'm just saying okay. If you've never
thought about doing anything on any of your family's
land, that's not totally abnormal, I would suppose. I
don't know what it's like to grow up with all of that."

"Where did you grow up?" It occurred to her then
that she actually didn't know.

"A ways from here," he said. He offered up nothing more.

Olivia looked out the window and took in the scenery. It was a beautiful piece of land. Pastoral, with a
heavy ridgeline of pine trees around the edge of the
fenced-in fields, mountains rising up beyond. "What
are you going to do with this place?"

She didn't know why on earth she should care. Only
that she did.

That was almost scarier than kissing him.

CHAPTER TEN

LUKE QUESTIONED WHY he had taken Olivia out here. Hell, he questioned everything he had done since he had walked into Sugar Cup and seen Olivia in there placing her order. He shouldn't have bought her a cinnamon roll. He sure as *hell* shouldn't have made it a sexual experience. He shouldn't have teased her.

Because it hadn't stayed teasing, not for long.

He couldn't keep it light with her. Not anymore. That kiss had changed things.

Now that pissed him off. He wasn't inexperienced. Not in the least. He didn't let women get under his skin.

What he was realizing was that Olivia Logan had been under his skin for such a long damn time, like a dormant infection or some shit. And now it was no longer dormant. And there was nothing that he could do about it.

He didn't characterize himself as controlled. Not at all. It was just that he didn't struggle against things often. But this… This he was trying to struggle against. He was doing a piss-poor job.

And now he was bringing her to this ranch. This place that felt like a strange, spiky dream that had more pricks and pitfalls than it had promise.

"I want my own ranch," he said.

"What are you going to ranch?" she asked.

"Cattle, probably. It's what I have the most experience with. Back when I first came to town that was what Quinn used to have. And there's fewer cows now than there used to be, since the focus has shifted, but that's what I always liked best."

"Really?"

"Oh yeah," he said, slowing down as they took another curve on the long driveway. "I like driving cattle. Riding the range. Cowboy stuff."

He saw her shake her head out of the corner of his eye. "Sounds like a lot of work."

"I like work. I like hard work. It's like science."

"Science?" she asked, her tone skeptical.

"Sure. Every action has a reaction, right? It's about the only time I've ever really used anything from school. But that I remember. I've always remembered that. And it's true. You do something on the land, the land rewards you. Or it doesn't, but it does *something*. It always changes. And yet, it's the same, too. The weather can be predicted, unless it can't be. Things work a certain way with animals, until they don't. There something comforting in that. That something can be new every morning when you step outside and the sun is rising up above the hills. It gives that same old view a new promise. That's what I want. A place of my own."

He hadn't exactly meant to spill his guts quite to that degree. Hell, he hadn't known he had that much in them to spill. But it was true. It was all true.

Suddenly he wanted to give her more.

"I grew up in Eugene," he said. "Suburbs, mostly. Not really nice suburbs. But everybody who had parents who took them on vacations for spring break, road trips to nice places…they would talk about going and staying out in Gold Valley. And… Well, when the time was right for me to move, I figured I wanted to see it, too."

"Your mom and dad never took you to Gold Valley? It's not a very long drive from Eugene."

"I know," he said.

Olivia had both of her parents. She had a good family, a good life. She wouldn't understand a situation like his. And he didn't need her to. He didn't need anyone to.

"It was never on the agenda," he said. "But I spun a lot of fantasies about it. About what it would be like to see a place like that. A place that was like those old Westerns that I used to watch on cable. I wanted something like that. Where it didn't matter where you came from, didn't matter what you started with—all that mattered was what you made of yourself." They came to the end of the driveway, where a small, modest cabin sat. He stopped the truck and turned off the engine. "I figured I might find something in a place like that. Or at least, I had a better chance of not finding the same as I'd always had."

"It's not *exactly* like a Western," she pointed out.

"Closer than what I grew up with. I saw an ad for a job at Get Out of Dodge and figured that was my chance. My chance to be a cowboy."

"You wanted to be a cowboy." She sounded amused. He liked that. Her sounding amused rather than like she wanted to smack him.

"I did," he confirmed. "And hell, I guess I am. Quinn has been good to me. The whole family has been good to me. So, not Bennett so much this morning. But I can't blame him. Still, I think it's time for me to do something for myself. If I don't do it now, I probably never will. And that wouldn't be the worst thing. I love where I'm at. But this… I think this is right."

"You're going to have to make the house bigger," she said.

"What for?"

"You know. If you ever have a wife and children…" She trailed off and her eyes met his. Immediately, color flooded her face and she looked embarrassed. Regretful.

"I don't want a wife, kiddo," he said.

She shook her head. "No. I mean, I figured that. A man and his cows. There's a Western for you."

"I guess so." He turned to look at her and it felt like the air in the cabin went away and the space between them seemed to close in.

"So we should…" She fumbled for her seat belt and got out of the truck. "We should walk around."

She shut the door, and he had a feeling she had just been looking to get some distance between them.

He was going to behave. He had promised her that. Moreover, he had promised himself that.

Still, he hadn't been doing the best job of doing what he set his mind on lately.

He got out of the truck, too, the sheer silence of the setting closing in around them. It was set so far back off the highway, so deep in the trees, past any other person anywhere, that the quiet had weight to it. It made him conscious of just how much noise was around him all the time, even in a small town like Gold Valley. Even on a small ranch like Get Out of Dodge.

He could picture it. A new barn, the house restored. Cows in the field. Horses in the stable. Yes, it would be a lot of work, but it would be his work.

He and his mother had only ever rented houses. He wondered what she would think of her son owning his own ranch. All this land. This piece of a state, of a town, that felt like it was part of him.

He would always have to wonder what she'd think. He couldn't ask her. She was gone. And that was the reason he was here. The reason he was even able to entertain the idea of buying the ranch.

The reason that his sense of home could never be simple.

"This is perfect for my purposes," he said, ignoring the tightness in his chest.

"I think there's a river down here," Olivia said, frowning. "It's been forever since I've been here, but I do remember coming as a kid." She turned a small circle, the breeze blowing her glossy brown hair.

This was Logan land. Land that was in her blood. He wondered what it would be like to have ties like that.

Luckily for him, you could just buy ties if you had the cash. And that's what he was going to do. Buy himself a piece of Gold Valley. Buy himself a bit of that belonging that had always eluded him.

He was determined in that. But even so, he couldn't shake that feeling that Olivia seemed to belong here. Seemed to effortlessly fit into the surrounding scenery.

Even in her leggings and ridiculous oversize sweater.

"This way," she said, taking off ahead of him through the fields, the tall blades of grass bending themselves to get out of her way. Luke followed after her, heading toward the trees that stood sentry at the edge of the field.

They were about halfway across when he started to hear the sound of rushing water, and as they got closer, it became clearer.

"Which river is this?" he asked.

"Tioga," she said, "I think. It runs into the Skokomish."

And that ran out into the sea. Another connection. Another thing that made this land feel significant. Weighty.

Made him feel like he could do something significant with that money that had always been more like a millstone than a life preserver.

"I can pay a lot of money for the property," Luke said. "So you don't have to worry about me offering too little to your dad. I promise I'm not asking you for that big of a favor."

Olivia looked up at him, shading her eyes from the unseasonably bright sun. "I figured as much. You're also the kind of man who's devoted the past twenty years of his life to doing hard labor at Get Out of Dodge."

He had. That was true.

She'd noticed, apparently.

He walked through the grove of trees, down to the edge of the water. The air smelled damp. Like earth and the course gray sand that lined the edge of the riverbed. Like moss and pine.

He turned to look at Olivia and saw that she was studying him. "What?"

She shook her head. "Nothing."

He had half a mind to tell her that she was playing a dangerous game. That she shouldn't look at him like that. Except he wanted her to look at him like that. Curious. Hot. He wanted it more than he wanted to breathe right about now, and he damn well shouldn't.

Why did she get under his skin like this? This prickly little control freak in her big sweater and her leggings. He couldn't answer the question, and that bugged the hell out of him.

"Do you like it?" she asked, her hands clasped, her expression hopeful now.

"Hell, yeah," he responded, keeping his tone casual. "I could bring some lawn chairs down here. Some red Solo cups. Beer."

She rolled her eyes. "Why am I not surprised that you consider that the height of celebration?"

"That feels a little bit judgmental."

A smile played around the corners of her lips. "It was supposed to."

The wind kicked up, ice-cold in spite of the sun that shone somewhere above the canopy of trees, sending a gentle whisper through the pine trees, the smell of wet earth and cold water mixing together, rising up around them.

There was no one here. No one to see this. To see him standing with Olivia Logan. She looked softer somehow, standing there in her flat shoes, her face clear of any makeup. Her dark hair blowing gently in the breeze. She looked just right to fit in his arms.

But he wasn't going to do anything about it. Because he had promised that he wouldn't.

Instead he turned, so that he was facing her square on. She looked at him out of the corner of her eye, then startled and looked at him more fully. There was a question in her dark eyes, one that he could see she was afraid of verbalizing.

Bennett wanted to protect her. Luke didn't. He wanted to wrap his arms around her, crush her to his chest and kiss the prickles right out of her. He wanted to kiss her until she was soft and pliant again, like she had been in his truck. Like he had fantasized about every night since.

He didn't want to protect her, no. He wanted to strip her bare. Wanted to see what was beneath all that reserve of hers. Wanted to see Olivia. The woman she was, not the woman she showed the world.

He wanted to see who she was when she first woke

up in the morning. Before she'd had her coffee. Before she'd put on a stitch of makeup or fixed her hair.

Before she transformed into the character the town expected to see.

Her eyes clashed with his, and a spark flared in them. Heat. Fear.

"Luke…" She took a step away from him, and then bit her bottom lip.

Then she sighed, all of the air rushing out of her body, her petite shoulders sagging. She stood frozen for a moment, indecision on her face, then she took two strides toward him, so that she was standing close, so that her breasts were nearly brushing up against his chest. She was breathing hard, her eyes darting back and forth like she was afraid she was about to be caught at any moment.

He clenched his hands into fists, clenched his teeth. Because he was about to catch her. And he had promised he wouldn't. But she was pushing it. She was pushing it hard.

Whatever she was used to, whatever she thought… She didn't know him. She didn't know him as a man. He wasn't careful; he wasn't thoughtful or protective.

He imagined that she expected him to be, when push came to shove, seeing as her dating experience, as far as he knew, basically boiled down to Bennett. And he knew exactly how Bennett felt about her.

"Be very careful, Liv," he said, his tone full of warning.

Warning was the kindest thing he could give.

"Please," she said. "Would you touch me, Luke?"

And then she reached out, pressed her palm flat against his chest, right over his heart. He knew full well what she felt. His heart raging out of control, because of her. Because she was touching him. Because she was tempting him.

He was sure she had no idea what she was tempting. Oh, she might have some pale idea, but if she could see just how filthy his thoughts were from such a simple touch, she would probably run the opposite direction.

But he wasn't protective.

And he wasn't going to protect her now.

Instead, he reached out and slipped a strand of silken brown hair behind her ear, the simple touch echoing through him like a shout. "Where do you want me to touch you?"

She looked down, her sooty lashes fanning over her cheek. "I don't... I don't know." She looked up at him, her brown eyes glittering. "Will you just kiss me again?"

He didn't need to be asked twice.

He wrapped his arms around her and pulled her against him, lowering his head and not holding back at all as he claimed her mouth for his own. She was so soft. Soft and enticing, and everything that a man who'd had a life made of dirt and gravel, barbed wire and nails had missed out on. Everything that a man like him didn't know quite how to handle.

She felt so fragile in his arms, and for a moment he was afraid he might break her. For a moment, he felt like he might actually be more protective than he'd realized.

She curled her fingers around the fabric of his shirt, clinging to him, making little sounds in the back of her throat. Needy sounds, that told him she wanted more of what he had to give.

He might not be what she was used to, but he was certainly something that she wanted.

He pressed his palms flat between her shoulder

blades, slid them down to her hips, where he held her tightly, drew her up against his body and let her feel the evidence of what she did to him.

This woman, who had been off-limits to him for so long. Who had been a clear no-go zone. That woman, she was in his arms now. Kissing him like she would die if she couldn't have more.

He was starting to feel the same.

He moved one hand to cup her head, angling so that he could take the kiss deeper, so that he could taste her, all that sweet coffee flavor that still lingered, and the flavor that was just her. Olivia. A woman he hadn't even let himself fantasize about.

That made her different in ways she would probably never understand.

That he had drawn a line around her. That he had tried. Truly tried, to be decent.

Oh well. He was past decency now.

With any luck they both were.

She shifted in his arms, flattening her hands on his chest, dragging them down to his stomach, to the edge of his jeans. He growled, her tentative, innocent exploration lighting a fire in his body he was sure was about to rage out of control.

He moved his hand from her hip to her ass, squeezing her through that woolly sweater of hers that rendered her leggings useless in his opinion. What was the point if they covered everything?

But now she was in his arms, under his hands, so he could feel her.

Could feel the delicate press of her small breasts against his chest, could feel the way her breath had quickened because she wanted him. Because she was as into this as he was.

But unless she was into getting laid down by the river, or pushed up against the tree, having those leggings torn right off in the open air… It had to stop. Right now, it had to stop.

He was so hard he was in pain, wanted her so badly he could scarcely breathe around it, and yet, somewhere he had found it in himself to think of her.

To think that Olivia, the woman who had been so horrified by the fact that he might have been with a woman in the Gold Valley Saloon bathroom that she'd nearly disintegrated from the force of her disgust, would probably not want to get screwed outdoors.

She probably wanted soft pillows, blankets and romance. He would give it. If it meant having her, he would give it.

He gripped her face, running his thumbs over her delicate cheekbones, and then pulled away, meeting her gaze. "Liv," he said, his voice rough.

Suddenly, her cloudy gaze went wide, and then got a little bit horrified. She took a step back, putting her fingertips over her lips. "I'm sorry."

"Don't be sorry. But I can clear my schedule for the rest of the day if you want to come over."

"If I want to come…over…to…" She swallowed hard. "No. I can't. Luke… It would be wrong."

She wanted him; he knew it. He didn't know why she wouldn't just have him. It wasn't like she was with Bennett now. And yeah, it probably all came back to the cinnamon roll analogy.

That she wasn't the type of person to indulge, just for the sake of it. That she probably imagined she needed feelings and a commitment, things like that.

"Why not?"

"Because. I don't love you," she said, shaking her head. "And I'm not going to—"

"You love Bennett."

That made his stomach twist. He didn't like it. He flat-out didn't. Because he might not want forever, he might not want commitment. But he wanted her. Wanted her more than he wanted to take his next breath, and considering he wanted to live for a good while longer, that was pretty damned bad.

And it was selfish and shortsighted to think that that should take precedence over true love, or whatever the hell she imagined she had with Bennett Dodge. But right now it felt like it should. Right now, it felt like wanting her, having her, might be more important than anything that lay ahead in the future.

Right. Except you're supposed to be convincing her to put a good word in with her father. If you try and convince her to let you ravish her, it's probably not going to go over well.

This land. This land was more important. He knew that. Making that money go to something worthwhile. This was the thing. The thing that was finally going to get him out from under his past. From underneath the crushing weight of the settlement that he'd been left with at sixteen rather than having a mother.

If there was ever going to be a place that stood as tribute to Rose Hollister, it would be this place. He felt it down to his bones.

And that certainty was the only reason that he took a step back. The only reason that he moved away from Olivia.

The only spot of clarity in his lust-addled brain.

The only thing stronger than his desire to simply say *to hell with it* and push her back up against the tree, kiss her again until she forgot why she was protesting. Until she could no longer think of any good reason that the two of them should resist.

She might wish she wanted Bennett only, forever and ever. But it didn't shock him much to know that sometimes lust was stronger than love. He'd never been in love, so he couldn't really say. But he had always been a lot more interested in lust. So the theory suited him.

"Yes," she confirmed. "I love Bennett."

"Great." He pushed his hand through his hair, letting out a long, slow breath.

"Are you mad at me?"

He looked down at her, genuinely shocked by the question. "What?"

"You seem upset."

"Kiddo, I'm in pain."

"What?" She blinked.

"I am so damned hard, I'm in pain. Taking it this far and stopping hurts."

She bit her lip, delicate color flooding her cheeks. "It kind of does."

That innocent response lanced through him. How was the pain of breaking off the promise of sex new to her?

Well, maybe she just *didn't* resist Bennett. She loved him, after all. And it seemed to him that for her love might be necessary. Like she thought hunger was necessary to eating a cinnamon roll. So maybe that was it. She just gave in to Bennett whenever and hadn't had to experience the frustration of a thwarted sexual encounter.

The thought made him grind his teeth together. He didn't want to think about her with Bennett. He didn't want to think about her with anyone. Anyone but him.

"I'm sure you feel a little bit crabby, too, if you're honest with yourself," he growled.

The idea that she might be just fine was unacceptable.

"Maybe," she said, tucking her hair behind her ear, suddenly looking very young. Too young for him.

He tried repeating that in his head a few times. Just to see if it would deter him. To see if it would magically make him not want her. No such luck.

"We'd better go," he said.

"Why?"

"Because, Olivia, if we don't get out of here I'm going to do my damnedest to change your mind, and I don't think you want that."

She shrank back. "You said you wouldn't do anything I didn't want."

"I won't. But I would make you want things you'd wish you hadn't asked for later. On that, you can trust me."

She looked away from him and scurried the opposite direction, headed out of the trees and back to the field. He followed her slowly, doing his best to keep a careful distance between them.

It was fitting that this had happened here. Because it was a reminder. Of what his actual goals were.

Goals that went beyond satisfying the ache he felt for Olivia Logan.

The ranch was more important.

He paused for a moment and looked around. Saw the cabin in the distance, the trees back behind him. This piece of a dream he knew his mother had had for him.

Yes. This ranch was the only thing that mattered.

CHAPTER ELEVEN

OLIVIA WASN'T SURE how she made it through the ride from her dad's property back to her car out in front of Sugar Cup. By the time she got back home she was shaking. She had kissed Luke again.

He had kissed her.

He had made it very plain that he wanted more.

She had asked him to kiss her. Asked him to touch her. She couldn't even say what insanity had gripped her when she'd said that to him. They'd been standing by the river and there was something on his face she'd never seen before.

Even while he was joking about Solo cups and beer, it was there. This deep sadness and a burning *hunger* that resonated inside of her. She'd wanted to touch it. Had wanted to take it on board for him. Or just feel. Feel that deeply. With that much rawness.

And she had. Oh, she had.

She was a jumbled-up mess. She couldn't deny that. It didn't make sense. Feeling like she did about Bennett… Like he was supposed to be the future, and also wanting Luke with so much strength she thought she might die of it.

Bennett was stability. He was the key to that happy life she had spent so many years imagining. Luke was the itch underneath her skin that she couldn't scratch.

Was she really no better than this? No better than she had spent so many years trying to be?

She and Vanessa were twins. Right now, she wondered if they were as different as she'd always believed. Or if, for her, the need to please had simply been stronger than her impulses. Maybe they were really all there inside her.

There was a very firm knock on her front door and she startled, an image of Luke flashing behind her eyes. Was he here? Was he here to try and… Convince her?

The real question was: Could she be convinced?

Seduced.

That was the word. *Seduced.*

Luke wasn't talking about doing more kissing. Luke was talking about *sex.*

She shivered.

Sex made her… Well, more than a little bit nervous. She had spent so long putting it off, so long trying to cultivate control, trying to make sure that she was the creative director of her own life, that the idea of stripping everything away and getting naked with somebody seemed…

Too much. Like it would strip away all the layers she counted on to protect herself. To keep herself safe and sane.

And something that was off in the future. Something that wouldn't happen until Bennett put a ring on her finger.

There was another knock, and she realized that she had not gone to the door, but was standing there ruminating. Heart in her throat she moved quickly to the door, flinging it open. And her heart plummeted into her feet when she saw not Luke, but Bennett.

"What are you doing here?" She realized that she

hadn't spoken two words to him since that day they had broken up at the Copper Ridge Christmas Tree Lighting, in front of an entire crowd of people.

And her first words to him were *What are you doing here?*

That would *not* be a story for the grandchildren. Assuming there were grandchildren. She frowned. Why was she doubting this?

"I need to talk to you," he said.

"Well, I didn't figure you were selling Girl Scout cookies," she said, feeling testy.

He arched a brow. "Was that sarcasm, Olivia?"

She returned the raised eyebrow. "Yes it was, Bennett. Come in."

She stepped away from the door and moved to the side so that he could walk through.

She hadn't been this close to him in well over a month. He smelled the same. Like basic soap and hay. Hard work.

His sleeves were pushed up his forearms, revealing his muscles, and the scars on his hands from where he'd taken some teeth from the animals he cared for. Her eyes fell to a particularly deep groove on the back of his hand that he'd gotten courtesy of a distressed Australian shepherd.

A wound and a situation he'd taken with steady calm, as he did most everything. He was a good man. There was no question.

He used to be hers.

The familiarity of him made her chest ache. Those brown eyes that she used to gaze into, those lips she had kissed countless times. The square jaw she had traced with her fingertips whenever she had gotten the chance.

He was beautiful.

And he didn't make her feel reckless. Didn't make her feel out of control. He made her feel *nice*. Made her feel like there was a beautiful, stable future spread out in front of her. Made her think of things like home and family. Children, lovely ranch houses.

He made her think of golden retrievers.

They would definitely have a golden retriever. Maybe a golden retriever and a lab. Bennett loved animals.

She thought they were only okay, but they made a very nice mental image in her domestic fantasy.

He didn't make her think of getting naked. Didn't make her think of sweat and tangled-up bedsheets.

Unbidden, her mind went back to that kiss from a few minutes earlier, down by the river.

Made her think of Luke.

Luke made her think about tangled bedsheets.

"I'm here to talk to you about Luke," he said, and for a moment she was afraid he could read her mind.

"What about him?" she asked, feeling grouchy and combative. Not at all how she'd imagined she might feel in this situation.

"You shouldn't be seeing him," Bennett said, shaking his head.

"Why?"

"He's not good for you. And he's allergic to commitment. Olivia, I know how much you want a commitment."

"Not a generic commitment, Bennett," she said. "I wanted a commitment from you." She really, truly had. But she wasn't sure at all if that was still true.

That made her feel like she was falling into a pit. Endless and dark. Nothing to pull her back.

He frowned. "Right."

"I'm a grown woman, you know." Even if she didn't

feel like one. Even if she felt like an irrational child who had no clue what she was doing.

"I *do* know," he said. "I also know that you don't have any experience with men. I know that I was a damn sight more patient with you than most other guys in my position would have been. I respected the hell out of you, and believe me when I tell you men who are willing to do that aren't in easy supply. I doubt Luke is interested in waiting for anything."

"Luke hasn't asked me to do anything I didn't want to," she said, speaking with total honesty.

Because everything that had happened with Luke might have scared her a little bit, but she had certainly wanted it at the time.

Bennett scrubbed his hand over his forehead and let out a long, slow breath. "Let's get back together, Olivia," he said. The words were heavy. Decisive. But not filled with any kind of happiness. "Being apart any longer is stupid. You want to get married, and I want you to be happy."

"You do?"

His words spread over her like sunshine on a cold day. And she waited to feel the warmth. But she didn't. She felt numb. He was offering her what she wanted. He had just said the words she had fantasized about hearing him say ever since she had first broken up with him. And she didn't feel happy. Not even a little.

"I want you safe," he said. "I want to take care of you."

He hadn't said he loved her. And if she had been as over-the-moon elated as she had initially imagined she might be when she'd fantasized about this moment, she might not have noticed that.

But she was more than numb. She was rational. And

rational Olivia definitely noticed the absence of declarations of deep emotion.

"You want to take care of me?"

"Yes," he confirmed.

"You want to keep me *safe*?" she asked, incredulous.

"Yes, Olivia, that's what I just said."

Suddenly, rage sparked through her. Pure, unmitigated rage. Unexpected as it was welcome. "I am not a *hen*, Bennett," she said, advancing on him.

He frowned, his dark brows knitting together, a crease appearing in the center of his forehead. "You're not a hen. What the hell does that mean?"

"I'm not a...a little *chicken* that you need to protect. I am a woman. I don't want you to baby me. I don't want you to placate me. Is that what you're here to do? To offer to wrap me in cotton wool for the rest of my life?"

"We're a good match, Olivia. You know that. Everybody knows that." He shook his head. "What's wrong with wanting to keep you safe? Why does that bother you? I thought it was what you wanted."

"Do you love me?" The question fell from her lips before she could stop it. And then she realized she didn't even want to stop it.

She deserved an answer.

Suddenly, the answer was everything.

"Olivia..."

"You don't," she said, fully seeing it now. Fully understanding.

"We make sense," he said, lifting a shoulder. "For me that's good enough."

"It's not good enough for me." And she realized that, until recently, it had been. Bennett had never said that he loved her. She had ignored that. She ignored it because she had been so certain that he probably did, he just hadn't verbalized it. But mostly, the image of what the relationship could be mattered more than what it actually was.

"Are you rejecting me because of Luke?"

"Maybe," she said, feeling angry now. "Maybe I am. And it's none of your business if I do. Not at all. I could dance naked with him down Main Street and it wouldn't be your business. I can do whatever I want with him."

"I really, really don't want you to do that," he said. He dragged his hand over his face, and she suddenly noticed lines by his eyes, his mouth, that she'd never seen before. She wondered if they were new. Or if she was just suddenly seeing that he was human, and not the superhero she'd glossed him into for the past decade. "He's going to hurt you. The idea of seeing you hurt…" He let out a frustrated breath. "That's not what I want."

"*You* hurt me," she said. "You let me think that you loved me."

He frowned. "I never meant to hurt you. I never meant to make you believe something that wasn't true. And it would be easy for me to lie to you now, Olivia. It would be easy for me to give you the words. But it's not you, it's me. I'm not ever going to love someone. But I definitely wanted that life. The life that we both want."

Her actions over the past month suddenly seemed glaring, humiliating, in light of the revelation about Bennett's feeling. She had been making a spectacle of herself for *this*. Over a man who wanted to swaddle her rather than love her passionately.

She wanted to be good. She had spent so many years trying to be. But she had thought that somewhere in that would be the reward of having a man who loved her to distraction. The way that her father loved her mother.

She had been certain that she could have both. That she could behave and have passion. Passion in its place.

But standing there looking at Bennett now she was keenly aware that they didn't actually have any.

"You wasted a year of my life," she said. "You didn't tell me that you *couldn't fall in love*. Whatever that's supposed to mean."

"Olivia…" He broke off for a moment, his gaze fixed on the white clock on the wall. "There are things about me that you don't know."

More anger flooded her then, a relief, because it was better than the crushing sadness and hint of humiliation she'd felt a moment earlier.

"Does Kaylee know them?" she asked.

"Kaylee doesn't have anything to do with this," he said through gritted teeth.

"She might. I really think she might. You were closer to her than you ever were to me. I was your *girlfriend*, but she's the person that you spend all of your time with. She's the person you confide in. You *protect* me. And that's not the same. We don't… Bennett, we never had a real relationship. I thought that we did. I was honest with you. I told you everything about me. You know about Vanessa. You know that I…that I've never been with anyone. You know exactly why I wanted to wait until we were engaged."

"Yes," he said, his voice hard as he found some of his own anger. "You wanted to wait until we were engaged because you were trying to hold it over my head. Just like you were trying to force me into proposing when you broke up with me. Don't think I didn't realize that."

Her cheeks flamed. He was right. To a degree, he was right. And she couldn't deny it. It all seemed small and silly now. Like something someone else would do, but not her. "Okay. So maybe I tried that. But, I had feelings for you, too. It isn't like it was a cold-eyed calculation. It made sense to me."

"And that's why I let you get away with it," he said. "I'm not the kind of guy that lets somebody manipulate them, Olivia. I went into it with my eyes open. Because you did mean something to me. Our relationship meant something to me."

"Why?" If it wasn't love, she sure as hell couldn't figure out what.

"You're special. I wanted to keep you safe."

"Why?" she pressed.

"Because your father asked me to."

She felt like the room was spinning. Like the floor was waving beneath her feet. "My father asked you to *date* me?"

"When he had the heart attack a few years ago, he asked me to look after you. He was afraid…after that he felt like there was no guarantee he would be around for you. I waited, because you're so young. But then… The time seemed right. He had recovered, but it still seemed like the right thing to do."

"My *father* asked *you* to *date me*." Each word tasted like a curse. "He asked you to take care of me. And you agreed. I'm your charity girlfriend. And you were going to let me be your charity wife."

"It was beneficial for both of us, Olivia. I didn't see the problem with it."

Olivia exploded. "No wonder you were so happy to let me have my little manipulations. You saw right through them anyway. And you never cared. It was never hard for you because you *don't want me*. Which I bet you laugh about over beers with the woman you actually do confide in." She closed her eyes. "Are you sleeping with Kaylee?"

"Hell, no," he said. "I haven't touched another woman since you and I got together, or since we split up. Which is more than I can say for you."

"We're not together anymore. So I can touch Luke Hollister all I want. Not because my father asked him to touch me, either. He wants me. He actually wants me. And maybe it'll end badly, Bennett. But right now I don't really care. I would rather take my chances with him than deal with you."

"Olivia…"

"Get out of my house."

She pointed toward the front door. They stood for a moment, staring at each other. Bennett's jaw was locked, his expression stoic, and she had a feeling that for her part she looked like a rumpled creature with red cheeks and wild hair. But she didn't care.

She didn't need to look good for Bennett. Not anymore.

Bennett nodded once, then turned and walked out of her house, shutting the door firmly behind him.

She sat on the couch, her entire face cold, pinpricks dotting her skin. Bennett had called her out on her manipulations. They were real, and she couldn't deny them. She had been using him. Using him because she had been convinced that he was the key to her happiness. Oh, with all of that she had also been convinced she loved him. But she couldn't deny the other things.

It had just never occurred to her that he had been using her, too. Or worse, doing her father a favor.

Suddenly, she wanted to rage at everyone. Against the whole world. Against the dad that she loved so much, against the past year of her life, and every moment she had ever labored under the illusion that she might be heartbroken.

She wanted to do something dangerous.

And the most dangerous thing she could think of was Luke Hollister.

CHAPTER TWELVE

LUKE HAD JUST kicked off his boots, and was on his way to the fridge to grab a beer. It had been a long day of work at the ranch, and that short interval he'd spent with Olivia hadn't really helped. The break hadn't left him feeling relaxed, not in the least. Instead, it had put him square on edge, his toes pressed against the ledge of a cliff, a slight breeze likely to push him off.

Then he had gone back to Get Out of Dodge and had punished himself with physical labor until the sun had gone down. And then he had worked some after that, too. It was late, he was tired and he was cranky as hell.

But he was about to have some alcohol.

At least, that was the plan until he heard a knock on the door.

He looked around the spare cabin that he called home. He rented the place on a remote plot of land outside of Gold Valley, and rarely did anyone come to visit him. There was no reason to. He went out if he wanted to associate with people, or they had gatherings at the Dodge place, which was big and civilized and wasn't slapped together with rough-hewn logs.

He didn't spend all that much time at home. Just the evenings. He worked seven days a week at the ranch in some capacity, and if he ever did have a day off he usually spent the time outdoors anyway.

That meant he didn't need much. Didn't matter that he could have afforded more, it wasn't necessary.

Still, it didn't make his place the ideal location for house parties or, really, visitors of any kind, and he couldn't imagine who had come out all this way to see him at eight o'clock at night.

Unless it was Bennett, looking to cave his face in. Which sounded about right.

His interactions with Wyatt had been strained today, too, but he knew that Wyatt wasn't going to go getting himself involved, either. He had thought initially that he might, but if he hadn't at this point, he wasn't going to.

Bennett, though—he might be out looking for a fight.

But Luke could still feel the way Olivia's lips had felt pressed against his, the way she had sighed with pleasure as he had curved his hand around to cup her head and take the kiss deeper.

Yeah, if he was about to get punched in the face, he could honestly say that it was worth it.

So the hell with it.

He jerked the door open, ready to dodge a blow if need be, and was shocked to see Olivia standing there, looking nearly drowned by the downpour that was happening outside. Her dark hair hung in heavy chunks down past her shoulders, her arms wrapped around her slender body, a sweater the only thing she had to shield her from the elements.

He looked her over. "You'd better come in."

She nodded jerkily and traipsed in the door, still holding on to her elbows.

"What are you doing here, kiddo?"

She didn't say anything. Instead, she treated him to an expression he imagined was supposed to be fearsome, her brows drawing together, her lips pulled down into a frown.

"I see," he said.

He turned away from her, moving to the old freestanding cabinet that was in the living room area. A rickety piece of furniture that had been there when he moved in. He figured it was for China plates or some other fancy bullshit. He used it for alcohol.

He opened up the cabinet and regarded it for a moment, then took out a bottle of whiskey that Quinn Dodge had given him for Christmas a few years ago. It was good stuff. Not the kind of thing he indulged in on a nightly basis. But Olivia looked like she was in a Serious Whiskey Space.

He took two glasses down and poured a small amount of the amber liquid into them. He didn't wait for her to protest or to confirm that she wanted any. He grabbed hold of the top of the glass and held it out to her.

She took hold of it with both hands, clutching it tightly, as though it might offer her some security. Which, fair enough. He found alcohol offered him a fair measure of security at any given point in time. And confidence. It was good for that, too.

She wordlessly lifted the glass to her lips and took a sip. She grimaced, opening her mouth and sticking her tongue out, making a distressed sound. "It's like drinking a campfire."

"Now that you mention it, it kind of is. But I consider that part of its charm."

"No, thank you," she said crisply, handing the glass back to him.

He chuckled, but took it from her and set it back down on the cabinet. "Okay. So you didn't come here to have a drink with me. What exactly are you here for?"

She looked up at him, her expression so helpless it might have been funny if it didn't reach down inside of him, grab hold of his heart and pull hard. Luke Hollister was no sucker, and he wasn't a softy, either. But there was something about Olivia. Olivia and this strange vulnerability that he could see in her eyes. Olivia, who was usually about as vulnerable as a cactus.

Her expression was expectant, as though she was hoping he might hazard a guess, so that she wouldn't have to say what was on her mind.

He could start trying to guess, but he didn't want to give her any outs. Didn't want to offer an option that seemed more palatable to whatever she was here for. And he didn't want to say anything so shocking it might scare her off.

Plus, Olivia could do with some personal responsibility. With some consequences for her actions.

That was why he had said if she wanted to be touched she was going to have to ask.

He wasn't going to play the part of aggressor and allow her to be the helpless maiden. While it was a fine thing in terms of role-play, it was also a great way for her to pretend that he was the brute, and she had no stake in any of what had happened between them.

No. He wasn't giving her that kind of relief.

Maybe that was moot. Maybe she had another flat tire. Maybe that was all she needed him for. Maybe, she just wanted to talk about her feelings. But that look in her eyes, that wild, helpless look, made him think it was something a lot deeper than that.

And he would be damned if he gave her any excuse later to do anything but own it.

"Something happened," she said, beginning to pace, water dripping from her hair.

"Why are you so wet?"

She turned to him. "Oh. I stood outside in the rain about five minutes before I knocked on your door." She said this as though it was completely normal.

"Why?"

"Because I was considering running into the woods. Starting my life over as a squirrel."

"I don't recommend that," he said, keeping his voice grave.

"Squirrels seem happy," she said. "Their life seems simple."

"Indecisive squirrels often end up as roadkill. Remember that."

"Bennett asked to get back together," she said.

His stomach constricted, his skin suddenly feeling tight. That was why she had come. To tell him that whatever was going on between them—which wasn't really anything, since it was just a show they were putting on for Bennett's benefit—was over.

"Well," he said, "congratulations."

"I didn't…"

"I might skip the wedding. But I can send you a toaster. Assuming you need a toaster."

She made a short, frustrated sound, bouncing up and down with frustrated energy. And then she took one stride forward, reaching up and grabbing hold of his face, pulling him down so that he was a scant half inch from her mouth. "I told him to take a hike," she said, her brown eyes fixed on his.

He could smell her. That scent that was woman and rain, vanilla and Olivia. And he wanted to inhale her. Indulge himself. With every inch of her beautiful body.

But instead, he simply stayed like he was, the tips of their noses nearly touching, her eyes glittering.

"You did?"

"Yes," she said, her tone intense.

"Why the hell did you do that? You want him. That's what you told me. That you want to be with him. You had your chance. Why the hell didn't you take it?"

"He dated me because my dad told him to," she said, her expression turning furious, mutinous. And she was still holding on to his face. Her fingernails were digging into his temples, and he didn't even care. "Do you have any idea how humiliating that is? He never cared about me. Ever. He cared about the idea of us. And it's all…it's all about keeping me safe, and keeping me living this…this life that I'm supposed to live and I don't know if I want to live that life anymore."

Her voice was trembling with rage. He wasn't sure he had ever seen her so upset, and considering that he had in the past made a near living out of annoying Olivia, that was saying something.

"I'm not charity," she said. "And I'm not a hen. I don't need to be protected, I don't need to be coddled. I need… I need something else."

In spite of himself, he lifted his hand, cupped her chin gently and tilted her face up just a little more, bringing her lips a bit closer to his own. He could feel her breath, warm and unsteady, and he wanted to drink it in.

"Sadly, kiddo, I would say you are a hen. And you walked into the fox's house."

She shivered, from cold or something else he didn't know. "Fine. Maybe I am. But I came here on purpose." A spark lit deep in those brown eyes, turning them a whiskey gold, like the drink she had rejected earlier. Twice as likely to get him drunk, too, that was sure.

"What exactly are you saying? Just say it. And don't expect me to make it easy for you."

"You haven't made anything easy for me. Not from the first day I met you. I wouldn't expect you to start now." She tilted her face up just a fraction, and now their lips were so close a breeze could barely pass through them.

"Fair enough. Since you've made things very, very hard for me." He wasn't sure if she got the double entendre in that, but he'd meant it. Since she had shown up at the door he had been hard. Painfully so.

Restraint. Teasing. He didn't go in for all that, and that was all he'd had with Olivia over the past weeks.

"I'm tired of being good," she said. "It hasn't gotten me anything."

"Did you come here to be bad? Because you already failed at step one. You rejected the alcohol. That's not taking to peer pressure very well."

"I'm not here for a drink."

The hold on his face softened, and she dragged her fingertips down his cheeks, along his jaw, pressing both her thumbs against his lower lip, and then tracing it in opposite directions.

"You have to say it, Liv," he said, the words hoarse, broken.

"I want you," she said, her voice almost a whisper.

"Not just kissing," he said. "Let's make that very clear."

She shook her head. "No. Not just kissing."

"This is because you're mad at Bennett?" He asked himself, very seriously, at least for a moment, if that was a problem. It burned in his gut, like he'd been stabbed with a red-hot poker, but his desire for Olivia burned a hell of a lot hotter. And it was going to win.

Pride be damned.

This woman was under his skin in a way no other woman had ever been. He couldn't wait. And he sure as hell couldn't live in a world where he would never know how soft her skin was all over. Where he never had a chance to see what she looked like uncovered. What color her nipples were. What she would taste like between her thighs when she was wet with her desire for him.

He could deal with being a revenge lay. But not having Olivia?

He didn't think he could live with that.

"It wasn't worth it," she said. "He wasn't worth it."

It was admittance enough of her anger. Of the fact that she was reacting to the confrontation with him. But he didn't care. He really, really didn't care.

"I'm going to tell you something," he said, tightening his hold on her chin. "I'm not worth it, either. But I'm going to make tonight worth it. I'm going to make damn sure that this, this revenge that you're taking, makes it all worth it. That months from now, years from now, you're going to be lying in bed at night, and you're going to think of this. You're going to think of me. I'm not worth it. But the sex sure as hell will be."

She gasped, but he swallowed it, pulling her face toward his and claiming her mouth. He kissed her deep, he kissed her hard, he kissed her knowing that this wasn't going to end in frustration and a hard cock.

No, tonight he was going to end up inside of her.

That thought tested the limits of his control, made him feel at the end of it already, when all they were doing was kissing. When she still had her hands on his face, and he had one hand on her chin. They hadn't even begun to explore each other's bodies. Everybody was fully dressed.

It was already the hottest damned encounter of his life.

"You're cold," he said, when she shivered against him. "Let me warm you up."

He didn't wait for her to ask how, didn't wait for her to say anything. He gripped the wet hem of her sweater and pulled it up over her head, leaving her standing there in a lacy bra that showed off small, perky tits that just about brought him to his knees.

Her cheeks turned pink, that beautiful flush spreading all the way down to the shadow between her breasts. She wrapped her arms around herself, like she had done when she had first come in to see him. He grabbed hold of her wrist, drawing her arm back down. "No," he said. "I get to see you."

Her eyes widened, but she put her hands down at her sides, curling them into fists, looking like it was taking every bit of her strength to stay rooted to the spot, rather than scurrying under a piece of furniture.

He could tell that it was an effort for her to stand there like that, underneath his gaze. He liked that. Couldn't say why. Except that she affected her. In a way that shocked her, he must, otherwise it would be no big deal for her to whip her top off in front of him and let him see her bra.

Whatever Bennett had made her feel, he made her feel something else. Or maybe it was just the fact that she felt it with him that she found off-putting. But he would take it. He would take being different.

He would take it and go from there. Because by the time he was done with her, she was going to be screaming his name and never remember if she had cried out anyone else's.

He reached out, put both hands on her shoulders and then slid them down her arms, taking her hands in his, squeezing them. Her eyes met his, and they were suspiciously bright, but he ignored that. Because he wanted to focus on that deep, taut ache in his groin, and not the tightness in his chest.

Then he pulled her to him, bringing her heart against his chest, relishing the feel of all that skin pressed against him, her bare back beneath his hands. And he still had his clothes on. She still had her bra on.

He had to get a grip. Or he was going to lose it in about thirty seconds flat and not be able to make good on that promise to make this memorable. Well, it would be memorable, but not in the way that he had meant it.

Of course, in that case, he could spread her out on his floor and make a feast of her until he was hard again.

That thought did nothing to help him rein in his libido. Not at all.

He kissed her. Kissed her like it was going to save them both, even though odds were it would only ruin them. Kissed her because he wanted to. And she wanted him.

Olivia Logan. She was going to be his. His finally. He was done pretending that he hadn't wanted it since she was eighteen years old. Since it was legal, but messed up enough to make him lose every friend and associate in good standing in the town of Gold Valley.

He had wanted her. And he had resisted.

He told himself he wasn't good with resistance, but he had resisted her for the past seven years. Because she was better than him, and then had belonged to a better man than him.

But tonight he didn't want to be a better man; he just wanted to be the man she was with. Tonight, he was going to bring her down to his level, get that halo a little dirty, and maybe she would regret it later. It was entirely possible what he'd said about not being worth it was true. Not for a long-term investment.

But he'd make it good. He'd make it good for both of them. Make it worth that wait.

That long, impossible wait that he had reached the end of. He didn't have restraint anymore. Didn't have anything left in him but his desire for her. But the fire in his veins that was about to spark a blaze hot enough to burn them both to the ground.

He lifted one hand from her lower back, brought it around and undid the button on her jeans. Then, he slowly drew the zipper down, sliding his hands back around to grab hold of her bare ass beneath the fabric of her jeans and her panties, then he drew her up hard against him, kissing her as he pressed his hips against hers, letting her feel how hard he was. How much he wanted her.

Damn, she was soft. He squeezed her, not too gently either, because she was in his hands and he was all out of restraint. Restraint that he hadn't fully appreciated until now. That he hadn't fully realized he possessed. Funny how being aware of it made it seem unreasonable.

He let his other hand drift up the line of her spine, to the band of her bra. He made quick work of it with one hand, then wrenched the insubstantial fabric down her arms, casting it down to the floor. She sucked in a sharp breath, right in time with his.

He swore, the sound as reverent as a word like that could be. He dragged his thumb over one tightened nipple and Olivia's head fell back, the motion almost helpless, unconscious. A small, tortured sound of pleasure on her trembling lips as he continued to stroke her.

He pressed his hands down firmly against her lower back, then lowered himself down to his knees, kissing the valley between her breasts, down to the waistband of her pants. She was panting heavily, her stomach rising and falling with each labored breath. He looked up at her, saw that she was watching him with an almost-horrified expression. He treated her to a half smile and slowly peeled one side of her jeans open, then the other, eye level with the lacy white panties she was wearing. Then he slowly pushed the denim down her legs, revealing each inch of skin, torturing himself because part of him kind of liked it. His chest hurt, his throat was dry and part of him wanted to exist in this torment forever.

This place between the hell of wanting her and the heaven of having her.

He could see dark curls through the wispy fabric of her underwear, and he lifted his hand, pressing one fingertip beneath the edge of her panties, tracing a line from her hip bone down between her legs, that crease between her thigh and the most intimate part of her. She gasped, her breathing getting harder, faster as he teased her, as he pressed his finger deeper and found her wet with her desire for him.

He groaned, shifting position, hooking his finger across that filmy fabric and drawing it aside before cupping her in his hand, pressing his middle finger deep, parting her lips so that he could have greater access.

He grabbed her ass with his free hand and dragged her toward him, lowering his head and tasting her deeply as he continued to tease her with his fingers.

She made a short, shocked sound, her hands coming

up, grabbing hold of his head, tugging his hair. He ignored her, nuzzling his nose against that most sensitive part of her before sliding his tongue down her crease as he pushed a finger inside of her.

"Luke," she said, her voice breathless. "You can't…" She gasped. "You really can't." But she was bucking her hips against him, and she might be saying that he couldn't, but her body was begging him to

"Sure I can, Liv," he said, "just watch me."

He angled his head, tasting her deeply like he had done with her mouth earlier. She was sweeter than he had ever imagined. Better than anything. He could satisfy himself this way for hours. Olivia, under his mouth, under his hands, wet and hot and slick, her internal muscles beginning to pulse around that finger pushed inside of her. She was rocking against him, the sounds she was making increasingly distressed, as if pleasure was a foreign thing, a near enemy.

But then, he wondered if for a woman like Olivia it was. God knew he had practice being out of control. He liked to drink. He liked to have a good time. Control wasn't always part of the equation. Oblivion mattered to him a hell of a lot more than control. But not Liv. He knew that for sure.

He imagined she liked to be in charge. That she liked to have pleasure on her own terms.

But the hen was in the fox's house now.

He gripped her more firmly, pulling her harder against his mouth as he increased the pace. And she quit pulling against him and lowered her hands to his shoulders, fingernails digging into his skin as she surrendered. As she gave into him. Into this. Pleasure washed through him, more than he'd ever had without a woman's hand in his pants. He had no experience with this. With enjoying her pleasure more than he wanted to satisfy his own.

He pressed another finger inside of her and a sharp, intense cry escaped her lips as she rolled her hips forward, as her internal muscles tightened around him, spasmed as her orgasm overtook her. It was sweeter than he remembered it being. Better than that time in his truck. Because he could feel it. Could taste it.

And in the end, he was going to know what it was like to feel all of this need, her hot, wet body, pulsing around him, and that was enough to set him off then and there.

She slumped against him, boneless, and he stood, lifting her up off the ground, holding her in his arms as he walked through the small living area, down the narrow hallway and into his bedroom. Typically, when he hooked up with a woman, they did it over at her place. But his bed was big enough. It would do.

He set her down in the center of his bed, on his well-worn, flannel comforter that looked like a work shirt, and didn't look near fine enough for Olivia Logan's pretty, naked body.

But he already knew that he wasn't good enough. Already knew that he never would be. But she was embracing him, so he didn't see why the hell he shouldn't embrace this thing happening between them.

He leaned forward, grabbing the sides of her panties and drawing them down all the way, throwing them to the floor. "You're so beautiful," he said, the words thick, difficult to squeeze out of his tightened throat.

She shifted, her knees pressed tightly together, drawing one leg up slightly, as though she was trying to cover that beautiful, shadowed triangle there at the apex of her thighs.

He didn't even scold her, because every inch of her body was a joy to look at, and there would be plenty of time to examine that part of her later.

He walked around to the side of the bed with his nightstand, opened up the drawer and grabbed the unopened box of condoms inside. He ripped the top off, tearing one condom off the strip of them, and setting it down on the bed. Then he pulled his T-shirt up over his head. She watched him, watched every movement he made, those brown eyes fixed on him, not angry anymore.

Anger might have propelled her here, but it was desire that kept her going now. And even if it meant letting go of all his pride to know that she was at his house, in his bed, to get back at another man… That wasn't what kept her here.

He undid the button on his jeans, drew the zipper down slowly, and then pushed his pants and his underwear down to the floor. Olivia might be shy, but he wasn't.

Her eyes widened, her mouth dropping open. "Careful," he said, "you're going to make my ego bigger."

"I don't think any part of you needs to be bigger," she said, the words strangled.

Then he joined her on the bed, pressing her back against the mattress, every inch of his skin against every inch of hers. Her thighs parted, as if by instinct, and his erection settled there against her slick skin. He arched his hips forward, moving through her folds, teasing them both.

He shivered, pressing his forehead against hers.

Delicate fingertips came up and pressed against his cheek. "Are you cold?" she asked, her teeth chattering slightly.

"Burning up," he answered. "How about you."

"I'm not cold," she answered, her whole body trembling beneath his.

He held her chin, looked into her eyes, didn't ignore the sheen of tears in them this time. "You okay?"

She nodded wordlessly. "I want you."

She said it with that kind of grim determination that let him know this was another Olivia plan, rather than an act of passion. And that was unacceptable. He wanted her back the way she had been in the living room. Boneless and sated and beyond control.

He kissed her, rocking his hips against her again, wrapping his hand around his length, guiding it through her slickness, over her where she was most sensitive, repeating the motion until she was clinging to him, until she was making small sounds of pleasure, like she had done earlier.

He kissed her neck, her collarbone, down to her breasts, sucking one nipple into his mouth, sliding his tongue around that sensitive flesh in time with the motion of his hips. Then he moved on to the other one, drawing a harsh cry from deep inside of her. She was on edge again. And best of all, she wasn't thinking.

He reached to the side, grabbing the condom packet, tearing it open and rolling the latex over himself before moving back into position between her legs. He pressed his thick head against the entrance to her body, rocking forward slowly.

She gripped his shoulders, then down lower, her hands moving almost frantically as he pressed himself into her. He grabbed hold of her wrists, pushed her hands up overhead, forcing them down to the mattress as he bucked forward, taking her completely, a sound of wrenching pain coming from her as he did.

And that was when he realized that Olivia Logan was a virgin. Or had been, until a second ago.

She wasn't anymore. Because he was inside of her.

She had been so angry at Bennett that she had gone to give her virginity to Luke.

He couldn't process that.

On a good day, he wouldn't be able to process it, but this was a damned great day. He was inside of the woman he had wanted for years, and rational thought wasn't in his grasp.

She was a virgin.

He was sure that there was something to be angry about in that, but right now all he felt was triumph. Pure masculine, possessive triumph.

He didn't care what it meant. Not now. Because nothing mattered except having more of her.

All of her.

The only man to ever have this. He shuddered, eased himself out a couple of inches before thrusting back in. She groaned, lowering her head, burying her face in his neck as he tried to establish a rhythm that was gentle enough for her.

"Tell me if it hurts," he whispered against her lips. "Tell me what you want."

"Just you," she said, the words watery, unsteady.

He kept hold of her wrists as he moved inside of her, as he found exactly what she liked, listening to the sounds she made, paying attention to the subtle ways the movements of her body changed as he found ways to make contact with the source of her pleasure.

And then he could feel her release beginning to build again. He was familiar with it now. And he couldn't hold back his own any longer. His control snapped completely as she shivered and shuddered beneath him, her internal muscles pulsing around him as she climaxed, deeper and more intense than last time.

His blood roared in his ears, his restraint gone completely. He forgot to be gentle. He forgot to hold her steady. He let go of her wrists, held on to her hips and pounded himself into her, conscious now of nothing beyond his own need. This need that he had held back in his truck, against the tree, earlier in the living room.

The moment he had become conscious that she was a woman. A woman that he wanted. A woman he couldn't have.

But he was having her. He was having Olivia Logan right there in his bed, in his shitty cabin that was hardly fit for company. And she had been incandescent with pleasure in his arms.

He came on a growl, digging his fingers more firmly into her hips, knowing that he might leave marks behind, not able to do anything to stop himself. He should have been more gentle with her. From the beginning.

But this was all part of him living up to the only promises he had ever made her. That he wouldn't be good enough. That he wasn't right for a woman like her.

But none of it mattered. None of it mattered at all as pleasure burst through him like a bomb.

He could only hope it didn't blow them both to pieces.

CHAPTER THIRTEEN

SHE HAD BEEN right to be afraid of this.

As Olivia lay on Luke's bed, his large, naked body pressed over the top of her, buried inside of her, the bed soft beneath her and him hard above her, her chest feeling like it would crack in two... That was all she could think of.

That sex was every inch as terrifying as she had been scared it might be.

Everything had been so hot. So bright and real, sweaty and incredibly clear. In her mind, it had always been a foggy thing. Hidden behind the mists of secrecy, shrouded in mystery. Yes, she had known about how sex worked. But there had been a certain measure of fantasy in her thoughts about it. Whenever she had let herself think about having it with Bennett she hadn't focused on body parts. Hadn't focused on the physical act itself. But on feelings. On how nice it would be for the two of them to be so close. On what it would symbolize.

She hadn't thought about skin. Sweaty, close, intimate. Hadn't thought of what it would be like to have something so hard, so male, inside of her. And how close that really made you with someone.

Hadn't thought about large, strong hands that would hold her so tight she was afraid she might be bruised, and the kind of strange, overheated pleasure that made that somehow seem like a good idea.

She really hadn't thought about the possibility of anyone putting their mouth where Luke had. Again, not that she philosophically didn't understand that happened, it was just that she hadn't thought about it. She had avoided. Avoided and pushed to the side and covered it all up.

But here she was, uncovered, naked in his arms, a completely different creature to the one that she would say she had been all of her life. Except, this was her. There was no denying it. This was her with no makeup, no clothes and no defenses at all. She had no idea what to do with that.

She wanted to curl up into a ball and disappear, but that was impossible to do with that hard, rangy body still on top of her. Those intense, green eyes burning into hers.

She was about to say something, about to tell him that she needed to get up, but he pressed his palm to her cheek. Then he kissed her. It was tender, in comparison with everything that had come before it. Shockingly, impossibly, it stoked the fire inside of her again. A fire she would have said didn't exist, then would have said had been extinguished handily by Luke in the past few minutes. But there it was again. All it took was that firm mouth on hers. The slick sweep of his tongue.

Too soon, the kiss stopped, and he pushed himself up and away from her, withdrawing from her body. She gasped. She wasn't prepared for the way that her heart twisted, for the way that the loss of him felt. As if he had taken part of her with him.

As overwhelming as it had been to be joined, being separated again was worse. She had felt fine before. Now she felt like something was missing.

He turned away from her, and she took that opportunity to study his naked body. She had never seen a naked man in person before. His back was muscular—which she had known already, because she had seen him without a shirt before—but then, the muscle continued, all the way down. To his butt, which was a thing of art, and his thighs, which were sculpted and made her mouth water. Which was weird, because she had never devoted any time to thinking about a man's thighs before.

He walked out of the room without saying anything and she let out a long breath she hadn't realized she'd been holding in. She looked up at the ceiling, at the unfamiliar wooden slats, then over at his nightstand. The condom box was sitting on the bed in front of it, looking half demolished. The nightstand itself had very little on it. A lamp and what looked like a phone charger.

His whole house was sparse.

It didn't contain a single thing that she would identify as being Luke. Which fit, really. Because Luke couldn't be contained in a cabin. Not even pieces of him.

She realized after a breath that she was lying there completely naked, on her back with her legs spread, and her arms flung out to the side. Her clothes were… Well, everywhere. Some in the living room, some in here.

She hadn't anticipated that, either.

She scurried up to the top of the bed and situated herself beneath the covers, drawing the blankets up to her chin.

A moment later, Luke reappeared in the doorway. Completely naked. Still naked, and not at all ashamed. Not like her.

But then Luke had probably been naked in front of a lot of women. Like the woman in the bathroom at the saloon, for instance.

Thinking about that made her stomach twist, an intense, vile feeling that she didn't like at all.

But even as she battled that, she took the opportunity to admire him. The man was the mysteries of the universe revealed as far as she was concerned. The answer to the question of what a naked man looked like. The answer to the question of what an orgasm felt like, what sex was actually all about.

So strange that she had associated it with romance.

What had happened between them had not felt romantic. It had felt like willingly throwing herself down on a knife's edge. Far too sharp. Far too intense.

And yet, somehow, even as it ached from the unfamiliar invasion, her body seemed to want more.

He walked across the room and sat on the edge of the bed, looking over at her. "Something that you want to talk about?" he asked.

"Quite the rainstorm outside," she said, curling up into a ball and burrowing deeper into the bedding. "Otherwise, it's been a fairly mild January."

"Not the weather, little squirrel girl, try again."

"I've never done that before," she said, the words sticking in her throat. "Sorry I didn't tell you. I thought that maybe you had guessed."

"I knew that you were inexperienced. I didn't think you were lacking in experience entirely. I figured... Bennett."

She shook her head. "No."

"He's a fucking idiot."

The response was so shocking that Olivia laughed. She would have said that was impossible a split second ago, but the absurdity of all of it gripped her. And she found herself giggling helplessly, naked beneath the covers in Luke's bed, while he sat on the edge of the mattress with nothing covering him at all, looking at her like she had lost her mind.

Maybe she had.

Well, she definitely had. She had lost her mind the moment she had left her house tonight, intending to go to Luke's to seduce him.

She'd had something completely different in mind. She was supposed to come in looking confident and sexy. She was supposed to tease him, flirt with him. Take control of everything. She was supposed to destroy that part of her life that was Bennett Dodge, and all the aspirations she had with him with a simple stroke, so to speak.

But that wasn't how it had gone. Starting with the fact that she had stood out in the rain until she had been dripping wet and had effectively ruined any seductive appeal she might have had.

So already, by the time she had knocked on the door she was not in the space she had hoped to be. But then… Then, it hadn't gone any closer to plan from there.

She hadn't seduced anyone. No, Luke had effectively seduced her. He had put any and all claims to control she had ever made to terrible, red-faced shame. He had obliterated all thoughts of Bennett from her mind, had made revenge so low on the list of reasons she had come, she wasn't sure it was even there anymore.

And by the time he had slid inside of her… There hadn't been anyone else. There hadn't been another person on earth as far as she was concerned, much less a man who had driven her into Luke's arms.

Luke had driven her into Luke's arms.

That thought hit her fully then. The realization washing over her like a wave. All of this, all of the fictions that she had carefully constructed over the past few weeks… Reasons to spend time with Luke. Reasons they had to touch, reasons that kissing him had been rational.

It had been about Luke. Bennett had been the palatable excuse.

He was right.

She didn't care. Not really. She had no more passionately loved Bennett than he had loved her. If she had, she would have curled up on the floor of her house and wept all evening, she wouldn't have run straight to Luke's cabin.

She was a woman who considered herself reasonable, above all else. Who considered herself controlled and rational and above all the romantic entanglements her friends had had over the past few months. She had judged everyone from a place of imperious superiority. When Clara had started sleeping with her late older brother's best friend Alex, with no promise of commitment, Olivia had scoffed. When Sabrina had engaged in a physical-only relationship with the man who had once broken her heart, Olivia had been skeptical and not entirely supportive.

Now here she was. Certainly not above the kinds of decisions her friends had made. No different from most other people when confronted with real, serious attraction. Physical need that made cerebral decision making seem like a pointless exercise. Because what could be more important than the next kiss? The next touch?

The next release?

She hadn't believed she was so fallible.

"Thank you," she said slowly. "But you know... It wasn't him. It was me."

Luke nodded slowly. "He's still an idiot."

"How exactly do you figure that?"

"Because I'm here. He's not. You're with me. Somewhere along the way he went wrong."

Luke made a very masculine sound of satisfaction and stretched out on the bed beside her, above the covers, still unconcerned with the fact that he didn't have anything on. She was a bit concerned by it. Because she couldn't concentrate with him like that. Not at all.

"I think that's the sex talking," she said, her tone crisp.

"You're an expert now, are you?"

"Just because I hadn't had sex doesn't mean I don't know about it," she said, feeling a bit prickly and ridiculous even as she said it, because there was no bluffing Luke at this point. He knew exactly what she knew about sex. And what she didn't know.

"All right, but I'm going to need you to educate me on a few things, Olivia. Because you're clearly never at a loss."

He was teasing her, that wicked smile that she was so accustomed to curving his lips upward. It was so strange. Being here with him like this, seeing that familiar expression in this wildly unfamiliar position. With both of them naked, and her body still buzzing with the aftereffects of their recent intimacy.

"I'll do my best," she said, craning her neck above the covers.

"Why didn't you ever sleep with Bennett?" He shifted, and her eyes were drawn to the play of muscles on his chest, the bunch and shift of his abs. "Eyes up here, kiddo. Focus." She looked up and made eye contact, her stomach hollowing out when she did. "Don't tell me it's because you were waiting for marriage. If you had been, you never would have come here tonight, and we both know it. Because if there's one thing I know about you, it's that you put your mind to something and you get it. Hell, even if you don't get it, you're willing to go down in a blazing, bloodied knuckled glory. So I don't buy that you were just waiting."

"I wanted to be engaged to Bennett first," she said,

lowering her head, part of the comforter blocking her mouth, muffling her words.

"Right. But here we are, not engaged."

"Because I… I was mad when I came over. But that's not really why this happened. I'm attracted to you."

The infuriating man had the nerve to laugh at her. "No shit."

"Luke," she said, frustrated, pulling her hand out of the covers and slapping him on the shoulder. "Try not to be a jackass."

"I could try, but I feel like it would give you false expectations."

"I mean, I've been attracted to you." His green gaze went serious then. His lips pulling down into a line. "All this time… I didn't like it. Bennett… Bennett was safe."

"Wow. Did you tell him that?"

"No."

"Probably for the best. That's right up there with finding out your dad told somebody to date you."

"Do you remember my sister? I mean, I know that you know about her. It's not like the whole town isn't fully aware that I'm a twin. And it isn't like there aren't rumors about Vanessa."

"Yeah," he said. "She hasn't lived in Gold Valley for a long time."

"No. Do you know why?"

"Why?"

"Because my parents sent her away. They sent her away because she was getting into so much trouble. They thought that it would help. It didn't. It just… It just made her cut ties with all of us." Her throat tightened, tears filling her eyes. "It's because of me. They sent my sister away because of me."

CHAPTER FOURTEEN

SHE HATED THIS. Hated remembering it. Hated talking about it. Hated absolutely everything about the subject of Vanessa. She and her parents avoided the topic, and when they had to discuss her it was usually coded.

She hadn't known life without her sister for the first sixteen years. They had been in the womb together, born together. Every birthday party, every milestone shared. She had been Olivia's other half in so many ways.

The bright spark to Olivia's steady rock. When they hit adolescence, it hadn't been an easy relationship. Olivia was too boring for Vanessa a lot of the time. Vanessa was always daring. Adventurous. Vivacious and fun. She had definitely added sparkle to their house. But she had also been the one who was consistently rebellious. Part of Olivia had envied her.

Vanessa had always worn loud, trendy clothes, and if somebody said they didn't like them, Vanessa was the first to tell them where to shove their opinions. She had thought nothing of charging headfirst into various schemes, preferring to ask for forgiveness rather than permission. But then, as she had gotten older she hadn't even asked for forgiveness.

She had stopped wanting to spend time with Olivia. And Olivia had been… Angry. Jealous. Vanessa was like a magnet, and she drew people to her. And at the same time shoved Olivia aside.

Olivia had done a lot of stewing about it while she had thrown darts down in the basement, when Vanessa had been out at night with groups of friends doing God knows what, and Olivia wasn't invited.

That was when she had concocted her plan to be included. The plan that had ultimately wrecked everything.

That had proven to her the importance of staying on her own path.

"I didn't mean to," Olivia said, her voice small. As small as she felt whenever she thought about Vanessa. Whenever she thought about that horrible day when, after talking to her father in his office, they had a family meeting in the living room and Vanessa's fate had been handed down.

She could still remember the look on her sister's face. Could still remember the venom in her voice.

This is your fault. I hate you.

"Of course you didn't mean to do anything that hurt anyone," Luke said, so willing to believe her.

It was strange, because she wouldn't have said that Luke would defend her, or her motives, but there he was. Doing just that. It felt right, too. Like it was the natural thing for him to be on her side.

"I was being self-righteous," Olivia said. "It's my natural setting, or haven't you noticed?" She laughed, a brittle sound.

"You like things a certain way," he said. "You have a strong sense of what you think is right and wrong. I'm pretty flexible on a lot of those things, but let me tell you, I find you refreshing. Because I always know where I stand. And so do you."

"Right now, I'm lying," she said, raising both hands

off the covers and spreading her arms wide. "So, I think maybe we were both wrong."

"Tell me about Vanessa," he said, his eyes serious.

"She didn't like hanging out with me anymore. When we were thirteen, she and a group of our friends decided they wanted to go skinny-dipping when we were hanging out at one of the ranch properties during this big barbecue. The creek was hidden in the woods, but there were people there and I... I didn't want to. Vanessa said..." She cleared her throat. "She said I might as well because we were identical so once everyone saw her it would be the same as seeing me. I was afraid we'd get caught. But I didn't want to be left out. I wanted... I wanted so much to take a chance and be accepted. I didn't do it, but I agreed to be a lookout." Olivia shook her head. "A boy saw them. And he went and told everyone that the girls were naked in the creek. And at that point everyone scattered. My mom was furious. She asked me who was involved and she said she couldn't believe I'd allowed something so inappropriate to happen. She said...she said she expected it of Vanessa, not of me." Her throat felt scratchy and her eyes were dry. It was such a small thing, a silly thing. Keeping a lookout while the other girls were naked in a creek. It wasn't like anyone had been hurt. But even now the memory of how she felt made it feel enormous. Like she'd let her parents down. Like she'd somehow let herself down because she was supposed to know better. To be better.

She continued. "She asked for the names of everyone involved, so she could talk to their parents and I... I gave them to her. After that I had a reputation for being a tattletale. Nobody wanted my sister to invite me to anything, and my sister didn't want to, either."

"Maybe you were a little bit of a tattletale," Luke

said, sounding defensive of her, "but they pressured you to do something that made you uncomfortable."

"I think they call that being a teenager, Luke. And you can see how that didn't make me very popular. I wasn't fun." She took a deep breath. "When we were in high school, Vanessa never wanted to spend time with me at all. She had a different group of friends, and I wasn't included. She was always getting in trouble, and whenever there were waves…my parents were worried we were both getting into bad situations. Vanessa got detention, she'd get grounded and go out anyway. Then my grades might slip and I'd get the same punishment Vanessa would get if she were caught with beer. I felt like I was walking on eggshells with everyone."

"That's not fair," Luke said.

"Maybe not. But I think they were afraid I could be influenced to behave like Vanessa if they didn't crack down. And Vanessa…they couldn't control her at all. So they focused on me. It was hard, and in all that, I missed my sister. I was angry because I was home alone all the time and…and I wanted to be part of the group again. I wanted a chance to prove I wasn't just an annoying tattletale. I thought that if I could get myself invited to one of the parties that she was going to maybe I could fix our relationship. Maybe I could find a way to bridge the gap between us. And I think… I think deep down part of me was jealous."

It was like spitting out nails, admitting that. Because it made everything that followed more murky. Made her less of the benevolent good child and more the petulant, angry sister who got treated like she might rebel at any moment without getting any of the fun of rebellion.

"I was spending Friday nights at home alone study-ing, trying to please our parents, and she was going out partying. I felt hungry for that. For friends. For fun. But it scared me, because I wanted to do the right thing, too. I wanted to do what my parents wanted. I was tutoring this girl that Vanessa used to hang out with in math, and I ended up weaseling an invite to one of the parties out of her. Or more, I weaseled the information out of her—she didn't explicitly say that I could show up. But I did."

Shame, sadness, all came crashing down on her chest.

"What happened?" he asked.

"I went to the party and there was drinking. I was prepared for that."

"You had all of your ways to say no firmly in place," he said, the corner of his mouth lifting upward slightly.

"You joke, Luke, but I did."

"Of course you did."

"I had been prepared for there to be drinking. But I wasn't prepared for the drugs. And I'm not talking marijuana. There was some harder stuff. Someone had stolen Oxy off of their parents, and everyone was taking pills. Vanessa took some," Olivia said. "I knew that we had gotten further apart, but I had no idea that she was doing stuff like that. I went straight home, and I told my parents."

In part because she'd been scared. But...

"The next day, when Vanessa came home, we had a meeting. And my father announced that he was sending her to a school for troubled girls."

"That's why she left," Luke confirmed.

"Yes. But I'm sure that you've heard all the rumors about that."

He lifted a shoulder. "Sure. There certainly weren't

any rumors that she had gone off to an art academy or anything."

"I think at that point everybody knew that Vanessa Logan was trouble." Olivia swallowed hard. "And I was the good one."

"And you still are," he said.

She nodded. "Yes. The good sister, that's me. It was easier with her gone though. And that…that's the worst part. That I enjoyed her being gone, because it seemed like they weren't quite as hard on me without Vanessa around making them worry. It was all fine when I imagined that being at the school might save her. That it might pull her out of risky behaviors and all of that."

"Let me guess," he said, his voice heavy. "It didn't."

"No. It didn't. If anything, it just gave her more access to people who had done more things. She ran away from the school. And my parents had trouble tracking her down. They looked, of course, sent out search parties down in Southern California, where she was, but they didn't find her. And then they quit looking."

She looked up at the ceiling, counted the wooden slats there. "She would resurface from time to time, just to give a phone call and let us know she was alive. And then she was eighteen, and there was nothing anyone could do about it. She wasn't missing. Not really. Oxy became heroin. And then everything else. We used to be identical. Drugs took that from us, too."

Her face and throat felt hot and scratchy. She wished she could cry. But she'd had too much practice with not crying over Vanessa. How could she? She had a stake in this place her sister had ended up.

Her mother and father had the right to cry.

Olivia had the right to behave.

"It's been about six months since we've heard from

her now though. God only knows. She could be dead of an overdose somewhere, and nobody would care, Luke. No one would care at all. Because she's a junkie. Except she's still my sister."

"And you think you have to be good enough for both of you now? This is why you have to text your parents and make sure they don't worry?"

She sat up, clinging to the blankets. "They have a daughter they have to worry might die in an alley somewhere," she said, shaking her head. "Shouldn't I make it easy for them? Shouldn't I let them know where I am? And yes, I do need to be good. Because if I'm not, then what was the point of being such a rigid, awful little tattletale? If I'm not everything that I've always pretended it was so easy to be, if it's actually not easy when you're faced with your own particular brand of temptation, then where did I ever get off?" She looked at him. "I guess I never had a leg to stand on. Because you seem to be my brand of temptation, Luke Hollister, and I resisted you all of two weeks."

"Technically," he said, "you've known me for a long time. Factoring in age of consent and all of that, I'd say you resisted for about seven years."

"You know what I mean." She frowned.

Luke let out a slow, heavy breath and reached out, cupping her chin in his hands. "I'm going to tell you something, Olivia, and I want you to take it to heart as much as you can. You can't make choices for someone else. And being good, never making a mistake, is never going to erase the mistakes your sister made. It's never going to erase what you're afraid are your mistakes. You did the right thing, as far as you could see it at the time. Your parents did, too. Were you supposed to look away and let her continue on in addiction right in front of you? You would blame yourself for that, too. But in the end, you can't blame yourself for any of it. Because you didn't inject anything into her veins, you didn't make her smoke anything or snort anything, didn't make her take off her clothes to go skinny-dipping in the first place all those years ago. She made her choices and you made yours. End of story."

He lay back, closing his eyes. "You can't make someone walk a path they don't want to be on. You can't even make them breathe if they don't want to anymore. That is their choice. And it's their life. You can't make your whole existence a fucking monument to that. Otherwise, what's the point in your good behavior? What's the point in continuing to be alive if you're not really living? You were going to marry some guy you weren't even tempted to jump into bed with because... Why?"

"Because I thought that it would make me safe," she said. Her throat had gone unbearably tight, her eyes stinging with unshed tears. "Because deep down I'm afraid that if I put one step out of line I'll end up like her. We're twins. What separates the two of us from each other? Genetically, almost nothing. I know my parents were worried about that. It's why they were so hard on me. I'm not sorry about it, either. It was that hardness that gave me the life I have, and it's better than the life Vanessa has, let me tell you."

"You thought marriage would protect you?"

"I don't know if I'd put it that way. But I knew it would...make my life settled. For me. For my parents. Then I can have all those things, and in the right place. I can have sex, and I could have it with commitment. And if I got pregnant, then at least I would have a husband."

"That's a lot of flawed reasoning there, darlin'," he said.

"Yes," she said slowly. "And when I say it out loud

I can see that. But when I felt it inside of me, when it was just a whole lot of pressure crushing down on my brain, it seemed reasonable enough. Bennett was safe. That was the beginning and end of it. I never really thought of it in all those different terms until just now."

"And what about me?" He brushed her hair back away from her eyes. "What am I?"

"I don't know. The first thing I've ever let myself have that I just wanted. The first time I've ever indulged."

"I can do that. I can be that."

"Okay," she said, her lips feeling numb.

He was the first person she had ever said all of these things to. She had admitted it to herself at the same moment she had admitted it to him.

And she had already committed one of those grave sins she had tried to keep herself from committing. Had already dropped her guard, released her hold on her control, let herself feel, instead of think.

Luke was… He was safe. As rebellions went. She knew him. He would never hurt her, not on purpose. He certainly wasn't going to marry her, and she didn't want to marry him, either.

They had chemistry. It might be fun to chase that for a while.

To hold it. To have this small, reckless thing that she could claim as her own, and then set aside when they were finished.

"Okay?"

"I mean… Please," she said. "Please be my reckless thing."

He smiled slowly, and for just one second it looked to her like the smile didn't reach his eyes. But then it arrived, and she didn't ponder that anymore.

"With pleasure."

CHAPTER FIFTEEN

LUKE THOUGHT HE deserved a damned medal for the restraint he showed early the next morning, when he woke up with Olivia's soft body curled around him, her breath fanning across his chest. The medal for not rolling her onto her back and having her again.

Once. He had only taken her the one time.

She had fallen asleep, and he had spent the rest of the night lying next to her, hard and aching and feeling extraordinarily benevolent.

She had been a virgin, and he had to be sensitive about that.

He didn't know how to be sensitive. He didn't know how to be protective. Apparently, when it came to Olivia it was just natural.

It was early, and the sun hadn't quite come up yet, but he had to get over to the ranch right about the time the first rays of morning light crested the top of the mountains. And he had a feeling Olivia would have to be getting to work, as well, though not anywhere near as early as him,

He also had a feeling that Olivia wouldn't want to go straight from his place over to the winery.

He paused at the coffeepot in the kitchen, which ran on a predictable, extremely necessary timer that meant he didn't have to spend more than a couple of minutes uncaffeinated when he rolled out of bed in the morning and poured himself a generous mug.

Then he walked quietly back into the bedroom.

He could see her feet. Sticking out the bottom of the comforter, her toes curled in. And he could see the top of her head, her dark brown hair resembling a bird's nest, covering her face.

He didn't wake up with women. One had never spent the night at his house. And, since he by and large tended to hook up at the woman's house, he had total control over whether or not he spent the night there. He did not.

He preferred to get his and get gone.

But after having Olivia, after he had discovered that he was the first man she had ever been with, after she had told him all about Vanessa and the weight that she carried on her petite little shoulders, there had been no turfing her out.

Not that he wanted to. But in an ideal world, spending the night in bed with her would have meant trying to make a dent in the hunger that he felt for her.

No such luck.

That brought him back to pondering his own innate goodness, which he had never thought existed. At the moment he was considering launching a campaign for sainthood.

"Olivia," he said, pushing away from the door and walking into the bedroom.

She let out a muffled sound and her feet disappeared beneath the covers as she curled into a ball.

He walked over to her side of the bed—which was technically his side, but she had colonized it and he wasn't about to argue with her—and set his mug down on his nightstand, crouching down low so that he was eye level with her. Or rather, tangled hair level, since he still couldn't see her face. "Olivia, you need to wake up, kiddo."

She nuzzled her face into the pillow, and then one eye appeared, looking sleepy and cloudy. Then, that eye widened.

She rolled over and sat up, holding on to the blankets. "What time is it?"

"It's five-thirty. It's early. But, I didn't know what your schedule was today, and I have to take off soon."

She blinked, looking around the room, a bit bewildered. "I… I slept here."

"Yes, you did," he said.

"In your bed."

"Yeah," Luke said. "But only after we had sex."

Olivia made a sound that put him in mind of a distressed vole and covered her face with her hands. "Right."

"It's a bit late for regrets, honey," he said.

She popped back up. "I don't have regrets." She sounded defiant. Mutinous.

"Good," he said. "Because it's too late."

"I know that," she snapped, climbing out of bed and taking the blanket with her, trailing it behind her as she marched over to where he had discarded her panties last night, and then into the living room, where the rest of her clothes still were.

That, he supposed would impact his candidacy for sainthood. If he were truly a good man, he would have brought her clothing to her, left it folded neatly on the foot of the bed. And he certainly wouldn't have stood behind her, living for that little glimpse of her ass that he caught when the fabric fell and exposed her.

Too bad. He was fine with not being commemorated

in stained glass as long as he had the chance to stare at Olivia Logan's bare behind for a while.

Sacrifices had to be made. And if his choices fell somewhere between good and Olivia's naked body, he knew which one he was going to pick.

She bent down, retrieving the clothing, and marched back into his bedroom. He followed.

"A little privacy?" she asked.

"It's a bit late for that, too."

Her face turned a particularly attractive shade of scarlet. "That's not fair."

"I didn't say I was fair, honey. You know what's not fair." He sat down on his bed and reclined. Then, he grabbed hold of his coffee mug, keeping his eyes fixed on her. "You stayed at my place for free last night. Now you have to pay up."

"I think I did pay up already," she said, muted.

"No. That was mutual pleasure. Wasn't any kind of transaction. This," he said, "might be somewhat transactional. But, if you drop the blanket I will give you a cup of coffee."

"Then I'll be back to owing you."

"I'm okay with that."

"I'm not sure I am."

He frowned. "You don't want to be in my debt?"

"Not especially." But she slowly released her hold on the plaid comforter and let it fall to a downy heap on the floor. Then she slowly took her white lace panties and stepped into them gingerly, pulling them up her legs and covering up that delicious triangle between her thighs. His breath hissed out through his teeth and he took a sip of his coffee, the warm liquid settling with regret in his stomach. Regret, because what he really wanted to do was push her back down onto the bed and make better use of the morning.

But he had a feeling she was not here for that, and also he really did have to get to work.

He watched with avid interest as she put on the rest of her clothes—a little reverse striptease that was as hot as it was disappointing—and neither of them said anything.

When she was dressed completely, he decided to initiate conversation.

"So, I don't know where this leaves things," he said. "Bennett. The land. All of that."

"I don't know," Olivia said. "Well, I know some. I don't want Bennett. I know that. I was…naive to think that I did. To think that what I felt for him was the right kind of thing to feel for a guy you were going to marry. As for the land… Offer for it. I'll tell my dad that I think you would do good things with it."

"And probably shouldn't mention that I took your virginity?"

"Probably not."

She frowned. "It would probably be best if no one knew."

"I hate to break it to you, but we kind of already made a spectacle about town."

She looked regretful and filled with distress. "But that was when it was fake."

"You mess with the bull, sometimes you get the horns."

Olivia scrunched up her face. "Who's the bull in this scenario?"

"It's more about what. We figured we could tempt this thing between us. We lost."

She worried her bottom lip between her teeth. "I didn't realize there was a thing between us."

"Sorry," he said, "I would have warned you if I would have known that you were a virgin who didn't recognize that kind of thing."

She treated him to a very cranky expression and stomped out of the bedroom and into the kitchen.

"Typically," he said, following her and keeping the relentlessly perky tone in his voice, "people are in a better mood after sex."

"I don't know what mood I'm in. I don't know what I am at all."

"You don't need to answer that question," he said.

"But I do," she said plaintively. "I don't know how to not have a plan. I don't understand uncertainty."

He chuckled. "Welcome to life for the rest of us."

"It sucks," she said.

"Sure. No one said it didn't."

"I have to go," he said.

"Of course you do," she responded.

"I'm not abandoning you," he said, his tone careful. "If I had wanted to do that I would have left last night. I have to go to work."

"I know," she said. "And even if you were abandoning me it would be fine. Because I'm busy, too. I have to go to work in a few hours."

"I figured you probably did. And that you would probably want to get ready at home. Unless you want to go in last night's clothes."

She wrinkled her nose. "Not especially."

"I didn't think so. Plus, I don't have an extra eyelash curler or anything for you to use."

"I don't use eyelash curlers. How do you even know what those are?"

He simply looked at her, arching his brow until her cheeks turned pink. Then she sniffed. "I don't need to hear about your past escapades."

"I have zero escapades that specifically involve an eyelash curler, I have just been in many a female bathroom. Never had an eyelash curler on my bathroom counter. So you know."

She frowned, then nodded slowly. "Okay. Good to know."

"Do you understand what I'm telling you?"

"Kind of." She clasped her hands and looked up at him, her expression searching. "But maybe be specific."

"I've never had a woman spend the night here. And, I don't do relationships."

"Well, the relationship thing I observed, having known you for about twenty years. But, I will take the assurance on the other thing. Since, you know… You're a first for me. And I can't pretend otherwise. It's nice to be a little bit of something special to you."

Luke's chest seized up tight. "You're special to me, Olivia." He took hold of her chin, which he was developing a real fondness for, and pressed a soft kiss to her lips. Just a brief one, because anything more and he was going to lose control, say to hell with their mutual schedules and drag her back into the bedroom.

Her eyes fluttered open, then she looked at him sleepily. "Thank you."

He didn't know quite what she was thanking him for. And he wasn't going to ask. Instead, he just nodded and grabbed his hat off the hook by the door and made his way out to his truck.

Olivia's little car was parked in his driveway next to his old clunker, and there was something strange and intimate about that, seeing it there in the early morning hour. He chose not to examine that terribly closely.

He jerked open the truck door and got in, keeping his eye on her little car and the light in the kitchen window as long as he could before he turned around and headed out of the driveway.

He wondered how long she would stay. If she would drink his coffee. Use one of the mugs. If she would sit on the couch for a while, or if she would just leave right away, anxious to get back to her own space, rather than inhabiting his.

It was a strange line of thinking, and one he couldn't quite see the point of. And yet, even as he pulled into Get Out of Dodge, he was still imagining her in his house. Maybe even wrapped back up in the blanket.

He parked out back by the heavy equipment barn and got out, the cold morning air a welcome slap in the face.

He breathed in deep. The smell of dirt and animals as soothing as he imagined potpourri was for other people. This was the mark of a good life to him. Not dried rose petals and scented candles.

The fresh air, infused with pine and wood. Horse sweat and manure.

Worked for him.

He made his way across the property and over to the main house. He stood in front of the place, staring up at the massive porch, the green sheet metal roof and the heavy, natural wood beams that extended down from the gutters to the ground.

He had lived on this property, but never in this house.

Part of the family, but not.

Bennett had said it himself. Luke wasn't one of them. And truthfully, it was time he had a talk with Wyatt about it.

He walked up the steps and paused at the door, then decided that he would knock. He didn't usually, but it seemed like today's conversation called for it.

When Wyatt jerked the door open, his expression was surprised. "Why the hell are you knocking?"

"I need to talk to you."

"Well, hell. That's awfully formal." He rubbed the back of his neck.

"It kind of is."

He waited for Wyatt to invite him in. And it seemed to take Wyatt a moment to realize that's what was happening. Finally, he stepped to the side, allowing Luke entry. "If we're going to be formal, we might as well go into the living room," he said.

Luke followed Wyatt through the entryway and into the living room area. The ceiling was high, pointed into an A with windows that ran from floor to ceiling and a large fireplace that went down the middle of them. There was a loft floor that overlooked part of the room, with Pendleton blankets draped over the railing, a hold-over from when Quinn had lived here.

Luke had a feeling that Wyatt kept it the same because his father and his new wife, Freda, did come back from time to time, and Wyatt didn't want it to look too much like he had overhauled the place the moment his father had left. He was doing it slowly. Incrementally. But the blankets were still in the same spot.

"Have a seat," Wyatt said, gesturing to one of the leather couches with the big brass nails on the armrests.

"I'll stand," Luke said.

"Okay," Wyatt said, remaining standing himself, rocking back on his boot heels.

Luke looked out past Wyatt, to the windows, to the

sky that was turning a blush color, illuminating the evergreen trees that grew thick along the mountains.

"I'm thinking of leaving."

"Leaving?" Wyatt asked. "What the hell does that mean?"

"The ranch," Luke clarified.

"You're leaving the ranch?" Wyatt looked incredulous. "Right now? Right when we're undergoing all these changes? Luke, I didn't plan on doing this without you. I need you for this. Get Out of Dodge needs you. You can't just abandon the ranch."

"I want to get a piece of land that belongs to me," Luke said, tamping down the defensiveness that rose up inside of him.

He didn't owe Wyatt Dodge his whole life. And if he wanted to leave his job, he sure as hell didn't owe the guy an explanation. He was talking to him because Wyatt was like family to him, and it was a courtesy as far as Luke was concerned.

"I know you and Bennett have some shit going down, but I thought you could both deal with it. If this is about Olivia..."

And that did it. It just *did it*. It was one thing to call twenty years of loyalty into question and accuse him of abandonment, but it was another damned thing to bring Olivia into it.

"All right, you want to talk about abandonment and loyalty? Let's talk about that. Because you don't have a right to talk about Olivia, that's for damn sure. If Bennett wants to come have a fight about it, he's welcome to, but you need to keep out of it."

"Fine, then," Wyatt said, looking pissed now. "The why doesn't matter. But this place is yours, too. You're part of the family, Luke, and leaving now—"

"Yeah," Luke interrupted. "It's mine, too. Even though I'm the one who devoted every ounce of work to the place. The only one who didn't have another job. The one who didn't get married and get a job in town, or go to veterinary school or run off to the rodeo circuit. You want to talk about abandonment? How long are you here for, Wyatt? How long until you can't stand the fact that living here means you aren't a big deal cowboy anymore? How long until you decide that compressed disks and bum knees don't matter if you can get just a little more glory? A few more buckle bunnies."

"I'm done," Wyatt said, his jaw hard, his brown eyes shining with a dangerous light. "I'm here now. And if you expect me to apologize for going away and earning more money to inject back into this place…"

"Oh, that's why you did it?" Luke asked. To hell with treading gently. "For everyone else? This is the thing, Wyatt, I'm well aware I'm not family. If I were I'd have had a room in the house. If I were, I'd be the one running this place now, not you. I was the one who was here all those years, not you. No, I'm not family. And this place isn't mine."

"So what? Without a stake in the ranch, twenty years of friendship, of eating dinner together, celebrating holidays together…it's nothing? Is that what you're saying?"

"No. I'm saying it's different. I refuse to take lectures on abandonment from the man who left his dad in the lurch to chase his dream and get trampled by bulls."

"You don't know jack shit," Wyatt said. "And anyway, Dad needed money for the place more than he needed me."

"Because I was cheap labor?"

"He had you. And it's not like I didn't come back in the off times of year."

"Incidentally when there was less work to be done on the ranch," Luke pointed out.

"I'm not looking for a lecture from you."

"No," Luke said. "You were looking to give one. Save it for your brothers. I could have just left, but I wanted to let you know my plans. I'm buying that piece of property owned by the Logan family, if all goes according to plan, and I'm going to establish my own ranch."

"With what money?" Wyatt asked. "Like you said, you're pretty cheap labor."

Luke let out a laugh that was not at all filled with humor. "Everyone is so worried about my financial situation. And thank you," he said, "but I'm good. I happen to be a grown man who isn't an idiot. I know what I can afford."

"It's just," Wyatt said, "I've seen the books. I know what we pay you."

"And I'm telling you," Luke said, "I'm good. I can pay cash for the place, thank you very much."

Wyatt's eyebrows shot upward, and Luke felt gratified by that. He also felt somewhat of a mix of gratitude and irritation that Wyatt didn't press for details.

"What's going on?"

Luke turned to see Bennett standing in the doorway, his arms crossed over his chest, his expression combative.

"Luke is thinking about leaving," Wyatt said.

"I'm not thinking about it," Luke said. "I am. I'm buying that plot of land that Cole Logan has for sale on the outskirts of town."

"You've talked to him?" Wyatt asked.

"No," Luke said.

"You son of a bitch," Bennett growled.

"What?" Luke asked.

"It's a coincidence that you're with Olivia now, and you want to buy a plot of land from her dad? Are you using her to get that land?"

"Fuck you, Bennett," Luke said. "Is that the best that you think of me?"

"Why would I think better of you? Give me a reason," Bennett said. "Explain this in a way that doesn't look like shit."

"I don't need to explain this to you. Olivia has nothing to do with the land." It was true enough. Yes, he had ended up talking to her about talking to her father, but it had nothing to do with their actual relationship. Had nothing to do with the fact that they were sleeping together. And giving out any of the actual reasons he had started hanging out with Olivia in the first place would be exposing her. And he wasn't going to do that.

"I would think that knowing me for the past twenty years might help out," Luke said.

"Do I know you?" he asked. "You've been around, sure. But you're not a guy that people can actually know, Luke. You show up with a smart-ass smile on your face and kick along without making waves."

"I've been here," Luke said, gesturing to the space around him.

"Sure," Bennett said. "Doesn't mean we know you. Not really. You have just been here all this time, and suddenly you want to make a move, and that happens to involve my ex-girlfriend."

Luke knew that at this point a smile would get him a better reaction than anything else. So he did just that. "Your ex-girlfriend involved herself with me, and that might bother you, Bennett, but it's her choice. She's not a kid. She's a woman whether you want to know that or not. Hell, I'd say you didn't know it. You treated her like… I don't know. Like a brass ring. And she's not."

"No. I guess she's the cosigner on the deed to your new ranch," Bennett spat.

"I'm not having this fight with you. I'm not having a fight with you at all. The lady chose. Deal with it. I don't have to justify a damned thing to you. Hell, I've been in bar fights with you guys, you ought to know me better than that."

Luke turned to walk out of the room, and Bennett's voice stopped him.

"Yeah," he said, "you've backed us up in fights. But what do you fight for, Luke? That's what I don't know. You slide through things so easy. You don't give a fuck about anyone. About anything. Sure as hell not about Olivia. So don't stand there like I ought to give you credit, like I should know you, when you've never demonstrated what kind of man you are."

"A man who backs up his buddies isn't good enough for you?" Luke asked.

"A man who backs up his buddies is doing the easy thing," Bennett said, "isn't he?"

"I'll remember that next time you're about to get your ass beat down at the saloon." He smiled. "I'll remember that you think I should improve my character by doing the hard thing and get your teeth knocked out."

He walked out of the living room, out the front door and was halfway down the steps when he heard Wyatt behind him.

"Hey," he said, coming down the steps and moving to stand beside Luke. "Just give him time to cool off. He's been bent out of shape since the breakup."

"Well, that's just too damn bad. I guess he should have figured out how to hang on to a woman," Luke said, not feeling like giving Bennett any quarter at that point.

"You have your secrets," Wyatt said. "We all do. I don't want you to leave. But I understand that sometimes leaving is the only thing. I get that you're pissed at me for getting in your business, but that's what family does. So you're just going to have to deal with it."

"Still sticking with the family thing, are you?"

"This family has been through a lot," Wyatt said, his expression grim. "We've lost enough. We don't need to lose you, too. My dad doesn't treat us all the same. And he's...he's not perfect, Luke, but he loves the hell out of you."

"I know that," Luke said. He did. It had been asinine of him to bring up the fact that Quinn hadn't sold part of the ranch to him. That things had gone to Wyatt. He had never talked to Quinn about it. He had never asked Quinn if he could live in the house. And he had a pretty good sense of things, enough to know that Quinn pretty purposefully didn't push to hand things to Luke. Because he knew Luke would reject them.

"Until the ranch comes together for you, you know that you have a place here. Hell, after, I would love to have you here."

"Why are you being nice to me? I mean, why aren't you on Bennett's side?"

Wyatt shrugged and put his cowboy hat on his head, moving past Luke. Then he stopped and turned toward him. "I may not have seen what you'd choose to throw a punch for. But I've seen what you sweat for. This place. For us. For my dad, and for everything he gave you. That tells me enough."

CHAPTER SIXTEEN

"ARE YOU IN a philosophical space that allows you to visit Get Out of Dodge?"

Lindy's sudden question shocked Olivia, and it sent her mind straight to Luke. Not that her mind had been far from Luke at any point during the day. An interesting change from when any mention of Get Out of Dodge would have put her in mind of Bennett, and no one else.

But, no. Her brain was completely fixed on Luke now.

Luke's body, Luke's lips, the way that Luke felt moving inside of her. Yes, she was having a full-fledged obsession, but really, a girl could hardly be blamed when she was twenty-five and had only just lost her virginity the night before.

"I am philosophically and physically able," Olivia said, looking up from the spreadsheet she had been examining, trying not to sound too eager.

"Great. I'm taking samples over to Get Out of Dodge. Wine, and some Donnelly cheese, as well. Just trying to get Wyatt on board with this whole joint venture thing."

"Yes. I can do that."

"I find the whole thing with Wyatt difficult," Lindy confessed.

"Why? Because he's friends with your ex?"

"He hates me," Lindy confessed. "I mean, he just really doesn't like me. Never has. From the first mo-

ment I met him when I went on a partial tour with
Damien years ago, we met in a bar and…he just took
against me."

"You want to partner with him why?"

"Because. Get Out of Dodge is the only dude ranch
in the area, and he's trying to revamp it. We are between Copper Ridge and Gold Valley, and I feel like
we should reap the benefits of both."

"I admire your avarice," Olivia said.

"Thank you," Lindy said. "It's one of my best quali-
ties. Okay. I have all the boxes loaded up in the back
of the truck. Now we just need to drive down there."

Olivia drifted behind Lindy, across the gravel lot.
She toed some of the gray rocks with her brown ankle
boots and looked around them at the towering pines,
still defiantly green, even in the dead of winter.

Olivia wanted to be defiant in that way, suddenly.
Wanted to weather these changes, this season, and
maintain her color and life.

Or more honestly, get it back.

They both got into the truck and Olivia placed her
elbow on the armrest and looked out the window as
they drove down to the highway.

"You still seem awfully quiet," Lindy said. "Is the
whole thing with Bennett…"

"He asked if we could get back together," Olivia
said. "I refused."

The words sent a little buzz through her. She really
had refused him. And she had gone after Luke, who
made her blood hot and her heart race fast. She'd satisfied herself for now, and who knew what would happen
in the future. But she felt good. Resolute, if nothing else.

Lindy slapped the steering wheel. "Good for you. I
don't think he appreciated you."

"Really?"

"Actually," Lindy relented, "he always seemed like a really nice guy, and he treated you like a princess. But, there was something missing."

"Chemistry," Olivia said. "Which… I know I can't ignore anymore."

"I see," Lindy said, carefully. "What brought about this change of heart?"

"I…" Olivia swallowed. "I slept with someone last night."

"I see," Lindy repeated, this time clearly not seeing at all.

"For the first time."

"The first time *ever* with that person, or the first time ever?"

"The first time *ever*," Olivia said.

She had felt very much like an outsider during the conversations her friends were having about love and sex over the past few months. Now she just wanted to talk.

"It was so much different than I thought it would be," she continued. "And he's so different than the kind of man I thought I'd be with. My feelings are…so complicated. I can't stop thinking about him."

"I'm having déjà vu," Lindy said. "This is the second time someone has confessed virginity loss to me in my car."

"Oh," Olivia said. "Is that really a lot?"

"Considering it's all been in the past couple of months? Yes. Which, more power to you guys. It's been so long for me I can hardly remember what it's like. Anyway, I would be too tired to have a relationship even if one presented itself. All this work on the winery. Every night when I get into bed I'm so sore I can hardly move. The other night I actually considered using my vibrator as a massager. For my shoulders. Because my predominant need is to relieve the aches and pains in my muscles, not anywhere else."

Olivia's face warmed slightly, but she found the line of conversation didn't mystify her as much as it might have before last night. Or maybe even before she had kissed Luke in the back of the truck.

Suddenly, a whole lot more things made sense to her. Like why people made rash, impulsive decisions that would only hurt them when sex was involved. Like why it was difficult to go without once you started.

That specter loomed large in front of her, made her feel slightly terrified. Just because she'd had sex with Luke once didn't mean it would keep happening. Or maybe it would happen a few more times, but then he would get bored and it would end. And then what? She would have to find someone else. Someone else that she felt this way about. It had taken her twenty-five years to find a man she felt this way about. She didn't want to wait twenty-five more.

"Was it Luke Hollister by any chance?" Lindy asked gently.

Olivia's head whipped around to look at Lindy's profile. "How did you know?"

"Because I saw you with him that morning he brought you to work. And I know you said there was nothing going on, but, Olivia, the way he looks at you…"

"How does he look at me?" Olivia asked, suddenly desperate to pry apart every detail about the way Luke might see her.

"Like he's starving and you're food. Like he'll die if he can't touch you."

Olivia felt like her breath had been sucked right out of her. "You got all of that from a look?"

"And more. Men are not very subtle. And he really isn't." Lindy laughed.

Olivia frowned. "I was such a virgin."

"Nothing wrong with that. But that man wanted to eat you alive. I'm glad he finally got to."

Olivia's face went hot at that. Because it put her in mind of a very literal interpretation of what Lindy meant metaphorically. Which had happened. And shocked her at the time. But delighted her in hindsight.

Okay, it still shocked her a little bit, too.

"Luke is probably going to be at the ranch," Olivia said, trying to sound casual.

"Well, as long as you don't take off on me when I'm trying to deal with Wyatt."

"I promise I won't."

They turned into the drive that led to Get Out of Dodge and Lindy parked the truck right in front.

Olivia went around to the back with her and lowered the tailgate, taking one of the boxes of wine, while Lindy took the other.

"Right now they're probably in the mess hall," Olivia said. "It's time for their midmorning coffee and carbs."

"You're going to have to show me where that is," Lindy said.

"Follow me," Olivia said, pleased at least to feel like an authority on one thing. The rest of the world felt like a big endless mystery all of a sudden. Which was funny, because she had labored under the assumption that she had it all figured out for the last twenty-five years or so. That plans and control were all she needed. And all it had taken was that wildfire attraction to Luke Hollister to prove to her that she had been laughably wrong.

Suddenly, she saw so much more nuance in life. So many more variables. Understood why people made bargains with themselves about certain things and why they committed grave sins in the name of pleasure.

For a moment she wondered if it were the same with drugs for some people as it was with sex. If it all felt worth it for that momentary high.

It was so much easier to stand in judgment. She had liked her moral high ground.

But now that she had proven herself human, too, it was difficult to get back up on it.

She paused in front of the door to the mess hall and knocked gently. And a moment later Wyatt flung the door open. He looked at her, and then his eyes settled on Lindy. And Olivia suddenly understood what Lindy had meant only a moment before.

What it looked like when a man wanted to eat you alive.

But, just as soon as that heat in Wyatt's eyes had appeared, it cooled.

"I wasn't expecting you," Wyatt said, his tone casual.

"I left a message," Lindy responded.

"I didn't confirm." Wyatt leaned against the door frame, the muscles on his forearms shifting as he crossed them over his broad chest.

"I didn't wait for you to confirm," Lindy said, breezing past both Olivia and Wyatt and heading into the hall with her box of wine. "This is heavy," she said, moving toward one of the large picnic-bench-type tables and setting it down in the center. "I brought you wine and cheese."

"Lucky me," Wyatt said. "As you can see and have probably guessed, I'm a big fan of having a glass of wine and a delicate cheese in the middle of my day spent shoveling shit."

Olivia sneaked in past Wyatt and he followed behind.

"Everybody likes wine and cheese, Wyatt." Lindy straightened, her blond hair flipping back over her shoulder. "It's what makes shoveling shit bearable."

The clash between the two of them was almost electric, and Olivia was caught up in it enough that she almost didn't notice when the door opened again and Luke came walking in. Almost. Because whatever electricity was arcing between Wyatt and Lindy, it was nothing compared to what she felt as soon as she saw Luke.

The breath rushed out of her lungs, and her whole body went tingly.

"Hi," she said, her voice sounding dangerously girlish.

She was not good at this.

"Good morning," Luke said, making the decision to cross the space and come close to her, not kissing her, but touching her hand. "How are you today?"

It wasn't a casual ask. But one laden with meaning. How was she today, specifically, the morning after they'd first slept together.

"Good," she said, smiling shyly.

She realized then that they had attracted the attention of Wyatt and Lindy, who had stopped sparring long enough to watch their interaction.

Wyatt turned away quick enough, but Lindy kept her eyes on them.

Olivia took a deep breath and set her own box down on the table. "We brought samples. In case you want to stock wine here for the guests. And arrange vineyard tours and things."

"Sure, sounds good," Luke said. "Though I probably won't be here anymore."

"I know," Olivia said. "Have you talked to my dad yet?"

"No," Luke answered, keeping his voice low. "But soon. I will soon."

"Good." She took a deep breath. "I'm still going to vouch for your character."

"I would think at this point you're well aware that it's disreputable."

"That's kind of what I like about it," she said.

A slow smile spread across his face. "Are you flirting with me?"

"I might be."

"Make your sales pitch, ladies," Wyatt interrupted, looking from Olivia to Lindy. "I have work to do."

"*Shoveling*," Lindy said. "I'm aware. All right, you want a sales pitch, Dodge, a sales pitch you'll get. I'm willing to give you a deep discount on the wine, the Donnelly brothers are willing to give a large discount on cheese—friends and family discount, seeing as they are now almost family to me, or close enough by marriage. I would also like to arrange for tours. And I know that you have been doing trail riding expeditions. If you'd like to, I'm willing to arrange for rides through the vineyard. That would be a nice thing to put on your website, don't you think?"

"It would be," Wyatt answered, "considering wine tourism is a big deal now."

"Oh, I'm well aware," Lindy said. "And I'm doing everything in my power to make Grassroots Winery the most successful in the area. Damien was cautious, and he didn't want to expand. The only PR vision he had was for the rodeo, Wyatt, and wine isn't a bull. I have a vision for how all this is going to work. We have the tasting room down in Copper Ridge, as well, so that will help direct some business from there to you. We have a long reach. We're a more established business than Get Out of Dodge is at this point, more synonymous with tourists. Of course, we will return the favor by putting brochures about the ranch in our shop."

"Sounds like a good deal to me," Wyatt said, clearly surprising Lindy with his easy acquiescence. "But let me taste what you brought, and get together some figures on pricing and let you know."

"Good," Lindy said. "Very good. We'll be in touch then."

"I expect we will," Wyatt said. "See you around." He tipped his hat and walked out of the mess hall, leaving Olivia and Lindy there with Luke.

"Well, I guess our work here is done." Lindy looked between Luke and Olivia. "I'll return her to you later," she said to Luke.

Olivia blushed. "I'm not his lost sweater. You do not need to return me to him."

"I would appreciate it," Luke said, smiling wickedly.

Olivia rolled her eyes. "God save me from alpha males." She looked at Lindy. "And meddling bosses."

"Yeah, well," Lindy said, "this meddling boss is going to wait out in the truck so that you can say goodbye to each other."

She waved slightly, and then walked out of the mess hall, leaving Olivia alone with Luke, who promptly took the opportunity to pull her into his arms and kissed her so hard it made her dizzy.

When they parted, she sighed happily.

"It feels like I haven't seen you in forever," she said, immediately embarrassed to have said that, because it was incredibly revealing if nothing else. Both to her and to him.

"It does," he agreed, immediately putting her at ease.

"So, you talked to Wyatt about leaving?"

"Yes. And nearly got hit by Bennett, but that's to be expected. He doesn't like the idea of me being with you."

She waited for there to be any kind of thrill over that. For her to feel anything at all. She did, but it was mostly just irritation.

"Too bad for him," she said.

Luke chuckled and slung his arm around her, kissing her on top of the head. "I expect you have to go back to work," he said, his tone sounding resigned.

"I do."

"See you tonight?" he asked.

She wasn't sure how to answer that. If she spent the night with him too often, her mother was going to notice. It wasn't like she was ashamed of what was happening with Luke, she just didn't know if she wanted to offer explanations to her mother right now.

It was different now that it was real. Because it felt fragile and fresh, because it felt personal. Like something she wanted to hold against her chest and examine all on her own without anyone else's opinion or eyes on it at all.

"If it's that difficult of a question to answer," Luke said, "I can wait till it's easy."

She shook her head. "No. I'll come over."

She was resolute. She was going to have this on her own terms. And while that meant everybody and their mom would know about it, it also meant that she couldn't do or not do what she wanted just because of what someone else might see or not.

In that, she was determined.

"All right then," he said, "I'll see you tonight."

LUKE DIDN'T HAVE any experience talking to the father of a girl he was sleeping with. Hell, he hadn't had entanglements with women that were serious enough for it to ever get there. And that wasn't the reason he was having a conversation with Olivia's father, either.

Still, he felt like he was going to ask for her hand in marriage or some kind of old-fashioned nonsense. Instead of going to talk about a business matter. He felt like *I took you daughter's virginity* was stamped on his forehead. Ideally, he would have met with Cole Logan a little later than twenty-four hours after that event, but the man had said he'd see him today, so Luke didn't want to reschedule the appointment simply because of that kind of discomfort.

Cole Logan was a tall man, age not doing a thing to diminish his presence and his appearance of strength. If anything, he was probably more authoritative now than he had been in his youth, and that only made him look more intimidating.

He invited Luke into the house, and took him back to his home office, which resembled a hunting lodge more than it did an office.

It had natural wood paneling and ducks mounted on the wall, frozen in midflight.

Luke had the strong feeling that he could easily find himself nailed to the wall if the older man ever found out what he had done to his daughter.

He figured it was best not to think about that.

"I hear that you're interested in the property just outside of town?" Cole said, sitting back and regarding Luke with a critical eye.

"I am," Luke said. "And I know that you've been hanging on to it for a long time out of interest for what happens to it. I understand that you didn't want there to be any major developments or anything like that made on the property. And I appreciate the way that you've worked to preserve the community."

"Is that so?" Cole laughed. "Luke, I know that Quinn Dodge has a high opinion of you. In fact, after you got in touch with me, I gave him a call and mentioned that you were interested in the place. He told me that there wouldn't be a harder worker for the land. That's why I've held on to it all this time. It's part of my family history. I don't need it, I can't put it to use. So I don't want it sitting there forever unused. If I kept on owning it, it would just be for the sake of that. But if I sell it to somebody who doesn't have a sense for this place, for this town and the county, then I felt like it would lose its integrity. You want to have a ranch on it—is that correct?"

"Yes," Luke said. "I intend to do a cattle ranch. It's the work I enjoyed best at Get Out of Dodge. And, now that Wyatt is taking it more in the dude ranch direction again, I'm not as interested. I have money from a…" Luke cleared his throat. "A settlement. I'm more than able to pay a fair price."

Cole regarded him closely. "I wasn't worried about that. I figured that you knew your finances."

"Well, I wanted to make it clear I'm not even waiting for financing. I'm able to pay cash."

Cole nodded in approval. "That's a point in your favor."

"I thought it might be."

"You've lived in Gold Valley for a long time," Cole said. "And you put a lot of work into Quinn's place.

He said that you work as hard as his own sons on that land, if not harder."

"Harder," Luke said, nodding in confirmation. "Just a fact. I haven't had any other vocation. I've poured everything I have, everything I am into that place. But now I want a place that carries my name."

"Make sense to me," Cole said.

He named his asking price and Luke agreed to it easily, finding it more than fair for his plans. It struck him, right then, that this had been so much easier than he had imagined. That Cole Logan was willing to give this to him based on his merit. Based on the work he had done on the ranch, work that he was beginning to think had gone unnoticed.

"Now," Cole said, "a bit of unofficial business. I hear you were out with my daughter the other night."

He should have figured that was going to come up. He'd thought he might have dodged it.

"That is true," Luke said, speaking slowly.

"You know she was pretty hung up on Bennett Dodge," Cole commented.

"Yeah," Luke said, "I know. She also knows that you talked to Bennett about dating her," Luke said, wondering if his honesty was a little bit too much, but he had always been honest about the things he chose to talk about, so it was too late for him to change that now. "She wasn't too happy about that."

"Things get a little bit frantic when you're staring down your mortality," Cole said. "I don't know if you know, but I had a heart attack, and I was worried about Olivia. Worried that she wouldn't have anyone to take care of her. You know, my other daughter has gone down a very bad road. And Olivia has always been... responsible. Responsible but sheltered, and sometimes that is scary in its own way. We were hard on her. Strict. More so than we should have been sometimes, I think. And I just don't want anything to happen to her. So, I made the best decision I could at the time, and when the two of them did start dating it seemed to me that it might all work out."

"You like him," Luke commented.

"I do," Cole said. And then he fixed his brown eyes, very similar in color and determination to his daughter's, on Luke. "I like Olivia's happiness more than I like any one person. Just so we're clear."

Luke nodded. "Her happiness matters to me, too."

"As I said before," Cole said, "Quinn Dodge said you were a good man. Quinn Dodge doesn't hand out compliments easy. And you have to do a hell of a lot more than smile nice to impress him. I trust that what he says is true."

"All right then," Luke said.

"You know what else I like about you?" Cole said. "You're honest."

Not that the whole thing with Olivia had started out with honesty, but then, the attraction between them sure had. There were no lies between them in the bedroom. None at all. "I aim to be."

"And you aim to put down roots."

"I do," Luke said. "This was the place I always wanted to be. I came to Gold Valley because it seemed like the promised land, and it's turned out to be that for me. I want to make it permanent."

"Glad to help with that."

But as Luke left, he couldn't help but ponder the fact that all this was a bit convenient for Cole, if he thought that Luke and Olivia might have a future together. To keep her here, to keep her close.

And that was a tricky situation. A minefield. He and Olivia had been pretty honest with each other about the situation, such as it was, but he was afraid that it would ultimately look like he hadn't been completely honest with her father.

Like he had been manipulating the situation in order to get the land.

He wasn't sure why he cared. Olivia knew better. Olivia knew that he wanted her, and that the land had come up separately. But he really didn't want that kind of a rumor circulating around town. That Olivia Logan had compromised herself with Luke Hollister so he could get her father's land.

Now that he thought about it, he knew that he would be suspicious of himself if he were an observer.

Dammit.

He needed to talk to Olivia. He just needed to make sure that she understood. And that she didn't need to talk to her father. Yeah, that would be the last thing he needed. Her talking to her father and compounding everything.

It had been one thing when it was fake. But now that there was actually something happening between them...

It was different. It was just a hell of a lot different.

CHAPTER SEVENTEEN

APPARENTLY, CHOOSING LINGERIE was harder than choosing an outfit the whole world was going to see.

It had always been a whole production to choose an outfit to go out with Bennett, but at least she hadn't had to worry about what she was wearing underneath her clothes, too.

Now she felt supremely worried about it. Did she need sexier lingerie? Should it match? What cut did Luke prefer?

These were questions that she felt she needed answers to. But she also didn't want to ask the questions.

Truly, it was concerning.

But she had a few hours to deal with it. At least, that was what she thought. Until there was a knock on her door.

Her mom? Bennett?

She didn't really want to deal with either of them.

No, it couldn't be her mother because her mother had just been texting her from the doctor, while she was waiting for her routine physical, and there was no way that she would be done with that so quickly.

That was a whole thing. Texting her mother while pondering the underwear she was going to wear to seduce her...

What was Luke to her?

He wasn't her boyfriend. He was...

Her lover. She supposed. Which sounded very mature and worldly. Descriptors she did not tend to apply to herself.

She didn't want it to be Bennett, either. She didn't want to have another fight with him. Luke had mentioned that Bennett had been irritated earlier that day. But as difficult as it had been to face him down *prior* to her sleeping with Luke, it would be almost impossible today.

She crossed her fingers before she jerked the door open.

Luke.

It was Luke. Relief, excitement and just a bit of apprehension wound through her.

Did he expect to have sex in the middle of the day? That seemed indulgent. Like a cinnamon roll. A cinnamon roll that you ate when you weren't even hungry.

Maybe that wasn't such a bad thing.

She let out a slow breath, trying to dispel the tension in her stomach. "I didn't expect to see you," she said.

"I just went and talked to your dad."

Just like that, any remaining air in her body rushed out, leaving her deflated. "You did?"

"He sold me the land. He's going to draw up an agreement. He accepted my offer."

"Luke!" She flung her arms around his neck. "That's great."

Then she took a step back, but he grabbed her arm and held her steady, kissed her on the lips. Then he released his hold on her.

"It is," he said. "He knows that we're...seeing each other."

Olivia went warm all over, little pinpricks dotting the back of her neck. "Does he?"

"Well, I should say that he knows we were seen together the other night, and I told him that was true. I just don't want him getting the wrong idea."

Her mind raced, as she tried to figure out what the wrong idea might be. "Right," she said, not willing to admit that she didn't quite understand. She was tired of feeling like she didn't understand everything.

"He was excited, I think. Because, with me buying the land he imagines it might give you roots close. In many ways, I feel like he might have thought he was selling it to me as a gift to you."

Suddenly, it hit her. Her father was now starting to imagine she might marry Luke.

The idea flooded her with a kind of crazy, reckless adrenaline that sent her blood pressure shooting sky-high. Made her hands shake.

She didn't *hate* the idea. That was the thing. The idea of spending the rest of forever with Luke Hollister. The man who made her feel safe, but not overprotected, all at the same time. The man who made her feel like she was something precious and special, to be treasured, but also to be lavished with passion.

Luke seemed to understand that she was a controlling, controlled, crazy person. And he seemed to not mind it so much.

She blinked, trying to get those thoughts out of her head. She really, really needed to not entertain things like that. It was her default setting. Wanting security. Wanting forever. Because she didn't want to face the prospect of heartbreak. Of the aftermath of something like that.

Of loss.

Losing another person that she could never have back. This thing with Luke wasn't a marriage thing. She knew it. She obviously had a problem with wanting commitment immediately from any man she could find.

Resolutely, she pushed any warm fuzzy feelings away.

"I see," she said.

"That kind of didn't become clear until after. After we had agreed. And I just wanted you to know that I don't want you to talk to him for me. I don't want you to say anything." He cleared his throat. "I see the merit now in not flaunting the relationship," he continued.

"Right," she said, hollow.

"Because what are people going to say? When I end up with that land that your father was notoriously reluctant to sell and then…"

"And then we're done," she said, "I get it. Fox. Sad little hen."

"You know it's what they'll say."

She nodded. And she wished that she could tell him she didn't care. Right now, she felt like she didn't, but maybe she would. And anyway, he wouldn't believe it. Not when appearances had always been important enough to her, because of what Vanessa had put her parents through.

"Okay," she said. "But I want you to know that I don't think that," she said. "I know that all of this… It doesn't have anything to do with the land. I mean, I know we made a deal. About Bennett. And that I would help you. But I also know that the real stuff… I know you're not using me, Luke," she said. "I do." A strange expression crossed his face and her stomach tightened.

"I appreciate that."

"Take me to the ranch," she said, feeling impulsive. "I want to see it now. Now that it's yours."

"Okay," he said slowly.

He honestly looked like he had expected things to go a different way. "Luke, did you really think that I would be afraid that you were using me for the land?"

"It's been said to me more than once over the past couple of weeks that I'm difficult to know."

"I suppose that could be considered true in some ways," she said. Because it wasn't like she knew a whole lot about Luke's past or anything, but she knew him. She had seen him naked, after all. She hadn't seen anyone else naked. And no one else had seen her naked.

"But I feel like I know you," she said. She took a step forward, placing her hand flat on his chest. "I trust you."

"That feels a little bit misplaced."

"We're both getting what we want." She did her best to look at him, to make eye contact. "I know this isn't forever, Luke. I know that we are not headed toward a great big happy ending. I'm okay with that. Whatever anyone else thinks… We can't control that. I'm tired of trying to control everything all the time. Myself. Everyone. So let's just have this. And not think about the future. That sounds nice to me."

He nodded slowly. "Okay."

"Now, take me to your ranch, cowboy."

THERE WAS A strange feeling of pride swelling in Olivia's chest as they drove down the road to the ranch that now belonged to Luke. Or would soon. It was a curious thing.

She had never felt that way for someone before. It struck her then how much her relationship with Bennett had been about her. About what she wanted. About her plans.

She hadn't really considered Bennett in them much at all. If she had, she wouldn't have been badgering him mercilessly about getting engaged as if his time-line didn't exist or matter.

And yes, this relationship with Luke, this relation-ship that was about sex and satisfaction, that had started to make someone else jealous… It felt different. She cared so much about this ranch that seemed to mean the world to him. Cared so much that it worked out for him.

And she didn't want to do anything to get in the way of it or to compromise it. Or to ruin the moment.

She had wanted so badly to reassure him, to have nothing spoil that moment of triumph for him.

And she had wanted to share it with him.

This ranch that wouldn't be for her. That would maybe be for another woman someday. Whatever woman he decided to marry. He said he didn't want to get married, but with a place like this, and plans and a future ahead of him… That would change. She was sure of it.

They were going down the driveway, toward a home that had nothing to do with her goals. And she just… Her chest felt full with her need for him to be happy. Her need for him to feel satisfied. To have good things.

Unconsciously she reached across the space between them in that old truck of his that was starting to feel fa-miliar, and she rested her hand on his leg.

Feeling a little bit possessive, perhaps because she had just been thinking about some other woman being in his life.

They didn't speak as he pulled the truck up to the house and they both got out.

They stood in front of the place, and she put her arm around his waist, leaning her head against his shoul-der. "It's yours."

"I've got the keys to the house," he said.

"Let's go in," she said, feeling excited.

"I was warned it was rough," he said. "I'm probably going to get a new construction going."

She looked at him. "You can still afford to get a new house built?"

He laughed. "Yes."

Olivia scrunched up her face as she regarded his completely cool expression. "Did you... Are you a hit man or something?"

"No," he said, laughing.

She squinted. "A male prostitute?"

That made him laugh again. "No."

"Luke, I just realized I don't know that much about you."

His expression turned irritated. "Didn't we just talk about this?"

"Yes. But that isn't what I mean. I don't mean about who you are. I know who you are. You seem like you don't care, but you do. You care about every square inch of dirt in this county, I think. You care most of all about the land that's Get Out of Dodge. And you care a lot about this place. You're going to make it yours. And you're going to work it with everything you have, because that's what you do. You paste a smile on your face and make it look like you're not trying at all while you throw your heart and soul into whatever you do. Even if it's making Bennett Dodge jealous. I know what kind of man you are. But I don't know the details about your life. And I've seen you naked. I want something that's more than naked."

He frowned. "What's the point of that, Liv? When we know that it's not forever?"

Those words stabbed her in the chest, but she kept on going. "Maybe that's the best reason. I spent a really long time keeping everything to myself. Because control was very important to me. And not letting anyone see the cracks in who I am. I didn't want my parents to see me as vulnerable. I didn't want to worry anyone. But… I'll worry you. That's fine. This has been my safe space. This thing that's just you and me. There's never been anything like it for me. Not even close." She felt silly saying that, because she knew that he wouldn't be able to answer in kind. But it didn't matter. "So, I just want to know. I want to feel like I know you that way, too."

"Not a gigolo," he said. "Haven't killed anyone. No secret government contract work, either."

"Darn," she said.

The wind rustled through the pines, the cold air stinging her cheeks. And she waited. Waited for him to say something. Anything.

"It's an insurance settlement," he said.

"What kind?"

He sighed heavily. "Let's go in."

He took the keys out of his pocket, and the two of them walked up the rickety front porch and inside the little country house. The screen door swung shut behind them with a resounding crash.

It was a rough house. But it was cute.

They walked past the little living room, which still had some blue-and-white flowered couches and a knotty pine floor, into the kitchen, which was all yellow and white details. From the two-tone cabinets to the little flowers on the linoleum floor. There were lace curtains in the windows that were very cheery even though they were full of dust and probably a few spiderwebs.

The lace made them seem like fancy spiderwebs, at least.

There was a little breakfast nook with a Shaker-style table and chairs that looked out over the field. She imagined in summer the flowers in that field were yellow, too.

It made her think that a little farm family could come home at any moment.

It was like her dollhouse. This perfect, simple little place that had inhabited a part of her dreams since she was a child. So much more *her* than the cottage she lived in now.

She could imagine a life here far too well. Children, a couple who spent their time working on the lands together. Who invested in something together.

Her chest felt tight.

Her dream wasn't here. Her dream had been Get Out of Dodge and Bennett. Now it would have to be something new, but it couldn't be this.

She was a grown woman. She didn't need to move into a place that reminded her of a dollhouse. Couldn't afford to entertain fantasies of a life spent with a man who claimed not to want that.

"This isn't so bad," she said, looking around. They walked through the kitchen and into the hall, which had real wood floors, and a narrow staircase with a yellow-and-white banister up the side.

"It's definitely not modern," he said.

"It's not," Olivia agreed. "It's like a little snapshot of another time. Perfect." Oh, so very perfect.

"I promise that if I build a new house I won't get rid of this one," he said, his gaze suddenly intense on hers. "Promise."

She didn't know why it mattered so much that he'd made that promise to her, all sincerity and seriousness. But it did.

"Thank you," she said softly.

He walked through and rested his hand on the stair rail. "I grew up in a house that was nothing like this one. A little place in Eugene. Tract housing from the sixties." He looked around the room. "I dreamed about places like this. Those places that seem simple, but you don't realize at the time actually are very expensive. I dreamed of the kind of life where I could work with my hands and fix my situation." He turned to look at her. "Nobody knows this, Olivia." And she could hear the unspoken question in the statement that told her she needed to stay the only person that knew.

She nodded slowly.

"I never knew my dad. My mom was single always, as far as I know. Maybe she didn't even know who my dad was. She never talked about him. But it didn't take me long to start realizing that my mom wasn't quite like other kids' moms. She didn't have a lot of energy, and it was difficult for her to see to everyday tasks sometimes. Some days she didn't get out of bed at all. And on those days, I just expected that I would have to feed us both. I learned how to make pancakes when I was six. We ate a lot of pancakes. I loved my mom. I really didn't mind taking care of her. And it was easy enough to get myself to school most days. I could ride my bike, so that was simple. By the time I got old enough, I just started forging her signature on school documents so that I didn't have to miss out on field trips and things. Because keeping track of all that paperwork was too difficult for her."

Olivia thought of her own family. Of the way that her mother and father had always been so involved in her life. Her mother had volunteered in her class always. Her father such a presence that she couldn't imagine simply not having a father at all. It hurt her just to think about it.

Luke hadn't just been without one parent, he had been the caregiver for the one he had.

And he talked about it with a strange kind of affection that she could hardly understand. Maybe it hadn't been her fault in some ways, but she'd left a little boy to his own devices. It made Olivia want to shelter him. Protect him.

But he didn't seem upset.

He cleared his throat. "It was a combination of permanent disability and government housing that paid for where we lived. Food stamps. I took a lot of charity. Coats for Kids, that kind of thing. It all worked. It worked fine enough. But I definitely dreamed of bigger things. I watched a lot of Westerns." He looked around the room. "I loved everything about them. The idea you could forge your own way. Like you said. I wanted to be a cowboy."

"Yeah," she said, her stomach tightening with dread, because she could sense that this wasn't going to a happy place.

"When I was sixteen I went into my mother's room and I found her unresponsive. She had taken an entire bottle of sleeping pills. It wasn't accidental."

"Luke," she said, the word coming out in a breath of horror.

"Don't do that," he said, "don't give me sad eyes and sorries. I've never told anyone this." He reiterated that part, and Olivia went silent. "I just need to say it. My mother killed herself. She killed herself two days after she and I got in a big fight and I asked what the hell she was doing. What the hell she was doing with her life. With our lives. That she couldn't ever be there for me."

He took a deep breath and looked across the room. "I understand that I didn't make her do it. Because fighting with your mom…that's normal," he said, resolute. "That's normal life stuff. It's normal teenage stuff. But our lives were never normal. I lied about my age when the police came by, but I knew it wouldn't take long for them to figure out I was a minor. I dodged a social worker after that, called the office and said I was looking for relatives. Then I found out about the insurance money."

Olivia bit her lip, trying to do what he had asked her to do. Trying to keep silent so that he could just tell his story.

"She'd taken out a policy a few years before. Which is interesting to note because there's a time frame, often, with suicide. If you take the policy out and kill yourself within a couple of years, your remaining family doesn't get the money. And all I can think sometimes… Is that she thought I would be better off with the money than with her. I got so angry at her, and I yelled at her. And I told her how messed up our lives were. And how she didn't do anything for me. So I think she figured I could have money instead."

"You can't know that," she said, the words rushing from her mouth before she could stop them. He hadn't wanted her to say anything, but she couldn't just let him stand there and say that. Not when it hurt so much. Not when it was hurting them both. "She's not here, so you can't ask her."

"I know," he said, his words scratchy, his green eyes pained. "That's why it's so damned hard. That's why I *have* to wonder. Because she's not here. Because she left the money instead. Because whatever the reasoning was, if she had any reasoning at all, or if it was just another dark moment in a lifetime filled with them, and this time the darkness won... I don't know. All I know is that I was left with money. A hell of a lot of money. And no mother."

Her heart felt like lead. Pounding against her chest. Pounding so hard she couldn't breathe. Could hardly speak. She wanted so badly to fix it. To go back in time and take care of the boy that he'd been.

So much of her life she'd been about control. About fixing. But she couldn't fix this.

She hated it. Imagining this man, this gorgeous, strong, laid-back man, alone and vulnerable, made her ache all the way down.

"Why didn't you end up in foster care?" she asked.

"Because I disappeared. And nobody really looked that hard for me. I'm not a missing person or anything. I just left that house. Quinn had that ad in the paper... Hiring a ranch hand. In Gold Valley. It was the place I'd dreamed about. I needed to go. I needed to...to see if it was what I hoped it would be. There was nothing behind me, nothing around me. There was only going forward." Luke shook his head. "I thought maybe it was my chance to have that life. That life that I'd seen in those movies. But I never wanted to use my mother's money. I was much happier working my ass off, much happier getting no more than what I had earned off my own back. But the problem with money like that is that it sits there. It just sits there. And if you do nothing with it... Well, what if that was why she killed herself? What's worse than using it to make a better life? Not using it, right? Not honoring that twisted sacrifice. But I don't even like to think of it that way. I don't know how to think of it. That's why for twenty years that money has just been there. Until this place."

This place. This ranch. The thing that was the ultimate realization of his dream. He had put that off; he had buried it deep, just as he had done with everything else. She could see that now. He had always seemed to her like a man who didn't worry much about what anyone thought. A man who seemed supremely unbothered in general by life. But she knew now that wasn't the case. He cared. He cared so much about so many things.

But it was painful. And that was why he chose to smile instead.

She had felt like she had known him before he had told her this, but it was different now. It truly was. Because now all those separate little pieces of him had come together. This one thread weaving into the complete picture of Luke Hollister. Just another mystery about the man solved. But it had opened up so much more.

Her image of him had shifted. She didn't just see the man standing in front of her, but the boy he'd been. Grieving. Guilty. Alone. Moving hours away, taking a chance on a job. Leaving his home. It made all that ease he possessed seem so much stronger. So much deeper. Because she knew now that it had come from hardship, from pain she'd never even imagined.

"You came to Gold Valley all alone," she said. "And you were sixteen."

"Yes. I lied about my age, but I think Quinn suspected it. And obviously I don't claim to be older than I am now, so he's certainly figured it out at this point. He let me stay on the property… He never asked me why I came there. But I think he recognized the loss in me. Because he experienced loss himself. Sometimes I think you see that in each other."

"Do you?"

His eyes connected with hers. "I think we see it in each other, don't you?"

The words landed precisely in her heart, made it throb. "You can hardly compare my loss to yours."

"Yes I can," he said. "I can't imagine having a twin sister pull away from you like that. Hell, I don't have any siblings. When my mother died, it left just me. So I went and I made another family. But the loss is still there. You have friends, you have a life, you have a close relationship with your parents, but it doesn't mean the loss of Vanessa isn't still there."

She looked away, twisting her hands together. "I suppose so."

"We have a lot of things in us that are different," he said, reaching out, his thumb brushing against her cheek. "But I think we have some of that same pain."

She reached up and placed her hand over his, encouraged him to flatten his palm over her cheek. "We make each other feel some of the same pleasure, too," she said softly.

She was entranced by that thought. That for all their differences—his age, his experience, his seemingly easygoing attitude compared to her—that at their core there was something that the other recognized. And maybe that was where they ignited. All those other things struck the sparks, but that right there was the fuel. It was what made it undeniable. It was what made it endless.

"I think that might be so."

"Look at this place," she said, turning around in a circle, looking around the room. "I bet you anything that your mother would be so happy to know that you have it."

He took a deep breath, and she could see that it

was cutting into him. That it was painful. "I think she would. I think if there had been a time when she could have figured out a way to get on top of that demon that was always on her back, this is the kind of place she would've wanted. I think it's the right place."

"For your roots," she said.

"Yes, ma'am," he responded.

He took hold of her hand and the two of them walked out of the house, back out to the driveway. It was starting to get dark now, twilight settling over the tops of the mountains, the inky black at the center of the sky bleeding down to the tops of the pines.

She didn't want tonight to end. Didn't want this time to end. She wanted to be here with him, on the verge of this new step he was taking. Now that she knew how big this was for him. How much it meant.

More selfishly, she wanted him to remember her being in that house. Wanted him to remember her standing in the driveway. Wanted him to remember her down by the river, and in every other piece of the land.

"Can you show me the barn?" she asked.

He looked over at her, his expression inscrutable in the dim light. "Sure."

He opened up his truck, retrieved a battery-powered lantern from the back, twisting the knob and illuminating the gravel around them, a shaft of light on part of his face. He was so beautiful she ached.

She wanted him. Suddenly, so very much, that she felt desperate for it. For him.

He took her hand and started to lead her toward the field. "Wait," she said. "I'm cold."

"I have a blanket in the truck," he said.

She nodded and he reached in and grabbed it, handing it to her. She wrapped it around her shoulders, a plan and a shiver winding through her as he gripped her hand and led her through the field, toward the edge of the trees where the old barn stood.

It was old and rickety, probably past the point of repair. This would most likely have to be demolished to make room for a new structure. One that didn't have large gaps in the siding that let in the cold night air, and the same gaps in the ceiling that revealed a smattering of stars coming forward, a light in the darkness.

The ground was dusty, but dry, and there was a small amount of hay spread out around them. There was a pile of it in the corner, too, and she had a feeling that it was probably worse for wear from the weather that no doubt got in through the cracks.

"I think this will do," he said.

Olivia's heart was pounding hard. And she tightened her hold on the blanket and looked from Luke to the floor of the barn. Yes. It would do perfectly. For tonight. Tonight with him.

She felt… It was an amazing thing. Feeling like she knew him like this. In the house, he had laid bare his soul to her. He had told her things about himself that nobody knew. They had traded that information, as she had given hers to him. Luke Hollister was the only man on earth who knew how she felt about Vanessa. Who knew the guilt she carried and knew the burden that she felt to be the good one. To be the one that never caused any trouble. To be the one that her parents could count on. She knew that his smile was a mask for loss. For pain. That the man who seemed like he didn't care much about anything, cared hell of a lot about everything. That his loyalty to the Dodge family came from a place of knowing what family meant. Of how painful losing family could be.

And it was too cold to skinny-dip. Otherwise, she had half a mind to drag him down to the creek, so that she could do something to express the ways in which she felt changed. By him. By this. So that she could strip off her clothes in front of the whole world and declare that connection. Those feelings.

Feelings that were raw, tender and frightening. The kinds of feelings that she had always tried to choke out.

And it might be a little cold in this barn, too, but she knew what she wanted. Knew that after their conversation, after the confession that he had given to her, that no one else on earth had, she wanted to give him something that no one else had ever had of her.

She unwrapped the blanket from her shoulders and laid it across the floor. He turned away from where he was looking in the barn and gave her a questioning glance.

Heart thundering heavily, she kicked off her boots, and then undid the buttons on her coat.

"Olivia?"

"Let me," she said.

She pulled her top up over her head and threw it down onto the floor, goose bumps breaking out over her skin as the cold washed over her. Then she undid her jeans, pushed them down her legs before she could lose her nerve. And in one quick breath she did the same to her panties, leaving herself standing there naked in the dimness, a bit of the lantern light shining over her.

She could see a hungry glittering in Luke's eyes and it didn't shock her. It made her feel good. Made her feel excited.

"I want you," she said.

"You said you were cold."

"Not anymore."

And it was like a clap of thunder had sounded. Like the truth of it all was suddenly so bright, so clear.

She loved him. She loved him with everything she was. With everything she ever would be.

She had spent a lot of years trying not to. She had spent a lot of years making sure he never got close enough for those feelings inside of her to have a chance to turn into this. Somehow, some part of her must have known that all it would ever take was the slightest bit of water on that seed, and it would grow into a tree that would be so large and so strong it could never be shaken, could never be uprooted.

That part of her had been wise. Wise and intuitive.

Because here she was, having slept with him once, and totally and permanently in love with him.

She wasn't going to say that though. She was just going to show him.

"You want me *now*?" he asked, a hint of that amused smile on his face, but not the whole thing. As if he couldn't quite force it out.

Always. "Right here," she said. "Right now."

She almost smiled because that very confident, sex kitten voice didn't feel like her. But it did, too. In some ways. Because he made her feel like she could reach new parts of herself. Like she was stretching out inside of herself for the first time and taking up all the space she could, instead of shoving herself into one corner.

She closed the distance between them and placed her palm on his cheek, stretching up on her toes, pressing her naked body against his entirely clothed one as she kissed him.

It was so strange, kissing him while she knew she

loved him. While she knew she was in love with Luke Hollister with everything in her.

It made her want to cry. But she was going to try to keep it all together.

She'd never been in love before. That thought went through her like a lance through her stomach. That this was a first for her in so many ways, regardless of what she had imagined before.

This was love. This was hope for the future, a pain in her heart, her chest, her lungs, coming together with desires in her body. This was honesty. It was two people who connected on every level. Skin to skin, soul to soul.

She had thought that she could have a relationship that cherry-picked those things, that she could care and call it love, that she could hold on to secrets and call it love. That she could keep her control and call it love. But Luke had shown her that for her at least, for them, that wasn't enough. She wanted to be closer. She wanted to strip everything that was between them away so that they could connect. This thing that had frightened her for so long... Suddenly, it wasn't enough. Suddenly, it wasn't scary. It was *necessary*.

The buttons on his shirt abraded her nipples as she arched against him. His large, rough hand moved to cup her butt as he drew her up against him.

When she pulled away, she examined his expression. It was raw, almost uncivilized. She liked him like that. Liked that she—Olivia Logan, the consummate civilized lady—could reduce him to this.

And that he could reduce her, too. To a creature of need and desire rather than one of logic and control.

But then, that was the beauty of this. This all-encompassing feeling that she was choosing it over control. That she chose it above everything. Because it was everything and so was he. Because it was better. Because the risk was worth the potential reward.

The present was so blindingly beautiful she didn't have to live for a hypothetical future. The journey was so amazing she didn't have to obsess about the destination.

She unbuttoned the top two buttons on his shirt, kissed his throat, down lower. Then she undid the next button and the next. Slowly, she pressed her hand beneath the fabric of his shirt, feeling his hot skin, his chest hair, his muscles. He was so beautiful. So undeniably, incredibly masculine.

From the solidity of his frame to the deep, rumbling sound he made when she kissed him at the hollow of his throat.

She finished unbuttoning his shirt, lowering herself down with each button as she went, and then finally came to kneel in front of him. Butterflies jostled around in her stomach as she reached up and undid the button on his jeans. She could see that most masculine part of him outlined to perfection there beneath the denim. She knew what he looked like already, had already had him inside of her once. But not like this. She was afraid she would do it wrong. That she wouldn't be anywhere near as good as the girl he'd been with in the bathroom at the saloon. That she wouldn't be as good as any of the women he'd been with at all.

But none of those women knew about his past. None of them knew where he had come from. She did. On some level, that had to matter.

She lowered the zipper slowly, her heart pounding in her throat as she drew the fabric down, revealing his arousal to her gaze.

"Olivia..." His name on her lips was a warning, but

it was one that she wasn't going to heed. After all, she was intending exactly what he suspected she was.

She had a feeling he didn't realize that. But she was.

She curved her fingers around his length, and then leaned forward, tasting him tentatively.

She had never imagined herself doing this. Had never imagined wanting to. But with him it hadn't even been much of a consideration. She just wanted to make him feel good. And she wanted…

She wanted him to remember her, to remember this. However many women came after her, she wanted him to remember her most of all.

This wasn't a loss of control. It never really had been. This was her, a woman of supreme control, deciding to surrender to something wholeheartedly.

Olivia was the kind of person who got exactly what she set her mind to. And this would be no different.

She shifted, tightening her hold on him, and taking more of him into her mouth. And then she was lost. In the feral sounds that he made as she pleasured him with her mouth, in the flavor of him on her tongue, in the fact that she felt so connected to him. But nothing felt shocking or dirty about what was happening between them. It felt good. It felt right.

And it turned her on. That she could make him feel like this. She could make a man like him shake.

He bucked his hips and a wave of pleasure washed over her. When she realized just how close he was to losing his control. When she realized just how efficiently she had brought him to the brink. It reminded her of the way he had done the same to her in his truck that first night. When a kiss and a little bit of intimate contact had made her lose herself completely. Because the pull between them was so strong. Because the chemistry was so real.

"Olivia," he rasped, his voice completely frayed.

"Shhh," she said, "I'm enjoying myself." She took him in deeper, pleasure bursting through her like a firework, popping along her veins. Her breasts felt heavy, an ache growing, deepening inside of her.

"This has to stop now." He grabbed hold of her shoulders and lifted her up, and no amount of protest could stop him. "I need you. Not just this. You. All of you. I need to be in you, Liv. So deep. So deep I can't see straight. So deep I can't think anymore." Then he picked her up, grabbing hold of both thighs and wrapping her legs around his waist as he brought her down on the blanket, settling himself between her thighs. He kissed her deeply, rocking his slick erection against that place where she was wet and needy for him.

She gasped, those simple motions nearly bringing her to the brink.

"Gotta get a condom," he said, pressing his lips against her neck as he contorted, reaching into his back pocket and producing his wallet. "I was hoping," he said, his tone apologetic as he pulled out the condom. "Just so you know this is in there because I was hoping this would happen with you. Not anyone else."

A smile curved her lips upward. "I know," she said, lacing her fingers through his hair and kissing his chin, loving the way it prickled beneath her lips.

"Do you?"

She did. She really did. Because if there was one thing she was confident in now it was that she had him. Right now, she had all of him.

"I do."

She took the packet from him and tore it open, her

fingers shaking as she struggled to figure out which side of the protection went up, and once she figured it out she placed it over the head of his arousal and began to roll it down over his length.

She wanted to do this. Wanted to be an active participant in all of it. She might not have experience, but she had desire in spades.

She was going to make sure it counted for something.

He rocked his hips backward, then pressed the head of him against the entrance to her body, teasing her with a slight push forward and a pull away.

It shocked her how different it felt this time. How ready she was for him. How it didn't hurt.

No, this time, she thought she would die if she didn't have him.

When he finally did join himself to her, there was none of the tearing pain that she had felt the first time. It was just... Perfect. Like being home. It might not be being good, but whatever it was it was what she wanted to be. This woman who had Luke Hollister, at least for now, body and soul.

That was the woman she wanted to be. Hers. His.

This wasn't about anyone else. Not about performing or pleasing anyone but each other.

She closed her eyes and rode on a wave of satisfaction as her orgasm crashed through her, as he followed closely behind. She clung to him after, shaking and sweating, feeling absolutely and completely undone by what had passed between them.

When it was over, Luke rolled to his side and pulled her up against him, and she laid her head on his chest, taking in the feeling of his heart beating against her cheek, his skin beaded with sweat beneath where she had rested her palm. She liked that, too, and she would have said she didn't.

She would have said that a lot of this couldn't have possibly excited her before Luke. That the absolute possession of his body, the sweat and heavy breathing, wasn't appealing at all.

Except with him it was more than appealing. It was a craving.

"You're probably cold," he said, curving his arm around her and rubbing his hand over her arm.

"Not really," she said.

The moment he said that, she became more conscious of the chill in the air, but before that she hadn't noticed it at all.

"Still, I'd better get you home," he said.

Those words sat funny in her chest, all while she got dressed, and while he adjusted his clothes. Then when they got back into the car she realized why.

"Are you... You're taking me to *my* home?"

"Yeah," he responded. "I have to be up early tomorrow. And it was great to bring you out to look around here, but I expect you'll want some time to yourself."

He hadn't asked her if she wanted time to herself. He was just assuming. Well, that made her wonder some things. If he was just giving her time, or if he had got sex so didn't need anything else from her.

She didn't want to beg, though. Well, she did want to beg. But she also didn't want to make it all about her. Because this reaction had something to do with him. Him and his emotions. And the woman that she had been with Bennett, the woman who had wanted a very specific relationship that served her very specific needs, would have badgered him. She would have tried as hard as she could to get her way. To finagle a sleepover invitation so that she wouldn't have to be uncomfortable.

The way she had done with Bennett and the marriage proposals.

She wasn't going to do that now. Even though it hurt her feelings a bit to have him put her off, she also wanted very much to make sure that he got what he needed.

She wished that what he needed was her, holding him all night. Talking to him. Being with him.

Clearly it wasn't what he needed right now. So there was no point making an issue.

"Okay," she said, "that's fine with me."

They were silent the rest of the way, and when he dropped her off he kissed her, which made her feel slightly more at ease. Just slightly.

"See you tomorrow, Liv," he said.

That confidence filled her with a sense of happiness. That he figured he would see her tomorrow. That he hoped to. Maybe things weren't so dire after all. Maybe it really was just a matter of giving him his space. After all, the conversation they'd had about his mother had been quite intense, and he probably needed a chance to deal with it. She didn't have the right to be upset about that.

He had given her what she had asked for, and now she needed to give him that unspoken thing.

"See you tomorrow, Luke," she said, getting out of the truck.

Luke walked her up the porch steps and stopped her at the door, leaning in and kissing her again. Chaste. Sweet compared to the other times they'd kissed. And then he tipped his hat, like he hadn't just ravished her silly on the floor of a barn.

Like he was a real, old-fashioned gentleman and she was a lady.

She sighed, trying to ignore the tender feeling in her chest. Just tender. That was all. It wasn't painful. Not really.

Well, it was a little bit painful. Being in love was a little bit painful all around.

She walked into the house, closing and locking the door behind her. Then she walked to the window, pushed one of the lace curtains to the side and watched Luke drive away. Watched until she couldn't see his truck anymore.

She fought the urge to text him. Right away. To make sure he was okay and everything was okay and he still liked her and wanted to make love with her again.

Instead, she sent a text to her mother to let her know that she was home, and then gave her a call and chatted with her idly, trying not to let her mind stray back to the intimate few hours she had spent with Luke at his property.

She would love to talk to her mother about Luke, but right now she didn't really know what to say. Because she couldn't find a middle ground between keeping it all to herself and wanting to shout that she was in love from the mountaintops.

Being in love was strange. And a whole lot different than she had thought. She had been completely rational when it came to her feelings for Bennett. Completely able to talk about them to people.

With Luke, it felt so important it seemed like something she needed to keep to herself. And so big she wasn't sure that she could, not without exploding.

There was nothing simple about love. There was nothing controlled about love.

As she got into the shower, the words that had struck her yesterday after she and Luke had made love for the first time rolled through her head on repeat.

She had been right to be afraid of this. But she was pretty sure she was going to embrace it anyway.

CHAPTER EIGHTEEN

LUKE HADN'T TEXTED Olivia or called her that day, and he was starting to feel a little bit like an ass. But, he hadn't wanted her to come spend the night at his place after that conversation about his mother. He had never told anyone about that. Had never talked about the money, the complex blame that he felt. The complex anger.

The way that he blamed his mother and himself for everything that had happened.

The way the money felt like more of a curse than a blessing, but a curse that he had to use to try and fashion it into something of a blessing, because if he didn't, it would just be another failure as a son.

Then that encounter in the barn, which had been explosive as hell, Olivia dropping to her knees in front of him and taking him in her mouth.

Beautiful Olivia Logan, on her knees for him. Yeah, that was an image that was going to live in his mind until he was dead.

Maybe even after.

If you got to watch a reel of your greatest hits in the afterlife, he was pretty sure that one was going to be on his.

And then he slid inside of her and the whole world fell away. It had just been the two of them, and it had been so raw and focused that he hadn't been able to handle the idea of going to *sleep* with her, too.

He had never thought of himself as a coward. But he was beginning to question that.

"You interested in going out drinking tonight?" Wyatt asked.

They had just wrapped up a long day out in the field, and it was only four o'clock. Still, Luke could barely walk after a whole day spent riding, and then fixing the fence, which was worse than a day of squats in the gym. He assumed. He'd never had a need to go to the gym, since he spent all day, every day, doing hard labor.

"Not particularly."

"I talked Grant into going out," Wyatt said.

Damn. Luke could hardly turn his friend down in that case. And he ignored the part of himself that whispered in his ear that he was rationalizing, that he was trying to get out of doing the right thing, which was making contact with Olivia, by pretending that he needed to be there to hold Grant's hand.

But, in fairness to him, Grant hadn't gotten out there and done a night out in a while. And the guy needed to get out.

Having known Grant for the past eight years, he knew that he wasn't as mired in his grief as he had been back in the beginning. But it was bad enough.

"How did you do that?"

"He just said that he wanted to. So, far be it from me not to oblige him."

"Hell, no," Luke agreed.

"You might have to play designated driver," Wyatt said.

"Oh, come on," Luke said. "You're gonna do that designated driver crap on me?"

"We can draw straws, but I think we have to let Grant

drink. He can't go out for the first time in who knows how long and have to be DD."

"That really is bull pucky," Luke said.

"I'm a bad friend," Wyatt said, shrugging.

"You really are." Luke took a deep breath, looking around the property. At the guest cabins that were coming together nicely, at the flower beds that had been prepared, the wood chips that had been laid down to create clean, easy walkways between the various outbuildings.

This place was getting ready for a whole new life. One that didn't require him. It was a good thing. Especially all things considered. But it was strange, too. The end of an era in his life.

The first time that had happened the choice had been made for him. His mom had killed herself and there had been no other decision for him to make. Nothing that he had a say in. He simply had to do something. Anything. Had to move on, because there was no place to stay.

But this was his decision, and it was twenty years in the making.

"I got the property," he said. "Cole Logan agreed to sell."

"Really?" Wyatt looked at him in surprise. "Well... Congratulations. Really. I'm not psyched about losing you around here. But, I'm happy for you."

"You don't sound that happy."

"I figured we would do this together," Wyatt said, looking around the spread. "Make this place new again. Because I know that you love it as much as I do. Because I know that you..." Wyatt cleared his throat. "You put so much into this place, Luke. You're right. I left. I left, and I didn't spend hours working the land. I didn't spend all my time working with Dad. You did. Grant got married. Bennett went off to school. You're right.

This places is in your bones. And if you really hate what I'm doing with it…"

"I don't," Luke said. "I don't hate it. It's just not me. I need a place of my own. And it was more than kind of your dad, of you, to make this place feel like home to me for as long as you did. But I just need to move on to something else. I need something that's mine."

"Then I'm glad you have it."

"It doesn't mean I'm dying. It doesn't mean I'm not going to visit."

Wyatt looked at him for a moment, then nodded. "Glad to hear that. Anyway, if you weren't planning on visiting, we'd hog-tie your ass and drag you back for family barbecues even if you didn't want to come."

Luke barked out a laugh. "Good to know."

"We love you," Wyatt said, his voice getting sincere. Just for a moment. "But not so much that we'd respect your wishes if they were in opposition to ours. Our wishes that we get to see you still."

Luke laughed. "That is very good to know. So, should we go get that drink?"

"Well, you get to have soda."

"You're an awful friend."

Wyatt clapped his hand on Luke's shoulder. "I'm really more of a brother."

WHEN THEY WALKED into the bar, it was full of people. Crowded because it was Friday night and half the town was there to drink off the long workweek. Head into the weekend in style. Or, they were ranchers who had to get up early the next day no matter what, which was an even better reason to drink, as far as Luke was concerned. And certainly the reason they were all there drinking.

Wyatt was scanning the room, probably looking for

his type of woman. Buckle bunnies who wanted to ride a cowboy and nothing more. Grant looked grim, his hat pulled down low over his face, his eyes fixed firmly on the bar, and on Laz.

Obviously Grant had been more interested in alcohol than sex.

Luke didn't have an interest in alcohol, not really. And he didn't have an interest in generic sex at all. He wanted Olivia. Wanted to be in Olivia's quiet house with her, or in his cabin. Or on the floor of a barn.

Again, guilt tugged at him for not making contact with Olivia. He should have. But then, she hadn't texted him, either.

Probably because you told her that you didn't want her to spend the night.

Maybe. But he'd also told her that he would see her today. And, he had kissed her good-night.

Still, she hadn't contacted him. So, maybe she really did need her space, like he'd suggested to her last night.

He'd made his decision. He'd gone out with Wyatt and Grant, and if nothing else, that promised to be interesting. So he was going to focus on that, and not on the fact he had to spend a sober evening away from the one person he wanted.

He walked across the distressed barn wood floor, passed a few vacant high round tables toward the back of the room where people were gathered around the pool table, the TVs and the dartboard.

And that was where he saw Olivia. For a second, he thought he was hallucinating because he couldn't figure out why the hell Olivia would be there. But she was. Leaning up against the wall with Bennett right in front of her, his face scant inches from hers.

Then Bennett raised his hand and brushed a piece of Olivia's glossy brown hair back from her face.

And Luke saw red.

There was no rational thought. There was nothing but pure male rage that drove him forward. He grabbed Bennett by the back of the shoulder and pulled him back. "What the hell is going on here?"

Olivia's eyes flew wide. "Luke."

"What the hell is this?" Luke asked.

"I'm sorry," Bennett said, "you don't have any right to come in here and question my actions with her."

"I sure as hell do," Luke said.

"Why is that? Were you her boyfriend for a year? Did you plan on marrying her?"

Luke grabbed hold of Bennett's shirt and slammed him up against the wall. "I'm her lover, asshole," Luke said. "And you wanted to know what I would throw a punch for? You're about to find out."

Bennett shoved him back and Olivia screeched. "Luke," she said. "Stop it. We were talking."

"Then *he* should've said that," Luke said. "But he's been spoiling for a fight for weeks now, so maybe this is a good time."

"Why should *he* have to say it?" Olivia said. "*I* said it. I don't need you to act like a posturing ape. You should listen to me."

But he couldn't listen, because the ring in his ears was so loud. Because the anger so far surpassed anything he had ever felt. The possessiveness. She had been his. Finally. And now to see her standing there with Bennett—Bennett, who he had already taken her from... He couldn't handle it.

She was his. Olivia Logan was *his*.

Finally.

And he wasn't going to lose her to another man.

"Olivia can speak for herself," Bennett said, "and you need to back off."

He was torn then. Between throwing that punch he promised and hauling Olivia out of there. He figured that since Wyatt was there, he probably shouldn't start a bar fight with his younger brother. Because that was going to be weighted decidedly in Bennett's favor. Wyatt and Grant might be his friends, but they were going to have to stand with their brother in a fistfight. That was just how it was. Luke didn't even begrudge them that.

He also didn't want to be in the middle of it.

So, he did the only logical thing there was.

He picked Olivia up, like he was Kevin Costner to her Whitney, and carried her toward the bathroom.

"You've lost your mind," she squeaked, clinging to his shoulders as they crossed the bar.

"Maybe I have," he said. "But I'm starting to think I didn't lose it soon enough."

He opened the bathroom door and carried her in, then slammed it behind them before locking it and setting her on her feet.

"What are you doing?" she demanded, facing him with furious brown eyes, her hands on her hips.

He wrapped his arm around her waist and pulled her up against him. "Maybe they'll carve your name up there, next to mine, what do you think?"

"Luke Hollister, I swear." She was looking at him angrily, but she didn't push him away.

There was a heavy knock on the door, and he had a feeling that it was Bennett.

"Hang on," Olivia said. She whirled around, unlocking the door and cracking it. "We're busy."

He heard a muffled male voice. Definitely Bennett.

"No, I don't need you to come in. We're fine." She slammed the door and locked it again, turning her focus back to Luke.

"Why didn't you go with him?"

"Because I don't want to," she said. "You are the stupidest man, Luke. Seriously, the stupidest one."

"I'm not used to being an overachiever," he said. "So I'll take that."

"You shouldn't be proud of it. What did you think was happening when you came in?"

"He was *touching* you," Luke said.

"Yes," Olivia said, "but not… It doesn't mean anything with him. It doesn't even feel like anything."

"You're in love with him." He didn't even believe that, but he was angry, and he was looking for ways to justify that anger. Anger he could see now was just pure jealousy. Like he'd never felt before. Oh yeah, he'd felt twinges of envy when he'd seen Bennett with Olivia, but that had been different. This was an all-out testosterone-fueled jealous rage.

"I don't love him," she said. "I never did. Luke, I chose *you*. I chose to sleep with you. I… After last night how can you doubt that?"

Because he doubted *everything*. Something about her made him feel more certain of things than he had ever felt his entire life, and more unsure about other things. The kinds of things he was usually confident as hell in. Like his ability to hold on to a woman as long as he wanted to. And the fact that he would be fine if she walked away.

He had no idea who in the hell he was, or what in the hell was going on with him. Except that she was in his blood, and she was some kind of crazy madness that he couldn't reason out.

He didn't have anything to say, so he just kissed her. Because he didn't have the right words, and he didn't think he ever would. He kissed her until the ringing in his ears stopped. Until the anger was replaced by desire. Until he forgot that Bennett—or a whole bar full of people—was on the other side of that door.

It didn't take long for her to wrap her arms around his neck, for her to push her fingers through his hair and kiss him back. Hard and deep and with all the anger he knew she felt. The anger and the desire.

"You're a fool," she hissed when they parted. "How could you think that I wanted him? Did you think this was just a game? That it was advanced-level Make Bennett Jealous stuff?"

"You've been convinced that you loved him for a long time," Luke said. "And convinced that you didn't *like* me very much for even longer."

Her expression softened then, those dark eyes going liquid and touching something inside him that he wished wasn't touched at all. "I do like you, you idiot."

"Is that a term of affection now?"

"It is when the man that you…" She cleared her throat. "The man that you're sleeping with is being an idiot." She softened her words, then pressed her fingers against his lips and traced the outline of them. "I didn't know what it meant to want somebody until you. That matters. You matter."

"That's it," he said. "We have to go now."

"We do?"

He picked her up, and she squeaked again. He unlocked the bathroom door and held her against his chest while they stood there in front of it. "Unless you want to do it in here."

"Not especially."

He cracked open the bathroom door and she held on to him more tightly. "Luke," she whispered. "Everyone will know."

He looked at her, and out at the room full of people. People who knew them. Knew him and that he was from nowhere, knew her and that she was town royalty. And he was fine with that. "Good."

And then he took them out of the bathroom, and carried her across the saloon. People were craning their necks watching them, and a few men stood up from their chairs like they were thinking of rescuing her. But he didn't stop. He took her straight out the front door.

"My parents are going to get phone calls," she said, throwing her arm over her eyes.

"Good," he said again.

She uncovered her face. Their eyes clashed. Then held. And it was like something broke between them. She kissed him then, on the street, where anyone could see them. Where everyone in the bar most certainly saw them, as they were definitely looking.

Then he carried her to his truck and deposited her in the passenger seat. "We'll get your car tomorrow."

She didn't even argue. He started the engine and began to drive out toward her place. "Why are you at the bar in the first place?"

She ducked her head. "I was upset with you. I was trying not to be. I figured that you needed space."

"I was giving *you* space," he said.

She waved a hand. "Sure. But that was crap. You knew I didn't need space. *You* needed space."

Her words, her confidence, hit him like a slap. "I never need space."

"You need all the space, all the time," she said, scoffing. "And you know it."

"What exactly does that mean, Liv?"

"Your entire life is you building space between yourself and others. With that ridiculous, smart-ass smile of yours. That one that makes my stomach flip over. Because it makes me want to jump on you and slap you in the face all at the same time."

"You could try slapping me in the face while you jump on me," he said, keeping his tone light. "It might be fun. I might like it. Maybe I'm kinky."

"*That*. That kind of thing," she said. "You were so upset just a few minutes ago, and now you're joking."

"What do you want from me? You want me to keep raging? Do you want me to tell you how I about put my fist through your ex-boyfriend's face just for talking to you? You make me feel like a caveman? Like someone I don't even know?"

"Yes," she responded. "I would like you to tell me that. Tell me that you almost put your fist through his face. Because let me tell *you*, Luke, no man has ever wanted me like that before."

"Olivia…" He shook his head. "You make me crazy, do you know that?"

"Good."

"*Not* good," he said. "It's very unenlightened."

"I didn't ask you for enlightenment. I'm sick of obligations and doing the right thing, Luke. I don't want to be a thing you're protecting. I would rather have feelings."

He huffed out a laugh. "You've got 'em, babe."

They drove on in silence, and Luke sighed heavily,

feeling the tension in the cab of the truck like a band across his chest.

"Olivia…"

"We don't have to talk," she said, reaching across and brushing her fingertips against his thigh. He liked that. There was something almost routine about this. Her riding in his truck. Touching his leg. Like there was real intimacy between them. Like maybe she owned part of him, and he owned her, too.

He didn't understand this thing inside of him, and he wasn't sure he wanted to. He just wanted to be in it. That was how he liked to do things. To jump right in with both feet, to just revel in it. It was better than thinking ahead. When things would inevitably fall apart. To when they would end. He didn't want to think about those things, so he didn't.

He looked out at the highway and focused on the way the road cut a winding path through the thick trees, focused on the way her fingertips felt against his thigh. If the world was only this, it wouldn't be so bad.

When they arrived at the house, they got out of the truck and he took her hand, and they walked into her house together.

"Aren't you worried that your mom is going to see?" he asked.

"I'm much more worried my mom is going to come over, having heard that some Neanderthal carried her daughter out of the Gold Valley Saloon. Possibly after shagging her senseless in the bathroom."

"Darlin', I haven't begun to shag you senseless."

"I hope you begin soon," she said, treating him to a smile that was vixenish, but still every inch Olivia. She was such a funny creature, his girl. It was the thing about her that had captivated him from the beginning.

That she was so utterly unique. Not like anyone or anything else. There was no peer pressuring Olivia Logan. She was who she was. She did absolutely everything the way that she wanted it done. Except for him. He seemed to be the one thing that ruffled her. That disrupted her calm. And damned if he didn't like that. He liked it a hell of a lot.

He took a moment to look around Olivia's house, which he hadn't done yet. It was very her. White and pristine, neatly in order. As if the various knickknacks on the shelves would never dare to collect dust, not as long as Olivia Logan was present.

There was a little cupboard with plates on display, plates that looked like they had never been used, which was exactly the kind of thing he expected to see in a little cottage like this. There were doilies and frilly things laid across every surface, blankets on each couch and chair.

Imagining her curled up beneath those made him smile. Maybe on a rainy day, with her legs curled up to her chest, with a cup of coffee. He wanted to see her like that, but somehow wanted also to not be there, so he wouldn't interrupt the moment. The moment that wasn't even real. He'd lost his mind, and he wasn't sure he cared.

He walked through the living area and into her little kitchen, compelled to see more of the place. More of Olivia.

"What are you doing?" she asked.

"Looking around," he responded. Then he looked at the counter and saw a metal tin with a plastic lid over the top. He took a step closer. "Cinnamon rolls."

"I had a craving," she said, sounding defensive.

There were two cinnamon rolls gone, and he assumed that she had eaten them. In the middle of the day.

"Cinnamon rolls without me," he said, making his tone faintly disapproving. "That's no good, honey."

"You corrupted me," she admonished.

"I wish I could say I was sorry," he said.

"No you don't," she said.

"No I don't," he returned cheerfully.

He didn't wait for her to come to him. Instead, he closed the distance between them, kissed her, pressed her back against the edge of her counter and braced his hands on the surface of it, taking the kiss deep, hard. He needed her. It was more than want. It was more than anything he had ever experienced in his whole life. In his mind, he replayed every moment that he had seen Olivia with Bennett over the course of the past year.

What shocked him the most was that so many images of the two of them were burned into his brain. That he remembered them so clearly. And what stood out the most was his own position in those memories. Him standing there watching them, hands curled into fists. Because he had *cared*. He had cared even then. Had wanted to wrench her out of Bennett's arms and take her in his. What had happened today was just him letting that come forward.

She was everything. Absolutely everything.

His life had revolved around *places* for years. When he'd come to Gold Valley and made it his home it had been about the place. About Get Out of Dodge. About land and livestock. About work.

The first sixteen years of his life had been different. It had revolved around a person.

But apparently, it revolved around one again. Olivia. How had this happened? How long had it been her?

The answer was suddenly clear.

Always.

From the moment he had first seen her as a woman. Always.

He kissed her with that word on repeat in the back of his mind. Joining the one that had echoed there from the first moment her lips had touched his. Finally. Finally Olivia. Always Olivia.

She looped her arms around his neck, held on to him tightly and kissed him back. It was sweet, like always. But there was more bite to the kiss this time. More intensity. He was already changing her. Teaching her. *Corrupting* her, as she'd said. And he knew he should feel some regret over that.

Well, he did. Some. Not a lot. It was hard to regret anything when he was kissing her like this.

"Please tell me," he rasped, kissing her neck, down to her collarbone, "that you have a frilly little princess bed that I get to demolish."

She laughed. "Yes. I absolutely do."

"Thank God," he said, hauling her up against him and lifting her feet up off the ground.

"You have a bad habit of picking me up."

"You have a bad habit of being very pickupable."

"You can't have a habit of *that*," she pointed out as he scooped her into his arms. "And you don't know where my bedroom is."

"I think I can find it."

He looked out of the kitchen, and down the narrow hall. "Let me guess—it's at the end."

"I'm not sure that I like what that says about you," she said as he carried her toward her room. "That you're able to guess the location of women's bedrooms in charming cottages so unerringly."

"It says that I'm a very, very bad man," he responded. "But you already knew that. Because you know me."

"I do," she said, placing her hand on the side of his face and kissing him as he continued to walk down the hall. She didn't quite get his lips; she moved to his neck, his cheek and on down.

"Olivia," he groaned as she scraped her teeth down his tendon.

"What?" she asked, blinking wide eyes at him.

"You are not that innocent. A fact I can attest to. You know exactly what you're doing to me."

"I suppose I do," she said. "But do you know what you're doing to me?"

"I hope it's the same thing."

He opened the door to her room, and indeed, she had a frilly little princess bed. Replete with layers of white bedding, like a snowdrift made from lace.

He set her down at the center, ran his fingers through her hair. "You have to take your clothes off," he said, "because I have to see this."

They had made love once in his cabin, and then again on the floor of a barn. And not any one of those times had he felt that she had something that suited her. That was worthy of her. This was it. This soft, pure setting. For the softest, most elegant woman he had ever known.

He wanted to see her naked against this bed. Wanted to see her as she was, beautiful and too good for the likes of him. But his all the same.

She quickly stripped her top off, followed by her jeans, leaving her in a pair of pale pink underwear that he thought made a nice contrast to the white bedding.

But not nice enough for him to want to keep them on her. He leaned forward, hooking his fingers in the sides of her panties and pulling them down her thighs, then he reached behind her and unhooked her bra, pulling it off quickly with one hand and discarding it on the floor. He looked his fill, her pale skin against the white bed, her nipples tight and pink, perfect. Edible. He let his eyes wander down to that dark touch of curls between her legs, that he knew was so delicious, and already wet for him.

And he felt… It wasn't like anything he had ever known before; it was an excitement. It wasn't entitlement or the kind of masculine satisfaction he expected to feel when he looked at a naked woman.

It was humility. Awe. It was something bigger than both of those things combined.

He had never felt anything like he did right now. Like he was cracking open. Like he would die if he didn't have her, and die if he did.

"Hey," she said, "my turn."

"I'm looking," he growled. "Give me a minute."

"How long does it take for you to look?"

"There will never be enough time," he said, the words slipping out before he could stop them.

There wouldn't be. There would never be enough hours in the day, in a year, in a *lifetime* for him to look at Olivia Logan.

"Luke?" Her expression became vulnerable, her gaze questioning. And that did something to him. Reached inside his chest and twisted hard. He didn't want her to ever worry again. Not about anything. He never wanted her to be hurt. He never wanted her to be unsure. He wanted to hold up the sky for her if it threatened to fall. And he didn't know what in the hell to do with those feelings. He already knew that if the sky needed holding up he wouldn't be able to do it. That it would all crumble and break around them, the world falling to pieces. He wasn't a savior. He never had been.

She made him want to be.

But *wanting* wasn't enough. He knew that. He knew that better than he knew anything else in the whole world.

He stripped his shirt off, watching as she looked at him, taking satisfaction in her open appraisal. There was something incredible about the fact that he was the only man she had seen naked.

But right about then he had the feeling she might be the only woman who had ever seen him. At least in any way that mattered.

She *knew* him. Knew where he had been weak when he should have been strong. Knew about his darker moments, knew about his pain.

She knew him. Every scar, in a way that no one else ever had.

And he didn't feel any more like he knew what he was doing than she did. Didn't feel any more experienced. He wanted to give her something more than sex, and sex was all he knew. Intimacy was something else, and he didn't know it.

This was all new to him. This feeling. This feeling that told him he wasn't enough, while desperately making him desire to be more.

It was easier to smile. It was easier to make a joke.

It was easier to let the object of your desire walk off with another man because it would be better for her if he would let her.

He unfastened his jeans, pushed them down his hips, stood naked before her, enjoying the avid way that she visually explored him from her perch. Then he reached down and grabbed his wallet out of his jeans, taking care of protection before joining her on the bed. He held her. Pressing her bare chest to his, her stomach to his. Hips locked together, legs woven within each other. He sifted her hair through his fingers, kissed her on the mouth. And he could have done it all night, with no thought to his own satisfaction. Because just tasting her, the slow, languid movements of their mouths, was more, was deeper, than the best sex he'd ever had before this.

She began to thrust her hips gently against his, urging him to give her more, the silent demand something that he couldn't refuse. Not her. Not Olivia. Right then, he didn't want to refuse her anything.

He couldn't deny himself. The immediacy of his need to be inside of her shocked him, but it was almost that same feeling he'd had when he had walked into the saloon and seen her standing there with Bennett. It was beyond logic. It was beyond familiar. It was something new and elemental that lived in a place inside of him he hadn't known existed. Something reserved just for her. A space that he hadn't realized was there. Waiting. All this time.

This wasn't desire. It was need. Pure and simple.

The need to be inside of her. To possess her. The need for her to belong to him. Olivia. His Olivia.

He shifted, parted her thighs and slipped between them, pressing into her slowly, gritting his teeth as he did, trying to keep hold of his control. Of his sanity.

There was precious little of it left. He had lost most of it when he had walked into that bar tonight. Or maybe, he had lost it before then. Maybe she had laid claim to it years ago; he was coming to collect now.

But then, he didn't have the ability to worry about it anymore. Because he had nothing left in him but need.

But feeling. He wanted more. Needed more. Deeper. Harder. All of him and all of her. And maybe if it were possible, her inside of him a little bit. It wasn't enough. He didn't know what would be. That terrified him. That feeling that he would *always* want her. That there would be no end to it. That this was what he was, for the rest of his life. This mountain of need and unsatisfied longing.

She arched against him, wrapping slim legs around his hips, her heels digging in his lower back, urging him on.

He looked down at her and his heart stopped. She had her head thrown back, moving side to side, her eyes closed. She bit her lip, the color rising higher in her cheeks. He could see her pleasure. See her desire.

She was wild. His Olivia. Undone. For him.

Any control he thought to stake claim on was gone now. He had no more finesse. No more measure left in his thrusts. All he could do was desperately chase the release that was snarling at him from deep inside. Demanding satisfaction.

He gripped her hips, moving hard inside of her, meeting her every hip flex with a hard, decisive thrust of his own. Her fingernails dug into his skin, and he welcomed it. Welcomed any sense of discomfort that might take the edge off this pleasure. Because the pleasure was what might kill him. Was what might make it impossible to go back to life the way it had been.

This life that had been fine. At least until Olivia had shown him there could be more. Until Olivia had become his reason for breathing.

She curved her face into his neck, her internal muscles pulsing around him as she found her release, and then he found his own. Was blinded by it. Deaf to everything but the roaring in his ears and the sound of his own heart thundering like a spooked horse inside of his chest.

And Olivia was whispering words in his ears. Soft words. Sweet words. Words he hadn't heard since he was a child.

Words no one had ever spoken to him. But he couldn't translate it. All he could do was feel. Like a battering ram in his chest, trying to break out.

And suddenly, all the words ordered themselves in his mind, and he was able to understand.

Just in time for her to press her lips to his cheek, one last sweet whisper in his ear.

"Luke. I love you, Luke."

CHAPTER NINETEEN

SHE HADN'T MEANT to say it. She had been overwhelmed by her feelings, completely swept away on a tide of pleasure and something so much deeper. She hadn't been able to hold it inside. Not anymore. She loved him. Really, and truly. The kind that made her not care if there was heartbreak on the other side. The kind that made her reckless.

She hadn't gone skinny-dipping with her sister and her friends, because it hadn't mattered to her. That had seemed silly. Certainly not worth risking her pride, worth risking getting caught, being humiliated. But this was worth that. It was worth all that and more. Luke was. He was everything. And if she didn't have him she was going to break apart. If she didn't have him, then the rest of it didn't matter. Whether or not she was good, whether she was bad.

She wouldn't have him. And that was the only thing that mattered right now.

She had insulated herself with Bennett. Had sought to use him as this thing to keep her in line, to complete her life. An asset to all of her good behavior. To give herself the life her parents wanted her to have.

The cottage, not the farmhouse.

She didn't want it anymore.

She didn't want an asset. She didn't want a life that looked like that perfect image that had lived in her head for so long. Didn't want that golden retriever. Not if she didn't also have Luke. Everything but Luke was negotiable.

It hit her then, for the very first time, that everything was negotiable but love.

The rest... Well, the rest would have to cover itself.

"I love you," she said again.

"Olivia," he said, that firm, decisive tone that he was using just because he was about to explain to her how things work. That was what Luke did. He teased her, and then he took on that tone that told her he was going to tell her all about how the world worked.

She didn't want to hear how Luke Hollister thought the world worked. Didn't want to hear how he thought love might work, not when she had a feeling that the two of them were going to disagree.

"Don't tell me that I can't," she said. "Don't tell me that I don't. Luke..." She stood up, naked, and really not caring. Not for the first time. She was naked, and she wasn't embarrassed. Naked, and not ashamed. "I... Made a lot of mistakes in my relationship with my sister. Or maybe I didn't. Maybe what I did was the nicest thing I could have done. I don't know the answer to that. But I did what I did because I loved her. I loved her, and I wanted her to be safe. So I made the best decision that I could. But everything went to hell after that. And I have spent so many years since trying to make up for that. Trying to be the daughter my parents needed. Or that I thought they needed." She swallowed hard. "I was keeping myself safe that way. So many excuses that I used as armor. And I don't know what the future holds now. I don't know if all this is going to crumble around me or if it will upset my parents. I don't have a lot of answers. And I know that I love you. And that I might get hurt because of it. But I wouldn't change it. Because loving you…"

She looked down at her fingers, locked them together, twisted them. "Loving you wrenched me open." She looked up at him. "I was closed off for so many years. I had this one thing in mind. To be good. And that would make me happy. And it would make everyone around me happy. I don't feel… I don't feel happy right now. I'm terrified. I'm terrified and my chest hurts and everything feels impossible. But it's me. It's me unafraid. Of making mistakes. It's me learning to look outside of myself. That's the funniest thing I've realized. In my effort to be everything my parents wanted me to be, I used other people. I used Bennett. And I didn't mean to. I wanted him to make my dreams come true. I wanted him to make me the person that I saw myself being. I didn't care what he wanted. Not really. It was all about me. At the heart of it. But last night I wanted to argue with you when you sent me home, because I wanted to be with you. But I wanted to give you what you needed more. I've never experienced anything like that. Because I've never been in love before. I told you that. I don't love Bennett. I never did. I realized last night that I love you. And… Oh, I ran from that hard for so long, Luke."

He was staring at her, not saying anything, a muscle in his jaw jumping, his entire demeanor tense. He was naked, lying there on her bed, that impossibly feminine bed that was made of lace and frills, with that hard, muscular man lying across it, all angles and lines and delectable masculinity. He didn't fit. And yet he fit. Wonderfully, and possibly perfectly. And he was worth this. Worth this risk. Worth this moment where everything might fall to pieces. Where she reached inside of

herself, inside those new, recently invigorated places
that wanted and needed more.

"When Bennett asked to have me back, he said that
he didn't love me. And that was when I realized that the
life in my head wasn't enough. It was my wake-up call. I
thought that it could be. I thought it would be. I thought
I could love that idea enough that I could love Bennett,
too. That he *could* love me. But it doesn't work like
that. I'm learning… And all I keep thinking is that… I
was right to be afraid of this. Luke, this is bigger than
I could have ever imagined. It's tearing me up inside.
I was right to be afraid of you. I was. I was protecting
myself with Bennett, protecting myself from another
loss, another potential heartbreak. Hiding behind this
idea that I needed to be good, because what good really means is *safe*." She swallowed hard. "I don't want
to be safe anymore. At least, not above all else. I can't
be. Not when I know that none of it matters if I don't
have you. If I don't have your love."

He wasn't saying anything. He was just staring at her.
There was no smart-ass smile. There was no easy grin.
There was nothing. Nothing but a hard stare that she
couldn't decode. An expression that looked nothing like
the Luke that she knew. And nothing like the vulnerable boy she had imagined him being twenty years ago.

This was hard. It was merciless. It was blank and
cold.

And it terrified her.

"Olivia… I told you what this was."

"I don't care," she said. "Because we both lied to
each other for years. Do you think that you like picking on me because you're an overgrown child? I don't
believe that. I just don't. I think that you pick on me
because you care about me. Because you love me. Be-

cause you've always wanted me, no matter what either of us think. It's bigger than us. And our plans. I'm pretty sure it always has been."

"I can't," he said.

"You can't or you won't?" she insisted.

"It doesn't matter which," he said.

"Yes it does. If you can't love me... If this is just sex and years of the two of us wanting sex with each other, and then us finally having it the minute that we got close enough for it to happen... I could walk away from that. I walked away from Bennett when he said he didn't love me. I could walk away from you, too. But I think you do love me. And I think you could give a life with me a chance. I think we could love each other. Real, serious love. Maybe not safe love. But real love. And that... That matters. That's everything."

He swallowed hard, a muscle in his throat working. And she could see that he was deciding what to say. Luke, who prided himself on his honesty. Who said nothing when he couldn't say the truth, who fell back on sarcasm when the truth was too heavy.

He got up off the bed and began to collect his clothes.

"Luke," she said. "You have to say something."

He looked over at her, his eyes holding a deep resolve she didn't recognize. "I don't, kiddo," he said.

He continued to collect his clothes, and got dressed. She was too numb to take all that in. To register what was happening exactly. It was surreal. It was painful.

It was like the world was falling apart in front of her with each new piece of clothing Luke Hollister put on his body. He pulled his jeans up and a piece of her was stripped away. His shirt. Socks and boots. And that hat. That cowboy hat that made her feel so fluttery inside. Until he looked just as he had when he'd walked into the saloon tonight. Until he was put back together, and she was left ragged and destroyed. Naked in every way that counted.

"Luke," she said, "tell me that you don't love me."

He just looked at her with those green eyes. So flat and desolate and unreadable. Then he walked out of her bedroom.

Olivia sat there for a moment, stunned. Then she rallied. Scrambling up and moving after him, into the living room. She caught him just as he put his hand on the front door.

"Luke Hollister," she said, the words coming out as frayed and shaky as she felt. "As I live and breathe, if you don't give me an answer right now then you're nothing but a coward."

"The answer doesn't matter," he said. "Because it wouldn't be enough either way."

He opened the front door and started to walk out.

"Answer me," she screamed, past the point of caring about pride, past the point of caring about anything but this. But him. "You owe me a fucking explanation."

She had never said that word in her entire life. But she would scream it a thousand times now if it would make him stop.

Then his eyes connected with hers, and she felt it like a blow. "I don't love you." Then he walked out the door and closed it behind him.

And Olivia Logan, who had once suffered a horrible breakup on a public street on Christmas Eve and hadn't let it destroy her, fell to her knees in the dark quiet of her house and wept as if she would never stop.

CHAPTER TWENTY

LUKE DIDN'T KNOW how many shots of whiskey it took for a man to die of alcohol poisoning.

He was tempted to find out.

He grunted. Even in his whiskey-addled mind he knew that wasn't an acceptable line of thinking, even if it wasn't sincere. Even if it was just in his mind.

He had loved someone who had drowned her life away like that, and he didn't intend to do that.

But for the first time he could understand the hopelessness. The feeling that you would be in a dark tunnel for the rest of your life with no end, so what was the damned point of taking the next breath.

As he lay there on the floor by his bed—because beds were for people who weren't horrible human beings, and the floor was for liars—he wondered if he had been in that tunnel all of his life, and had emerged for just a moment the first time Olivia Logan's lips had touched his. Or maybe that day when he had pulled over and helped her with that flat tire.

Maybe then.

Maybe that was the first time he had seen the sun in twenty years and now he had simply been plunged back into darkness.

What a fine time to realize it. What a fine time to be alive.

He would rather be unconscious.

He rolled over to his side, pressing the heel of his palm against his pounding forehead.

She had made him lie to her. He didn't lie Not directly. Not like that. He prided himself on being a pretty up-front guy.

But he had never cared enough about anyone, or anything, to lie. Except for Olivia, apparently.

Because it had kind of been a lie when the two of them had tried to make Bennett jealous. Except so much of it had been the truth since he had wanted to be with her, even then.

But the words he'd spoken to her before he had walked out of her house had been an outright lie. A damned lie straight out of hell. He loved her.

He had loved her for... God knew how long. Months. *Years*.

But it wasn't enough. That was the problem.

And she'd said that him not loving her would be the one thing that would make her walk away from him, so he'd said he didn't, even though it wasn't true.

Even though when those words, those three simple words, had fallen from her lips, it was like the whole world had lit up. Like he suddenly saw her, and himself, and their feelings for each other exactly as they were for the first time.

It still wasn't enough.

Because in the end love didn't change a damn thing, and he knew it. It couldn't keep someone with you when they decided they didn't want to be there. It couldn't erase that terrible darkness that had lived inside of his mother. His love wasn't enough.

Olivia didn't know that because she'd never been with him for long enough. But he knew it.

She thought love was everything. That it could protect you in hard times. She talked about being fearless but it was only because she didn't understand.

Love was weak. It was helpless as a sixteen-year-old boy crying over his mother's body.

It was a sword that could be turned against you and used at a moment's notice. Like he had done to his mother. The way he had wielded his words with devastating accuracy when she had been at a moment that was so low she couldn't recover. When she had brandished it against him, taken herself from him. Proven that the love she supposedly felt for him wasn't enough to keep her there.

Love wasn't enough.

And that was the problem.

He loved Olivia Logan with everything he possessed, every last part of himself. And in the end, it was futile.

And it always would be.

He rolled back over and poured himself another measure of whiskey, then let his arms fall slack.

He was pathetic. And at the moment he didn't much care.

Because love might not be enough to save him, but he had a feeling it might be enough to destroy him.

CHAPTER TWENTY-ONE

OLIVIA WAS SURPRISED she got as much isolation as she did, but even so, when there was a knock on her door early the next morning, she felt jolted and cranky and not at all ready to deal with anyone.

She scowled and looked at her phone, and saw a raft of text messages from her mother.

The last one said: Olivia, I'm coming over.

For a moment, she froze, debating whether or not she should let her mother see what a freaking disaster she was. She wasn't the kind of person to let all that hang out. She kept it contained. She didn't want to worry her parents, after all. But... Well, her mom had come by without waiting for the okay, and Olivia just didn't have the energy to pretend to be okay. Not now.

She sighed heavily and shuffled to the door. She was still wearing her pajamas, and she knew she looked like a small disaster. She had to be at work in a couple of hours, and while she knew Lindy would be somewhat sympathetic to her breakup situation, she also knew that her boss would need her for a shift, broken heart or not.

She frowned. She had been brokenhearted a lot lately. The first time, though, it had been largely performative. Designed to convince both herself and the man who she felt had broken her heart that her love had indeed been true.

She'd been so, so wrong. And had somehow walked

herself into a much bigger heartbreak while trying to patch up the old one.

It was funny now, in hindsight.

Or would have been had anything been funny at all to her right now.

Nothing was funny. And it never would be again. Because she was heartbroken. Really and *truly* heartbroken.

She jerked open the door and saw her mother standing there, looking concerned and soft. Not angry like she should have been, since she'd no doubt heard about the incident with Luke at the Saloon.

Olivia couldn't stand it. She burst into tears.

"Mom," she said, her voice wobbling.

"Olivia?" Tamara Logan stepped inside and pulled Olivia into a hug, holding on to her tightly while Olivia wept plaintively into her shoulder.

She put her arm around Olivia's shoulder and walked her into the living room. "Sit down, sweetheart."

Olivia complied, taking a seat on the couch and pulling a blanket over her lap. Her mother went into the kitchen, and Olivia heard the sound of running water. She assumed her mother was putting some tea on. Because that was her mother's solution to all bad feelings. A warm drink.

Olivia felt that as solutions went it was a pretty good one. It wouldn't do anything to fix the broken heart, of course, but it was still better than nothing. Brokenhearted without a warm drink was decidedly worse than a broken heart *with* one.

"Talk to me," her mother said, coming into the room, her expression one full of concern.

"I…"

"Olivia," her mother said, crossing her arms and

looking stern. "You haven't gotten involved in... There's nothing going on with drugs?"

Olivia sat bolt upright. "Mother," she said, "I am twenty-five years old. If I was going to have a drug-addled rebellion I probably would have done it before now, don't you think?"

"But you've been acting out of character," her mom said.

"Have I? Maybe I've been acting in character. Maybe I've spent the past nine years playing a part." That realization washed over her, strongly, intensely. As she sat here in her house, feeling miserable, it all hit her fully. That she had been playacting since she was a teenager. Trying to do her best to make sure that she played the part of dutiful daughter. To keep herself safe—yes— because she and Vanessa were identical, so how easy would it be for her to slip down the same road as her sister had done? But more than that, because it had always felt like she had to stay in line or upset her parents.

They had constantly been on the lookout for slipping grades, for her being ten minutes late coming home, and she had taken all of that and done her very best to comply with the letter of their law. To use it as a guideline to keep herself safe, and to earn their approval.

Once Vanessa was gone, once she had been sent away to school, it was how she had gotten her attention. And it was how she had felt... Validated. But it wasn't her.

Luke hadn't needed any of that. That man who had seemed like he didn't like her half the time. Luke knew that she was crazy, that she was difficult and that she wasn't half as good as she pretended to be. And Luke had been with her anyway. But then, he had left her. So maybe that was the end result of Olivia being herself.

But she knew that she couldn't go back, either.

Not with him, not with her mother, not ever.

"Does this have anything to do with Luke Hollister carrying you out of the Gold Valley Saloon last night?"

Olivia sighed. "I guess there's gossip?"

"Yes," her mom said, "and, it's a concerning thing to hear, that a man physically removed your daughter from a bar."

"I went willingly."

"I realize that," her mom said. "Don't think for one second your father wouldn't have beaten down Luke's door if that weren't the case. He was the one that stopped me from coming over here last night. He says you're a grown woman."

"He is correct," Olivia said, her tone brittle.

"But, I have every right to worry about you."

Olivia pressed her hand to her forehead, leaning over. "Of course you do. Of course you do, because you're my mother. Because Vanessa is off doing God knows what, God knows where. And we all worry. But I'm not her."

"I know that," her mom said.

"I don't know if you do. I'm not sure that I do. I'm not her. I'm not in danger of becoming her. But I've been… All of my life… I was never as funny as she was. Never as popular. And the older we got the more distant she became. I couldn't get her attention, I couldn't get your attention. Then she started getting into all of that trouble, and I just kept… I kept being good. But you were so hard on me. Anytime I stepped out of line even just a little bit I got grounded."

Her mother sat down. "Olivia," she said, "we didn't mean to have a double standard, but we had already lost touch with Vanessa at that point. Grounding wasn't going to work. She used to sneak out. There was no keeping her in her room, and we already knew it. Any-time something small happened with you we probably overreacted because we didn't want to lose you, too."

"I know," Olivia said, her voice breaking. "I know. I never wanted you to worry about me. I took that seriously. But it just… It took on a life of its own. And suddenly, I'm in this life that I don't even want. I almost married Bennett Dodge because it seemed like the best thing to do. It seemed like the ultimate trophy for my good behavior. The thing that I could do to make you proud of me."

She felt so small and petty saying those words. Like a silly girl. Admitting she was trying to earn her parents' approval with her actions. Admitting that she had been trying to earn their attention, their good favor. And yes, part of it was that she hadn't wanted them to worry. But some of it was definitely that she had just wanted that unconditional love. Had wanted to be assured of it. Had wanted to make sure she had clinched it.

"Olivia," her mother said, the word coming out breathless. "I don't want you marrying somebody that you don't love because you think it's going to make us approve of you. I've always approved of you."

"Yes, because I've always done what you wanted me to do. Because I've never rebelled. Because I've never done anything wrong. But still, you come in here and I look like a mess and the first thing you do is ask me if I'm taking drugs."

"I'm sorry," her mom said. "I worry. I worry because I parented you and Vanessa the same for the first fifteen years of your lives. You were identical. Identical in every way. The same dresses, the same faces. And somehow, she went completely off the path that we hoped she would stay on. Somehow, we lost touch with her completely. And after that, I think I was too hard on you, but I was afraid. I didn't know what I had done to make Vanessa act out that way. And I just… Doubled down with you because it wasn't too late. Because I could still reach you. And I know that I hover. I know that sometimes I'm overbearing with you even now, but it's just because I want to… Olivia, I don't want you to stop loving me."

Olivia felt like she had been hit with a brick. "Mom, I'm never going to stop loving you."

"I don't want to lose our relationship. I watched one daughter turn into a stranger and for the life of me I don't know why it happened. And I feel like I made a lot of mistakes with you in my desperation. In my fear."

All of the breath rushed out of Olivia's body. "I've been… Trying to make sure that I didn't lose my relationship with you and Dad. I've been trying so hard. And I'm… I wasn't happy. I didn't realize it. But I was too afraid to do anything to change it."

"I'm so sorry," Tamara said, reaching out and squeezing Olivia's hand. "I had no idea you felt that way."

"I didn't, either," Olivia said. "I had settled into it. That life. That person. And then… I asked Luke if he would help me make Bennett jealous," Olivia said, her cheeks turning hot. "He agreed. But… Things with Luke got complicated quickly. And it ended up not being a game anymore. And it had nothing to do with Bennett. I love him. I love him, and he doesn't love me back. And I feel like I might die. So, yes. I'm a mess. I'm an absolute mess. I decided that I was going to have a sex-only relationship with a hot-looking man because I was sick of being good. And this is where it got me. And I'm sure that you're disgusted with me now, and I've made the entire town gossip about me and you think

I'm a drug addict. So… I guess this is the worst-case scenario." Olivia let out a long, slow breath and melted beneath the blanket. "I'm officially the cautionary tale I tried never to be. And I don't even care. Because I'm heartbroken and that's the worst part. I can't even care about gossip. I can't even really care that much if you're disappointed in me. I have too much to worry about. My own feelings. If that's selfish… But I guess for a little while I'm going to feel selfish."

She looked back at her mom, challenging her to get angry with her. To storm out. To say that she didn't love her. Something.

"I see," her mom said, instead of any of that.

"I had sex with him," Olivia restated. "A physical-only fling. And yes, I did fall in love with him. But I didn't mean to." She sniffed. "I was irresponsible."

"Did you want me to yell at you?" Tamara asked.

"Not particularly," Olivia responded, sheepish.

"It seems to me that your consequences are doing all the punishing for you. If I got angry at you it would just be rubbing it in."

"I'm not perfect." Olivia looked up at the ceiling. "I never could be."

"You don't have to be," her mom said. "Olivia, I love you, perfect or not. I wanted to protect you. I wanted to keep you safe. Of course I'm not happy that you're heartbroken, I hurt for you. But I'm not going to scold you. I'm not going to disown you just because there's a small situation with gossip in town. I might advise you to not let men carry you out of bars in the future."

"I doubt that's going to happen again anytime soon," Olivia said, feeling miserable.

"What do you want?" her mom asked. "From me. What can I do to make things better between us."

Olivia blinked. "I don't… I don't know. It's all… It's me. It's me being afraid. Afraid that if I don't end up with the life you and Dad have, you'll think that I'm a failure. You will be disappointed in me. And that I'll have caused you more pain, when Vanessa already did. And then I'll have lost you, too. I could never be the sister that she wanted me to be. I could never be fun and carefree. I lost her already. And if I lose you and Dad…"

Her mother leaned off the chair and pulled Olivia in for a hug. "I think that's what we were both afraid of, too. That we would lose you. That if we weren't strict with you, if we weren't hard on you, we might lose you the way that we did Vanessa. But that's not fair, Olivia. You never did anything to earn that. It was just us being afraid."

That word washed over her, and it felt important. Like the key to something. The key to everything. "Yes," Olivia agreed. "I've been afraid of so many things for so long. For good reason. Because, I mean, here I am heartbroken because I opened myself up to Luke, and he rejected me." She sighed. "But I can't go back. I can't shove all of this down again. I can't go back to how things were."

"Olivia, from the moment you were born, you and Vanessa, you were the two most precious things in my world. I love Vanessa, even now. I feel like I haven't done a good job of making sure you know that, because again… I was afraid that if I seemed too accepting of her behavior you might follow suit. The same as I was afraid if I didn't monitor your behavior all the time you might get involved in the same kinds of things. But I love her. Unconditionally. And I love you, too. Don't you know that?

"No," her mom said, "I mean, do you really know

that? Whether you're with Bennett, or with Luke, or all by yourself. Whether you're well behaved or gossip fodder, do you know that I love you?"

Olivia's heart twisted. "I feel like…like I know I need to change, but I'm not sure that I really want to. I did something bold for the first time and got hurt. And I don't know what's going to happen next. I don't know if this was the wrong choice. If I made a mistake getting involved with him, or loving him. But I wouldn't take it back. I don't know what I want now. I don't know what's going to happen and that…terrifies me."

"Whatever happens," her mom said, slowly. "You're my daughter. I love you. I want you to be happy. That's all. I would like it if that were here near me. I would like it if your happiness and your path to it didn't scare me. But if it did, I would cope with it, Olivia. You don't belong to me. You belong to yourself. And whatever you choose to do…I support you. And I'm proud of you."

Olivia's eyes felt scratchy, and her heart—that broken, bruised little heart—felt like it might have started to get put back together. "I believe you," Olivia said. "I'm sorry. For just… Not talking to you. All of this Vanessa stuff… We should've talked about it sooner. We were too careful not to make each other cry."

"Well, let's not be in the future," she said.

Olivia nodded. "Okay."

"Now," her mom said, getting up. "I'm going to check on your tea."

"Thank you," Olivia said.

"And I saw cinnamon rolls in there."

Olivia was about to refuse them. Because in light of everything, she didn't think she could eat cinnamon rolls. They would only make her think of Luke. Of Luke and his encouragement for her to indulge herself. And then she thought… Why not? She might not be able to have Luke at the end of all this, but she wouldn't be the same person either way. She couldn't go back now. She had uncovered too many things about herself that she'd had buried before. She expected more. She wanted more.

She wasn't going to live for other people's happiness. Not anymore. It was so strange to have sat here with her mom and finally had an honest conversation. To discover they had both been scared of losing each other. That they were clinging so tightly it had been suffocating.

But she was done with that.

She wanted a cinnamon roll.

"Let's have some."

CHAPTER TWENTY-TWO

LUKE WAS IN a mean mood and had a terrible headache by the time he got down to Get Out of Dodge the next day. He had a feeling that no amount of manual labor was going to fix it for him, either. Which made him angrier. Because that was what he had counted on for most of his life. Physical punishment.

But so far he had mucked every stall, dug new holes for fence posts, exercised three horses, and he still didn't feel any closer to dealing with the anger that was swirling around inside of him. The regret. All directed at himself.

He had opted to go and move river rock that Wyatt was transferring from one part of the property to another for landscape, because hefting giant-ass stones from a pile into the back of his truck was both painful and somehow metaphorical for the weight inside of him.

He was still angry. So it was almost a relief when he saw Bennett crossing the property and heading toward him. Because that would give him a place for some of his anger to go.

Right. Because that's completely reasonable. Yell at Bennett.

Oh well. He wasn't in the market for reasonable. He was in the market for blood and mayhem. "We need to talk about this," Bennett said, striding across the rocky ground and heading straight toward Luke.

"About what?"

"You carrying Olivia out of the saloon last night like she was a bag of feed."

Luke snorted and picked up another rock. "Don't be ridiculous. I'd have slung a bag of feed over my shoulder." He walked over to his truck and slammed the boulder down on the tailgate before pushing it back into the bed against the rest of them.

Then he turned and wiped the sweat off his brow. "She wanted to go," he said. "Or she wouldn't have come with me."

"I realize that." Bennett shook his head. "But I never figured you'd be one for putting on a show for the town."

Luke shrugged. "Neither did I."

Bennett stared at him for a moment, the crease between his dark brows deepening. Then he let out a slow breath. "You really care about her," he said.

"Doesn't matter," Luke returned.

"What do you mean it doesn't matter? You just about started a fight with me last night in front of the entire town. It mattered plenty then."

"Well," Luke responded, "it doesn't matter now. Don't you have a cow who needs a hand stuck up her ass or something?"

Bennett shook his head. "Not at the moment. I thought you were using her for that land."

"Damn, I wish," Luke bit out.

"And she was using you because she was mad at me."

Luke nodded once. "Well, she was. At first."

"But not after a while," Bennett said, his eyes fixed on Luke's.

Luke looked away. "Like I said. Doesn't matter. It's done now."

"I swear, Luke, if you hurt her…"

"I did," Luke said, picking up another rock and turn-ing, dropping it in the back of his truck with a loud crash. He turned back to Bennett, dusting his hands off on his jeans. "I did, because that's the only thing I know how to do to people I love. How about that?"

Bennett looked like Luke had just hurled one of the rocks in that pile right at his head. "You love her?"

"I sure as hell do," Luke responded, almost laugh-ing because the whole thing was ridiculous. So damned ridiculous. "Do you know what's terrible about that? There is nothing in the whole world that I can do to make that enough. It is the biggest emotion I have, the biggest damn emotion anyone has and it's not enough. I don't... I don't know what else to do. I don't know what else I can give to her. Except for me." He picked up an-other rock. "I already know I'm not enough."

"What are you talking about?" Bennett asked, look-ing genuinely confused.

Luke dropped the rock back on the ground, between his feet. "Do you want to know who my family is?"

Bennett looked hard at him. "I actually do."

So this was the second time in just a few days he was going to talk about this. Cut his chest open and let it all bleed out. And why the hell not? He'd lost Olivia already. Nothing else mattered.

"I never knew my father," Luke said. "When I was sixteen my mother killed herself."

Bennett's expression shifted, his jaw going slack.

"Shit. Man, I had no idea." Bennett looked genuinely stricken. "You never...you never told us your mother was dead."

"It didn't matter."

"Our mother is dead, too," Bennett said. "If anyone would have understood..."

"It didn't matter to me. I just wanted a place to be. A new place. Somewhere I could have a different life. But that's why I have money. You wanted to know? Now you do. I had money from my mother's life insurance settlement. That's why I came here in the first place. Because I didn't have anyone. Because I might as well have been an orphan. I loved my mother, Bennett. It still ended the way it did."

"And you think… What? Living with you is going to make Olivia depressed?"

"I just can't… I don't deserve it. I don't deserve for her to love me. And it won't fix anything. It won't fix me."

Bennett shrugged. "You can't accept love."

"No," Luke said.

"Not at all?" he pressed.

"You have a point, Bennett?" Luke snapped.

"I do. What do you think this is?" Bennett asked, gesturing around them.

"A fucking ranch," Luke responded.

"Not the ranch, dumb-ass. All of it. Us. Wyatt, Grant. My father and Jamie. What do you think holds us here? What do you think holds it all together?"

Luke gritted his teeth. "That's different."

The Dodges were the best family Luke had ever known. Not that he'd known many. Not perfect, not like *Leave It to Beaver*, but they loved each other. And Quinn Dodge was his father figure, sure as hell. The man was made of grit. He'd raised his kids mostly alone and had taken Luke onto the ranch when he was a surly teenager.

"Is it? If I didn't love you like a brother, Luke, I would have flattened your ass the minute I saw you with Olivia."

"You said I wasn't like you."

"Because I was pissed," Bennett said. "And I was jealous, which is bullshit, because you're right. I'm not in love with her. I feel protective of her, and that's not the same thing. If you're really in love with her, and she's in love with you, then dammit, man, you've got to do something with that."

"Why? You were going to marry a woman you didn't love. You clearly don't believe in it, either."

Bennett shook his head. "I cared for her. I've never expected more than that. I wanted to protect her, and I mean that. I never would have hurt her. But you obviously have *something* with her. Something that has you acting all kinds of messed up. Something that has her acting crazy. I've never known Olivia to act crazy in my life. So it has to be something serious. That kind of thing my dad had with my mom. And that he has with Freda. My dad believes in love, even though he was hurt. Even though he lost someone."

"Your mom's death is different than mine. It just is."

"I'm not going to pretend I understand exactly how you feel," Bennett said. "But I know loss. I understand what it does to you." Bennett spoke with such depth that Luke had to wonder if he was still talking about the loss of his mother, or if there was something else. Bennett had said Luke didn't know everything about him. That made him wonder. "I think that's what's holding you back. You're afraid of losing someone you care about."

"Well, I lost Olivia, so your theory doesn't really hold up."

"You lost her on your terms, man. That's not the same thing."

Luke scowled. "I don't need a lecture from you, Bennett. Run along."

"Shut up," Bennett said. "Luke, I'm sorry that you lost your mother. And I'm even sorrier that I didn't know about it until now. I know that losses like that leave scars, but I can't let you sink into that. I wouldn't be family to you if I didn't put aside the anger I've had for you for the past couple of weeks. If I didn't put aside any lingering issues I have with Olivia and tell you that you should be with her. Because any woman who makes you look *that* miserable obviously matters. Any woman who makes you just about start a bar fight matters. Matters in a way that goes way beyond anything I've ever felt. You should be with her. Because she deserves that. Deserves a man who looks this miserable when he's not with her. That man isn't me."

"I know it's not," Luke said. "But that doesn't change things. Olivia deserves everything. I want to…give her everything I have. I want to give her diamonds and that little farmhouse on the property I just bought that made her eyes light up like she was looking at the most beautiful mansion in the world. I want to pull down the sky and give her the stars. But it doesn't change who I am. It doesn't change anything."

"You deserve her, too," Bennett said. "You don't deserve to live this half life, hanging on to the past. You always deserved to be here, always deserved to be part of our family. And you deserve to be with the woman you love."

It was a strange thing, having the man he had just gotten in a fight with twenty-four hours ago standing there looking at him and telling him he deserved to be happy. But then, all of this was strange.

"I just can't see how it's going to be enough," Luke said, feeling weary down to his soul. And it had nothing to do with moving boulders.

"It's not love that fails people. It's fear," Bennett said. "I know a little something about that. And right now, you're letting fear win. So stop it."

"I…" Revelation washed over Luke like a tide, and any words he'd been about to speak froze in his throat. "It can't be that easy." He finished the sentence by tearing those words out from deep inside himself.

"Why not?" Bennett asked. "Nothing is broken between you two. You haven't destroyed anything. You've…changed each other for the better. Hell, I've never seen anything like it. She's happier with you, Luke. Take it from the guy who was with her before."

Then Bennett tipped his hat and walked away, leaving Luke standing there feeling like the grade A asshole he was.

He stared at Bennett's retreating figure, backlit by the sun that was piercing through the furious gray clouds slowly breaking into pieces above the mountains. Mountains he knew by heart. Mountains that encircled this land he knew better than his own heart.

For years, this place had been his heart. This place, and the people on it.

It wasn't love that failed.

Suddenly it all hit him with blinding clarity. He had love all around him. It was easy for him to think that he'd had it and lost it when his mother had died. But that wasn't it.

He had been loved from the moment he had stepped onto the Get Out of Dodge Ranch. Had been embraced and accepted by them. And if there had been any distance, it had been on his part. Because he had resisted caring too much. He had loved this land with all of himself. And he had found a new ranch, a new place to love.

And there was Olivia.

He had loved her from the beginning. From the moment he had first begun to see her as a woman. And in all that time, that love had sustained him. The love of this place, the love of the Dodge family. And now, his love for Olivia. It had been enough.

Suddenly he couldn't breathe, pain slicing through his chest like the sharp edge of one of his whiskey tumblers had broken off and stuck in there last night when he'd tried to drink all this away.

It wasn't that love had failed the day his mother had killed herself.

It was that fear had won.

His mother's fear of the future. Her fear of walking through that darkness she'd been in for the next ten years, twenty. The fear that it would never get better. And maybe even that it would never get better for him if she didn't do something drastic.

On that day, fear had been stronger, and there had been nothing he could do to combat it. But right now he had a choice. A choice between love and fear. He couldn't have both. He knew it. They couldn't exist side by side.

One had to win. He had seen that play out.

But today it was his choice which one got the victory.

He pictured Olivia's face, the way that he had left her, curled up on the floor, and the way he had spent the night curled up on the floor after. He had made them both miserable because of his choice. And he wanted to fix it. He just had to hope that she would let him.

Love was going to have to be enough. It was all he had. But he had it. And for the first time in twenty years he was ready to embrace it.

When he had driven himself to Get Out of Dodge at sixteen, in that old beater car of his, his heart torn to pieces, he'd imagined that love had let him down. But all this time he'd missed that love hadn't failed him. Love was what had held him up.

And now it was the only thing strong enough to make him move forward.

CHAPTER TWENTY-THREE

"MEN ARE IDIOTS," Sabrina Leighton said, as she passed Olivia a glass of wine.

"Serious idiots," Lindy agreed.

"They're okay," Clara Campbell said.

"No they aren't," Sabrina protested. "They're pigs."

"Even Alex and Liam?" Clara asked.

"They have their moments," Sabrina said, speaking of both her and Clara's fiancés.

Olivia appreciated very much that her friends were giving her an after-hours pick-me-up at the little cheese restaurant down in town. They had all worked together at Grassroots for a couple of years, and they had been incredibly patient with Olivia and her general lack of social skills during that time.

During that time, Olivia had seen Clara and Sabrina fall in love and go through the initial uncertainty of it, but both were incredibly happy now. Olivia wished she could have similar confidence. But right now, Clara and Sabrina were seated on one side of the table, with Olivia and Lindy on the other. And Olivia had a feeling that was symbolic in some ways.

Bellissima was a vaguely Italian restaurant that was somewhere at the crossroads of fancy and family style on the edge of Main Street in Gold Valley. Grassroots supplied most of the wine, which meant that the Grassroots team made occasional deliveries there during the week. And this week, after the winery had closed, the group of them had decided that they would stay and have drinks and bread.

They had said it was because they had not been together in months—Clara no longer worked at Grassroots, so they only saw her when she was able to get away from the ranch—but Olivia knew it was because of her sadness, and not so much because they were all suddenly spurred by a desire to hang out.

"I appreciate the support," Olivia said. "And he is an idiot. But I'm kind of an idiot, too. I… It's not like I was terribly in touch with my feelings until him, really. He's the one that made me like this. He's the one that made me feel things. He's the one that made me care."

"Burn the witch," Sabrina said.

"Yes, this is his fault," Lindy said.

"Stop it," Olivia said. "You're making me want to defend him. And that's the worst."

"Okay," Clara said. "Then I'm sure he had a very good reason for rejecting you and stomping on your heart after he took your virginity."

Olivia wrinkled her nose. "That's not really better." She sighed heavily and tore a piece of bread off the remaining loaf in the center of the table. "I'm sorry," Olivia said.

"Sorry for what?" Clara asked, lifting a can of Coke to her lips.

"I'm sorry that I've been kind of a difficult friend over the past couple of years. You've all been wonderful, and I've been difficult to get to know."

"You haven't been," Sabrina said. "Anyway, we all have our things. It's not like any of us are the easiest group of people."

"Speak for yourself," Lindy said. "I am a delight."

"An endless delight," Sabrina said. "But, also a bit prickly at times."

"I'm your boss," Lindy pointed.

"Yeah," Sabrina said cheerfully. "But you're not going to fire me. I'm family."

"You were family," Lindy corrected, her tone lacking heat. "I divorced your brother. I can get rid of you, too."

"No you can't," Sabrina said. "You like me."

Lindy snapped her fingers. "Dammit!"

Olivia smiled in spite of herself. "I just… I'm learning. I'm learning something from all of this. That I'm not perfect, and that's okay. I was afraid of that. I was afraid of what it might mean if I admitted that." She explained the entire situation with her sister, and how it had affected her. Hurt her. How she had been afraid that if she didn't keep tight control on everything, the worst part of her nature would come out, and then ruining her sister's life would be for nothing.

"You make yourself sound terrible," Clara said. "And we know you're not. You've always listened whenever we had problems, even if you had your own opinions on how we should handle things."

"I'm judgmental," Olivia said. "Mostly because I was afraid that if I wasn't…"

"You would fall into bed with the first hot cowboy that you saw?" Clara asked.

"Now that you mention it," Olivia mumbled.

"I mean, that's what I did," Clara said. "No judgment here."

"Same," added Sabrina.

"You're *human*," Lindy said. "Welcome. It's terrible."

"Apparently," Olivia grumbled.

"None of us are all good or all bad," Lindy said. "We're just doing our best."

Olivia looked down at the bread in her hand, and suddenly it looked like sawdust. "Well, my best apparently isn't good enough for Luke Hollister."

"Then he's an idiot," Sabrina said, circling back to her earlier statement.

Lindy's phone buzzed and she looked down at the screen, scowling. "I have to get going," Lindy said. "I have some paperwork to get from Damien and I'd rather die, but I also want all of this settled once and for all. Down to car titles. Of all things."

Sabrina grimaced. "I could go with you. He *is* my asshole brother, after all."

Lindy studied her manicured fingers. "No. That's okay. I'd rather have an alibi than witnesses."

"We'll say you were with us all night," Clara said.

"My word would have been more helpful a few weeks ago," Olivia said. "Prior to me destroying my reputation as a levelheaded paragon."

Lindy shrugged. "I probably won't kill him. I haven't yet." Lindy looked around, searching for the waitress so they could collect their bill.

"I'll put it on your tab, Lindy." Janine, the owner of Bellissima, popped her head out of the kitchen.

"Okay," Lindy said, waving, and the group of them got up and walked out of the restaurant and onto the sidewalk.

Olivia still felt miserable. Hanging out with her friends hadn't magically healed her broken heart. But the conversation with her mother earlier this morning, the long workday and then this conversation had made her feel... Not alone.

Part of her wanted to cling to the idea that her heartbreak was singular, and that no one had ever been through anything like it before, but there was also something therapeutic in knowing that they had. Though, for Sabrina and Clara, and for her mother, all of it had worked out in the end.

Lindy, for her part, was still rebuilding her life. But she was doing it.

When Clara and Sabrina said goodbye and headed off to their cars, Lindy paused and turned to Olivia. "I know it's hard, because it worked out for them," Lindy said. "It's hard for me sometimes. This whole being alone thing."

"It's not hard," Olivia lied.

"It is," Lindy said. "I don't miss Damien, but I miss being with someone. And accepting that everything went wrong sucks. It really does. To have believed in something with all of yourself only to have it blow up in your face is awful." She smiled. "You can't let them make you bitter. Don't let this make you shut yourself off again. This is just the first relationship. The first *real* one. In a line of what I know will be good ones."

"I have to go through a whole line of them?" Olivia sighed heavily.

"Maybe not," Lindy said. "But if you do, you'll be fine. You don't need a man to have that happy ending that you're looking for."

"I need Luke to have a happy ending I want," she protested.

"I know it feels that way right now. Right now, I'm currently involved in a passionate love affair with the winery. Unexpected. And kind of awesome. And you know what? Better than my marriage. So. I thought I would never get over it, but here I am. I'm over it." Then she shrugged. "Okay. I'm mostly over it. Whenever I have to go see him I feel a lot less over it."

"You were married for ten years. If you were over it…"

"I know," Lindy said.

"So what do I do now? Have a fling? Luke kind of was my fling to get over my boyfriend, and then I fell in love with him even harder. But then, Luke is also the only man I've ever slept with."

"I haven't graduated to fling stage yet," Lindy said. "If I do, I'll let you know."

Olivia felt affirmed by that, because she really didn't want to go out and find another guy. Actually, she found it kind of interesting that she didn't even want to do anything to try and win Luke back through subterfuge, like she'd tried with Bennett. She *wanted* Luke back. But… It needed to be because he loved her.

That was the other difference when it was real, she supposed.

"Thank you," Olivia said, leaning in to give Lindy a hug.

"No problem." Lindy gave her a half wave. "See you tomorrow."

Olivia nodded and walked the opposite direction from Lindy, heading toward her car. Now that she was without her friends, she felt a little bit depleted. Maybe she would call her mom and talk to her on the way home so she didn't have to be left alone with her thoughts and her sadness. That seemed like a pretty good solution.

She shook her head and slipped her coat on, buttoning it up to brace herself against the cold.

Then she started to walk down the sidewalk, one foot in front of the other. The streetlights had started to turn on, pools of light showing the cracks in the sidewalk. The shop windows were dim, showing the outlines of chairs and window displays. There were no Christ-

mas lights anymore. The season was over. And that
felt somehow metaphorical for where she was at now.

Christmas was over. Now it was just winter. And she
had to hope that on the other side of it would be spring,
because it had always come in the past.

But right now it felt like it wouldn't. Right now, it
felt like it would be like this, cold, and gray, for the rest
of forever. In her heart and outside.

The bar was starting to fill up with people, because
it was Saturday, which was an even bigger drinking day
than Friday. She thought about going in for a second.
Throwing darts. That just made her think of Luke and
kissing whiskey off his lips.

She didn't even want to play darts. The man really
had broken her.

This whole town was filled to the brim with Luke
Hollister. Everywhere she looked. Everywhere she had
been. He was part of it.

She ached to tell him that, because she knew that in
a lot of ways he would find that pleasing. That he was
synonymous with the town. That he had roots here,
even if he didn't know it.

But she *couldn't* tell him. Because he didn't love her.

She was going to have to walk down the streets, go to
all these places they had been together. She was going
to have to run into him at the grocery store.

In line for coffee.

She was going to have to pretend that he had never
seen her naked. That he had never kissed her, tasted
her. That they hadn't been intimate. That he didn't have
a piece of her heart buried deep inside of him that she
would never be able to get back.

How was she going to do that? How was she going
to do it without folding in on herself completely?

She knew how she had done it in the past. She had closed parts of herself off. Had given herself goals. But she didn't want to be that person anymore, either. So she supposed she just had to endure this. Be one with her pain and all of that.

It was overrated.

"Olivia Logan," came the sound of a rough voice to her left. "As I live and breathe."

She turned and saw Luke, the window rolled down in the passenger seat of his truck, him staring across the bench seat at her.

"What are you doing?" she asked.

"Driving," he said simply.

"You're talking to me."

"If you know what I'm doing, then why did you ask me?"

He was *not* doing this to her. Not now. She stomped her foot and whirled to fully face him. "Luke Hollister, how dare you tease me? Don't you do it. I will… I will throw my purse at you."

"Don't do that. I'll just keep it until you agree to talk to me."

She frowned. "Why would I want to talk to you?"

"A question for the ages. But then I'm not quite sure why you wanted to kiss me. Why you wanted to touch me. Why you wanted to be with me at all."

"Because I *loved* you," she said, choking on tears that were threatening to rise up. "And you know that. So don't act confused now."

"Did you stop loving me that quickly?" he asked, his expression losing the amusement it had held only a moment before.

She gritted her teeth. "You don't have the right to ask me that." She wrapped her coat more firmly around herself and began to walk more resolutely down the street. Luke's truck engine rumbling along with her.

"Olivia," he said, "I need to talk to you."

"I don't care."

"Olivia…" She kept on walking. *"Olivia!"*

She stopped and whirled around on her heel. "What? What do you think I have to say to you?"

"Maybe nothing. And that's okay. I understand. But I have something to say to you," he said. "You did a lot of talking last night, and you don't owe me anything more than what you already gave me. But I let you down, and I want a chance to fix that. I've been doing a lot of driving around. A lot of lifting heavy rocks. A lot of thinking."

"I don't tend to like where your thinking leads," she said.

"I'm sorry about that," he responded. "I'm sorry about a lot of things. About a lot of damn things. You're right. I've always loved you. From the time you were eighteen years old. It tore me up inside. Caring about you like that. I didn't want to care about anybody like that. Let alone you. This pretty little rich girl who had a plan for her life. Who had everything all set out before her. I knew that I wouldn't do anything but disappoint you. There was no other alternative for that. Ever. And I felt… I felt certain that love… My love was never going to be good enough. Not for the likes of you. It wasn't good enough for my own mother, Olivia. How could it be good enough for you?" He shook his head. "I failed at love."

A sharp honk came from behind Luke breaking that sense of isolation she'd been shrouded in, that feeling that they were the only two people in the world. Olivia looked back and saw a battered old truck behind Luke with the engine idling. Luke hung his head out his window and shouted, "Wait a damned second, Hank! I'm busy."

Luke turned back to Olivia. "I was wrong, Liv. I was flat-out wrong. I want the chance to explain myself."

Hank honked his horn again. Luke hit the side of his truck with his open palm and hung his head out the window again. "Hank! I'm declaring my love here. Don't make a scene."

"I think we're the ones making a scene," Olivia said, looking around, suddenly conscious of the fact that she was standing on the sidewalk, with Luke blocking the whole of Main Street, right in front of the Saloon, the big picture windows offering everyone inside a prime view of the proceedings.

"I think we're owed a scene. Look at me," he said, his voice frayed. "*Me.* I'm cool about everything. I don't make scenes. I don't care enough about anything. Not until you. I almost punched Bennett Dodge out last night. I carried you out of the saloon like a caveman, in front of God and everybody. And here I am, blocking traffic." He looked behind him at the one truck backed up in the lane behind him. "Such as it is."

She did her best to hold back the tears that were building in her eyes. "You hurt me. So much."

"I know, kiddo," he said, his voice pained. "I know I did. I'm sorry. Give me a chance to explain. Give me a chance to make it up to you."

She had a feeling the old her would've closed herself off now. Out of fear. Would have clung tightly to all that hard-won control. To goals and logic. But she didn't care about any of that now. And she wasn't the old her. She was different. Changed forever by Luke. So, she figured she should give him a chance.

"Okay," she said, climbing into the truck. Anyway, now Hank could go. She buckled the seat belt and took a deep breath, trying to ignore the feeling of rightness welling up beneath the pain in her chest. Even though he'd hurt her, even though it was all uncertain, it was better to be close to him than to be away from him.

"I have half a mind to sit here and make him wait for being obnoxious."

"I hate to break it to you," she said. "You're the one being obnoxious."

"But I'm doing it for you," he pointed out. "That has to mean something."

"It means something to me," she said softly.

He started driving down the road then, and Hank honked at them a couple of times just for good measure. They were silent on the drive, and it didn't take long for Olivia to realize he was driving her out to the new property. To the ranch.

They were silent all the way down the dirt road, and then he parked in front of the house. That house that had felt so instantly perfect to her when she had walked inside. "Come out here with me," he said.

Then they stood out there, in front of the house, the porch light casting a golden glow onto the ornate wooden scrollwork that ran between the support beams, casting shadows made of lace onto the ground below.

Luke walked toward her and took her hand, the warmth of his touch washing away her pain, her doubts.

"Suddenly, it seemed like this place was perfect," he said slowly. "Right around the time you asked me for help, it seemed like the time to use that money I'd held on to for twenty years. I told myself it was because I couldn't leave it sitting there forever. That this was the right property. That it was the right time. Just because the money had been there so long, and it needed to be used. That wasn't it." He let out a heavy breath. "Come with me."

He led her across the gravel, out to the field that stretched between the house and the barn. The grass was damp from condensation, seeping through her pants as they walked out toward the center. "Look up," he said. "All the stars. The view out here is perfect. No lights coming from town. No noise from traffic."

"It's beautiful," she said, turning her focus back to him, "but I'm not sure I understand."

"I thought earlier today… I wanted to give you everything. That I wanted to pull the stars down from the sky and give them to you, and I would if I could. Then I realized I might not be able to bring them down to earth, but I can give them to you all the same."

"Luke, I don't understand," she said, *desperate* to understand. Desperate to erase this distance between them. It had been there long enough. The two of them had cultivated that distance over years, because they'd known on some level where closeness would lead. Now that she'd experienced life without it, without space, without clothes between herself and Luke, moving back to distant was intolerable.

"It was never for me," he responded. "This. It was never the right time to spend the money for *me*. It was because of you. This is for you, Liv. That's why it was right. It was finally time to get a place of my own because it was time for me to have a wife. It was time for me to make my move. To claim that life with you. The life that I always wanted. Dammit, watching you with him… Watching you *want* him… It tore me up inside, but there was nothing I could do about it. I wouldn't even let myself acknowledge it, because I had to protect you from everything I couldn't give. But I was just such a dumb-ass. Bennett made me see it. Bennett, of all people."

"Bennett?" she asked, incredulous. "What did he say to you?"

"It's not love that fails, Liv," he said. "It's fear. And that changed everything. All this time, I believed that the love my mother had for me, the love I had for her, wasn't enough. That it failed in some way." His voice deepened, went rougher. "It was just that fear had the victory that day that she died. It doesn't mean love never mattered. It doesn't mean that life we had wasn't *something*. And knowing that has made a difference in me. I have a choice. *We* do. To let fear win, or to let love win. This whole road was leading me to you. It was leading me here.

"I am such a fool," he said, shaking his head. "To think that it just so happened that a property owned by Cole Logan was the one where I wanted to hang my hat. It's because this field, that barn, that house, it's yours, kiddo. Yours and mine. Not for my life, for our life. That money... That money was always about love. My mom loved me the best that she could. I saved it, but it wasn't worth using until I loved someone enough to spend it. And that was you. That was you, all this time."

Luke's words poured through her like rain, washing away all of her doubt. All of her pain. She didn't want to hold back. She didn't want control. She just wanted him.

Olivia flung herself into his arms, and he spun her around beneath that blanket of stars, her stars. *Their* stars. Wet grass whipped dewdrops up around them, but she didn't care. "I love you," she said. "It was always you for me, too. Always. Luke, I love you so much."

She clung to him, standing in the field, her heart

pounding so hard she thought it might go straight through her chest.

"Fear almost won," he said. "With me and with you."

"I know. It's why I avoided you. Why I was so mad at you all the time." She kissed his cheek, pressing her fingertips against his skin, tracing that beloved line of his jaw. "Luke, remember when we went to the beach? I was so mad at you that day. Because you looked so good, and I couldn't understand why I wanted a man that drove me crazy, and not the one that I thought I should be with."

"Oh, I remember that day," he said. "You had that prim little black swimsuit on that didn't even show all that much skin. It shouldn't have turned me on, but it did. But I just pretended it was because you were a pretty girl and I liked pretty girls." He cupped her cheeks with his big hands, staring down at her. "You're not just a pretty girl. There are millions of pretty girls. But there's only one you. And you have had me, had my heart, for a hell of a long time."

"You have mine. And I was going to ask for it back. But I think I'm going to let you keep it. As long as I can keep yours. Then I think we'll be pretty even."

"I think we will," he said.

"Can we make a deal?" she asked.

"Anything."

"If ever we're afraid, we can't push it down. We can't hide it. We have to tell each other. Fear is a part of life. We'll never get rid of it altogether. But we can choose how much power it has. I think bringing it into the light steals that power away. Talking to you, sharing with you, that's what changed me. I don't want to go back to holding it all inside."

"You have my word," he said. "You come first.

You're the only person that's ever known me. You're the only person that ever made sure I couldn't get away with keeping my secrets. And I'm never going to keep them, not from you."

He took her in his arms and kissed her, with all of the desire inside of him, and she thought she was going to explode from her love. She had been right to be afraid of this. Because it was so big, so powerful and so life-changing. She'd had to be ready to accept it. But now that she'd made fear step aside, it was all love. Brilliant and blinding. And everything that she needed.

"Come on," he said, taking hold of her hand and leading her back toward the truck. She felt reluctant to go. Reluctant to leave this place that was going to be theirs. *Theirs.* They were going to have a life. A future. And she was so blinded by happiness that she couldn't picture it clearly. Couldn't see any golden retrievers.

She didn't need to see that perfect picture. She only needed to see Luke's face.

She thought Luke was going to lead her back to the truck, but instead, he surprised her by guiding her up the steps and onto the front porch. Then, Luke got down on one knee. Her heart lurched in her throat, everything in her shivering in anticipation.

"Before I came looking for you, I came out here. I made sure the house was ready. That the power was turned on, that it was clean. Then I stopped at a jewelry store. I chose this because it's classic. An antique, actually. But it reminded me of you. Because it's a little bit old-fashioned, beautiful through and through. And one of a kind." He pulled a ring from his shirt pocket and held it up toward her. It was ornate, with a beautiful gold setting and diamonds that glittered beneath the simple porch light.

"Will you marry me?" he asked, the uncertainty on that handsome face, a face that was never uncertain, sending a shock wave of love through her.

A terrible thought occurred to her then, as she looked down at the man of her dreams, offering her a ring after being together for such a short time. "You don't have to ask me so quickly."

She had the reputation of being the girl who broke up with men because they wouldn't marry her. And now he felt like he had to.

"I want to do it so quickly," he said. "Anyway, it's not that quick. I've loved you for years, woman. I'm just finally awake. Marry me. So that I don't lose you again. Marry me, Olivia. Be my roots. Be my family. Be my home."

The word welled up inside of her, the answer she'd been dying to give to a proposal for so long. This wasn't the way she'd imagined it. Not when she'd been with Bennett. When she'd hoped for a proposal during a crowded Christmas celebration, with all manner of fanfare and attention.

This was just her and the man she loved. It was more than enough.

He slipped the ring on her finger, then swung her up into his arms.

"I told you," she said, clinging to him. "It's becoming a habit."

"Good," he said. "And anyway, I need to practice this." He carried her up the front porch steps, toward the door of the house. "Practice carrying my wife over the threshold."

And that was exactly what he did. Carried her through the front door and into their life together.

Olivia supposed it could be argued that it was irresponsible to get engaged so quickly. And up until Luke Hollister, Olivia had always been responsible. But with Luke, she wasn't responsible. She was just in love.

She had been incredibly peeved that day when her tire was flat, that Luke Hollister had been the salvation she hadn't wanted. But oh, that bad boy had been the salvation the good girl had desperately needed.

Since her big breakup with Bennett, she'd been slowly learning what she wanted out of her own life. But in the end she'd found something even better. She'd found a way to their life. Hers and Luke's.

All of the fear, all of the uncertainty, that bound up feeling inside of her faded away. She didn't need to be *good*. She just needed to be her. Because Luke Hollister loved her, and she loved him.

And that was as good as it got.

EPILOGUE

LUKE PUT THE finishing touches on a brand-new carving on the bathroom wall of the Gold Valley Saloon, right next to a similar carving that was ten years old. The words he'd carved just now stood out more boldly than the slightly faded and darkened *Luke Hollister* it was next to, but Luke felt like that was how it should be.

Olivia was the brightest thing in his life, after all.

And he… Well, he was her scandal.

The bathroom door opened and his fiancée emerged, her gaze immediately turning suspicious. "Luke," she said, "what did you do?"

She turned toward the wall, her mouth dropping open. "Luke Hollister and Olivia Hollister," she read. "We aren't married yet!"

"But we will be. Soon. The sooner the better."

"Laz is going to be mad that you carved up his bar!" she scolded.

"Sorry," he said. "Except I'm not sorry. I had to make sure that my story was complete. And without you… it just isn't."

"People are going to think we hooked up in the bathroom!" she protested.

"Marriage is long, kiddo. I can't promise that someday we won't. Might want to spice things up in our golden years."

Olivia sniffed and leaned into him. He put his arm

around her and she buried her face against him. "I'm a lady."

"Yes. But you're my lady. Which means that you're just a little bit wicked sometimes. At least with me."

That earned him a smile.

There had been a time when he'd thought everyone in town had liked him, except for Olivia. But now... Well, everyone in town might like him, but Olivia loved him.

When he was sixteen years old, he had come to Gold Valley with the idea he might find a way to fulfill his dreams.

He had thought his dream was to be a cowboy. But his dream had been Olivia all along. And now he had her.

Finally. Forever.

* * * * *

Seduce Me, Cowboy

CHAPTER ONE

HAYLEY THOMPSON WAS a good girl. In all the ways that phrase applied. The kind of girl every mother wished her son would bring home for Sunday dinner.

Of course, the mothers of Copper Ridge were much more enthusiastic about Hayley than their sons were, but that had never been a problem. She had never really tried dating, anyway. Dates were the least of her problems.

She was more worried about the constant feeling that she was under a microscope. That she was a trained seal, sitting behind the desk in the church office exactly as one might expect from a small-town pastor's daughter—who also happened to be the church secretary.

And what did she have to show for being so good? Absolutely nothing.

Meanwhile, her older brother had gone out into the world and done whatever he wanted. He'd broken every rule. Run away from home. Gotten married, gotten divorced. Come back home and opened a bar in the same town where his father preached sermons. All while Hayley had stayed and behaved herself. Done everything that was expected of her.

Ace was the prodigal son. He hadn't just received forgiveness for his transgressions. He'd been rewarded. He had so many things well-behaved Hayley wanted and didn't have.

He'd found love again in his wife, Sierra. They had
children. The doting attention of Hayley's parents—a
side effect of being the first to supply grandchildren,
she felt—while Hayley had...

Well, nothing.

Nothing but a future as a very well-behaved spinster.

That was why she was here now. Clutching a newspaper in her hand until it was wrinkled tight. She hadn't
even known people still put ads in the paper for job listings, but while she'd been sitting in The Grind yesterday
on Copper Ridge's main street, watching people go by
and feeling a strange sense of being untethered, she'd
grabbed the local paper.

That had led her to the job listings. And seeing as
she was unemployed for the first time since she was
sixteen years old, she'd read them.

Every single one of them had been submitted by
people she knew. Businesses she'd grown up patroniz-
ing, or businesses owned by people she knew from her
dad's congregation. And if she got a job somewhere like
that, she might as well have stayed on at the church.

Except for one listing. Assistant to Jonathan Bear,
owner of Gray Bear Construction. The job was for him
personally, but would also entail clerical work for his
company and some work around his home.

She didn't know anything about the company. She'd
never had a house built, after all. Neither had her mother
and father. And she'd never heard his name before, and
was reasonably sure she'd never seen him at church.

She wanted that distance.

Familiar, nagging guilt gnawed at the edges of her
heart. Her parents were good people. They loved her
very much. And she loved them. But she felt like a beloved goldfish. With people watching her every move

and tapping on the glass. Plus, the bowl was restricting, when she was well aware there was an entire ocean out there.

Step one in her plan for independence had been to acquire her own apartment. Cassie Caldwell, owner of The Grind, and her husband, Jake, had moved out of the space above the coffee shop a while ago. Happily, it had been vacant and ready to rent, and Hayley had taken advantage of that. So, with the money she'd saved up, she'd moved into that place. And then, after hoarding a few months' worth of rent, she had finally worked up the courage to quit.

Her father had been… She wouldn't go so far as to say he'd been disappointed. John Thompson never had a harsh word for anyone. He was all kind eyes and deep conviction. The type of goodness Hayley could only marvel at, that made her feel as though she could never quite measure up.

But she could tell her father had been confused. And she hadn't been able to explain herself, not fully. Because she didn't want either of her parents to know that ultimately, this little journey of independence would lead straight out of Copper Ridge.

She had to get out of the fishbowl. She needed people to stop tapping on her glass.

Virtue wasn't its own reward. For years she'd believed it would be. But then…suddenly, watching Ace at the dinner table at her parents' house, with his family, she'd realized the strange knot in her stomach wasn't anger over his abandonment, over the way he'd embarrassed their parents with his behavior.

It was envy.

Envy of all he had, of his freedom. Well, this was her

chance to have some of that for herself, and she couldn't do it with everyone watching.

She took a deep breath and regarded the house in front of her. If she didn't know it was the home and office of the owner of Gray Bear Construction, she would be tempted to assume it was some kind of resort.

The expansive front porch was made entirely out of logs, stained with a glossy, honey-colored sheen that caught the light and made the place look like it was glowing. The green metal roof was designed to withstand harsh weather—which down in town by the beach wasn't much of an issue. But a few miles inland, here in the mountains, she could imagine there was snow in winter.

She wondered if she would need chains for her car. But she supposed she'd cross that bridge when she came to it. It was early spring, and she didn't even have the job yet.

Getting the job, and keeping it through winter, was only a pipe dream at this point.

She took a deep breath and started up the path, the bark-laden ground soft beneath her feet. She inhaled deeply, the sharp scent of pine filling her lungs. It was cool beneath the trees, and she wrapped her arms around herself as she walked up the steps and made her way to the front door.

She knocked before she had a chance to rethink her actions, and then she waited.

She was just about to knock again when she heard footsteps. She quickly put her hand down at her side. Then lifted it again, brushing her hair out of her face. Then she clasped her hands in front of her, then put them back at her sides again. Then she decided to hold them in front of her again.

She had just settled on that position when the door jerked open.

She had rehearsed her opening remarks. Had practiced making a natural smile in the mirror—which was easy after so many years manning the front desk of a church—but all that disappeared completely when she looked at the man standing in front of her.

He was… Well, he was nothing like she'd expected, which left her grappling for what exactly she had been expecting. Somebody older. Certainly not somebody who towered over her like a redwood.

Jonathan Bear wasn't someone you could anticipate.

His dark, glittering eyes assessed her; his mouth pressed into a thin line. His black hair was tied back, but it was impossible for her to tell just how long it was from where she stood.

"Who are you?" he asked, his tone uncompromising.

"I'm here to interview for the assistant position. Were you expecting someone else?" Her stomach twisted with anxiety. He wasn't what she had expected, and now she was wondering if she was what *he* had expected. Maybe he wanted somebody older, with more qualifications. Or somebody more… Well, sexy secretary than former church secretary.

Though, she looked very nice in this twin set and pencil skirt, if she said so herself.

"No," he said, moving away from the door. "Come in."

"Oh," she said, scampering to follow his direction.

"The office is upstairs," he said, taking great strides through the entryway and heading toward a massive curved staircase.

She found herself taking very quick steps to try and keep up with him. And it was difficult to do that when

she was distracted by the beauty of the house. She was
trying to take in all the details as she trailed behind him
up the stairs, her low heels clicking on the hardwood.

"I'm Hayley Thompson," she said, "which I know the
résumé said, but you didn't know who I was… So…"

"We're the only two people here," he said, looking
back at her, lifting one dark brow. "So knowing your
name isn't really that important, is it?"

She couldn't tell if he was joking. She laughed nervously, and it got her no response at all. So then she was
concerned she had miscalculated.

They reached the top of the stairs, and she followed
him down a long hallway, the sound of her steps damp-
ened now by a long carpet runner the colors of the nature that surrounded them. Brown, forest green and a
red that reminded her of cranberries.

The house smelled new. Which was maybe a strange
observation to make, but the scent of wood lingered in
the air, and something that reminded her of paint.

"How long have you lived here?" she asked, more
comfortable with polite conversation than contending
with silence.

"Just moved in last month," he said. "One of our de-
signs. You might have guessed, this is what Gray Bear
does. Custom homes. That's our specialty. And since my
construction company merged with Grayson Design,
we're doing design as well as construction."

"How many people can buy places like this?" she
asked, turning in a circle while she walked, daunted
by the amount of house they had left behind them, and
the amount that was still before them.

"You would be surprised. For a lot of our clients
these are only vacation homes. Escapes to the coast
and to the mountains. Mostly, we work on the Oregon

coast, but we make exceptions for some of the higher-paying clientele."

"That's…kind of amazing. I mean, something of this scale right here in Copper Ridge. Or I guess, technically, we're outside the city limits."

"Still the same zip code," he said, lifting a shoulder.

He took hold of two sliding double doors fashioned to look like barn doors and slid them open, revealing a huge office space with floor-to-ceiling windows and a view that made her jaw drop.

The sheer immensity of the mountains spread before them was incredible on its own. But beyond that, she could make out the faint gray of the ocean, white-capped waves and jagged rocks rising out of the surf.

"The best of everything," he said. "Sky, mountains, ocean. That kind of sums up the company. Now that you know about us, you can tell me why I should hire you."

"I want the job," she said, her tone hesitant. As soon as she said the words, she realized how ridiculous they were. Everybody who interviewed for this position would want the job. "I was working as a secretary for my father's…business," she said, feeling guilty about fudging a little bit on her résumé. But she hadn't really wanted to say she was working at her father's church, because… Well, she just wanted to come in at a slightly more neutral position.

"You were working for your family?"

"Yes," she said.

He crossed his arms, and she felt slightly intimidated. He was the largest man she'd ever seen. At least, he felt large. Something about all the height and muscles and presence combined.

"We're going to have to get one thing straight right now, Hayley. I'm not your daddy. So if you're used to a kind and gentle working environment where you get a lot of chances because firing you would make it awkward around the holidays, this might take some adjustment for you. I'm damned hard to please. And I'm not a very nice boss. There's a lot of work to do around here. I hate paperwork, and I don't want to have to do any form twice. If you make mistakes and I have to sit at that desk longer as a result, you're fired. If I've hired you to make things easier between myself and my clients, and something you do makes it harder, you're fired. If you pass on a call to me that I shouldn't have to take, you're fired."

She nodded, wishing she had a notepad, not because she was ever going to forget what he'd said, but so she could underscore the fact that she was paying attention. "Anything else?"

"Yeah," he said, a slight smile curving his lips. "You're also fired if you fuck up my coffee."

THIS WAS A MISTAKE. Jonathan Bear was absolutely certain of it. But he had earned millions making mistakes, so what was one more? Nobody else had responded to his ad.

Except for this pale, strange little creature who looked barely twenty and wore the outfit of an eighty-year-old woman.

She was… Well, she wasn't the kind of formidable woman who could stand up to the rigors of working with him.

His sister, Rebecca, would say—with absolutely no tact at all—that he sucked as a boss. And maybe she was right, but he didn't really care. He was busy, and right now he hated most of what he was busy with.

There was irony in that, he knew. He had worked

hard all his life. While a lot of his friends had sought solace and oblivion in drugs and alcohol, Jonathan had figured it was best to sweat the poison right out.

He'd gotten a job on a construction site when he was fifteen, and learned his trade. He'd gotten to where he was faster, better than most of the men around him. By the time he was twenty, he had been doing serious custom work on the more upscale custom homes he'd built with West Construction.

But he wanted more. There was a cap on what he could make with that company, and he didn't like a ceiling. He wanted open skies and the freedom to go as high, as fast as he wanted. So he could amass so much it could never be taken from him.

So he'd risked striking out on his own. No one had believed a kid from the wrong side of the tracks could compete with West. But Jonathan had courted business across city and county lines. And created a reputation beyond Copper Ridge so that when people came looking to build retirement homes or vacation properties, his was the name they knew.

He had built everything he had, brick by brick. In a strictly literal sense in some cases.

And every brick built a stronger wall against all the things he had left behind. Poverty, uncertainty, the lack of respect paid to a man in his circumstances.

Then six months ago, Joshua Grayson had approached him. Originally from Copper Ridge, the man had been looking for a foothold back in town after years in Seattle. Faith Grayson, Joshua's sister was quickly becoming the most sought after architect in the Pacific Northwest. But the siblings had decided it was time to bring the business back home in order to be closer to their parents.

And so Joshua asked Jonathan if he would consider bringing design in-house, making Bear Construction into Gray Bear.

This gave Jonathan reach into urban areas, into Seattle. Had him managing remote crews and dealing with many projects at one time. And it had pushed him straight out of the building game in many ways. He had turned into a desk drone. And while his bank account had grown astronomically, he was quite a ways from the life he thought he'd live after reaching this point.

Except the house. The house was finally finished. Finally, he was living in one of the places he'd built.

Finally, Jonathan Bear, that poor Indian kid who wasn't worth anything to anyone, bastard son of the biggest bastard in town, had his house on the side of the mountain and more money than he would ever be able to spend.

And he was bored out of his mind.

Boredom, it turned out, worked him into a hell of a temper. He had a feeling Hayley Thompson wasn't strong enough to stand up to that. But he expected to go through a few assistants before he found one who could handle it. She might as well be number one.

"You've got the job," he said. "You can start tomorrow."

Her eyes widened, and he noticed they were a strange shade of blue. Gray in some lights, shot through with a dark, velvet navy that reminded him of the ocean before a storm. It made him wonder if there was some hidden strength there.

They would both find out.

"I got the job? Just like that?"

"Getting the job was always going to be the easy part. It's keeping the job that might be tricky. My list of reasons to hire you are short—you showed up. The list of reasons I have for why I might fire you is much longer."

"You're not very reassuring," she said, her lips tilting down in a slight frown.

He laughed. "If you want to go back and work for your daddy, do that. I'm not going to call you. But maybe you'll appreciate my ways later. Other jobs will seem easy after this one."

She just looked at him, her jaw firmly set, her petite body rigid with determination. "What time do you want me here?"

"Seven o'clock. Don't be late. Or else…"

"You'll fire me. I've got the theme."

"Excellent. Hayley Thompson, you've got yourself a job."

CHAPTER TWO

HAYLEY SCRUBBED HER face as she walked into The Grind through the private entrance from her upstairs apartment. It was early. But she wanted to make sure she wasn't late to work.

On account of all the firing talk.

"Good morning," Cassie said from behind the counter, smiling cheerfully. Hayley wondered if Cassie was really thrilled to be at work this early in the morning. Hayley knew all about presenting a cheerful face to anyone who might walk in the door.

You couldn't have a bad day when you worked at the church.

"I need coffee," Hayley said, not bothering to force a grin. She wasn't at work yet. She paused. "Do you know Jonathan Bear?"

Cassie gave her a questioning look. "Yes, I'm friends with his sister, Rebecca. She owns the store across the street."

"Right," Hayley said, frowning. "I don't think I've ever met her. But I've seen her around town."

Hayley was a few years younger than Cassie, and probably a bit younger than Rebecca, as well, which meant they had never been in classes together at school, and had never shared groups of friends. Not that Hayley had much in the way of friends. People tended to fear the pastor's daughter would put a damper on things.

No one had tested the theory.

"So yes, I know Jonathan in passing. He's... Well, he's not very friendly." Cassie laughed. "Why?"

"He just hired me."

Cassie's expression contorted into one of horror and Hayley saw her start to backpedal. "He's probably fine. It's just that he's very protective of Rebecca because he raised her, you know, and all that. And she had her accident, and had to have a lot of medical procedures done... So my perception of him is based entirely on that. I'm sure he's a great boss."

"No," Hayley said, "you were right the first time. He's a grumpy cuss. Do you have any idea what kind of coffee he drinks?"

Cassie frowned, a small notch appearing between her brows. "He doesn't come in that often. But when he does I think he gets a dark roast, large, black, no sugar, with a double shot of espresso."

"How do you remember that?"

"It's my job. And there are a lot of people I know by drink and not by name."

"Well, I will take one of those for him. And hope that it's still hot by the time I get up the mountain."

"Okay. And a coffee for you with room for cream?"

"Yes," Hayley said. "I don't consider my morning caffeination ritual a punishment like some people seem to."

"Hey," Cassie said, "some people just like their coffee unadulterated. But I am not one of them. I feel you."

Hayley paid for her order and made her way to the back of the store, looking around at the warm, quaint surroundings. Locals had filed in and were filling up the tables, reading their papers, opening laptops and dropping off bags and coats to secure the coveted positions in the tiny coffee shop.

Then a line began to form, and Hayley was grateful she had come as early as she had.

A moment later, her order was ready. Popping the lid off her cup at the cream and sugar station, she gave herself a generous helping of both. She walked back out the way she had come in, going to her car, which was parked behind the building in her reserved space.

She got inside, wishing she'd warmed up the vehicle before placing her order. It wasn't too cold this morning, but she could see her breath in the damp air. She positioned both cups of coffee in the cup holders of her old Civic, and then headed to the main road, which was void of traffic—and would remain that way for the entire day.

She liked the pace of Copper Ridge, she really did. Liked the fact that she knew so many people, that people waved and smiled when she walked by. Liked that there were no traffic lights, and that you rarely had to wait for more than one car at a four-way stop.

She loved the mountains, and she loved the ocean.

But she knew there were things beyond this place, too. And she wanted to see them.

Needed to see them.

She thought about all those places as she drove along the winding road to Jonathan Bear's house. She had the vague thought that if she went to London or Paris, if she looked at the Eiffel Tower or Big Ben, structures so old and lasting—structures that had been there for centuries—maybe she would learn something about herself.

Maybe she would find what she couldn't identify here. Maybe she would find the cure for the elusive ache in her chest when she saw Ace with Sierra and their kids.

Would find the freedom to be herself—whoever that might be. To flirt and date, and maybe drink a beer. To escape the confines that so rigidly held her.

Even driving out of town this morning, instead of to the church, was strange. Usually, she felt as though she were moving through the grooves of a well-worn track. There were certain places she went in town— her parents' home, the church, the grocery store, The Grind, her brother's brewery and restaurant, but never his bar—and she rarely deviated from that routine.

She supposed this drive would become routine soon enough.

She pulled up to the front of the house, experiencing a sharp sense of déjà vu as she walked up to the front porch to knock again. Except this time her stomach twisted with an even greater sense of trepidation. Not because Jonathan Bear was an unknown, but because she knew a little bit about him now. And what she knew terrified her.

The door jerked open before she could pound against it. "Just come in next time," he said.

"Oh."

"During business hours. I was expecting you."

"Expecting me to be late?" she asked, holding out his cup of coffee.

He arched a dark brow. "Maybe." He tilted his head to the side. "What's that?"

"Probably coffee." She didn't know why she was being anything other than straightforward and sweet. He'd made it very clear that he had exacting standards. Likely, he wanted his assistant to fulfill his every whim before it even occurred to him, and to do so with a smile. Likely, he didn't want his assistant to sass him, even lightly.

Except, something niggled at her, telling her he wouldn't respect her at all if she acted like a doormat. She was good at reading people. It was a happy side effect of being quiet. Of having few friends, of being an observer. Of spending years behind the church desk, not sure who might walk through the door seeking help. That experience had taught Hayley not only kindness, but also discernment.

And that was why she chose to follow her instincts with Jonathan.

"It's probably coffee?" he asked, taking the cup from her, anyway.

"Yes," she returned. "Probably."

He turned away from her, heading toward the stairs, but she noticed that he took the lid off the cup and examined the contents. She smiled as she followed him up the stairs to the office.

The doors were already open, the computer that faced the windows fired up. There were papers everywhere. And pens sat across nearly every surface.

"Why so many pens?" she asked.

"If I have to stop and look for one I waste an awful lot of time cussing."

"Fair enough."

"I have to go outside and take care of the horses, but I want you to go through that stack of invoices and enter all the information into the spreadsheet on the computer. Can you do that?"

"Spreadsheets are my specialty. You have horses?"

He nodded. "This is kind of a ranch."

"Oh," she said. "I didn't realize."

"No reason you should." Then he turned, grabbing a

black cowboy hat off a hook and putting it firmly on his head. "I'll be back in a couple of hours. And I'm going to want more coffee. The machine is downstairs in the kitchen. Should be pretty easy. Probably."

Then he brushed his fingertips against the brim of his hat, nodding slightly before walking out, leaving her alone.

When he left, something in her chest loosened, eased. She hadn't realized just how tense she'd felt in his presence.

She took a deep breath, sitting down at the desk in front of the computer, eyeing the healthy stack of papers to her left. Then she looked over the monitor to the view below. This wouldn't be so bad. He wasn't here looking over her shoulder, barking orders. And really, in terms of work space, this office could hardly be beat.

Maybe this job wouldn't be so bad, after all.

BY THE TIME Jonathan made a run to town after finishing up with the horses, it was past lunchtime. So he brought food from the Crab Shanty and hoped his new assistant didn't have a horrible allergy to seafood.

He probably should have checked. He wasn't really used to considering other people. And he couldn't say he was looking forward to getting used to it. But he would rather she didn't die. At least, not while at work.

He held tightly to the white bag of food as he made his way to the office. Her back was to the door, her head bent low over a stack of papers, one hand poised on the mouse.

He set the bag down loudly on the table by the doorway, then deposited his keys there, too. He hung his hat on the hook. "Hungry?"

Her head popped up, her eyes wide. "Oh, I didn't

hear you come in. You scared me. You should have announced yourself or something."

"I just did. I said, 'hungry?' I mean, I could have said I'm here, but how is that any different?"

She shook her head. "I don't have an answer to that."

"Great. I have fish."

"What kind?"

"Fried kind."

"I approve."

He sighed in mock relief. "Good. Because if you didn't, I don't know how I would live with myself. I would have had to eat both of these." He opened the bag, taking out two cartons and two cans of Coke.

He sat in the chair in front of the table he used for drawing plans, then held her portion toward her.

She made a funny face, then accepted the offered lunch. "Is one of the Cokes for me, too?"

"Sure," he said, sliding a can at her.

She blinked, then took the can.

"What?"

She shook her head. "Nothing."

"You expected me to hand everything to you, didn't you?"

She shook her head. "No. Well, maybe. But, I'm sorry. I don't work with my father anymore, as you have mentioned more than once."

"No," he said, "you don't. And this isn't a church. Though—" he took a french fry out of the box and bit it "—this is pretty close to a religious experience." He picked up one of the thoughtfully included napkins and wiped his fingers before popping the top on the Coke can.

"How did you know I worked at the church?" she asked.

"I pay attention. And I definitely looked at the address you included on your form. Also, I know your brother. Or rather, I know of him. My sister is engaged to his brother-in-law. I might not be chummy with him, but I know his dad is the pastor. And that he has a younger sister."

She looked crestfallen. "I didn't realize you knew my brother."

"Is that a problem?"

"I was trying to get a job based on my own merit. Not on family connections. And frankly, I can't find anyone who is not connected to my family in some way in this town. My father knows the saints, my brother knows the sinners."

"Are you calling me a sinner?"

She picked gingerly at a piece of fish. "All have sinned and so forth."

"That isn't what you meant."

She suddenly became very interested in her coleslaw, prodding it with her plastic fork.

"How is it you know I'm a sinner?" he asked, not intending to let her off the hook, because this was just so fun. Hell, he'd gone and hired himself a church secretary, so might as well play with her a little bit.

"I didn't mean that," she insisted, her cheeks turning pink. He couldn't remember the last time he'd seen a woman blush.

"Well, if it helps at all, I don't know your brother well. I just buy alcohol from him on the weekends. But you're right. I am a sinner, Hayley."

She looked up at him then. The shock reflected in those stormy eyes touched him down deep. Made his stomach feel tight, made his blood feel hot. All right, he needed to get a handle on himself. Because that was not the kind of fun he was going to have with the church secretary he had hired. No way.

Jonathan Bear was a ruthless bastard; that fact could not be disputed. He had learned to look out for himself at an early age, because no one else would. Not his father. Certainly not his mother, who had taken off when he was a teenager, leaving him with a younger sister to raise. And most definitely not anyone in town.

But, even he had a conscience.

In theory, anyway.

"Good to know. I mean, since we're getting to know each other, I guess."

They ate in relative silence after that. Jonathan took that opportunity to check messages on his phone. A damn smartphone. This was what he had come to. Used to be that if he wanted to spend time alone he could unplug and go out on his horse easily enough. Now, he could still do that, but his business partners—dammit all, he had business partners—knew that he should be accessible and was opting not to be.

"Why did you leave the church?" he asked after a long stretch of silence.

"I didn't. I mean, not as a member. But, I couldn't work there anymore. You know, I woke up one morning and looked in the mirror and imagined doing that exact same thing in forty years. Sitting behind that desk, in the same chair, talking to the same people, having the same conversations... I just didn't think I could do it. I thought...well, for a long time I thought if I sat in that chair life would come to me." She took a deep breath. "But it won't. I have to go get it."

What she was talking about... That kind of stability. It was completely foreign to him. Jonathan could scarcely remember a time in his life when things had stayed the same from year to year. He would say one thing for poverty, it was dynamic. It could be a grind, sure, but it kept you on your toes. He'd constantly looked for new ways to support himself and Rebecca. To prove to child services that he was a fit guardian. To keep their dwelling up to par, to make sure they could always afford it. To keep them both fed and clothed— or at least her, if not him.

He had always craved what Hayley was talking about. A place secure enough to rest for a while. But not having it was why he was here now. In this house, with all this money. Which was the only real damned security in the world. Making sure you were in control of everything around you.

Even if it did mean owning a fucking smartphone.

"So, your big move was to be my assistant?"

She frowned. "No. This is my small move. You have to make small moves before you can make a big one."

That he agreed with, more or less. His whole life had been a series of small moves with no pausing in between. One step at a time as he climbed up to the top. "I'm not sure it's the best thing to let your employer know you think he's a small step," he said, just because he wanted to see her cheeks turn pink again. He was gratified when they did.

"Sorry. This is a giant step for me. I intend to stay here forever in my elevated position as your assistant."

He set his lunch down, leaning back and holding up his hands. "Slow down, baby. I'm not looking for a commitment."

At that, her cheeks turned bright red. She took another bite of coleslaw, leaving a smear of mayonnaise on the corner of her mouth. Without thinking, he leaned in and brushed his thumb across the smudge, and along the edge of her lower lip.

He didn't realize it was a mistake until the slug of heat hit him low and fast in the gut.

He hadn't realized it would be a mistake because she was such a mousy little thing, a church secretary. Because his taste didn't run to that kind of thing. At least, that's what he would have said.

But while his brain might have a conscience, he discovered in that moment that his body certainly did not.

CHAPTER THREE

IT WAS LIKE striking a match, his thumb sweeping across her skin. It left a trail of fire where he touched, and made her feel hot in places he hadn't. She was... Well, she was immobilized.

Like a deer caught in the headlights, seeing exactly what was barreling down on her, and unable to move.

Except, of course, Jonathan wasn't barreling down on her. He wasn't moving at all.

He was just looking at her, his dark eyes glittering, his expression like granite. She followed his lead, unsure of what to do. Of how she should react.

And then, suddenly, everything clicked into place. Exactly what she was feeling, exactly what she was doing...and exactly how much of an idiot she was

She took a deep breath, gasping as though she'd been submerged beneath water. She turned her chair sideways, facing the computer again. "Well," she said, "thank you for lunch."

Fiddlesticks. And darn it. And fudging graham crackers.

She had just openly stared at her boss, probably looking like a guppy gasping on dry land because he had wiped mayonnaise off her lip. Which was—as things went—probably one of the more platonic touches a man and a woman could share.

The problem was, she couldn't remember ever being

touched—even platonically—by a man who wasn't family. So she had been completely unprepared for the reaction it created inside her. Which she had no doubt he'd noticed.

Attraction. She had felt *attracted* to him.

Backtracking, she realized the tight feeling in her stomach that had appeared the first moment she'd seen him was probably attraction.

That was bad. Very bad.

But what she was really curious about, was why this attraction felt different from what she'd felt around other men she had liked. She'd felt fluttery feelings before. Most notably for Grant Daniels, the junior high youth pastor, a couple years ago. She had really liked him, and she was pretty sure he'd liked her, too, but he hadn't seemed willing to make a move.

She had conversations with him over coffee in the Fellowship Hall, where he had brought up his feelings on dating—he didn't—and how he was waiting until he was ready to get married before getting into any kind of relationship with a woman.

For a while, she'd been convinced he'd told her that because he was close to being ready, and he might want to marry her.

Another instance of sitting, waiting and believing what she wanted would come to her through the sheer force of her good behavior.

Looking back, she realized it was kind of stupid that she had hoped he'd marry her. She didn't know him, not really. She had only ever seen him around church, and of course her feelings for him were based on that. Everybody was on their best behavior there. Including her.

Not that she actually behaved badly, which was kind of the problem. There was what she did, what she showed the world, and then there were the dark, secret things that lived inside her. Things she wanted but was afraid to pursue.

The fluttery feelings she had for Grant were like public Hayley. Smiley, shiny and giddy. Wholesome and hopeful.

The tension she felt in her stomach when she looked at Jonathan…that was all secret Hayley.

And it scared her that there was another person who seemed to have access to those feelings she examined only late at night in the darkness of her room.

She had finally gotten up the courage to buy a ro-mance novel when she'd been at the grocery store a month or so ago. She had always been curious about those books, but since she'd lived with her parents, she had never been brave enough to buy one.

So, at the age of twenty-four, she had gotten her very first one. And it had been educational. Very, *very* educational. She had been a little afraid of it, to be honest.

Because those illicit feelings brought about late at night by hazy images and the slide of sheets against her bare skin had suddenly become focused and specific after reading that book.

And if that book had been the fantasy, Jonathan was the reality. It made her want to turn tail and run. But she couldn't. Because if she did, then he would know what no one else knew about her.

She couldn't risk him knowing.

They were practically strangers. They had nothing in common. These feelings were ridiculous. At least Grant had been the kind of person she was suited to.

Which begged the question—why didn't he make her feel this off-kilter?

Her face felt like it was on fire, and she was sure

Jonathan could easily read her reaction. That was the problem. It had taken her longer to understand what she was feeling than it had likely taken him. Because he wasn't sheltered like she was.

Sheltered even from her own desire.

The word made her shiver. Because it was one she had avoided thinking until now.

Desire.

Did she desire him? And if she did, what did that mean?

Her mouth went dry as several possibilities floated through her mind. Each more firmly rooted in fantasy than the last, since she had no practical experience with any of this.

And it was going to stay that way. At least for now.

Small steps. This job was her first small step. And it was a job, not a chance for her to get ridiculous over a man.

"Did you have anything else you wanted me to do?" she asked, not turning to face him, keeping her gaze resolutely pinned to the computer screen.

He was silent for a moment, and for some reason, the silence felt thick. "Did you finish entering the invoices?"

"Yes."

"Good," he said. "Here." He handed her his phone. "If anyone calls, say I'm not available, but you're happy to take a message. And I want you to call the county office and ask about the permits listed in the other spreadsheet I have open. Just get a status update on that. Do you cook?"

She blinked. "What?"

"Do you cook? I hired you to be my assistant. Which

includes things around the house. And I eat around the house."

"I cook," she said, reeling from the change of topic.

"Great. Have something ready for me, and if I'm not back before you knock off at five, just keep it warm."

Then he turned and walked out, leaving her feeling both relieved and utterly confused. All those positive thoughts from this morning seemed to be coming back to haunt her, mock her.

The work she could handle. It was the man that scared her.

THE FIRST WEEK of working with Hayley had been pretty good, in spite of that hiccup on the first day.

The one where he had touched her skin and felt just how soft it was. Something he never should have done.

But she was a good assistant. And every evening when he came in from dealing with ranch work his dinner was ready. That had been kind of a dick move, asking her to cook, but in truth, he hadn't put a very detailed job description in the ad. And she wasn't an employee of Gray Bear. She was his personal employee, and that meant he could expand her responsibilities.

At least, that was what he told himself as he approached the front porch Friday evening, his stomach already growling in anticipation. When he came in for the evening after the outside work was done, she was usually gone and the food was warming in the oven.

It was like having a wife. With none of the drawbacks *and* none of the perks.

But considering he could get those perks from a woman who wasn't in his house more than forty hours a week, he would take this happily.

He stomped up the front steps, kicking his boots

off before he went inside. He'd been walking through sludge in one of the far pastures and he didn't want to track in mud. His housekeeper didn't come until later in the week.

The corner of his mouth lifted as he processed that thought. He had a housekeeper. He didn't have to get on his hands and knees and scrub floors anymore. Which he had done. More times than he would care to recount. Most of the time the house he and Rebecca had shared while growing up had been messy.

It was small, and their belongings—basic though they were—created a lot of clutter. Plus, teenage boys weren't the best at keeping things deep cleaned. Especially not when they also had full-time jobs and were trying to finish high school. But when he knew child services would be by, he did his best.

He didn't now. He paid somebody else to do it. For a long time, adding those kinds of expenses had made both pride and anxiety burn in his gut. Adjusting to living at a new income level was not seamless. And since things had grown exponentially and so quickly, the adjustments had come even harder. Often in a million ways he couldn't anticipate. But he was working on it. Hiring a housekeeper. Hiring Hayley.

Pretty soon, he would give in and buy himself a new pair of boots.

He drew nearer to the kitchen, smelling something good. And then he heard footsteps, the clattering of dishes.

He braced his arms on either side of the doorway. Clearly, she hadn't heard him approach. She was bending down to pull something out of the oven, her sweet ass outlined to perfection by that prim little skirt.

There was absolutely nothing provocative about it. It

fell down past her knees, and when she stood straight it didn't display any curves whatsoever.

For a moment, he just admired his own commitment to being a dick. She could not be dressed more appropriately, and still his eyes were glued to her butt. And damn, his body liked what he saw.

"You're still here," he said, pushing away from the door and walking into the room. He had to break the tension stretching tight inside him. Step one was breaking the silence and making his presence known. Step two was going to be calling up one of the women he had associations with off and on.

Because he had to do something to take the edge off. Clearly, it had been too long since he'd gotten laid.

"Sorry," she said, wiping her hands on a dishcloth and making a few frantic movements. As though she wanted to look industrious, but didn't exactly have a specific task. "The roast took longer than I thought it would. But I did a little more paperwork while I waited. And I called the county to track down that permit."

"You don't have to justify all your time. Everything has gotten done this week. Plus, inefficient meat preparation was not on my list of reasons I might fire you."

She shrugged. "I thought you reserved the right to revise that list at any time."

"I do. But not today."

"I should be out of your hair soon." She walked around the counter and he saw she was barefoot. Earlier, he had been far too distracted by her backside to notice.

"Pretty sure that's a health code violation," he said.

She turned pink all the way up to her scalp. "Sorry. My feet hurt."

He thought of those low, sensible heels she always wore and he had to wonder what the point was to wearing shoes that ugly if they weren't even comfortable. The kind of women he usually went out with wore the kinds of shoes made for sitting. Or dancing on a pole.

But Hayley didn't look like she even knew what pole dancing was, let alone like she would jump up there and give it a try. She was... Well, she was damn near sweet.

Which was all wrong for him, in every way. He wasn't sweet.

He was successful. He was driven.

But he was temporary at best. And frankly, almost everyone in his life seemed grateful for that fact. No one stayed. Not his mother, not his father. Even his sister was off living her own life now.

So why he should spend even one moment looking at Hayley the way he'd been looking at her, he didn't know. He didn't have time for subtlety. He never had. He had always liked obvious women. Women who asked for what they wanted without any game-playing or shame.

He didn't want a wife. He didn't even want a serious girlfriend. Hell, he didn't want a casual girlfriend. When he went out it was with the express intention of hooking up. When it came to women, he didn't like a challenge.

His whole damned life was a challenge, and always had been. When he'd been raising his sister he couldn't bring anyone back to his place, which meant he needed someone with a place of their own, or someone willing to get busy in the back of a pickup truck.

Someone who understood he had only a couple free hours, and he wouldn't be sharing their bed all night.

Basically, his taste ran toward women who were all the things Hayley wasn't.

Cute ass or not.

None of those thoughts did anything to ease the tension in his stomach. No matter how succinctly they broke down just why he shouldn't find Hayley hot.

He nearly scoffed. She *wasn't* hot. She was… She would not be out of place as the wholesome face on a baking mix. Much more Little Debbie than Debbie Does Dallas.

"It's fine. I don't want you going lame on me."

She grinned. "No. Then you'd have to put me down."

"True. And if I lose more than one personal assistant that way people will start asking questions."

He could tell she wasn't sure if he was kidding or not. For a second, she looked downright concerned.

"I have not sent, nor do I intend to send, any of my employees—present or former—to the glue factory. Don't look at me like that."

She bit her lower lip, and that forced him to spend a moment examining just how lush it was. He didn't like that. She needed to stop bending over, and to do nothing that would draw attention to her mouth. Maybe, when he revised the list of things he might fire her for, he would add drawing attention to attractive body parts to the list.

"I can never tell when you're joking."

"Me, either," he said.

That time she did laugh. "You know," she said, "you could smile."

"Takes too much energy."

The timer went off and she bustled back to the stove. "Okay," she said, "it should be ready now." She pulled a little pan out of the oven and took the lid off. It was full of roast and potatoes, carrots and onions. The kind of home-cooked meal he imagined a lot of kids grew up on.

For him, traditional fare had been more along the lines of flour tortillas with cheese or ramen noodles.

Something cheap, easy and full of carbs. Just enough to keep you going.

His stomach growled in appreciation, and that was the kind of hunger associated with Hayley that he could accept.

"I should go," she said, starting to walk toward the kitchen door.

"Stay."

As soon as he made the offer Jonathan wanted to bite his tongue off. He did not need to encourage spending more time in closed off spaces with her. Although dinner might be a good chance to prove that he could easily master those weird bursts of attraction.

"No," she said, and he found himself strangely relieved. "I should go."

"Don't be an idiot," he said, surprising himself yet again. "Dinner is ready here. And it's late. Plus there's no way I can eat all this."

"Okay," she said, clearly hesitant.

"Come on now. Stop looking at me like you think I'm going to bite you. You've been reading too much *Twilight*. Indians don't really turn into wolves."

Her face turned really red then. "That's not what I was thinking. I don't… I'm not afraid of you."

She was afraid of something. And what concerned him most was that it might be the same thing he was fighting against.

"I really was teasing you," he said. "I have a little bit of a reputation in town, but I didn't earn half of it."

"Are you saying people in town are…prejudiced?"

"I wouldn't go that far. I mean, I wouldn't say it's on purpose. But whether it's because I grew up poor or it's because I'm brown, people have always given me a wide berth."

"I didn't… I mean, I've never seen people act that way."

"Well, they wouldn't. Not to you."

She blinked slightly. "I'll serve dinner now."

"Don't worry," he said, "the story has a happy ending. I have a lot of money now, and that trumps anything else. People have no issue hiring me to build these days. Though, I remember the first time my old boss put me on as the leader of the building crew, and the guy whose house we were building had a problem with it. He didn't think I should be doing anything that required too much skill. Was more comfortable with me just swinging the hammer, not telling other people where to swing it."

She took plates down from the cupboard, holding them close to her chest. "That's awful."

"People are awful."

A line creased her forehead. "They definitely can be."

"Stop hugging my dinner plate to your shirt. That really isn't sanitary. We can eat in here." He gestured to the countertop island. She set the plates down hurriedly, then started dishing food onto them.

He sighed heavily, moving to where she was and taking the big fork and knife out of her hands. "Have a seat. How much do you want?"

"Oh," she said, "I don't need much."

He ignored her, filling the plate completely, then filling his own. After that, he went to the fridge and pulled out a beer. "Want one?"

She shook her head. "I don't drink."

He frowned, then looked back into the fridge. "I don't have anything else."

"Water is fine."

He got her a glass and poured some water from the

spigot in the fridge. He handed it to her, regarding her like she was some kind of alien life-form. The small conversation had really highlighted the gulf between them.

It should make him feel even more ashamed about looking at her butt.

Except shame was pretty hard for him to come by.

"Tell me what you think about people, Hayley." He took a bite of the roast and nearly gave her a raise then and there.

"No matter what things look like on the surface, you never know what someone is going through. It surprised me how often someone who had been smiling on Sunday would come into the office and break down in tears on Tuesday afternoon, saying they needed to talk to the pastor. Everyone has problems, and I do my best not to add to them."

"That's a hell of a lot nicer than most people deserve."

"Okay, what do you think about people?" she asked, clasping her hands in front of her and looking so damn interested and sincere he wasn't quite sure how to react.

"I think they're a bunch of self-interested bastards. And that's fair enough, because so am I. But whenever somebody asks for something, or offers me something, I ask myself what they will get out of it. If I can't figure out how they'll benefit, that's when I get worried."

"Not everyone is after money or power," she said. He could see she really believed what she said. He wasn't sure what to make of that.

"All right," he conceded, "maybe they aren't all after money. But they are looking to gain something. Everyone is. You can't get through life any other way. Trust me."

"I don't know. I never thought of it that way. In terms of who could get me what. At least, that's not how I've lived."

"Then you're an anomaly."

She shook her head. "My father is like that, too. He really does want to help people. He cares. Pastoring a small church in a little town doesn't net you much power or money."

"Of course it does. You hold the power of people's salvation in your hands. Pass around the plate every week. Of course you get power and money." Jonathan shook his head. "Being the leader of local spirituality is power, honey, trust me."

Her cheeks turned pink. "Okay. You might have a point. But my father doesn't claim to have the key to anyone's salvation. And the money in that basket goes right back into the community. Or into keeping the doors of the church open. My father believes in living the same way the community lives. Not higher up. So whatever baggage you might have about church, that's specific to your experience. It has nothing to do with my father or his faith."

She spoke with such raw certainty that Jonathan was tempted to believe her. But he knew too much about human nature.

Still, he liked all that conviction burning inside her. He liked that she believed what she said, even if he couldn't.

If he had been born with any ideals, he couldn't remember them now. He'd never had the luxury of having faith in humanity, as Hayley seemed to have. No, his earliest memory of his father was the old man's fist connecting with his face. Jonathan had never had the chance to believe the best of anybody.

He had been introduced to the worst far too early.

And he didn't know very many people who'd had different experiences.

The optimism she seemed to carry, the softness combined with strength, fascinated him. He wanted to draw closer to it, to her, to touch her skin, to see if she was strong enough to take the physical demands he put on a woman who shared his bed.

To see how shocked she might be when he told her what those demands were. In explicit detail.

He clenched his jaw tight, clamping his teeth down hard. He was not going to find out, for a couple reasons. The first being that she was his employee, and off-limits. The second being that all those things that fascinated him would be destroyed if he got close, if he laid even one finger on her.

Cynicism bled from his pores, and he damn well knew it. He had earned it. He wasn't one of those bored rich people overcome by ennui just because life had gone so well he wanted to create problems so he had something to battle against.

No. He had fought every step of the way, and he had been disappointed by people in every way imaginable. He had earned his feelings about people, that was for damn sure.

But he wasn't certain he wanted to pass that cynicism on to Hayley. No, she was like a pristine wilderness area. Unspoiled by humans. And his first inclination was to explore every last inch, to experience all that beauty, all that majesty. But he had to leave it alone. He had to leave it looked at, not touched.

Hayley Thompson was the same. Untouched. He had to leave her unspoiled. Exploring that beauty would only leave it ruined, and he couldn't do that. He wouldn't.

"I think it's sad," she said, her voice muted. "That you can't see the good in other people."

"I've been bitten in the ass too many times," he said, his tone harder than he'd intended it to be. "I'm glad you haven't been."

"I haven't had the chance to be. But that's kind of the point of what I'm doing. Going out, maybe getting bitten in the ass." Her cheeks turned bright red. "I can't believe I said that."

"What?"

"That word."

That made his stomach feel like it had been hollowed out. *"Ass?"*

Her cheeks turned even redder. "Yes. I don't say things like that."

"I guess not… Being the church secretary and all."

Now he just felt… Well, she made him feel rough and uncultured, dirty and hard and unbending as steel. Everything she was not. She was small, delicate and probably far too easy to break. Just like he'd imagined earlier, she was…set apart. Unspoiled. And here he had already spoiled her a little bit. She'd said ass, right there in his kitchen.

And she'd looked shocked as hell by her own behavior.

"You don't have to say things like that if you don't want to," he said. "Not every experience is a good experience. You shouldn't try things just to try them. Hell, if I'd had the choice of staying innocent of human nature, maybe I would have taken that route instead. Don't ruin that nice vision of the world you have."

She frowned. "You know, everybody talks about going out and experiencing things…"

"Sure. But when people say that, they want control

over those experiences. Believe me, having the blinders ripped off is not necessarily the best thing."

She nodded slowly. "I guess I understand that. What kinds of experiences do you think are bad?"

Immediately, he thought of about a hundred bad things he wanted to do to her. Most of them in bed, all of them naked. He sucked in a sharp breath through his teeth. "I don't think we need to get into that."

"I'm curious."

"You know what they say about curiosity and the cat, right?"

"But I'm not a cat."

"No," he said, "you are Hayley, and you should be grateful for the things you've been spared. Maybe you should even go back to the church office."

"No," she said, frowning. "I don't want to. Maybe I don't want to *experience everything*—I can see how you're probably right about that. But I can't just stay in one place, sheltered for the rest of my life. I have to figure out…who I am and what I want."

That made him laugh, because it was such a naive sentiment. He had never stood back and asked himself who the hell Jonathan Bear was, and what he wanted out of life. He hadn't given a damn how he made his money as long as he made it.

As far as he was concerned, dreams were for people with a lot of time on their hands. He had to *do*. Even as a kid, he couldn't think, couldn't wonder; he had to act.

She might as well be speaking a foreign language. "You'll have to tell me what that's like."

"What?"

"That quest to find yourself. Let me know if it's any more effective than just living your life and seeing what happens."

"Okay, now you've made me feel silly."

He took another bite of dinner. Maybe he should back down, because he didn't want her to quit. He would like to continue eating her food. And, frankly, he would like to keep looking at her.

Just because he should back down didn't mean he was going to.

"There was no safety net in my life," he said, not bothering to reassure her. "There never has been. I had to work my ass off from the moment I was old enough to get paid to do something. Hell, even before then. I would get what I could from the store, expired products, whatever, so we would have something to eat. That teaches you a lot about yourself. You don't have to go looking. In those situations, you find out whether you're a survivor or not. Turns out I am. And I've never really seen what more I needed to know."

"I don't… I don't have anything to say to that."

"Yeah," he returned. "My life story is kind of a bummer."

"Not now," she said softly. "You have all this. You have the business, you have this house."

"Yeah, I expect a man could find himself here. Well, unless he got lost because it was so big." He smiled at her, but she didn't look at all disarmed by the gesture. Instead, she looked thoughtful, and that made his stomach feel tight.

He didn't really do meaningful conversation. He especially didn't do it with women.

Yet here he was, telling this woman more about himself than he could remember telling anyone. Rebecca knew everything, of course. Well, as much as she'd observed while being a kid in that situation. They didn't need to talk about it. It was just life. But other people…

Well, he didn't see the point in talking about the deficit he'd started with. He preferred people assume he'd sprung out of the ground powerful and successful. They took him more seriously.

He'd had enough disadvantages, and he wouldn't set himself up for any more.

But there was something about Hayley—her openness, her honesty—that made him want to talk. That made him feel bad for being insincere. Because she was just so...so damn real.

How would he have been if he'd had a softer existence? Maybe he wouldn't be as hard. Maybe a different life would have meant not breaking a woman like this the moment he put his hands on her.

It was moot. Because he hadn't had a different life. And if he had, he probably wouldn't have made half as much of himself.

"You don't have to feel bad for wanting more," he said finally. "Just because other people don't have it easy, doesn't mean you don't have your own kind of hard."

"It's just difficult to decide what to do when other people's expectations feel so much bigger than your own dreams."

"I know a little something about that. Only in my case, the expectations other people had for me were that I would end up dead of a drug overdose or in prison. So, all things considered, I figured I would blow past those expectations and give people something to talk about."

"I just want to travel."

"Is that it?"

A smile played in the corner of her lips, and he found himself wondering what it might be like to taste that smile. "Okay. And see a famous landmark. Like the Eiffel Tower or Big Ben. And I want to dance."

"Have you never danced?"

"No!" She looked almost comically horrified. "Where would I have danced?"

"Well, your brother does own a bar. And there is line dancing."

"I can't even go into Ace's bar. My parents don't go. We can go to the brewery. Because they serve more food there. And it's not called a bar."

"That seems like some arbitrary shit."

Her cheeks colored, and he didn't know if it was because he'd pointed out a flaw in her parents' logic or because he had cursed. "Maybe. But I follow their lead. It's important for us to keep away from the appearance of evil."

"Now, that I don't know anything about. Because nobody cares much about my appearance."

She cleared her throat. "So," she said. "Dancing."

Suddenly, an impulse stole over him, one he couldn't quite understand or control. Before he knew it, he was pushing his chair back and standing up, extending his hand. "All right, Hayley Thompson, Paris has to wait awhile. But we can take care of the dancing right now."

"What?" Her pretty eyes flew wide, her soft lips rounded into a perfect O.

"Dance with me, Hayley."

CHAPTER FOUR

HAYLEY WAS PRETTY sure she was hallucinating.

Because there was no way her stern boss was standing there, his large, work-worn hand stretched toward her, his dark eyes glittering with an intensity she could only guess at the meaning of, having just asked her to dance. Except, no matter how many times she blinked, he was still standing there. And the words were still echoing in her head.

"There's no music."

He took his cell phone out of his pocket, opened an app and set the phone on the table, a slow country song filling the air. "There," he said. "Music accomplished. Now, dance with me."

"I thought men *asked* for a dance, I didn't think they demanded one."

"Some men, maybe. But not me. But remember, I don't give a damn about appearances."

"I think I might admire that about you."

"You should," he said, his tone grave.

She felt… Well, she felt breathless and fluttery, and she didn't know what to do. But if she said no, then he would know just how inexperienced she was. He would know she was making a giant internal deal about his hand touching hers, about the possibility of being held against his body. That she felt strange, unnerving sensations skittering over her skin when she looked at him. She was afraid he could see her too clearly.

Isn't this what you wanted? To reach out? To take a chance?

It was. So she did.

She took his hand. She was still acclimating to his heat, to being touched by him, skin to skin, when she found herself pressed flush against his chest, his hand enveloping hers. He wrapped his arm around her waist, his palm hot on her lower back.

She shivered. She didn't know why. Because she wasn't cold. No. She was hot. And so was he. Hot and hard, so much harder than she had imagined another person could be.

She had never, ever been this close to a man before. Had never felt a man's skin against hers. His hand was rough, from all that hard work. What might it feel like if he touched her skin elsewhere? If he pushed his other hand beneath her shirt and slid his fingertips against her lower back?

That thought sent a sharp pang straight to her stomach, unfurling something inside her, making her blood run faster.

She stared straight at his shoulder, at an innocuous spot on his flannel shirt. Because she couldn't bring herself to raise her eyes and look at that hard, lean face, at the raw beauty she had never fully appreciated before.

He would probably be offended to be characterized as beautiful. But he was. In the same way that a mountain was beautiful. Tall, strong and unmoving.

She gingerly curled her fingers around his shoulder, while he took the lead, his hold on her firm and sure as he established a rhythm she could follow.

The grace in his steps surprised her. Caused her to

meet his gaze. She both regretted it and relished it at the same time. Because it was a shame to stare at flannel when she could be looking into those dark eyes, but they also made her feel…absolutely and completely undone.

"Where did you learn to dance?" she asked, her voice sounding as breathless as she had feared it might.

But she was curious about this man who had grown up in such harsh circumstances, who had clearly devoted most of his life to hard work with no frills, who had learned to do this.

"A woman," he said, a small smile tugging at the edges of his lips.

She was shocked by the sudden, sour turn in her stomach. It was deeply unpleasant, and she didn't know what to do to make it stop. Imagining what other woman he might have learned this from, how he might have held her…

It hurt. In the strangest way.

"Was she…somebody special to you? Did you love her?"

His smile widened. "No. I've never loved anybody. Not anybody besides my sister. But I sure as hell *wanted* something from that woman, and she wanted to dance."

It took Hayley a while to figure out the meaning behind those words. "Oh," she said, "she wanted to dance and you wanted…" That feeling in her stomach intensified, but along with it came a strange sort of heat. Because he was holding *her* now, dancing with her. *She* wanted to dance. Did that mean that he…?

"Don't look at me like that, Hayley. This," he said, tightening his hold on her and dipping her slightly, his face moving closer to hers, "is just a dance."

She was a tangle of unidentified feelings—knots

in her stomach, an ache between her thighs—and she didn't want to figure out what any of it meant.

"Good," she said, wishing she could have infused some conviction into that word.

The music slowed, the bass got heavier. And he matched the song effortlessly, his hips moving firmly against hers with every deep pulse of the beat.

This time, she couldn't ignore the lyrics. About two people and the fire they created together. She wouldn't have fully understood what that meant even a few minutes ago, but in Jonathan's arms, with the heat that burned from his body, fire was what she felt.

Like her nerve endings had been set ablaze, like a spark had been stoked low inside her. If he moved in just the wrong way—or just the right way—the flames in him would catch hold of that spark in her and they would combust.

She let her eyes flutter closed, gave herself over to the moment, to the song, to the feel of him, the scent of him. She was dancing. And she liked it a lot more than she had anticipated and in a way she hadn't imagined she could.

She had pictured laughing, lightness, with people all around, like at the bar she had never been to before. But this was something else. A deep intimacy that grew from somewhere inside her chest and intensified as the music seemed to draw them more tightly together.

She drew in a breath, letting her eyes open and look up at him. And then she froze.

He was staring at her, the glitter in his dark eyes almost predatory. She didn't know why that word came to mind. Didn't even know what it might mean in this context. When a man looked at you like he was a wildcat and you were a potential meal.

Then her eyes dipped down to his mouth. Her own lips tingled in response and she was suddenly aware of how dry they were. She slid her tongue over them, completely self-conscious about the action even as she did it, yet unable to stop.

She was satisfied when that predatory light in his eyes turned sharper. More intense.

She didn't know what she was doing. But she found herself moving closer to him. She didn't know why. She just knew she had to. With the same bone-deep impulse that came with the need to draw breath, she had to lean in closer to Jonathan Bear. She couldn't fight it; she didn't want to. And until her lips touched his, she didn't even know what she was moving toward.

But when their mouths met, it all became blindingly clear.

She had thought about these feelings in terms of fire, but this sensation was something bigger, something infinitely more destructive. This was an explosion. One she felt all the way down to her toes; one that hit every place in between.

She was shaking. Trembling like a leaf in the wind. Or maybe even like a tree in a storm.

He was the storm.

His hold changed. He let go of her hand, withdrew his arm from around her waist, pressed both palms against her cheeks as he took the kiss deeper, harder.

It was like drowning. Like dying. Only she didn't want to fight it. Didn't want to turn away. She couldn't have, even if she'd tried. Because his grip was like iron, his body like a rock wall. They weren't moving in time with the music anymore. No. This was a different rhythm entirely. He propelled her backward, until her shoulder blades met with the dining room wall, his hard body pressed against hers.

He was hard. Everywhere. Hard chest, hard stomach, hard thighs. And that insistent hardness pressing against her hip.

She gasped when she realized what that was. And he consumed her shocked sound, taking advantage of her parted lips to slide his tongue between them.

She released her hold on him, her hands floating up without a place to land, and she curled her fingers into fists. She surrendered herself to the kiss, to him. His hold was tight enough to keep her anchored to the earth, to keep her anchored to him.

She let him have control. Let him take the lead. She didn't know how to dance, and she didn't know how to do this. But he did.

So she let him show her. This was on her list, too, though she hadn't been brave enough to say it, even to herself. To know passion. To experience her first kiss.

She wanted it to go on and on. She never wanted it to end. If she could just be like this, those hot hands cupping her face, that insistent mouth devouring hers, she was pretty sure she could skip the Eiffel Tower.

She felt him everywhere, not just his kiss, not just his touch. Her breasts felt heavy. They ached. In any other circumstances, she might be horrified by that. But she didn't possess the capacity to be horrified, not right now. Not when everything else felt so good. She wasn't ashamed; she wasn't embarrassed—not of the heavy feeling in her breasts, not of the honeyed, slick feeling between her thighs.

This just made sense.

Right now, what she felt was the only thing that made sense. It was the only thing she wanted.

Kissing Jonathan Bear was a necessity.

He growled, flexing his hips toward hers, making it so she couldn't ignore his arousal. And the evidence of his desire carved out a hollow feeling inside her. Made her shake, made her feel like her knees had dissolved into nothing and that without his powerful hold she would crumple onto the floor.

She still wasn't touching him. Her hands were still away from his body, trembling. But she didn't want to do anything to break the moment. Didn't want to make a sound, didn't want to make the wrong move. She didn't want to turn him off or scare him away. Didn't want to do anything to telegraph her innocence. Because it would probably freak him out.

Right, Hayley, like he totally believes you're a sex kitten who's kissed a hundred men.

She didn't know what to do with her hands, let alone her lips, her tongue. She was receiving, not giving. But she had a feeling if she did anything else she would look like an idiot.

Suddenly, he released his hold on her, moving away from her so quickly she might have thought she'd hurt him.

She was dazed, still leaning against the wall. If she hadn't been, she would have collapsed. Her hands were still in the air, clenched into fists, and her breath came in short, harsh bursts. So did his, if the sharp rise and fall of his chest was anything to go by.

"That was a mistake," he said, his voice hard. His words were everything she had feared they might be.

"No, it wasn't," she said, her lips feeling numb, and a little bit full, making it difficult for her to talk. Or maybe the real difficulty came from feeling like her head was filled with bees, buzzing all around and scrambling her thoughts.

"Yes," he said, his voice harder, "it was."

"No," she insisted. "It was a great kiss. A really, really good kiss. I didn't want it to end."

Immediately, she regretted saying that. Because it had been way too revealing. She supposed it was incredibly gauche to tell the guy you'd just kissed that you could have kissed him forever. She tried to imagine how Grant, the youth pastor, might have reacted to that. He would have told her she needed to go to an extra Bible study. Or that she needed to marry him first.

He certainly wouldn't have looked at her the way Jonathan was. Like he wanted to eat her whole, but was barely restraining himself from doing just that. "That's exactly the problem," he returned, the words like iron, "because I *did* want it to end. But in a much different way than it did."

"I don't understand." Her face was hot, and she was humiliated now. So she didn't see why she shouldn't go whole hog. Let him know she was fully outside her comfort zone and she wasn't keeping up with all his implications. She needed stated facts, not innuendo.

"I didn't want to keep kissing you forever. I wanted to pull your top off, shove your skirt up and bury myself inside of you. Is that descriptive enough for you?"

It was. And he had succeeded in shocking her. She wasn't stupid. She knew he was hard, and she knew what that meant. But even given that fact, she hadn't really imagined he wanted... Not with her.

And this was just her first kiss. She wasn't ready for more. Wasn't ready for another step away from the person she had been taught to be.

What about the person you want to be?

She looked at her boss, who was also the most beautiful man she had ever seen. That hadn't been her immediate thought when she'd met him, but she had settled into it as the truth. As certain as the fact the sky was blue and the pine trees that dotted the mountains were deep forest green.

So maybe... Even though it was shocking. Even though it would be a big step, and undoubtedly a big mistake... Maybe she did want it.

"You better go," he said, his voice rough.

"Maybe I don't—"

"You do," he said. "Trust me. And I want you to."

She was confused. Because he had just said he wanted her, and now he was saying he wanted her to go. She didn't understand men. She didn't understand this. She wanted to cry. But a lick of pride slid its way up her spine, keeping her straight, keeping her tears from falling.

Pride she hadn't known she possessed. But then, she hadn't realized she possessed the level of passion that had just exploded between them, either. So it was a day for new discoveries.

"That's fine. I just wanted to have some fun. I can go have it with someone else."

She turned on her heel and walked out of the dining room, out the front door and down the porch steps as quickly as possible. It was dark now, trees like inky bottle brushes rising around her, framing the midnight-blue sky dotted with stars. It was beautiful, but she didn't care. Not right now. She felt...hurt. Emotionally. Physically. The unsatisfied ache between her thighs intensified with the pain growing in her heart.

It was awful. All of it.

It made her want to run. Run back to her parents' house. Run back to the church office.

Being *good* had always been safe.

She had been so certain she wanted to escape safety. Only a few moments earlier she'd needed that escape, felt it might be her salvation. Except she could see now that it was ruin. Utter and complete ruin.

With shaking hands, she pushed the button that undid the locks on her car door and got inside, jamming the key into the ignition and starting it up, a tear sliding down her cheek as she started to back out of the driveway.

She refused to let this ruin her, or this job, or this step she was taking on her own.

She was finding independence, learning new things.

As she turned onto the two-lane highway that would take her back home, she clung to that truth. To the fact that, even though her first kiss had ended somewhat disastrously, it had still shown her something about herself.

It had shown her exactly why it was a good thing she hadn't gotten married to that youthful crush of hers. It would have been dishonest, and not fair to him or to her.

She drove on autopilot, eventually pulling into her driveway and stumbling inside her apartment, lying down on her bed without changing out of her work clothes.

Was she a fallen woman? To want Jonathan like she had. A man she wasn't in love with, a man she wasn't planning to marry.

Had that passion always been there? Or was it created by Jonathan? This feeling. This *need*.

She bit back a sob and forced a smile. She'd had her first kiss. And she wouldn't dwell on what it might mean. Or on the fact that he had sent her away. Or on the fact that—for a moment at least—she had been consumed with the desire for more.

She'd had her first kiss. At twenty-four. And that felt like a change deep inside her body.

Hayley Thompson had a new apartment, a new job, and she had been kissed.

So maybe it wasn't safe. But she had decided she wanted something more than safety, hadn't she?

She would focus on the victories and simply ignore the rest.

No matter that this victory made her body burn in a way that kept her up for the rest of the night.

CHAPTER FIVE

HE HADN'T EXPECTED her to show up Monday morning.
But there she was, in the entryway of the house, hands
clasped in front of her, dark hair pulled back in a neat
bun. Like she was compensating for what had happened
between them Friday night.

"Good morning," he said, taking a sip of his coffee.
"I half expected you to take the day off."

"No," she said, her voice shot through with steel,
"I can't just take days off. My boss is a tyrant. He'll
fire me."

He laughed, mostly to disguise the physical response
those words created in him. There was something about
her. About all that softness, that innocence, combined
with the determination he hadn't realized existed inside
her until this moment.

She wasn't just soft, or innocent. She was a force to
be reckoned with, and she was bent on showing him
that now.

"If he's so bad why do you want to keep the job?"

"My job history is pathetic," she said, walking ahead
of him to the stairs. "And, as he has pointed out to me
many times, he is not my daddy. My previous boss was.
I need something a bit more impressive on my résumé."

"Right. For when you do your traveling."

"Maybe I'll get a job in London," she shot back.

"What's the biggest city you've been to, Hayley?"

he asked, following her up the stairs and down the hall toward the office.

"Portland," she said.

He laughed. "London is a little bit bigger."

"I don't care. That's what I want. I want a city where I can walk down the street and not run into anybody that I've ever seen before. All new people. All new faces. I can't imagine that. I can't imagine living a life where I do what I want and not hear a retelling of the night before coming out of my mother's mouth at breakfast the next morning."

"Have you ever done anything worthy of being recounted by your mother?"

Color infused her cheeks. "Okay, specifically, the incident I'm referring to is somebody telling my mother they were proud of me because they saw me giving a homeless woman a dollar."

He laughed. He couldn't help himself, and her cheeks turned an even more intense shade of pink that he knew meant she was furious.

She stamped. Honest to God stamped, like an old-time movie heroine. "What's so funny?"

"Even the gossip about you is good, Hayley Thompson. For the life of me, I can't figure out why you hate that so much."

"Because I can't *do* anything. Jonathan, if you had kissed me in my brother's bar... Can you even imagine? My parents' phone would have been ringing off the hook."

His body hardened at the mention of the kiss. He had been convinced she would avoid the topic.

But he should've known by now that when it came to Hayley he couldn't anticipate her next move. She was more direct, more up-front than he had thought she might be. Was it because of her innocence that she faced things so squarely? Because she hadn't experienced a whole range of consequences for much of anything yet?

"I wouldn't do that to you," he said. "Because you're right. If anybody suspected something unprofessional had happened between us, it would cause trouble for you."

"I didn't mean it that way." She looked horrified. "I mean, the way people would react if they thought I was… It has nothing to do with you."

"It does. More than you realize. You've been sheltered. But just because you don't know my reputation, that doesn't mean other people in town don't know it. Most people who know you're a good girl know I am a bad man, Hayley. And if anyone suspected I had put my hands on you, I'm pretty sure there would be torches and pitchforks at my front door by sunset."

"Well," she said, "that isn't fair. Because *I* kissed *you.*"

"I'm going out on a limb here—of the two of us, I have more experience."

She clasped her hands in front of her and shuffled her feet. "Maybe."

"Maybe nothing, honey. I'm not the kind of man you need to be seen with. So, you're right. You do need to get away. Maybe you should go to London. Hell, I don't know."

"Now you want to get rid of me?"

"Now you're just making it so I can't win."

"I don't mean to," she said, with that trademark sincerity that was no less alarming for being typical of her. "But I don't know what to do with…with this."

She bit her lip, and the motion drew his eye to that

lush mouth of hers. Forced him back to the memory of kissing it. Of tasting her.

He wanted her. No question about it.

He couldn't pretend otherwise. But he could at least be honest with himself about why. He wanted her for all the wrong reasons. He wanted her because some sick, caveman part of him wanted to get all that *pretty* dirty. Part of him wanted to corrupt her. To show her everything she was missing. To make her fall from grace a lasting one.

And that was some fucked up shit.

Didn't mean he didn't feel it.

"Well, after I earn enough money, that's probably what I'll do," she said. "And since this isn't going anywhere… I should probably just get to work. And we shouldn't talk about it anymore."

"No," he said, "we shouldn't."

"It was just a kiss."

His stomach twisted. Not because it disappointed him to hear her say that, but because she had to say it for her own peace of mind. She was innocent enough that a kiss worked her up. It meant something to her. Hell, sex barely meant anything to him. Much less a kiss.

Except for hers. You remember hers far too well.

"Just a kiss," he confirmed.

"Good. So give me some spreadsheets."

THE REST OF the week went well. If well meant dodging moments alone with Jonathan, catching herself staring at him at odd times during the day and having difficulty dreaming of anything except him at night.

"Thank God it's Friday," she said into the emptiness of her living room.

She didn't feel like cooking. She had already made

a meal for Jonathan at his house, and then hightailed it out of there as quickly as possible. She knew that if she'd made enough for herself and took food with her he wouldn't have minded, but she was doing her best to keep the lines between them firm.

She couldn't have any more blurred lines. They couldn't have any more…kissing and other weirdness. Just thinking about kissing Jonathan made her feel restless, edgy. She didn't like it. Or maybe she liked it too much.

She huffed out a growl and wandered into the kitchen, opening the cupboard and pulling out a box of chocolate cereal.

It was the kind of cereal her parents never would have bought. Because it wasn't good for you, and it was expensive. So she had bought it for herself, because she had her own job, she was an adult and she made her own decisions.

Do you?

She shut out that snotty little voice. Yes, she *did* make her own decisions. Here she was, living in her own place, working at the job she had chosen. Yes, she very much made her own decisions. She had even kissed Jonathan. Yes, that had been her idea.

Which made the fallout her fault. But she wasn't going to dwell on that.

"I'm dwelling," she muttered. "I'm a liar, and I'm dwelling." She took down a bowl and poured herself a large portion of the chocolaty cereal. Then she stared at it. She didn't want to eat cereal by herself for dinner.

She was feeling restless, reckless.

She was feeling something a whole lot like desperation.

Because of that kiss.

The kiss she had just proposed she wasn't going to think about, the kiss she couldn't let go of. The kiss that made her burn, made her ache and made her wonder about all the mysteries in life she had yet to uncover.

Yeah, *that* kiss.

She had opened a floodgate. She'd uncovered all this potential for passion inside herself, and then she had to stuff it back down deep.

Jonathan Bear was not the only man in the world. Jonathan Bear wasn't even the only man in Copper Ridge.

She could find another guy if she wanted to.

Of course, if she went out, there would be all those gossip issues she and Jonathan had discussed earlier in the week.

That was why she had to get out of this town.

It struck her then, like a horse kicking her square in the chest, that she was running away. So she could be who she wanted to be without anybody knowing about it. So she could make mistakes and minimize the consequences.

So she could be brave and a coward all at the same time.

That's what it was. It was cowardice. And she was not very impressed with herself.

"Look at you," she scolded, "eating cold cereal on a Friday night by yourself when you would rather be out getting kissed."

Her heart started to beat faster. Where would she go?

And then it hit her. There was one place she could go on a Friday night where nobody from church would recognize her, and even if they did recognize her, they probably wouldn't tell on her because by doing so they would be telling on themselves.

Of course, going there would introduce the problem of her older brother. But Ace had struck out on his own when he was only seventeen years old. He was her inspiration in all this. So he should understand Hayley's need for independence.

And that was when she made her decision. It was Friday night, and she was going out.

She was going to one of the few places in town where she had never set foot before.

Ace's bar.

CHAPTER SIX

"I'D LIKE A HAMBURGER," Hayley said, adjusting her dress and trying not to look like she was about to commit a crime.

"Hayley?" Her brother looked at her as if she had grown another head. "What are you doing in my bar?"

"I'm here to have a hamburger. And…a beer."

Ace shook his head. "You don't want beer."

Darn him for being right. She couldn't stand the smell of the stuff, and she'd honestly never even been tempted to taste it.

"No," she agreed. "I want a Coke."

"I will get you a Coke. Are Mom and Dad here?"

She sighed heavily. "No, they're not. I do go places without them. I moved out."

"I know. We talked about it last time Sierra and I went over for dinner."

Hayley's brother had never much cared about his reputation, or about what anyone thought of him. She had been jealous of that for a long time. For years, Ace had been a total hellion and a womanizer, until he'd settled down and married the town rodeo princess, Sierra West. Now the two of them had one child and another on the way, and Ace's position in the community had improved vastly.

"Right. Well, I'm just saying." She traced an imaginary pattern over the bar top with the tip of her finger. "Did I tell you I quit working at the church?"

Ace look surprised by that. "No."

"Well," she said, "I did. I'm working for Jonathan Bear. Helping out with things around the house and in the office."

Ace frowned. "Well, that probably isn't very much fun. He's kind of a grumpy sumbitch."

"I didn't know you knew him all that well."

"He's my future sister-in-law's brother," Ace said, "but no, I don't know him *well*. He's not very sociable. It's not like he comes to the West family gatherings."

"He said he knows you because he buys beer from you."

"That's how everybody knows me," Ace said.

"Except for me."

"You were *trying* to buy beer from me. I'm just not going to sell one to you."

"That's not fair."

"Sure it is," he said, smiling. "Because you don't actually want to buy beer from me. You're just trying to prove a point."

She scowled. She hated that Ace seemed to understand her so well. "Okay, maybe so. I'm kind of proving a point by being here, I guess."

"Well," he said, "it's all right by me."

"Good."

"I kind of wish you would have come on another night, though," he said, "because I have to go. I promised Sierra I would be home early, so I'm about to take off. But I'll tell Jasmine to keep an eye on you."

"I don't need anybody to keep an eye on me."

"Yes," Ace said, laughing, "you do."

Hayley frowned, and plotted how to order a beer

when her brother was gone. Ultimately, she decided to stick with Coke, but when the dancing started, she knew that while she might stay away from alcohol, she didn't want to stay seated. She had danced once. And she had liked it.

She was going to do it again.

JONATHAN DIDN'T KNOW what in blazes he was doing at Ace's. Sure, he knew what he'd told himself while getting ready, his whole body restless thanks to memories of kissing Hayley.

He had continued to push those thoughts down while pacing around the house, and then, after a while, he'd decided to go out and find someone to hook up with. He didn't do that kind of thing, not anymore. He had a couple of women he called; he didn't go trawling bars. He was too old for that.

But right now, he was too much of a hazard to his innocent assistant, and he needed to take the edge off.

And it occurred to him that if he went to Ace's bar and found somebody, the news might filter back to Hayley.

Even though she might find it upsetting, it would be beneficial in the long run. She didn't want to mess with a man like him, not really. It was only that she was too innocent realize the dangers. But she would, eventually, and she would thank him.

That decision made, he'd hauled his ass down to the bar as quickly as possible.

By the time he walked in, his mood had not improved. He had thought it might. The decision to find a willing woman should have cheered him up. But he felt far from cheered. Maybe because an anonymous body was the last thing he wanted.

He wanted *Hayley*.

Whether he should or not. But he wasn't going to have Hayley. So he would have to get the hell over it.

He moved to the bar and then looked over at the dance floor. His chest tightened up. His body hardened. There was a petite brunette in a formfitting dress dancing with no one in particular. Two men hovered nearby, clearly not minding as she turned to and away from each of them, giving them both just a little bit of attention.

She reminded him of Hayley. Out there on the dance floor acting like nothing close to Hayley.

Then she turned, her dark hair shimmering behind her in a stream, a bright smile on her face, and he could barely process his thoughts. Because it was Hayley. *His* Hayley, out there in the middle of the dance floor, wearing a dress that showed off the figure her clothes had only hinted at before. Sure, in comparison to a lot of women, there was nothing flashy about it, but for Hayley Thompson, it was damned flashy.

And he was… Well, he would be damned if he was going to let those guys put their hands on her.

Yeah, he was bad news. Yeah, he was the kind of guy she should stay well away from. But those guys weren't any better. College douche bags. Probably in their twenties, closer to her age, sure, but not the kind of men who knew how to handle a woman. Especially not one as inexperienced as Hayley.

She would need a man who could guide the experience, show her what she liked. A man who could unlock the mysteries of sex, of her body.

Dickwads that age were better off with an empty dorm room and a half bottle of lotion.

And there was no way in hell they were getting their hands on her.

Without ordering, he moved away from the bar and went out on the dance floor. "You're done here," he said to one of the guys, who looked at him as though Jonathan had just threatened his life. His tone had been soft and even, but it was nice to know the younger man had heard the implied threat loud and clear.

Hayley hadn't noticed his approach, or that the other guy had scurried off to the other end of the dance floor. She was too involved with the guy she was currently dancing with to notice. She was shaking her head, her eyes closed, her body swaying to the music. A completely different kind of dancing than the two of them had done last week.

Then her current dance partner caught Jonathan's eye and paled. He slunk off into the shadows, too.

If Jonathan hadn't already found them wanting when it came to Hayley, he would have now. If they were any kind of men, they would have stood up and declared their interest. They would have proclaimed their desire for her, marked their territory.

He still would have thrown punches, but at least he would've respected them a bit.

Not now.

"Mind if I dance with you?"

Her eyes flew open and she looked around, her head whipping from side to side, her hair following suit. "Where are..."

"Tweedledee and Tweedledum had somewhere to be."

"Where?"

"Someplace where I wouldn't beat their asses."

"Why are you going to beat their...butts?"

"What are you doing here, Hayley?"

She looked around, a guilty expression on her face.

"I was just dancing. I have to say, when I imagined getting in trouble in a bar, I figured it would be my dad dragging me outside, not my boss."

"I haven't dragged you outside. *Yet*." He added that last bit because at this point he wasn't sure how this night was going to end. "What are you doing?"

She lifted a shoulder. "Dancing."

"Getting ready to have your first threesome?"

Her mouth dropped open. "I don't even know how that would work."

He huffed out a laugh. "Look it up. On second thought, don't."

She rolled her eyes like a snotty teenager. "We were just dancing. It wasn't a big deal."

"Little girl, what you don't know about men could fill a library. Men don't *just want to dance*. And men don't *just want to kiss*. You can't play these kinds of games. You don't know the rules. You're going to get yourself into trouble."

"I'm not going to get myself into trouble. Did it ever occur to you that maybe some men are nicer than you?"

He chuckled, a low, bitter sound. "Oh, I know that most men are a lot nicer than me. Even then, they want in your pants."

"I don't know what your problem is. You don't want me, so what do you care if they do?"

"Hayley, honey, I don't *want* to want you, but that is not the same thing as not wanting you. It is not even close. What I want is something you can't handle."

"I know," she said, looking to the right and then to the left, as though making sure no one was within earshot. Then she took a step toward him. "You said you wanted to…be inside of me."

That simple statement, that repetition of his words, had him hard as an iron bar. "You better back off."

"See, I thought you didn't want me. I thought you were trying to scare me away when you said that. Because why would you want me?"

"I'd list the reasons, but I would shock you."

She tilted her head to the side, her hair falling over her shoulder like a glossy curtain. "Maybe I want to be shocked. Maybe I want something I'm not quite ready for."

"No," he said, his tone emphatic now. "You're on this big kick to have experiences. And there are much nicer men you can have experiences with."

She bared her teeth. "I was trying! You just scared them off."

"You're not having experiences with those clowns. They wouldn't know how to handle a woman if she came with an instruction manual. And let me tell you, women do not come with an instruction manual. You just have to know what to do."

"And you know what to do?"

"Damn straight," he returned.

"So," she said, tilting her chin up, looking stubborn. "Show me."

"Not likely, babe."

He wanted to. He wanted to pick her up, throw her over his shoulder and drag her back to his cave. He wanted to bury himself inside her and screw them both senseless, breathless. He wanted to chase every man in the vicinity away from her. He wanted to make it known, loud and clear that—for a little while at least— she was his.

But it was wrong. On about a thousand levels. And

the fact that she didn't seem to know it was just another bit of evidence that he needed to stay away.

"You're playing with fire," he said.

"I know. When you kissed me, that was the closest to being burned I've ever experienced in my life. I want more of that."

"We're not having this conversation in the middle of a bar." He grabbed her arm and hauled her off the dance floor, steering them both to the door.

"Hayley!"

He turned and saw one of the waitresses standing by the bar with her hands on her hips.

"Is everything all right?" she asked.

"Yes," Hayley responded. "Jasmine, it's fine. This is my boss."

Jasmine arched her brow. "Really?"

Hayley nodded. "Really. Just work stuff."

Then she broke free of him and marched out ahead of him. When they were both outside, she rounded on him, her words coming out on a frosty cloud in the night air.

"You're so concerned about my reputation, but then you wander in and make a spectacle."

"You were dancing with two men when I got there," he said. "And what's happening with that dress?"

"Oh please," she said, "I wear this dress to church. It's fine."

"You wear that to *church*?" He supposed, now that he evaluated it with more neutrality, it was pretty tame. The black stretch cotton fell past her knees and had a fairly high neckline. But he could see the curves of her breasts, the subtle slope of her waist to her hips, and her ass looked incredible.

He didn't know if hers was the sort of church that did

confession, but he would sure as hell need to confess if he were seated in a row behind her during service.

"Yes," she said. "And it's fine. You're being crazy. Because…because you…*like* me. You *like me* like me."

There she went again, saying things that revealed how innocent she was. Things that made him want her even more, when they should send him running.

"I don't have relationships," he said. He would tell her the truth. He would be honest. It would be the fastest way to chase her off. "And I'm betting a nice girl like you wants a relationship. Wants romance, and flowers, and at least the possibility of commitment. You don't get any of those things with me, Hayley."

She looked up at him, her blue eyes glittering in the security light. He could hear the waves crashing on the shore just beyond the parking lot, feel the salt breeze blowing in off the water, sharp and cold.

"What would I get?" she asked.

"A good, hard fuck. A few orgasms." He knew he'd shocked her, and he was glad. She needed to be shocked. She needed to be scared away.

He couldn't see her face, not clearly, but he could tell she wasn't looking at him when she said, "That's… that's a good thing, right?"

"If you don't know the answer, then the answer is no. Not for you."

The sounds of the surf swelled around them, wind whipping through the pines across the road. She didn't speak for a long time. Didn't move.

"Kiss me again," she said, finally.

The words hit him like a sucker punch. "What? What did I just tell you about men and kissing?"

"It's not for you," she said, "it's for me. Before I give you an answer, you need to kiss me again."

She raised her head, and the light caught her face. She stared at him, all defiance and soft lips, all innocence and intensity, and he didn't have it in him to deny her.

Didn't have it in him to deny himself.

Before he could stop, he wrapped his arm around her waist, crushed her against his chest and brought his lips crashing down on hers.

CHAPTER SEVEN

SHE WAS DOING THIS. She wasn't going to turn back. Not now. And she kept telling herself that as she followed Jonathan's pickup truck down the long, empty highway that took them out of town, toward his house.

His house. Where she was going to spend the night.

Where she was going to lose her virginity.

She swallowed hard, her throat suddenly dry and prickly like a cactus.

This wasn't what she had planned when she'd started on her grand independence journey. Yes, she had wanted a kiss, but she hadn't really thought as far ahead as having a sexual partner. For most of her life she had imagined she would be married first, and then, when she'd started wavering on that decision, she had at least imagined she would be in a serious relationship.

This was... Well, it wasn't marriage. It wasn't the beginning of a relationship, either. Of that, she was certain. Jonathan hadn't been vague. Her cheeks heated at the memory of what he'd said, and she was grateful they were driving in separate cars so she had a moment alone for a private freak-out.

She was so out of her league here.

She could turn around. She could head back to town, back to Main Street, back to her little apartment where she could curl up in bed with the bowl of cereal she'd left dry and discarded on the counter earlier.

And in the morning, she wouldn't be changed. Not for the better, not for the worse.

She seriously considered that, though she kept on driving, her eyes on the road and on Jonathan's taillights.

This decision was a big deal. She wouldn't pretend it wasn't. Wouldn't pretend she didn't put some importance on her first sexual experience, on sex in general. And she wouldn't pretend it probably wasn't a mistake.

It was just that maybe she needed to make the mistake. Maybe she needed to find out for herself if Jonathan was right, if every experience wasn't necessary.

She bit her lip and allowed herself a moment of undiluted honesty. When this was over, there would be fallout. She was certain of it.

But while it was happening, it would feel really, really good.

If the kissing was anything to go by, it would be amazing.

She would feel…wild. And new. And maybe sex with Jonathan would be just the kind of thing she needed. He was hot; touching him burned.

Maybe he could be her own personal trial by fire.

She had always imagined that meant walking through hard times. And maybe, conventionally, it did. But she was walking into the heat willingly, knowing the real pain would come after.

She might be a virgin, but she wasn't an idiot. Jonathan Bear wasn't going to fall in love with her. And anyway, she didn't want him to.

She wanted freedom. She wanted something bigger than Copper Ridge.

That meant love wasn't on her agenda, either.

They pulled up to the house and he got out of his

truck, closing the door solidly behind him. And she… froze. Sitting there in the driver's seat, both hands on the steering wheel, the engine still running.

The car door opened and cool air rushed in. She looked up and saw Jonathan's large frame filling the space. "Second thoughts?"

She shook her head. "No," she said, and yet she couldn't make herself move.

"I want you," he said, his voice rough, husky, the words not at all what she had expected. "I would like to tell you that if you are having second thoughts, you should turn the car around and go back home. But I'm not going to tell you that. Because if I do, then I might miss out on my chance. And I want this. Even though I shouldn't."

She tightened her hold on the steering wheel. "Why shouldn't you?" she asked, her throat constricted now.

"Do you want the full list?"

"I've got all night."

"All right. You're a nice girl. You seem to believe the best of people, or at least, you want to, until they absolutely make it so you can't. I'm not a nice man. I don't believe the best of anyone, even when they prove I should. People like me, we tend to drag people like you down to our level. Unfortunately. And that's likely what's going to happen here. I'm going to drag you right down to my level. Because let me tell you, I like dirty. And I'm going to get you filthy. I can promise you that."

"Okay," she said, feeling breathless, not quite certain how to respond. Part of her wanted to fling herself out of the car and into his arms, while another, not insignificant part wanted to throw the car in Reverse and drive away.

"I can only promise you two things. This—you and

me—won't last forever. And tonight, I will make you come. If you're okay with those promises, then get out of the car and up to my room. If you're not, it's time for you to go."

For some reason, that softly issued command was what it took to get her moving. She released her hold on the steering wheel and turned sideways in her seat. Then she looked up at him, pushing herself into a standing position. He had one hand on the car door, the other on the side mirror, blocking her in.

Her breasts nearly touched his chest, and she was tempted to lean in and press against him completely.

"Come on then," he said, releasing his hold on the car and turning away.

The movement was abrupt. It made her wonder if he was struggling with indecision, too. Which didn't really make sense, since Jonathan was the most decisive man she had ever met. He seemed certain about everything, all the time, even if he was sure it was a bad decision.

That certainty was what she wanted. Yeah, she was certain this was a bad decision, too, but she was going for it, anyway.

She had walked into this house five days a week for the past couple weeks, yet this time was different. Because this time she wasn't headed to the office. This time she was going to his bedroom. And she wasn't his employee; he wasn't her boss. Not now.

Her stomach tightened, her blood heated at the idea of following orders. His orders. Lord knew she would need instruction. Direction. She had no idea what she was doing; she was just following her gut instinct.

When they reached the long hallway, they stopped at a different door than usual. His bedroom. She had never been inside Jonathan's bedroom. It was strange to be standing there now. So very deliberate.

It might have been easier if they had started kissing here in the house, and let things come to their natural conclusion… On the floor or something. She was reasonably sure people did it on the floor sometimes.

Yeah, that would have been easier. This was so *intentional.*

She was about to say something about the strangeness of it when he reached out, cupped her chin and tilted her face upward. Then he closed the distance between them, claiming her mouth.

She felt his possession, all the way down to her toes.

He didn't wait for her to part her lips this time. Instead, he invaded her, sliding his tongue forcibly against hers, his arms wrapped tight around her like steel bands. There was nothing gentle about this kiss. It was consuming, all-encompassing. And all her thoughts about the situation feeling premeditated dissolved.

This time, she didn't stand there as a passive participant. This time, she wrapped her arms around his neck—pressing her breasts flush against his chest, forking her fingers through his hair—and devoured him right back.

She couldn't believe this was her. Couldn't believe this was her life, that this man wanted her. That he was hard for her. That he thought she might be a mistake, and he was willing to make her, anyway. God knew, she was willing to make him.

Need grew inside her, prowling around like a restless thing. She rocked her hips forward, trying to tame the nameless ache between her thighs. Trying to calm the erratic, reckless feeling rioting through her.

He growled, sliding his hands down her back, over

her bottom, down to her thighs. She squeaked as he gripped her tightly, pulling both her feet off the ground and picking her up, pressing that soft, tender place between her legs against his arousal.

"Wrap your legs around me," he said against her mouth, the command harsh, and sexier because of that.

She obeyed him, locking her ankles behind his back. He reversed their positions, pressing her against the wall and deepening his kiss. She gasped as he made even firmer contact with the place that was wet and aching for him.

He ground his hips against her, and her internal muscles pulsed. An arc of electricity lanced through her. She gripped his shoulders hard, vaguely aware that she might be digging her fingernails into his skin, not really sure that she cared. Maybe it would hurt him, but she wasn't exactly sure if he was hurting her or not. She was suspended between pleasure and pain, feelings so intense she could scarcely breathe.

And through all that, he continued to devour her mouth, the rhythm of his tongue against hers combining with the press of his firm length between her thighs, ensuring that her entire world narrowed down to him. Jonathan Bear was everything right now. He was her breath; he was sensation. He was heaven and he was hell.

She needed it to end. Needed to reach some kind of conclusion, where all this tension could be defused.

And yet she wanted it to go on forever.

Her face was hot, her limbs shaking. A strange, hollow feeling in the pit of her stomach made her want to cry. It was too much. And it was not enough. That sharp, insistent ache between her legs burrowed deeper with each passing second, letting her know this kiss simply wasn't enough at all.

She moved her hands up from his broad shoulders, sliding them as far as she could into his long, dark hair. Her fingers snagged on the band that kept his hair tied back and she internally cursed her clumsiness, hoping he wouldn't notice. She had enthusiasm guiding her through this, but that was about it. Enthusiasm and a healthy dose of adrenaline that bordered on terror. But she didn't want to stop. She couldn't stop.

Those big, rough hands gripped her hips and braced her as he rocked more firmly against her, and suddenly, stars exploded behind her eyes. She gasped, wrenching her lips away from his as something that felt like thunder rolled through her body, muscles she'd never been aware of before pulsing like waves against the shore.

She pressed her forehead against his shoulder, did her best to grit her teeth and keep herself from crying out, but a low, shaky sound escaped when the deepest wave washed over her.

Then it ended, and she felt even more connected to reality, to this moment, than she had a second ago. And she felt…so very aware that she was pressed against the wall and him, that something had just happened, that she hadn't been fully cognizant of her actions. She didn't know what she might have said.

That was when she realized she was digging her nails into his back, and she had probably punctured his skin. She started to move against him, trying to get away, and he gripped her chin again, steadying her. "Hey," he said, "you're not going anywhere."

"I need to… I have to…"

"You don't have to do anything, baby. Nothing at all. Just relax." She could tell he was placating her.

She couldn't bring herself to care particularly, because she needed placating. Her heart was racing, her hands shaking, and that restlessness that had been so all-consuming earlier was growing again. She had thought the earthquake inside her had handled that.

That was when she realized exactly what that earthquake had been.

Her cheeks flamed, horror stealing through her. She'd had... Well, she'd had an orgasm. And he hadn't even touched her. Not with his hands. Not under her clothes.

"I'm sorry," she said, putting her hands up, patting his chest, then curling her hands into fists because she had patted him and that was really stupid. "I'm just sorry."

He frowned. "What are you sorry about?"

"I'm sorry because I—I...I did that. And we didn't..."

He raised one eyebrow. "Are you apologizing for your orgasm?"

She squeezed her eyes tightly shut. "Yes."

"Why?"

She tightened her fists even more, pressing them against her own chest, keeping her eyes closed. "Because we didn't even... You didn't... We're still dressed."

"Honey," he said, taking hold of her fists and drawing them toward him, pressing them against his chest. "You don't need to apologize to me for coming."

She opened one eye. "I...I don't?"

"No."

"But that..." She looked fully at him, too curious to be embarrassed now. "That ruins it, doesn't it? We didn't..."

"You can have as many orgasms as I can give you.

That's the magical thing about women. There's no ceiling on that."

"There isn't?"

"You didn't know?"

"No."

"Hayley," he said, his tone grave, "I need to ask you a question."

Oh great. Now he was actually going to ask if she was a virgin. Granted, she thought he'd probably guessed, but apparently he needed to hear it. "Go ahead," she said, bracing herself for utter humiliation.

"Have you never had an orgasm before?"

"Yes," she said, answering the wrong question before he even got his out. "I mean... No. I mean, just a minute ago. I wasn't even sure what it was right when it was happening."

"That doesn't... Not even with yourself?"

Her face felt so hot she thought it might be on fire. She was pretty sure her heart was beating in her forehead. "No." She shook her head. "I can't talk to you about things like that."

"I just gave you your first orgasm, so you better be able to talk to me about things like that. Plus I'm aiming to give you another one before too long here."

"I bet you can't."

He chuckled, and then he bent down, sweeping her up into his arms. She squeaked, curling her fingers around his shirt. "You should know better than to issue challenges like that." He turned toward the bedroom door, kicking it open with his boot before walking inside and kicking it closed again. Then he carried her to the bed and threw her down in the center.

"Wait," she said, starting to feel panicky, her heart

fluttering in her chest like a swarm of butterflies. "Just wait a second."

"I'm not going to fall on you like a ravenous beast," he said, his hands going to the top button of his shirt. "Yet." He started to undo the button slowly, revealing his tan, muscular chest.

She almost told him to stop, except he stripped the shirt off, and she got completely distracted by the play of all those muscles. The sharp hitch of his abs as he cast the flannel onto the floor, the shift and bunch of his pectoral muscles as he pushed his hand over his hair.

She had never seen a shirtless man that looked like him. Not in person, anyway. And most definitely not this close, looking at her like he had plans. Very, very dirty plans.

"I'm a virgin," she blurted out. "Just so you know."

His eyes glowed with black fire. For one heart-stopping moment she was afraid he might pick up his shirt and walk out of the room. His eyes looked pure black; his mouth pressed into a firm line. He stood frozen, hands on his belt buckle, every line in his cut torso still.

Then something in his expression shifted. Nearly imperceptible, and mostly unreadable, but she had seen it. Then his deft fingers went to work, moving his belt through the buckle. "I know," he said.

"Oh." She felt a little crestfallen. Like she must have made some novice mistake and given herself away.

"You're a church secretary who confessed to having never had an orgasm. I assumed." He lowered his voice. "If you hadn't told me outright, I could have had plausible deniability. Which I was sort of counting on."

She blinked. "Did you…need it?"

"My conscience is screwed, anyway. So not really."

She didn't know quite what to say, so she didn't say anything.

"Have you ever seen a naked man before?"

She shook her head. "No."

"Pictures?"

"Does medieval art count?"

"No, it does not."

"Then no," she said, shaking her head even more vigorously.

He rubbed his hand over his forehead, and she was sure she heard him swear beneath his breath. "Okay," he said, leaving his belt hanging open, but not going any further. He pressed his knee down on the mattress, kneeling beside her. Then he took her hand and placed it against his chest. "How's that?"

She drew shaking fingers across his chest slowly, relishing his heat, the satiny feel of his skin. "Good," she said. "You're very…hot. I mean, temperaturewise. Kind of smooth."

"You don't have to narrate," he said.

"Sorry," she said, drawing her hand back sharply.

"No," he said, pressing her palm back against his skin. "Don't apologize. Don't apologize for anything that happens between us tonight, got that?"

"Okay," she said, more than happy to agree, but not entirely sure if she could keep to the agreement. Because every time she moved her hand and his breath hissed through his teeth, she wanted to say she was sorry. Every time she took her exploration further, she wanted to apologize for the impulse to do it.

She bit her lip, letting her hands glide lower, over his stomach, which was as hard and rippled as corrugated steel. Then she found her hands at the waistband of his jeans, and she pulled back.

"Do you want me to take these off?" he asked.

"In a minute," she said, losing her nerve slightly. "Just a minute." She rose up on her knees, pressed her mouth to his and lost herself in kissing him. She really liked kissing. Loved the sounds he made, loved being enveloped in his arms, and she really loved it when he laid them both down, pressing her deep into the mattress and settling between her thighs.

Her dress rode up high, and she didn't care. She felt rough denim scraping her bare skin, felt the hard press of his zipper, and his arousal behind it through the thin fabric of her panties.

She lost herself in those sensations. In the easy, sensual contact that pushed her back to the brink again. She could see already that Jonathan was going to win the orgasm challenge. And she was okay with that.

Very, very okay with that.

Then he took her hem and pulled the cotton dress over her head, casting it onto the floor. Her skin heated all over, and she was sure she was pink from head to toe.

"Don't be embarrassed," he said, touching her collarbone, featherlight, then tracing a trail down to the curve of her breast, to the edge of her bra. "You're beautiful."

She didn't know quite how to feel about that. Didn't know what to do with that husky, earnest compliment. She wasn't embarrassed because she lacked beauty, but because she had always been taught to treasure modesty. To respect her body, to save it.

He *was* respecting it, though. And right now, she felt like she had been saving it for him.

He reached behind her, undoing her bra with one hand and flicking the fabric to the side.

"You're better at that than I am," she said, laughing

nervously as he bared her breasts, her nipples tightening as the cold air hit her skin.

He smiled. "You'll appreciate that in a few minutes."

"What will I appreciate?" she asked, shivering. She crossed her arms over her chest.

"My skill level." Instead of moving her hands, he bent his head and nuzzled the tender spot right next to her hand, the full part of her breast that was still exposed. She gasped, tightening her hold on herself.

He was not deterred.

He nosed her gently and shifted her hand to the side, pressing a kiss to her skin, sending electric sensations firing through her. "Don't be shy," he said, "not with me."

She waited for a reason why. He didn't give one, but she found that the more persistent he was—the more hot, open-mouthed kisses he pressed to her skin—the less able she was to deny him anything. Anything at all. She found herself shifting her hands and then letting them fall away.

As soon as she did, he closed his lips over her nipple, sucking deep. She gasped, her hips rocking up off the bed. He wrapped his arm around her, holding her against his hardness as he teased her with his lips and tongue.

Every time she wiggled, either closer to him, or in a moment of self-consciousness, away, it only brought him more in contact with that aching place between her thighs, and then she would forget why she was moving at all. Why she wasn't just letting him take the lead.

So she relaxed into him, and let herself get lost. She was in a daze when he took her hand and pushed it down his stomach, to the front of his jeans. She gasped when his hard, denim-covered length filled her palm.

"Feel that? That's how much I want you. That's what you do to me."

A strange surge of power rocketed through her. That she could cause such a raw, sexual response... Well, it was intoxicating in a way she hadn't appreciated it could be.

Especially because he was such a man. A hot man. A sexy man, and she had never thought of anyone that way in her life. But he was. He most definitely was.

"Are you ready?" he asked.

She nodded, sliding her hand experimentally over him. He moved, undoing his pants and shoving them quickly down, hardly giving her a chance to prepare. Her mouth dried when she saw him, all of him. She hadn't really... Well, she had been content to allow her fantasies to be somewhat hazy. Though reading that romance novel had made those fantasies a little sharper.

Still, she hadn't really imagined specifically how large a man might be. But suffice it to say, he was a bit larger than she had allowed for.

Her breath left her lungs in a rush. But along with the wave of nerves that washed over her came a sense of relief. "You are... I like the way you look," she said finally.

A crooked smile tipped his mouth upward. "Thank you."

"I told you, I've never seen a naked man before. I was a little afraid I wouldn't like it."

"Well, I'm glad you do. Because let me tell you, that's a lot of pressure. Being the first naked man you've ever seen." His eyes darkened and his voice got lower, huskier. "Being the first naked man you've ever touched." He took her hand again and placed it around his bare shaft, the skin there hotter and much softer than she had imagined. She slid her thumb up and down, marveling at the feel of him.

"You're the first man I've ever kissed," she said, the words slurred, because she had lost the full connection between her brain and her mouth. All her blood had flowed to her extremities.

He swore, and then crushed her to him, kissing her deeply and driving her back down to the mattress. His erection pressed into her stomach, his tongue slick against hers, his lips insistent. She barely noticed when he divested her of her underwear, until he placed his hand between her legs. The rough pads of his fingers sliding through her slick flesh, the white-hot pleasure his touch left behind, made her gasp.

"I'm going to make sure you're ready," he said.

She had no idea what that meant. But he started doing wicked, magical things with his fingers, so she didn't much care. Then he slid one finger deep inside her and she arched away, not sure whether she wanted more of that completely unfamiliar sensation, or if she needed to escape it.

"It's okay," he said, moving his thumb in a circle over a sensitive bundle of nerves as he continued to slide his finger in and out of her body.

After a few passes of his thumb, she agreed.

He shifted his position, adding a second finger, making her gasp. It burned slightly, made her feel like she was being stretched, but after a moment, she adjusted to that, too.

That lovely, spiraling tension built inside her again, and she knew she was close to the edge. But every time he took her to the brink, he would drop back again.

"Please," she whispered.

"Please what?" he asked, being dastardly, asking

her to clarify, when he knew saying the words would embarrass her.

"You know," she said, placing her hand over his, like she might take control, increase the pressure, increase the pace, since he refused.

But, of course, he was too strong for her to guide him at all. "I need to hear it."

"I need... I need to have an orgasm," she said quickly.

For a moment, he stopped. He looked at her like she mystified him. Like he had never seen anything like her before. Then he withdrew his hand and slid down her body, gripping her hips roughly before drawing her quickly against his mouth.

She squeaked when his lips and tongue touched her right in her most intimate place. She reached down, grabbing hold of his hair, because she was going to pull him away, but then his tongue touched her in the most amazing spot and she found herself lacing her fingers through his hair instead.

She found herself holding him against her instead of pushing him away.

She moved her hips in time with him, gasping for air as pleasure, arousal, built to impossible heights. She had been on the edge for so long now it felt like she was poised on the brink of something else entirely. But right when she was about to break, he moved away from her, drawing himself up her body. He grabbed a small, round packet from the bedspread that she hadn't noticed until now, and tore it open, quickly sheathing himself before moving to position the blunt head of his arousal at her entrance.

He flexed his hips, thrusting deep inside her, and her arousal broke like a mirror hit with a hammer. She gritted her teeth as pain—sharp and jagged—cut through all the hidden places within her. But along with the pain came the intense sensation of being full. Of being connected to another person like she never had been before.

She reached up, taking his heavily muscled arms and holding him, just holding him, as he moved slowly inside her.

He was *inside* her.

She marveled at that truth even as the pain eased, even as pleasure began to push its way into the foreground again.

"Move with me," he said, nuzzling her neck, kissing the tender skin there.

So she did, meeting his every thrust, clinging to him. She could see the effort it took for him to maintain control, and she could see when his control began to fray. When his thrusts became erratic, his golden skin slick with sweat, his breathing rough and ragged, matching her own.

When he thrust deep, she arched her hips, an electric shower of sparks shimmering through her each time.

His hands were braced on either side of her shoulders, his strong fingers gripping the sheets. His movements became hard, rough, but none of the earlier pain remained, and she welcomed him. Opened her thighs wider and then wrapped her legs around his lean hips so she could take him even deeper.

There was no pain. There was no shame. There was no doubt at all.

As far as she was concerned, there was only the two of them.

He leaned down, pressing his forehead against hers, his dark gaze intense as his rhythm increased. He went shallow, then deep, the change pushing her even closer to the edge.

Then he pulled out almost completely, his hips pulsing slightly. The denial of that deep, intimate contact made her feel frantic. Made her feel needy. Made her feel desperate.

"Jonathan," she said. "Jonathan, please."

"Tell me you want to come," he told her, the words a growl.

"I want to come," she said, not wasting a moment on self-consciousness.

He slammed back home, and she saw stars. This orgasm grabbed her deep, reached places she hadn't known were there. The pleasure seemed to go on and on, and when it was done, she felt like she was floating on a sea, gazing up at a sky full of infinite stars.

She felt adrift, but only for a moment. Because when she came back to herself, she was still clutching his strong arms, Jonathan Bear rooting her to the earth.

And then she waited.

Waited for regret. Waited for guilt.

But she didn't feel any of it. Right now, she just felt a bone-deep satisfaction she hoped never went away.

"I..." He started to say something, moving away from her. Then he frowned. "You don't have a toothbrush or anything, do you?"

It was such a strange question that it threw her for a loop. "What?"

"It doesn't matter," he said. He bent down, pressing a kiss to her forehead. "We'll work something out in the morning."

She was glad he'd said there was nothing to worry about, because her head was starting to get fuzzy and her eyelids were heavy. Which sucked, because she didn't want to sleep. She wanted to bask in her newfound warm and fuzzy feelings.

But she was far too sleepy, far too sated to do anything but allow herself to be enveloped by that warmth. By him.

He drew her into his arms, and she snuggled into his chest, pressing her palm against him. She could feel his heartbeat, hard and steady, beneath her hand.

And then, for the first time in her life, Hayley Thompson fell asleep in a man's arms.

CHAPTER EIGHT

JONATHAN DIDN'T SLEEP. As soon as Hayley drifted off, he went into his office, busying himself with work that didn't need to be done.

Women didn't spend the night at his house. He had never even brought a woman back to this house. But when Hayley had looked up at him like that... He hadn't been able to tell her to leave. He realized that she expected to stay. Because as far as she was concerned, sex included sleeping with somebody.

He had no idea where she had formed her ideas about relationships, but they were innocent. And he was a bastard. He had already known that, but tonight just confirmed it.

Except he had let her stay.

He couldn't decide if that was a good thing or not. Couldn't decide if letting her stay had been a kindness or a cruelty. Because the one thing it hadn't been was the reality of the situation.

The reality was this wasn't a relationship. The reality was, it had been... Well, a very bad idea.

He stood up from his desk, rubbing the back of his neck. It was getting light outside, pale edges beginning to bleed from the mountaintops, encroaching on the velvet middle of the sky.

He might as well go outside and get busy on morning

chores. And if some of those chores were in the name of avoiding Hayley, then so be it.

He made his way downstairs, shoved his feet into his boots and grabbed his hat, walking outside with heavy footsteps.

He paused, inhaling deeply, taking a moment to let the scent of the pines wash through him. This was his. All of it was his. He didn't think that revelation would ever get old.

He remembered well the way it had smelled on his front porch in the trailer park. Cigarette smoke and exhaust from cars as people got ready to leave for work. The noise of talking, families shouting at each other. It didn't matter if you were inside the house or outside. You lived way too close to your neighbors to avoid them.

He had fantasized about a place like this back then. Isolated. His. Where he wouldn't have to see another person unless he went out of his way to do so. He shook his head. And he had gone and invited Hayley to stay the night. He was a dumb ass.

He needed a ride to clear his head. The fact that he got to take weekends off now was one of his favorite things about his new position in life. He was a workaholic, and he had never minded that. But ranching was the kind of work he really enjoyed, and that was what he preferred to do with his free time.

He saddled his horse and mounted up, urging the bay gelding toward the biggest pasture. They started out at a slow walk, then Jonathan increased the pace until he and his horse were flying over the grass, patches of flowers blurring on either side of them, blending with the rich green.

It didn't matter what mess he had left behind at the

house. Didn't matter what mistakes he had made last night. It never did, not when he was on a horse. Not when he was in his sanctuary. The house... Well, he would be lying if he said that big custom house hadn't been a goal for him. Of course it had been. It was evidence that he had made it.

But this... The trees, the mountains, the wind in his face, being able to ride his horse until his lungs burned, and not reach the end of his property... That was the real achievement. It belonged to him and no one else. In this place he didn't have to answer to anyone.

Out here it didn't matter if he was bad. You couldn't let the sky down. You couldn't disappoint the mountains.

He leaned forward to go uphill, tightening his hold on the reins as the animal changed its gait. He pulled back, easing to a stop. He looked down the mountain, at the valley of trees spread out before him, an evergreen patchwork stitched together by rock and river. And beyond that, the ocean, brighter blue than usual on this exceptionally clear morning, the waves capped with a rosy pink handed down from the still-rising sun.

Hayley would love this.

That thought brought him up short, because he wasn't exactly sure why he thought she would. Or why he cared. Why he suddenly wanted to show her. He had never shown this view to anybody. Not even to his sister, Rebecca.

He had wanted to keep it for himself, because growing up, he'd had very little that belonged to him and him alone. In fact, up here, gazing at everything that belonged to him now, he couldn't think of a single damn thing that had truly belonged to him when he'd been younger.

It had all been for a landlord, for his sister, for the future.

This was what he had worked for his entire life.

He didn't need to show it to some woman he'd slept with last night.

He shook his head, turning the horse around and trotting down the hill, moving to a gallop back down to the barn.

When he exited the gate that would take him out of the pasture and back to the paddock, Jonathan saw Hayley standing in the path. Wearing last night's dress, her hair disheveled, she was holding two mugs of coffee.

He was tempted to imagine he had conjured her up just by thinking of her up on the ridge. But if it were a fantasy, she would have been wearing nothing, rather than being back in that black cotton contraption.

She was here, and it disturbed him just how happy that made him.

"I thought I might find you out here," she said. "And I figured you would probably want your coffee."

He dismounted, taking the reins and walking the horse toward Hayley. "It's your day off. You don't have to make me coffee."

Her cheeks turned pink, and he marveled at the blush. And on the heels of that marveling came the sharp bite of guilt. She was a woman who blushed routinely. And he had... Well, he had started down the path of corrupting her last night.

He had taken her virginity. Before her he'd never slept with a virgin in his damn life. In high school, that hadn't been so much out of a sense of honor as it had been out of a desire not to face down an angry dad with a shotgun. Better to associate with girls who had reputations worse than his own.

All that restraint had culminated in him screwing the pastor's daughter.

At least when people came with torches and pitchforks, he would have a decent-sized fortress to hole up in.

"I just thought maybe it would be nice," she said finally, taking a step toward him and extending the coffee mug in his direction.

"It is," he said, taking the cup, knowing he didn't sound quite as grateful as he might have. "Sorry," he conceded, sipping the strong brew, which was exactly the way he liked it. "I'm not used to people being nice. I'm never quite sure what to make of it when you are."

"Just take it at face value," she said, lifting her shoulder.

"Yeah, I don't do that."

"Why not?" she asked.

"I have to take care of the horse," he said. "If you want story time, you're going to have to follow me."

He thought his gruff demeanor might scare her off, but instead, she followed him along the fence line. He tethered his horse and set his mug on the fence post, then grabbed the pick and started on the gelding's hooves.

Hayley stepped up carefully on the bottom rung of the fence, settling herself on the top rung, clutching her mug and looking at him with an intensity he could feel even with his focus on the task at hand.

"I'm ready," she said.

He looked up at her, perched there like an inquisitive owl, her lips at the edge of her cup, her blue eyes round. She was…a study in contradictions. Innocent as hell. Soft in some ways, but determined in others.

It was her innocence that allowed her to be so open—

that was his conclusion. The fact that she'd never really been hurt before made it easy for her to come at people from the front.

"It's not a happy story," he warned.

It wasn't a secret one, either. Pretty much everybody knew his tragic backstory. He didn't go around talking about it, but there was no reason not to give her what she was asking for.

Except for the fact that he never talked to the women he hooked up with. There was just no point to it.

But then, the women he usually hooked up with never stumbled out of his house early in the morning with cups of coffee. So he supposed it was an unusual situation all around.

"I'm a big girl," she said, her tone comically serious. It was followed by a small slurp as she took another sip of coffee. The sound should not have been cute, but it was.

"Right." He looked up at her, started to speak and then stopped.

Would hearing about his past, about his childhood, change something in her? Just by talking to her he might ruin some of her optimism.

It was too late for worrying about that, he supposed. Since sleeping with her when she'd never even kissed anyone before had undoubtedly changed her.

There had been a lot of points in his life when he had not been his own favorite person. The feeling was intense right now. He was a damned bastard.

"I'm waiting," she said, kicking her foot slightly to signify her impatience.

"My father left when I was five," he said.

"Oh," she said, blinking, clearly shocked. "I'm sorry."

"It was the best thing that had happened to me in all five years of my life, Hayley. The very best thing. He was a violent bastard. He hit my mother. He hit me. The day he left… I was a kid, but I knew even then that life was going to be better. I was right. When I was seven, my mom had another kid. And she was the best thing. So cute. Tiny and loud as hell, but my mother wasn't all that interested in me, and my new sister was. Plus she gave me, I don't know…a feeling of importance. I had someone to look after, and that mattered. Made me feel like maybe I mattered."

"Rebecca," Hayley said.

"Yeah," he replied. "Then, when Rebecca was a teenager, she was badly injured in a car accident. Needed a lot of surgeries, skin grafts. All of it was paid for by the family responsible for the accident, in exchange for keeping everything quiet. Of course, it's kind of an open secret now that Gage West was the one who caused the accident."

Hayley blinked. "Gage. Isn't she… Aren't they… Engaged?"

Familiar irritation surged through him. "For now. We'll see how long that lasts. I don't have a very high opinion of that family."

"Well, you know my brother is married into that family."

He shrugged. "All right, maybe I'll rephrase that. I don't have anything against Colton, or Sierra, or Maddy. But I don't trust Gage or his father one bit. I certainly don't trust him with my sister, any more now than I did then. But if things fall apart, if he ends up breaking off the engagement, or leaves her ten years into the marriage… I'll have a place for her. I've always got a place for her."

Hayley frowned. "That's a very cynical take. If Rebecca can love the man who caused her accident, there must be something pretty exceptional about him."

"More likely, my sister doesn't really know what love looks like," he said, his voice hard, the words giving voice to the thing he feared most. "I have to backtrack a little. A few months after the accident, my mom took the cash payout Nathan West gave her and took off. Left me with Rebecca. Left Rebecca without a mother, when she needed her mother the most. My mom just couldn't handle it. So I had to. And I was a piss-poor replacement for parents. An older brother with a crappy construction job and not a lot of patience." He shook his head. "Every damn person in my life who was supposed to be there for me bailed. Everyone who was supposed to be there for Rebecca."

"And now you're mad at her, too. For not doing what you thought she should."

Guilt stabbed him right in the chest. Yeah, he was angry at his sister. And he felt like he had no damn right to be angry. Shouldn't she be allowed to be happy? Hadn't that been the entire point of taking care of her for all those years? So she could get out from under the cloud of their family?

So she'd done it. In a huge, spectacular way. She'd ended up with the man she'd been bitter about for years. She had let go of the past. She had embraced it, and in a pretty damned literal way.

But Jonathan couldn't. He didn't trust in sudden changes of heart or professions of love. He didn't trust much of anything.

"I'll be mad if she gets hurt," he said finally. "But that's my default. I assume it's going to end badly because I've only ever seen these things end badly. I worked my ass off to keep the two of us off the streets. To make sure we had a roof over our heads, as much food in our stomachs as I could manage. I protected her." He shook his head. "And there's no protecting somebody if you aren't always looking out for what might go wrong. For what might hurt them."

"I guess I can't blame you for not trusting the good in people. You haven't seen it very many times."

He snorted. "Understatement of the century." He straightened, undoing the girth and taking the saddle off the bay in a fluid movement, then draping it over the fence. "But my cynicism has served me just fine. Look at where I am now. I started out in a single-wide trailer, and I spent years working just to keep that much. I didn't advance to this place by letting down my guard, by stopping for even one minute." He shook his head again. "I probably owe my father a thank-you note. My mother, too, come to that. They taught me that I couldn't trust anyone but myself. And so far that lesson's served me pretty well."

Hayley was looking at him like she was sad for him, and he wanted to tell her to stop it. Contempt, disgust and distrust were what he was used to getting from people. And he had come to revel in that reaction, to draw strength from it.

Pity had been in short supply. And if it was ever tossed in his general direction, it was mostly directed at Rebecca. He wasn't comfortable receiving it himself.

"Don't look at me like I'm a sad puppy," he said.

"I'm not," she returned.

He untied the horse and began to walk back into the barn. "You are. I didn't ask for your pity." He unhooked the lead rope and urged the gelding into his stall. "Don't go feeling things for me, Hayley. I don't deserve it.

In fact, what you should have done this morning was walked out and slapped me in the face, not given me a cup of coffee."

"Why?"

"Because I took advantage of you last night. And you should be upset about that."

She frowned. "I should be?" She blinked. "I'm not. I thought about it. And I'm not."

"I don't know what you're imagining this is. I don't know what you think might happen next..."

She jumped down from the fence and set her coffee cup on the ground. Then she took one quick step forward. She hooked an arm around his neck and pushed herself onto her tiptoes, pressing her lips to his.

He was too stunned to react. But only for a moment. He wrapped an arm around her waist, pressing his forefinger beneath her chin and urging the kiss deeper.

She didn't have a lot of skill. That had been apparent the first and second times they'd kissed. And when they had come together last night. But he didn't need skill, he just needed her.

Even though it was wrong, he consumed her, sated his hunger on her mouth.

She whimpered, a sweet little sound that only fueled the driving hunger roaring in his gut. He grabbed her hair, tilting her head back farther, abandoning her mouth to scrape his teeth over her chin and down her neck, where he kissed her again, deep and hard.

He couldn't remember ever feeling like this before. Couldn't remember ever wanting a woman so much it was beyond the need for air. Sure, he liked sex. He was a man, after all. But the need had never been this specific. Had never been for one woman in particular.

But what he was feeling wasn't about sex, or about

lust or desire. It was about her. About Hayley. The sweet little sounds she made when he kissed the tender skin on her neck, when he licked his way back up to her lips. The way she trembled with her need for him The way she had felt last night, soft and slick and made only for him.

This was beyond anything he had ever experienced before. And he was a man who had experienced a hell of a lot.

That's what it was, he thought dimly as he scraped his teeth along her lower lip. And that said awful things about him, but then so did a lot of choices in his life.

He had conducted business with hard, ruthless precision, and he had kept his personal life free of any kind of connection beyond Rebecca—who he was loyal to above anyone else.

So maybe that was the problem. Now that he'd arrived at this place in life, he was collecting those things he had always denied himself. The comfortable home, the expansive mountains and a sweet woman.

Maybe this was some kind of latent urge. He had the homestead, now he wanted to put a woman in it.

He shook off that thought and all the rest. He didn't want to think right now. He just wanted to feel. Wanted to embrace the heat firing through his veins, the need stoking the flame low in his gut, which burned even more with each pass of her tongue against his.

She pulled away from him, breathing hard, her pupils dilated, her lips swollen and rounded into a perfect O. "That," she said, breathlessly, "was what I was thinking might happen next. And that we might… Take me back to bed, please."

"I can't think of a single reason to refuse," he said— a lie, as a litany of reasons cycled through his mind.

But he wasn't going to listen to them. He was going to take her, for as long as she was on offer. And when it ended, he could only hope he hadn't damaged her too much. Could only hope he hadn't broken her beyond repair.

Because there were a couple things he knew for sure. It would end; everything always did. And he would be the one who destroyed it.

He just hoped he didn't destroy her, too.

CHAPTER NINE

IT WAS LATE in the afternoon when Hayley and Jonathan finally got back out of bed. Hayley felt... Well, she didn't know quite what she felt. Good. Satisfied. Jonathan was... Well, if she'd ever had insecurities about whether or not she might be desirable to a man, he had done away with those completely. He had also taught her things about herself—about pleasure, about her own body—that she'd never in her wildest dreams conceived of.

She didn't know what would happen next, though. She had fallen asleep after their last time together, and when she'd awoken he was gone again. This morning, she had looked for him. She wasn't sure if she should do that twice.

Still, before she could even allow herself to ponder making the decision, she got out of bed, grabbed his T-shirt from the floor and pulled it over her head. Then she padded down the hallway, hoping he didn't have any surprise visitors. That would be a nightmare. Getting caught wearing only a T-shirt in her boss's hallway. There would be a lot of questions about what they had just spent the last few hours doing, that was for sure.

She wondered if Jonathan might be outside again, but she decided to check his office first. And was rewarded when she saw him sitting at the computer, his head lowered over the keyboard, some of his dark hair falling over his face after coming loose from the braid he normally kept it in.

Her heart clenched painfully, and it disturbed her that her heart was the first part of her body to tighten. The rest of her followed shortly thereafter, but she really wished her reaction was more about her body than her feelings. She couldn't afford to have feelings for him. She wasn't staying in Copper Ridge. And even if she were, he wouldn't want her long-term, anyway.

She took a deep breath, trying to dispel the strange, constricted feeling that had overtaken her lungs. "I thought I might find you here," she said.

He looked up, his expression betraying absolutely no surprise. He sneaked up on her all the time, but of course, as always, Jonathan was unflappable. "I just had a few schematics to check over." He pushed the chair away from the desk and stood, reaching over his head to stretch.

She was held captive by the sight of him. Even fully dressed, he was a beautiful thing.

His shoulders and chest were broad and muscular, his waist trim. His face like sculpted rock, or hardened bronze, uncompromising. But she knew the secret way to make those lips soften. Only for her.

No, not only for you. He does this all the time. They are just softening for you right now.

It was good for her to remember that.

"I'm finished now," he said, treating her to a smile that made her feel like melting ice cream on a hot day.

"Good," she said, not quite sure why she said it, because it wasn't like they had made plans. She wondered when he would ask her to leave. Or maybe he wanted her to leave, but didn't want to tell her. "It's late," she said. "I could go."

"Do you need to go?"

"No," she said, a little too quickly.

"Then don't."

Relief washed over her, and she did her best not to show him just how pleased she was by that statement. "Okay," she said, "then I won't go."

"I was thinking. About your list."

She blinked. "My list?"

"Yeah, your list. You had dancing on there. Pretty sure you had a kiss. And whether or not it was on the list…you did lose your virginity. Since I helped you with those items, I figured I might help you with some of the others."

A deep sense of pleasure and something that felt a lot like delight washed through her. "Really?"

"Yes," he said, "really. I figure we started all of this, so we might as well keep going."

"I don't have an official list."

"Well, that's ridiculous. If you're going to do this thing, you have to do it right." He grabbed a sheet of paper out of the printer and settled back down in the office chair. "Let's make a list."

He picked up a pen and started writing.

"What are you doing? I didn't tell you what I wanted yet."

"I'm writing down what we already did so you have the satisfaction of checking those off."

Her stomach turned over. "Don't write down all of it."

"Oh," he said, "I am. All of it. In detail."

"No!" She crossed the space between them and stood behind him, wrapping her arms around his broad shoulders as if she might restrain him. He kept on writing. She peered around his head, then slapped the pen out of his hand when she saw him writing a very dirty word. "Stop it. If anybody finds that list I could be... incriminated."

He laughed and swiveled the chair to the side. He wrapped his arm around her waist and pulled her onto his lap. "Oh no. We would hate for you to be incriminated. But on the other hand, the world would know you spent the afternoon with a very firm grip on my—"

"No!"

He looked at her and defiantly put a checkmark by what he had just written. She huffed, but settled into his hold. She liked this too much. Him smiling, him holding her when they had clothes on as if he just wanted to hold her.

It was nice to have him want her in bed. Very nice. But this was something else, and it was nice, too.

"Okay, so we have dancing, kissing, sex, and all of the many achievements beneath the sex," he said, ignoring her small noises of protest. "So what else?"

"I want to go to a place where I need a passport," she said.

"We could drive to Canada."

She laughed. "I was thinking more like Europe. But... Could we really drive to Canada?"

"Well," he said, "maybe not today, since I have to be back here by Monday."

"That's fine. I was thinking more Paris than Vancouver."

"Hey, they speak French in Canada."

"Just write it down," she said, poking his shoulder.

"Fine. What next?"

"I feel like I should try alcohol," she said slowly. "Just so I know."

"Fair enough." He wrote *get hammered*.

"That is not what I said."

"Sorry. I got so excited about the idea of getting you drunk. Lowering your inhibitions."

She rolled her eyes. "I'm already more uninhibited with you than I've ever been with anyone else." It was true, she realized, as soon as she said it. She was more herself with Jonathan than she had ever been with anyone, including her family, who had known her for her entire life.

Maybe it was the fact that, in a town full of people who were familiar with her, at least by reputation, he was someone she hadn't known at all until a couple weeks ago.

Maybe it was the fact that he had no expectations of her beyond what they'd shared. Whatever the case, around him she felt none of the pressure that she felt around other people in the community.

No need to censor herself, or hide; no need to be respectable or serene when she felt like being disreputable and wild.

"I want to kiss in the rain," she said.

"Given weather patterns," he said slowly, "we should be able to accomplish that, too."

She was ridiculously pleased he wanted to be a part of that, pleased that he hadn't said anything about her finding a guy to kiss in the rain in Paris. She shouldn't be happy he was assuming he would be the person to help her fulfill these things. She should be annoyed. She should feel like he was inserting himself into her independence, but she didn't. Mostly because he made her independence seem...well, like *more*.

"You're very useful, aren't you?"

He looked at her, putting his hand on her cheek, his

dark gaze serious as it met hers. "I'm glad I can be useful to you."

She felt him getting hard beneath her backside, and that pleased her, too. "Parts of you are very useful," she said, reaching behind her and slowly stroking his length.

The light in his eyes changed, turning much more intense. "Hayley Thompson," he said, "I would say that's shocking behavior."

"I would say you're responsible, Jonathan Bear."

He shook his head. "No, princess, you're responsible for this. For all of this. This is you. It's what you want, right? The things on your list that you don't even want to write down. It's part of you. You don't get to blame it all on me."

She felt strangely empowered by his words. By the idea that this was her, and not just him leading her somewhere.

"That's very… Well, that's very… I like it." She furthered her exploration of him, increasing the pressure of her touch. "At least, I like it with you."

"I'm not complaining."

"That's good," she said softly, continuing to stroke him through the fabric of his pants.

She looked down, watched herself touching him. It was…well, now that she had started, she didn't want to stop.

"I would be careful if I were you," he said, his tone laced with warning, "because you're about to start something, and it's very likely you need to take a break from all that."

"Do I? Why would I need a break?"

"Because you're going to get sore," he said, maddeningly pragmatic.

And, just as maddeningly, it made her blush to hear him say it. "I don't really mind," she said finally.

"You don't?" His tone was calm, but heat flared in the depths of his dark eyes.

"No," she replied, still trailing her fingertips over his hardening body. "I like feeling the difference. In me. I like being so…aware of everything we've done." For her, that was a pretty brazen proclamation, though she had a feeling it paled in comparison to the kinds of things other women had said to him in the past.

But she wasn't one of those other women. And right now he was responding to her, so she wasn't going to waste a single thought on anyone who had come before her. She held his interest now. That was enough.

"There's something else on my list," she said, fighting to keep her voice steady, fighting against the nerves firing through her.

"Is that so?"

She sucked in a sharp breath. "Yes. I want to… That is… What you did for me… A couple of times now… I want to… I want to…" She gave up trying to get the words out. She wasn't sure she had the right words for what she wanted to do, anyway, and she didn't want to humiliate herself by saying something wrong.

So, with unsteady hands, she undid the closure on his jeans and lowered the zipper. She looked up at him. If she expected to get any guidance, she was out of luck. He just stared at her, his dark eyes unfathomable, his jaw tight, a muscle in his cheek ticking.

She shifted on his lap, sliding gracefully to the floor in front of the chair. Then she went to her knees and turned to face him, flicking her hair out of her face.

He still said nothing, watching her closely, unnervingly so. But she wasn't going to turn back now. She lifted the waistband of his underwear, pulling it out in order to clear his impressive erection, then she pulled the fabric partway down his hips, as far as she could go with him sitting.

He was beautiful.

That feeling of intimidation she'd felt the first time she'd seen him had faded completely. Now she knew what he could do, and she appreciated it greatly. He had shown her so many things; he'd made her pleasure the number one priority. And she wanted to give to him in return.

Well, she also knew this would be for her, too.

She slid her hands up his thighs, then curled her fingers around his hardened length, squeezing him firmly. She was learning that he wasn't breakable there. That he liked a little bit of pressure.

"Hayley," he said, his voice rough, "I don't think you know what you're doing."

"No," she said, "I probably don't. But I know what I want. And it's been so much fun having what I want." She rose up slightly, then leaned in, pressing her lips to the head of his shaft. He jerked beneath her touch, and she took that as approval.

A couple hours ago she would have been afraid that she'd hurt him. But male pleasure, she was discovering, sometimes looked a little like pain. Heck, female pleasure was a little like pain. Sex was somewhere between. The aching need to have it all and the intense rush of satisfaction that followed.

She shivered just thinking about it.

And then she flicked her tongue out, slowly testing this new territory. She hummed, a low sound in the back of her throat, as she explored the taste of him, the texture. Jonathan Bear was her favorite indulgence, she was coming to realize. There was nothing about him she didn't like. Nothing he had done to her she didn't love. She liked the way he felt, and apparently she liked the way he tasted, too.

She parted her lips slowly, worked them over the head, then swallowed down as much of him as she could. The accompanying sound he made hollowed out her stomach, made her feel weak and powerful at the same time.

His body was such an amazing thing. So strong, like it had been carved straight from the mountain. Yet it wasn't in any way cold or unmovable; it was hot. His body had changed hers. Yes, he'd taken her virginity, but he had also taught her to feel pleasure she hadn't realized she had the capacity to feel.

Such power in his body, and yet, right now, it trembled beneath her touch. The whisper-soft touch of her lips possessed the power to rock him, to make him shake. To make him shatter.

Right now, desire was enough. She didn't need skill. She didn't need experience. And she felt completely confident in that.

She slipped her tongue over his length as she took him in deep, and he bucked his hips lightly, touching the back of her throat. Her throat contracted and he jerked back.

"Sorry," he said, his voice strained.

"No," she said, gripping him with one hand and bringing her lips back against him. "Don't apologize. I like it."

"You're inexperienced."

She nodded slowly, then traced him with the tip of her tongue. "Yes," she agreed, "I am. I've never done this for any other man. I've never even thought about it before." His hips jerked again, and she realized he liked this. That he—however much he tried to pretend he didn't—liked that her desire was all for him.

"I think you might be corrupting me," she said, keeping her eyes wide as she took him back into her mouth.

He grunted, fisting his hands in her hair, but he didn't pull her away again.

The muscles in his thighs twitched beneath her fingertips, and he seemed to grow larger, harder in her mouth. She increased the suction, increased the friction, used her hands as well as her mouth to drive him as crazy as she possibly could.

There was no plan. There was no skill. There was just the need to make him even half as mindless as he'd made her over the past couple days.

He had changed her. He had taken her from innocence…to this. She would be marked by him forever. He would always be her first. But society didn't have a term for a person's experience after virginity. So she didn't have a label for the impact she wanted to make on him.

Jonathan hadn't been a virgin for a very long time, she suspected. And she probably wasn't particularly special as a sexual partner.

So she had to try to make herself special.

She had no tricks to make this the best experience he'd ever had. She had only herself. And so she gave it to him. All of her. Everything.

"Hayley," he said, his voice rough, ragged. "You better stop."

She didn't. She ignored him. She had a feeling he was close; she recognized the signs now. She had watched him reach the point of pleasure enough times that she had a fair idea of what it looked like. Of what it felt like. His whole body tensing, his movements becoming less controlled.

She squeezed the base of him tightly, pulling him in deeper, and then he shattered. And she swallowed down every last shudder of need that racked his big body.

In the aftermath, she was dazed, her heart pounding hard, her entire body buzzing. She looked up at him from her position on the floor, and he looked down at her, his dark eyes blazing with…anger, maybe? Passion? A kind of sharp, raw need she hadn't ever seen before.

"You're going to pay for that," he said.

"Oh," she returned, "I hope so."

He swept her up, crushed her against his chest. "You have to put it on my list first," she said.

Then he brought his mouth down to hers, and whatever she'd intended to write down was forgotten until morning.

CHAPTER TEN

SOMETIME ON SUNDAY afternoon Hayley had gone home. Because, she had insisted, she wasn't able to work in either his T-shirt or the dress she had worn to the bar on Friday.

He hadn't agreed, but he had been relieved to have the reprieve. He didn't feel comfortable sharing the bed with her while he slept. Which had meant sleeping on the couch in the office after she drifted off.

He just... He didn't sleep with women. He didn't see the point in inviting that kind of intimacy. Having her spend the night in his bed was bad enough. But he hadn't wanted to send her home, either. He didn't want to think about why. Maybe it was because she expected to stay, because of her general inexperience.

Which made him think of the moment she had taken him into her mouth, letting him know he was the first man she had ever considered doing that for. Just the thought of it made his eyes roll back in his head.

Now, it was late Monday afternoon and she had been slowly driving him crazy with the prim little outfit she had come back to work in, as though he didn't know what she looked like underneath it.

Who knew he'd like a good girl who gave head like a dream.

She had also insisted that they stay professional during work hours, and it was making it hard for him to concentrate. Of course, it was always hard for him to concentrate on office work. In general, he hated it.

Though bringing Hayley into the office certainly made it easier to bear.

Except for the part where it was torture.

He stood up from his chair and stretched slowly, trying to work the tension out of his body. But he had a feeling that until he was buried inside Hayley's body again, tension was just going to be the state of things.

"Oh," Hayley said, "Joshua Grayson just emailed and said he needs you to go by the county office and sign a form. And no, it can't be faxed."

For the first time in his life, Johathan was relieved to encounter bureaucracy. He needed to get out of this space. He needed to get his head on straight.

"Great," he said.

"Maybe I should go with you," she said. "I've never been down to the building and planning office, and you might need me to run errands in the future."

He gritted his teeth. "Yeah, probably."

"I'll drive my own car." She stood, grabbing her purse off the desk. "Because by the time we're done it will be time for me to get off."

He ground his teeth together even harder, because he couldn't ignore her double entendre even though he knew it had been accidental. And because, in addition to the double meaning, it was clear she intended to stay in town tonight and not at his place.

He should probably be grateful she wasn't being clingy. He didn't like to encourage women to get too attached to him, not at all.

"Great idea," he said.

But he didn't think it was a great idea, and he grumbled the entire way to town in the solitude of his pickup truck, not missing the irony that he had been wanting alone time, and was now getting it, and was upset about it.

The errand really did take only a few minutes, and afterward it still wasn't quite time for Hayley to clock out.

"Do you want to grab something to eat?" he asked, though he had no earthly idea why. He should get something for himself and go home, deal with that tension he had been pondering earlier.

She looked back and forth, clearly edgy. "In town?"

"Yes," he returned, "in town."

"Oh. I don't... I guess so."

"Calm down," he said. "I'm not asking you to Beaches. Let's just stop by the Crab Shanty."

She looked visibly relieved, and again he couldn't quantify why that annoyed him.

He knew they shouldn't be seen together in town. He had a feeling she also liked the casual nature of the restaurant. It was much more likely to look like a boss and employee grabbing something to eat than it was to look like a date.

They walked from where they had parked a few streets over, and paused at the crosswalk. They waited for one car to crawl by, clearly not interested in heeding the law that said pedestrians had the right-of-way. Then Jonathan charged ahead of her across the street and up to the faded yellow building. A small line was already forming outside the order window, and he noticed that Hayley took pains to stand slightly behind him.

When it was their turn to order, he decided he wasn't having any of her missish circumspection. They shouldn't be seen together as anything more than a boss and an assistant.

But right now, hell if he cared. "Two orders of fish and chips, the halibut. Two beers and a Diet Coke."

He pulled his wallet out and paid before Hayley could protest, then he grabbed the plastic number from the window, and the two of them walked over to a picnic table positioned outside the ramshackle building. There was no indoor seating, which could be a little bracing on windy days, and there weren't very many days that didn't have wind on the Oregon coast.

Jonathan set the number on the wooden table, then sat down heavily, looking up at the blue-and-white-striped umbrella wiggling in the breeze.

"Two beers?"

"One of them is for you," he said, his words verging on a growl.

"I'm not going to drink a beer." She looked sideways. "At least not here."

"Yeah, right out here on Main Street in front of God and everybody? You're a lot braver in my bedroom."

He was goading her, but he didn't much care. He was... Well dammit, it pissed him off. To see how ashamed she was to be with him. How desperate she was to hide it. Even if he understood it, it was like a branding iron straight to the gut.

"You can't say that so loud," she hissed, leaning forward, grabbing the plastic number and pulling it to her chest. "What if people heard you?"

"I thought you were reinventing yourself, Hayley Thompson."

"Not for the benefit of...the town. It's about me."

"It's going to be about you not getting dinner if you keep hiding our number." He snatched the plastic triangle from her hands.

She let out a heavy sigh and leaned back, crossing

her arms. "Well, the extra beer is for you. Put it in your pocket."

"You can put it in your own pocket. Drink it back at your place."

"No, thanks."

"Don't you want to tick that box on your list? We ticked off some pretty interesting ones last night."

Her face turned scarlet. "You're being obnoxious, Jonathan."

"I've been obnoxious from day one. You just found it easy to ignore when I had my hand in your pants."

Her mouth dropped open, then she snapped it shut again. Their conversation was cut off when their food was placed in front of them.

She dragged the white cardboard box toward her and opened it, removing the container of coleslaw and setting it to the side before grabbing a french fry and biting into it fiercely. Her annoyance was clearly telegraphed by the ferocity with which she ate each bite of food. And the determination that went into her looking at anything and everything around them except for him.

"Enjoying the view?" he asked after a moment.

"The ocean is very pretty," she snapped.

"And you don't see it every day?"

"I never tire of the majesty of nature."

His lips twitched, in spite of his irritation. "Of course not."

The wind whipped up, blowing a strand of dark hair into Hayley's face. Reflexively, he reached across the table and pushed it out of her eyes. She jerked back, her lips going slack, her expression shocked.

"You're my boss," she said, her voice low. "As far as everyone is concerned."

"Well," he said, "I'm your lover. As far as I'm concerned."

"Stop."

"I thought you wanted new experiences? I thought you were tired of hiding? And here you are, hiding."

"I don't want to…perform," she said. "My new experiences are for me. Not for everyone else's consumption. That's why I'm leaving. So I can…do things without an audience."

"You want your dirty secrets, is that it? You want me to be your dirty secret."

"It's five o'clock," she said, her tone stiff. "I'm going to go home now."

She collected her food, and left the beer, standing up in a huff and taking off down the street in the opposite direction from where they had parked.

"Where are you going?"

"Home," she said sharply.

He gathered up the rest of the food and stomped after her. "You parked the other way."

"I'll get it in the morning."

"Then you better leave your house early. Unless this is you tendering your resignation."

"I'm not quitting," she said, the color heightening in her face. "I'm just… I'm irritated with you."

She turned away from him, continuing to walk quickly down the street. He took two strides and caught up with her. "I see that." He kept pace with her, but she seemed bound and determined not to look at him. "Would you care to share why?"

"Not even a little bit."

"So you're insisting that you're my employee, and that you want to be treated like my employee in public.

But that clearly excludes when you decide to run off having a temper tantrum."

She whirled around then, stopping in her tracks. "Why are you acting like this? You've been...much more careful than this up till now." She sniffed. "Out of deference to my innocence?"

"What innocence, baby? Because I took that." He smiled, knowing he was getting to her. That he was making her feel as bad as he did. "Pretty damn thoroughly."

"I can't do this with you. Not here." She paused at the street corner and looked both ways before hurrying across the two-lane road. He followed suit. She walked down the sidewalk, passed the coffeehouse, which was closing up for the day, then rounded the side of the brick building and headed toward the back.

"Is this where you live?" he asked.

"Maybe," she returned, sounding almost comically stubborn. Except he didn't feel like much was funny about this situation.

"Here in the alley?" he asked, waving his hand around the mostly vacant space.

"Yes. In the Dumpster with the mice. It's not so bad. I shredded up a bunch of newspaper and made a little bed."

"I suspect this is the real reason you've been spending the night at my place, then."

She scowled. "If you want to fight with me, come upstairs."

He didn't want to fight with her. He wanted to grab her, pull her into his arms and kiss her. He wanted to stop talking. Wanted to act logical instead of being wounded by something he knew he should want to avoid.

It didn't benefit him to have anyone in town know what he was doing with Hayley. He should want to hide it as badly as she did.

But the idea that she was enjoying his body, enjoying slumming it with him in the sheets, and was damned ashamed of him in the streets burned like hell.

But he followed her through the back door to a little hallway that contained two other doors. She unlocked one of them and held it open for him. Then she gestured to the narrow staircase. "Come on."

"Who's the boss around here?"

"I'm off the clock," she said.

He shrugged, then walked up the stairs and into an open-plan living room with exposed beams and brick. It was a much bigger space than he had expected it to be, though it was also mostly empty. As if she had only half committed to living there.

But then, he supposed, her plan *was* to travel the world.

"Nice place," he said.

"Yeah," she said, "Cassie gave me a deal."

"Nice of her."

"Some people are nice, Jonathan."

"Meaning I'm not?" he asked.

She nodded in response, her mouth firmly sealed, her chin jutting out stubbornly.

"Right. Because I bought you fish and french fries and beer. And I give you really great orgasms. I'm a monster."

"I don't know what game you're playing," she said, suddenly looking much less stubborn and a little more wobbly. And that made him feel something close to guilty. "What's the point in blurring the lines while we walk through town? We both know this isn't a relationship. It's…it's boxes being ticked on a list."

"Sure. But why does it matter if people in town know you're doing that?"

"You know why it matters. Don't play like you don't understand. You do. I know you do. You know who I am, and you know that I feel like I'm under a microscope. I shared all of that with you. Don't act surprised by it now."

"Well," he said, opting for honesty even though he knew it was a damned bad idea. "Maybe I don't like being your dirty secret."

"It's not about you. Any guy that I was… Anyone that I was…doing this with. It would be a secret. It has to be."

"Why?"

"Because!" she exploded. "Because everyone will be…disappointed."

"Honey," he said, "I don't think people spend half as much time thinking about you as you think they do."

"No," she said. "They do. You know Ace. He's the pastor's son. He ran away from home, he got married, he got divorced. Then he came back and opened a bar. My parents…they're great. They really are. But they had a lot of backlash over that. People saying that the Bible itself says if you train up a child the way he should go, he's not going to depart from it. Well, he departed from it, at least as far as a lot of the congregants were concerned. People actually left the church." She sucked in a sharp breath, then let it out slowly. "I wanted to do better than that for them. It was important. For me to be…the good one."

Caring about what people thought was a strange concept. Appearances had never mattered to Jonathan. For him, it had always been about actions. What the hell did Rebecca care if he had been good? All she cared about was being taken care of. He couldn't imagine being bound by rules like that.

For the first time, he wondered if there wasn't some kind of freedom in no one having a single good expectation of you.

"But you don't like being the good one. At least, not by these standards."

Her eyes glittered with tears now. She shook her head. "I don't know. I just… I don't know. I'm afraid. Afraid of what people will think. Afraid of what my parents will think. Afraid of them being disappointed. And hurt. They've always put a lot of stock in me being what Ace wasn't. They love Ace, don't get me wrong. It's just…"

"He made things hard for them."

Hayley nodded, looking miserable. "Yes. He did. And I don't want to do that. Only…only, I was the good one and he still ended up with the kind of life I want."

"Is that all?" Jonathan asked. "Or are you afraid of who you might be if you don't have all those rules to follow?"

A flash of fear showed in her eyes, and he felt a little guilty about putting it there. Not guilty enough to take it back. Not guilty enough to stay away from her. Not guilty enough to keep his hands to himself. He reached out, cupping her cheek, then wrapped his arm around her waist and drew her toward him. "Does it scare you? Who you might be if no one told you what to do? I don't care about the rules, Hayley. You can be whoever you want with me. Say whatever you want. Drink whatever you want. Do whatever you want."

"I don't know," she said, wiggling against him, trying to pull away. "I don't know what I want."

"I think you do. I just think you wish you wanted something else." He brushed his thumb over her cheekbone. "I think you like having rules because it keeps you from going after what scares you."

He ignored the strange reverberation those words set off inside him. The chain reaction that seemed to burst all the way down his spine.

Recognition.

Truth.

Yeah, he ignored all that, and he dipped his head, claiming her mouth with his own.

Suddenly, it seemed imperative that he have her here. In her apartment. That he wreck this place with his desire for her. That he have her on every surface, against every wall, so that whenever she walked in, whenever she looked around, he was what she thought of. So that she couldn't escape this. So that she couldn't escape him.

"You think you know me now?" she asked, her eyes squinting with challenge. Clearly, she wasn't going to back down without a fight. And that was one of the things he liked about her. For all that she was an innocent church secretary, she had spirit. She had the kind of steel backbone that he admired, that he respected. The kind of strength that could get you through anything. But there was a softness to her as well, and that was something more foreign to him. Something he had never been exposed to, had never really been allowed to have.

"Yeah," he said, tightening his hold and drawing her against his body. "I know you. I know what you look like naked. I know every inch of your skin. How it feels, how it tastes. I know you better than anybody does, baby. You can tell yourself that's not true. You can say that this, what we have, is the crazy thing. That it's a break from your real life. That it's some detour you don't want anyone in town to know you're taking. But I know the truth. And I think somewhere deep down you know it, too. This isn't the break. All that other stuff… prim, proper church girl. That's what isn't real." He cupped her face, smoothing his thumbs over her cheeks. "You're fire, honey, and together we are an explosion."

He kissed her then, proving his point. She tasted like anger, like need, and he was of a mind to consume both. Whatever was on offer. Whatever she would give him.

He was beyond himself. He had never wanted a woman like this before. He had never wanted anything quite like this before. Not money, not security, not his damned house on the hill.

All that want, all that need, paled in comparison to what he felt for Hayley Thompson. The innocent little miss who should have bored him to tears by now, had him aching, panting and begging for more.

He was so hard he was in physical pain.

And when she finally capitulated, when she gave herself over to the kiss, soft fingertips skimming his shoulders, down his back, all the way to his ass, he groaned in appreciation.

There was something extra dirty about Hayley exploring his body. About her wanting him the way she did, because she had never wanted another man like she wanted him. By her own admission. And she had never had a man the way she'd had him, which was an admission she didn't have to make.

He gripped her hips, then slipped his hands down her thighs, grabbing them and pulling her up, urging her legs around his waist. Then he propelled them both across the living room, down onto the couch. He covered her, pressing his hardness against the soft, sweet apex of her thighs. She gasped as he rolled his hips forward.

"Not so ashamed of this now, are you?" He growled, pressing a kiss to her neck, then to her collarbone, then to the edge of her T-shirt.

"I'm not ashamed," she said, gasping for air.

"You could've fooled me, princess."

"It's not about you." She sifted her fingers through his hair. "I'm not ashamed of you."

"Not ashamed of your dirty, wrong-side-of-the-tracks boyfriend?"

Her eyes flashed with hurt and then fascination. "I've never thought of you that way. I never... *Boyfriend?*"

Something burned hot in his chest. "Lover. Whatever."

"I'm not ashamed of you," she reiterated. "Nothing about you. You're so beautiful. If anything, you ought to be ashamed of me. I'm not pretty. Not like you. And I don't even know what I'm doing. I just know what I want. I want you. And I'm afraid for anybody to know the truth. I'm so scared. The only time I'm not scared is when you're holding me."

He didn't want to talk anymore. He consumed her mouth, tasting her deeply, ramping up the arousal between them with each sweet stroke of his tongue across hers. With each deep taste of the sweet flavor that could only ever be Hayley.

He gripped the hem of her top, yanking it over her head, making quick work of her bra. Exposing small, perfect breasts to his inspection. She was pale. All over. Ivory skin, coral-pink nipples. He loved the look of her. Loved the feel of her. Loved so many things about her that it was tempting to just go ahead and say he loved *her*.

That thought swam thick and dizzy in his head. He could barely grab hold of it, didn't want to. So he shoved it to the side. He wasn't going to claim that. Hell no.

He didn't love people. He loved *things*.

He could love her tits, and he could love her skin, could love the way it felt to slide inside her, slick and tight. But he sure as hell couldn't love *her*.

He bent his head, taking one hardened nipple into his mouth, sucking hard, relishing the horse sound of pleasure on her lips as he did so. Then he kissed his way down her stomach, to the edge of her pants, pulling them down her thighs, leaving her bare and open.

He pressed his hand between her legs, slicked his thumb over her, teased her entrance with one finger. She began to whimper, rolling her hips under him, arching them to meet him, and he watched. Watched as she took one finger inside, then another.

He damn well watched himself corrupt her, and he let himself enjoy it. Because he was sick, because he was broken, but at least it wasn't a surprise.

Everyone in his life was familiar with it.

His father had tried to beat it out of him. His mother had run from it.

Only Rebecca had ever stayed, and it was partly because she didn't know any better.

Hayley didn't know any better, either, come to that. Not really. Not when it came to men. Not when it came to sex. She was blinded by what he could make her body feel, so she had an easy enough time ignoring the rest. But that wouldn't last forever.

Fair enough, since they wouldn't last forever, anyway. They both knew it. So there was no point in worrying about it. Not really.

Instead, he would embrace this, embrace the rush.

Embrace the hollowed out feeling in his gut that bordered on sickness. The tension in his body that verged on pain. The need that rendered him hard as iron and hot as fire.

"Come for me," he commanded, his voice hoarse. All other words, all other thoughts were lost to him. All he could do was watch her writhing beneath his touch, so hot, so wet for him, arching her hips and taking his fingers in deeper.

"Not yet," she gasped, emitting little broken sounds.

"Yes," he said. "You will. You're going to come for me now, Hayley, because I told you to. Your body is mine. You're mine." He slid his thumb over the delicate bundle of nerves there.

And then he felt her shatter beneath his touch. Felt her internal muscles pulse around his knuckles.

He reached into his back pocket, took out his wallet and found a condom quickly. He tore it open, then wrenched free his belt buckle and took down the zipper. He pushed his jeans partway down his hips, rolled the condom on his hard length and thrust inside her, all the way to the hilt. She was wet and ready for him, and he had to grit his teeth to keep from embarrassing himself, to keep it from being over before it had begun.

She gasped as he filled her, and then grabbed his ass when he retreated. Her fingernails dug into his skin, and he relished the pain this petite little thing could inflict on him. Of course, it was nothing compared to the pain he felt from his arousal. From the great, burning need inside him.

No, nothing compared to that. Nothing at all.

He adjusted their positions, dragging her sideways on the couch, bringing her hips to the edge of the cushion, going down on his knees to the hardwood floor.

He knelt there, gripping her hips and pulling her tightly against him, urging her to wrap her legs around him. The floor bit into his knees, but he didn't care. All he cared about was having her, taking her, claiming her. He gripped her tightly, his blunt fingertips digging into her flesh.

He wondered if he would leave a mark. He hoped he might.

Hoped that she would see for days to come where he had held her. Even if she wouldn't hold his hand in public, she would remember when he'd held her hips in private, when he'd driven himself deep inside her, clinging to her like she might be the source of all life.

Yeah, she would remember that. She would remember this.

He watched as a deep red flush spread over her skin, covering her breasts, creeping up her neck. She was on the verge of another orgasm. He loved that. Another thing he was allowed to love.

Loved watching her lose control. Loved watching her so close to giving it up for him again, completely. Utterly. He was going to ruin her for any other man. That was his vow, there and then, on the floor of her apartment, with a ragged splinter digging into his knee through the fabric of his jeans. She was never going to fuck anyone else without thinking of him. Without wanting him. Without wishing it were him.

She would go to Paris, and some guy would do her with a view of the Eiffel tower in the background. And she would wish she were here, counting the familiar beams on her ceiling.

And when she came home for a visit and she passed him on the street, she would shiver with a longing that she would never quite get rid of.

So many people in his life had left him. As far as he'd known, they had done it without a backward glance. But Hayley would never forget him. He would make sure of it. Damn sure.

His own arousal ratcheted up to impossible proportions. He was made entirely of his need for her. Of his need for release. And he forgot what he was trying to do. Forgot that this was about her. That this was about making her tremble, making her shake. Because he was trembling. He was shaking.

He was afraid he might be the one who was indelibly marked by all this.

He was the one who wouldn't be able to forget. The one who would never be with anyone else without thinking of her. No matter how skilled the woman was who might come after her, it would never be the same as the sweet, genuine urging of Hayley's hips against his. It would never be quite like the tight, wet clasp of her body.

He had been entirely reshaped, remade, to fit inside her, and no one else would do.

That thought ignited in his stomach, overtook him completely, lit him on fire.

When he came, it was with her name on his lips, with a strange satisfaction washing through him that left him only hungrier in the end, emptier. Because this was ending, and he knew it.

She wasn't going to work for him forever. She wasn't going to stay in Copper Ridge. She might hold on to him in secret, but in public, she would never touch him.

And as time passed, she would let go of him by inches, walking off to the life of freedom she was so desperate for.

Walking off like everyone else.

Right now, she was looking up at him, a mixture

of wonder and deep emotion visible in her blue eyes. She reached up, stroking his face. Some of his hair had been tugged from the leather strap, and she brushed the strands out of his eyes.

It was weird how that hit him. How it touched him. After all the overtly sexual ways she'd put her hands on him, why that sweet gesture impacted him low and deep.

"Stay with me," she said, her voice soft. "The night. In my bed."

That hit even harder.

He had never slept with her. He didn't sleep with women. But that was all about to change. He was going to sleep with her because he wanted to. Because he didn't want to release his hold on her for one moment, not while he still had her.

"Okay," he said.

Then, still buried deep inside her, he picked her up from the couch, brought them both to a standing position and started walking toward the door at the back of the room. "Bedroom is this way?"

"How did you know?"

"Important things, I know. Where the bedroom is." He kissed her lips. "How to make you scream my name. That I know."

"Care to make me scream it a few more times?"

"The neighbors might hear."

It was a joke, but he could still see her hesitation. "That's okay," she said slowly.

And even though he was reasonably confident that was a lie, he carried her into her bedroom and lay down on the bed with her.

It didn't matter if it was a lie. Because they had all night to live in it. And that was good enough for him.

CHAPTER ELEVEN

WHEN HE WOKE UP the next morning he was disoriented. He was lying in a bed that was too small for his large frame, and he had a woman wrapped around him. Of course, he knew immediately which woman it was. It couldn't be anyone else. Even in the fog of sleep, he wasn't confused about Hayley's identity.

She smelled like sunshine and wildflowers. Or maybe she just smelled like soap and skin and only reminded him of sunshine and wildflowers, because they were innocent things. New things. The kinds of things that could never be corrupted by the world around them.

The kinds of things not even he could wreck.

She was that kind of beautiful.

But the other reason he was certain it was Hayley was that there was no other woman he would have fallen asleep with. It was far too intimate a thing, sharing a bed with someone when you weren't angling for an orgasm. He had never seen the point of it. It was basically the same as sharing a toothbrush, and he wasn't interested in that, either.

He looked at Hayley, curled up at his side, her brown hair falling across her face, her soft lips parted, her breathing easy and deep. The feeling carved out in his chest was a strange one.

Hell, lying there in the early morning, sharing a toothbrush with Hayley didn't even seem so insane.

He sat up, shaking off the last cobwebs of sleep and extricating himself from Hayley's hold. He groaned when her fingertips brushed the lower part of his stomach, grazing his insistent morning erection. He had half a mind to wake her up the best way he knew how.

But the longer the realization of what had happened last night sat with him, the more eager he was to put some distance between them.

He could get some coffee, get his head on straight and come back fully clothed. Then maybe the two of them could prepare for the workday.

He needed to compartmentalize. He had forgotten that yesterday. He had let himself get annoyed about something that never should have bothered him. Had allowed old hurts to sink in when he shouldn't give a damn whether or not Hayley wanted to hold his hand when they walked down the street. She wasn't his girlfriend. And all the words that had passed between them in the apartment, all the anger that had been rattling around inside him, seemed strange now. Like it had all happened to somebody else. The morning had brought clarity, and it was much needed.

He hunted around the room, collecting his clothes and tugging them on quickly, then he walked over to the window, drew back the curtains and tried to get a sense of what time it was. She didn't have a clock in her room. He wondered if she just looked at her phone.

The sky was pink, so it had to be nearing six. He really needed to get home and take care of the horses. He didn't want to mess up their routine. But he would come back. Or maybe Hayley would just come to his place on time.

Then he cursed, realizing he had left his car at the other end of Main Street. He walked back to the living room, pulled on his boots and headed out the door, down the stairs. His vision was blurry, and he was in desperate need of caffeine. There were two doors in the hallway, and he reached for the one closest to him.

And nearly ran right into Cassie Caldwell as he walked into The Grind.

The morning sounds of the coffee shop filled his ears, the intense smell of the roast assaulting him in the best way.

But Cassie was staring at him, wide-eyed, as were the ten people sitting inside the dining room. One of whom happened to be Pastor John Thompson.

Jonathan froze, mumbled something about coming in through the back door, and then walked up to the counter. He was going to act like there was nothing remarkable about where he had just come from. Was going to do his very best to look like there was nothing at all strange about him coming through what he now realized was a private entrance used only by the tenant upstairs. It didn't escape his notice that the pastor was eyeballing him closely. And so was Cassie. Really, so was everybody. Damn small town.

Now, he could see why Hayley had been so vigilant yesterday.

If only he could go back and be vigilant in his door choice.

"Black coffee," he said, "two shots of espresso."

Cassie's gaze turned hard. "I know."

"I came through the wrong door," he said.

She walked over to the espresso machine, wrapped a damp cloth around the wand that steamed the milk and twisted it, a puff of steam coming out as she jerked the cloth up and down roughly, her eyes never leaving his. "Uh-huh."

"I did."

"And it's just a coincidence that my tenant happens to live upstairs. My tenant who works for you." She said that part softly, and he was sure nobody else in the room heard it.

"That's right," he said. "Just a coincidence."

Suddenly, the door to the coffee shop opened again, and Hayley appeared, wearing a T-shirt and jeans, her hair wild, like she had just rolled out of bed.

Her eyes widened when she saw her father. Then she looked over at the counter and her eyes widened even further when she saw Jonathan.

"Good morning," he said, his voice hard. "Fancy meeting you here before work."

"Yes," she said. "I'm just gonna go get ready."

She turned around and walked back out of the coffee shop, as quickly as she had come in. So much for being casual. If he hadn't already given it away, he was pretty sure Hayley's scampering had.

"You were saying?" Cassie said, her tone brittle.

"I'm sorry," he said, leaning in. "Is she your sister?"

"No."

"Best friend?"

"No."

"Is she your daughter? Because I have a feeling I'm about to catch hell from the reverend here in a few minutes, but I'm not really sure why I'm catching it from you."

"Because I know her. I know all about you. I am friends with your sister, and I know enough through her."

"Undoubtedly all about my great personal sacrifice and sparkling personality," he said.

Cassie's expression softened. "Rebecca loves you.

But she's also realistic about the fact that you aren't a love-and-commitment kind of guy. Also, I do believe Ms. Hayley Thompson is younger than your sister."

"And last I checked, I wasn't committing any crimes. I will just take the coffee. You can keep the lecture."

He was not going to get chased out of the coffee shop, no matter how many people looked at him. No matter how much Cassie lectured him.

He was not the poor kid he'd once been. He was more than just a boy who had been abandoned by both parents. He was a damned boon to the town. His business brought in good money. *He* brought in good money. He wasn't going to be treated like dirt beneath anybody's shoe.

Maybe Hayley was too good for him, but she was sleeping with him. She wanted him. So it wasn't really up to anybody to say that she shouldn't.

When he turned around after Cassie gave him his coffee, the pastor stood up at his table and began to make his way over to Jonathan.

"Hello. Jonathan, right?" the older man said, his voice shot through with the same kind of steel that Jonathan often heard in Hayley's voice. Clearly, she got her strength from her father. It was also clear to Jonathan that he was not being spoken to by a pastor at the moment. But by a fairly angry dad.

"Pastor John," Jonathan said by way of greeting.

"Why don't you join me for a cup of coffee?"

Not exactly the words Jonathan had expected, all things considered. He could sense the tension in the room, sense the tension coming off Hayley's father.

People were doing their very best to watch, without appearing to do so. Any hope Jonathan had retained that they were oblivious to what it meant that he had come down from the upstairs apartment was dashed by just how fascinated they all were. And by the steady intent on Pastor John's face.

If the old man wanted to sit him down and humiliate him in front of the town, wanted to talk about how Jonathan wasn't fit to lick the dust off Hayley's boots, Jonathan wouldn't be surprised. Hell, he welcomed it. It was true, after all.

"I think I will," Jonathan said, following the other man back to his table.

He took a seat, his hand curled tightly around his coffee cup.

"I don't think we've ever formally met," John said, leaning back in his chair.

"No," Jonathan said, "we wouldn't have. I don't recall darkening the door of the church in my lifetime. Unless it was to repair something."

Let him know just what kind of man Jonathan was. That's where this was headed, anyway. Jonathan had never met a woman's parents before. He had never been in a relationship that was serious enough to do so. And this wasn't serious, either. But because of this damn small town and Hayley's role in it, he was being forced into a position he had never wanted to be in.

"I see," the pastor said. "Hayley has been working for you for the past couple of weeks, I believe."

He was cutting right to the chase now. To Jonathan's connection to Hayley, which was undeniable. "Yes."

"I've been very protective of Hayley. Possibly over-protective. But when my son, Ace, went out on his own, he didn't find much but heartbreak. I transferred some of my fear of that happening again onto Hayley, to an unfair degree. So I kept her close. I encouraged her to keep working at the church. To live at home for as long as possible. You have a sister, don't you?"

Damn this man and his ironclad memory for detail. "I didn't think it was Christian to gossip. But I can see that you've certainly heard your share about me."

"I do know a little something about you, yes. My son is married to one of Nathan West's children, as I'm sure you know. And your sister has a connection to that family, as well."

Jonathan gritted his teeth. "Yes. My sister is with Gage. Though only God knows why. Maybe you could ask Him."

"Matters of the heart are rarely straightforward. Whether it's in the case of romantic love, or the love you feel for your children, or your sister. It's a big emotion. And it is scary at times. Not always the most rational. What you feel about Rebecca being with Gage I suppose is similar to the concerns I have about Hayley."

"That she's with a bastard who doesn't deserve her?"

The pastor didn't even flinch. "That she's involved deeply enough that she could be hurt. And if we're going to speak plainly, I suppose the question I could ask you is whether or not you would think any man was good enough for Rebecca, or if you would be concerned—no matter who it was—that he wouldn't handle her with the care you would want."

Jonathan didn't have much to say about that. Only because he was trying to be angry. Trying to take offense at the fact that the older man was ques tioning him. Trying to connect this conversation to what he knew to be true—everybody looked at him and saw someone who wasn't worthy. He certainly didn't deserve kindness from this man, not at all. Didn't deserve for him to sit here and try to forge some kind of connection.

Jonathan had taken advantage of Hayley. Regardless of her level of experience, she was his employee. Even if she had been with a hundred men, what he had done would be problematic. But, as far as he was concerned, the problem was compounded by the fact that Hayley had been innocent.

So he waited. He waited for that hammer to fall. For the accusations to fly.

But they didn't come. So he figured he might try to create a few.

"I'm sure there's a certain type of man you would prefer your daughter be with. But it's definitely not the guy with the bad reputation you'd want stumbling out of her apartment early in the morning."

John nodded slowly, and Jonathan thought—with a certain amount of triumph—that he saw anger flicker briefly in the older man's eyes.

"I told you already that I feel very protective of her," Pastor John said. "But I wonder if, by protecting her as much as I did, I shielded her too effectively from the reality of life. I don't want her to get hurt." He let out a long, slow breath. "But that is not within my control."

"Is this the part where you ask me about my intentions toward your daughter? Because I highly doubt we're ever going to sit around a dinner table and try to make small talk. This isn't that sort of thing." With those words, Jonathan effectively told Hayley's father that all he was doing was fooling around with her. And that wasn't strictly true. Also, he hated himself a little bit for pretending it was.

For saying that sort of thing to her father when he knew it would embarrass her.

But in a way, it would be a mercy. She cared what people in town thought about her. She cared about her father's opinion. And this conversation would make it so much easier for her to let Jonathan go when the time came.

She was always going to let you go. She has traveling to do, places to see. You were her dirty detour along the way. You're the one who needs distance. You're the one who needs to find a way to make it easier.

He ignored that voice, ignored the tightening in his chest.

"Why isn't it that sort of thing?" The question, issued from Hayley's father, his tone firm but steady, reached something deep inside Jonathan, twisted it, cracked it.

It couldn't be anything more than temporary. Because of him. Because of what he was. Who he was. That should be obvious. It would have been even more obvious if Pastor John had simply sat down and started hurling recriminations. About how Jonathan was beneath the man's pure, innocent daughter. About why a formerly impoverished man from the wrong side of the tracks could never be good enough for a woman like her.

It didn't matter that he had money now. He was the same person he had been born to be. The same boy who had been beaten by his father, abandoned by his mother. All that was still in him. And no custom home, no amount of money in his bank account, was ever going to fix it.

If John Thompson wouldn't look at him and see that, if he wouldn't shout it from across a crowded coffee shop so the whole town would hear, then Jonathan was going to have to make it clear.

"Because it's not something I do," he returned, his voice hard. "I'm in for temporary. That's all I've got."

"Well," John said, "that's a pretty neat lie you've been telling yourself, son. But the fact of the matter is, it's only the most you're willing to give, not the most you have the ability to give."

"And you're saying you want me to dig down deep and find it inside myself to be with your daughter forever? Something tells me that probably wouldn't be an ideal situation as far as you're concerned."

"That's between you and Hayley. I have my own personal feelings about it, to be sure. No father wants to believe that his daughter is being used. But if I believe that, then it means I don't see anything good in you, and that isn't true. Everybody knows how you took care of your sister. Whatever you think the people in this town believe about you, they do know that. I can't say you haven't been mistreated by the people here, and it grieves me to think about it."

He shook his head, and Jonathan was forced to believe the older man was being genuine. He didn't quite know what to do with that fact, but he saw the same honesty shining from John that he often saw in Hayley's eyes. An emotional honesty Jonathan had limited experience with.

The older man continued. "You think you don't have the capacity for love? When you've already mentioned your concern for Rebecca a couple of times in this conversation? When the past decade and a half of your life was devoted to caring for her? It's no secret how hard you've worked. I may never have formally met you until this moment, but I know about you, Jonathan Bear, and what I know isn't the reputation you seem to think you have."

"Well, regardless of my reputation, you should be concerned about Hayley's. When I came through that door this morning, it was unintentional. But it's important to Hayley that nobody realizes what's happening between us. So the longer I sit here talking to you, the more risk there is of exposing her to unnecessary chatter. And that's not what I want. So," he said, "out of respect for keeping it a secret, like Hayley wants—"

"That's not what I want."

CHAPTER TWELVE

HAYLEY WAS SHAKING. She had been shaking from the moment she had walked into The Grind and seen Jonathan there, with her father in the background.

Somehow, she had known—just known—that everyone in the room was putting two and two together and coming up with sex.

And she also knew she had definitely made it worse by running away. If she had sauntered in and acted surprised to see Jonathan there, she might have made people think it really was coincidental that the two of them were both in the coffeehouse early in the morning, coming through the same private door. For reasons that had nothing to do with him spending the night upstairs with her.

But she had spent the past five minutes pacing around upstairs, waiting for her breath to normalize, waiting for her heart to stop beating so hard. Neither thing had happened.

Then she had cautiously crept back downstairs and come in to see her father sitting at the table with Jonathan. Fortunately, Jonathan hadn't looked like he'd been punched in the face. But the conversation had definitely seemed tense.

And standing there, looking at what had been her worst nightmare not so long ago, she realized that it just...wasn't. She'd never been ashamed of Jonathan.

He was…the most determined, hardworking, wonderful man she had ever known. He had spent his life raising his sister. He had experienced a childhood where he had known nothing but abandonment and abuse, and he had turned around and given love to his sister, unconditionally and tirelessly.

And, yeah, maybe it wasn't ideal to announce her physical affair with him at the coffee shop, all things considered, but…whatever she had expected to feel… She didn't.

So, it had been the easiest thing in the world to walk over to their table and say that she really didn't need to keep their relationship a secret. Of course, now both Jonathan and her father were looking at her like she had grown a second head.

When she didn't get a response from either of them, she repeated, "That's not what I want."

"Hayley," Jonathan said, his tone firm. "You don't know what you're saying."

"Oh, please," she returned. "Jonathan, that tone wouldn't work on me in private, and it's not going to work on me here, either."

She took a deep breath, shifting her weight from foot to foot, gazing at her father, waiting for him to say something. He looked… Well, it was very difficult to say if John Thompson could ever really be surprised. In his line of work, he had seen it all, heard it all. While Protestants weren't much for confession, people often used him as a confessional, she knew.

Still, he looked a little surprised to be in this situation.

She searched his face for signs of disappointment. That was her deepest fear. That he would be disappointed in her. Because she had tried, she really had, to be the child Ace wasn't.

Except, as she stood there, she realized that was a steaming pile of bull-pucky. Her behavior wasn't about being what Ace hadn't been. It was all about desperately wanting to please people while at the same time wishing there was a way to please herself. And the fact of the matter was, she couldn't have both those things. Not always.

That contradiction was why she had been hell-bent on running away, less because she wanted to experience the wonders of the world and more because she wanted to go off and do what she wanted without disappointing anyone.

"Jonathan isn't just my boss," she said to her dad. "He's my... Well, I don't really know. But...you know." Her throat tightened, tears burning behind her eyes.

Yes, she wanted to admit to the relationship, and she wanted to live out in the open, but that didn't make the transition from good girl to her own woman any easier.

She wanted to beg her dad for his approval. He wasn't a judgmental man, her father, but he had certainly raised her in a specific fashion, and this was not it. So while he might not condemn her, she knew she wasn't going to get his wholesale approval.

And she would have to live with that.

Living without his approval was hard. Much harder than she had thought it might be. Especially given the fact that she thought she'd accepted it just a few moments ago. But being willing to experience disapproval and truly accepting it were apparently two different things.

"Why don't you have a seat, Hayley," her father said slowly.

"No, thank you," she replied. "I'm going to stand, because if I sit down… Well, I don't know. I have too much energy to sit down. But I—I care about him." She turned to Jonathan. "I care about you. I really do. I'm so sorry I made you feel like you were a dirty secret. Like I was ashamed of you. Because any woman would be proud to be involved with you." She took a deep breath and looked around the coffee shop. "I'm dating him," she said, pointing at Jonathan. "Just so you all know."

"Hayley," her father said, standing up, "come to dinner this week."

"With him?"

"If you want to. But please know that we want to know about your life. Even if it isn't what we would choose for you, we want to know." He didn't mean Jonathan specifically. He meant being in a physical relationship without the benefit of any kind of commitment, much less marriage.

But the way he looked at her, with nothing but love, made her ache all over. Made her throat feel so tight she could scarcely breathe.

She felt miserable. And she felt strong. She wasn't sure which emotion was more prominent. She had seen her father look at Ace like this countless times, had seen him talk about her brother with a similar expression on his face. Her father was loving, and he was as supportive as he could be, but he also had hard lines.

"I guess we'll see," she said.

"I suppose. I also imagine you need to have a talk with him," he said, tilting his head toward Jonathan, who was looking uncertain. She'd never seen Jonathan look uncertain before.

"Oh," she said, "I imagine I do."

"Come home if you need anything."

For some reason, she suddenly became aware of the tension in her father's expression. He was the pastor of Copper Ridge. And the entire town was watching him. So whether he wanted to or not, he couldn't haul off and punch Jonathan. He couldn't yell at her—though he never had yelled in all her life. And he was leaving her to sort out her own circumstances, when she could feel that he very much wanted to stay and sort them out for her.

Maybe Jonathan was right. Maybe she had never put a foot out of line because the rules were easier. There were no rules to what she was doing now, and no one was going to step in and tell her what to do. No one was going to pull her back if she went too far. Not even her father. Maybe that had been her real issue with taking this relationship public. Not so much the disappointment as the loss of a safety net.

Right now, Hayley felt like she was standing on the edge of an abyss. She had no idea how far she might fall, how bad it might hurt when she landed. If she would even survive it.

She was out here, living her potential mistakes, standing on the edge of a lot of potential pain.

Because with the barrier of following the rules removed, with no need to leave to experience things... Well, it was just her. Her heart and what she felt for Jonathan.

There was nothing in the way. No excuses. No false idea that this could never be anything, because she was leaving in the end.

As her father walked out of the coffeehouse, taking with him an entire truckload of her excuses, she realized exactly what she had been protecting herself from.

Falling in love. With Jonathan. With a man who

might never love her back. Wanting more, wanting everything, with the man least likely to give it to her.

She had been hiding behind the secretary desk at the church, listening to everybody else's problems, without ever incurring any of her own. She had witnessed a whole lot of heartbreak, a whole lot of struggle, but she had always been removed from it.

She didn't want to protect herself from this. She didn't want to hide.

"Why did you do that?" Jonathan asked.

"Because you were mad at me yesterday. I hurt your feelings."

He laughed, a dark, humorless sound. "Hayley," he said, "I don't exactly have feelings to hurt."

"That's not true," she said. "I know you do."

"Honey, that stuff was beaten out of me by my father before I was five years old. And whatever was left... It pretty much dissolved when my mother walked away and left me with a wounded sister to care for. That stuff just kind of leaves you numb. All you can do is survive. Work on through life as hard as you can, worry about putting food on the table. Worry about trying to do right by a kid who's had every unfair thing come down on her. You think you being embarrassed to hold my hand in public is going to hurt my feelings after that?"

She hated when he did this. When he drew lines between their levels of experience and made her feel silly.

She closed the distance between them and put her fingertips on his shoulder. Then she leaned in and kissed him, in full view of everybody in the coffeehouse. He put his hand on her hip, and even though he didn't enthusiastically kiss her back, he made no move to end it, either.

"Why do I get the feeling you are a little embarrassed to be with *me*?" she asked, when she pulled away from him.

He arched his brow. "I'm not embarrassed to be with you."

Maybe he wasn't. But there was something bothering him. "You're upset because everyone knows. And now there will be consequences if you do something to hurt me."

"When," he said, his tone uncompromising. "*When* I do something. That's what everyone is thinking. Trust me, Hayley, they don't think for one second that this might end in some fairy-tale wedding bullshit."

Hayley jerked back, trying to fight the feeling that she had just been slapped in the face. For whatever reason, he was trying to elicit exactly that response, and she really didn't want to give it to him. "Fine. Maybe that is what they think. But why does it matter? That's the question, isn't it? Why does what other people think matter more than what you or I might want?

"You were right about me. My choices were less about what other people might think, and more about what might happen to me if I found out I had never actually been reined in." She shook her head. "If I discovered that all along I could have done exactly what I wanted to, with no limit on it. Before now, I never took the chance to find out who I was. I was happy to be told. And I think I've been a little afraid of who I might be beneath all of these expectations."

"Why? Because you might harbor secret fantasies of shoplifting doilies out of the Trading Post?"

"No," Hayley said, "because I might go and get myself hurt. If I had continued working at the church, if I'd kept on gazing at the kind of men I met there from across the room, never making a move because waiting

for them to do it was right, pushing down all of my desires because it was lust I shouldn't feel… I would have
been safe. I wouldn't be sitting here in this coffee shop
with you, shaking because I'm scared, because I'm a little bit turned on thinking about what we did last night."

"I understand the turned on part," he said, his voice
rough like gravel. He lifted his hand, dragging his
thumb over her lower lip. "Why are you afraid?"

"I'm afraid because just like you said… There's a
very low chance of this ending in some fairy-tale wedding…nonsense. And I want all of that." Her chest
seized tight, her throat closing up to a painful degree.
"With you. If you were wondering. And that is… That's
so scary. Because I knew you would look at me like
that if I told you."

His face was flat, his dark eyes blazing. He was…
well, he was angry, rather than indifferent. Somehow,
she had known he would be.

"You shouldn't be afraid of not getting your fairy tale
with me. If anything, you should be relieved. Nobody
wants to stay with me for the rest of their life, Hayley,
trust me. You're supposed to go to Paris. And you're
going to Paris."

"I don't want to go," she said, because she wanted
to stay here, with him. Or take him with her. But she
didn't want to be without him.

"Dammit," he said, his voice like ground-up glass.
"Hayley, you're not going to change your plans because
of me. That would last how long? Maybe a year? Maybe
two if you're really dedicated. But I know exactly how
that ends—with you deciding you would rather be anywhere but stuck in my house, stuck in this town."

"But I don't feel stuck. I never did. It was all…me
being afraid. But the thing is, Jonathan, I never wanted

anything more than I wanted my safety. Thinking I needed to escape was just a response to this missing piece inside of me that I couldn't put a name to. But I know what it is now."

"Don't," he bit out.

"It was you," she said. "All of this time it was you. Don't you see? I never wanted anyone or anything badly enough to take the chance. To take the risk. To expose myself, to step out of line. But you... I do want you that badly."

"Because you were forced to take the risk. You had to own it. Yesterday, you didn't have to, and so you didn't. You pulled away from me when we walked down the street, didn't want anyone to see."

"That wasn't about you. It was about me. It was about the fact that...basically, everybody in town knows I've never dated anybody. So in my case it's a little bit like announcing that I lost my virginity, and it's embarrassing."

Except now she was having this conversation with him in a coffeehouse, where people she knew were sitting only a few feet away, undoubtedly straining to hear her over the sound of the espresso machine. But whatever. She didn't care. For the first time in her life, she really, really didn't care. She cared about him. She cared about this relationship. About doing whatever she needed to do to make him see that everything she was saying was true.

"I'm over it," she added. "I just had to decide that I was. Well, now I have. Because it doesn't get any more horrifying than having to admit that you were having your first affair to your father."

"You see," he said. "I wouldn't know. Nobody was all that invested in me when I lost my virginity, or why.

I was fifteen, if you were curious. So forgive me if your concerns seem foreign to me. It's just that I know how this all plays out. People say they love you, then they punch you in the face. You take care of somebody all of their damn life, and then they take off with the one person you spent all that time protecting them from. Yeah, they say they love you, and then they leave. That's life."

Hayley's chest tightened, her heart squeezing painfully. "I didn't say I loved you."

He looked stricken by that. "Well, good. At least you didn't lie to me."

She did love him, though. But he had introduced the word. Love and its effects were clearly the things that scared him most about what was happening between them.

Love loomed large between them. Love was clearly on the table here. Even if he didn't want it to be, there it was. Even if he was going to deny it, there it was.

Already in his mind, in his heart, whether she said it or not.

She opened her mouth to say it, but it stuck in her throat.

Because he had already decided it would be a lie if she spoke the words. He was so dedicated to that idea. To his story about who Jonathan Bear was, and who he had to be, and how people treated him. His behavior was so very close to what she had been doing for so long.

"Jonathan—"

He cut her off. "I don't love people," he said. "You know what I love? I love things. I love my house. I love my money. I love that company that I've spent so many hours investing in. I love the fact that I own a mountain, and can ride a horse from one end of my land to the other, and get a sense of everything that can never be taken from me. But I'll never love another person, not again." He stood up, gripping her chin with his thumb and forefinger. "Not even you. Because I will never love anything I can't buy right back, do you understand?"

She nodded, swallowing hard. "Yes," she said.

His pain was hemorrhaging from him, bleeding out of every pore, and there was nothing she could do to stop it. He was made of fury, of rage, and he was made of hurt, whether he would admit it or not.

"I think we're done then, Hayley."

He moved away from her, crossing the coffeehouse and walking out the door. Every eye in the room was on her, everybody watching to see what she would do next. So she did the only thing she could.

She stood up and she ran after Jonathan Bear for the entire town to see.

JONATHAN STRODE DOWN the street. The heavy gray sky was starting to crack, raindrops falling onto his head. His shoulders. Good. That was just about perfect.

It took him a few more strides to realize he was headed away from his car, but he couldn't think clearly enough to really grasp where he was going. His head was pounding like horse hooves over the grass, and he couldn't grab hold of a thought to save his life.

"Jonathan!"

He turned, looking down the mostly empty street, to see Hayley running after him, her dark hair flying behind her, rain flying into her face. She was making a spectacle of herself, right here on Main, and she didn't seem to care at all. Something about that made him feel like he'd been turned to stone, rooted to the spot, his heart thundering heavily in his chest.

"Don't run from me," she said, coming to a stop in front of him, breathing hard. "Don't run from us."

"You're the one who's running, honey," he said, keeping his voice deliberately flat.

"We're not done," she said. "We're not going to be done just because you say so. You might be the boss at your house, but you're not the boss here." Her words were jumbled up, fierce and ferocious. "What about what I want?"

He gritted his teeth. "Well, the problem is you made the mistake of assuming I might care what you want."

She sprang forward, pounding a closed fist on his shoulder. The gesture was so aggressive, so very unlike Hayley that it immobilized him. "You do care. You're not a mountain, you're just a man, and you do care. But you're awfully desperate to prove that you don't. You're awfully desperate to prove you have no worth. And I have to wonder why that is."

"I don't have to prove it. Everyone who's ever wandered through my life has proved it, Hayley. You're a little bit late to this party. You're hardly going to take thirty-five years of neglect and make me feel differently about it. Make me come to different conclusions than I've spent the past three decades drawing."

"Why not?" she asked. "That's kind of the point of knowing someone. Of being with them. They change you. You've certainly changed me. You made me...well, more me than I've ever been."

"I never said I needed to change."

"That's ridiculous. Of course you need to change. You live in that big house all by yourself, you're angry at your sister because she figured out how to let something go when you can't. And you're about ready to blow this up—to blow us up—to keep yourself safe."

She shivered, the rain making dark spots on her top, drops rolling down her face.

"There's no reason any of this has to end, Hayley." He gritted his teeth, fighting against the slow, expanding feeling growing in his chest, fighting against the pain starting to push against the back of his eyes. "But you have to accept what I'm willing to give. And it may not be what you want, what you're looking for. If it's not, if that makes you leave, then you're no different from anyone else who's ever come through my life, and you won't be any surprise to me."

Hayley looked stricken by that, pale. And he could see her carefully considering her words. "Wow. That's a very smart way to build yourself an impenetrable fort there, Jonathan. How can anyone demand something of you, if you're determined to equate high expectations with the people who abandoned you? If you're determined to believe that someone asking anything of you is the same as not loving you at all?"

"You haven't said you loved me." His voice was deliberately hard. He didn't know why he was bringing that up again. Didn't know why he was suspended between the desire for her to tell him she didn't, and the need—the intense, soul-shattering need—to hear her say it, even if he could never accept it. Even if he could never return it.

"My mistake," she said, her voice thin. "What will you do if I tell you, Jonathan? Will you say it doesn't matter, that it isn't real? Because you know everything, don't you? Even my heart."

"I know more about the world than you do, little girl," he said, his throat feeling tight for some reason. "Whatever your intentions, I have a better idea of what the actual outcome might be."

She shocked him by taking two steps forward, eliminating the air between them, pressing her hand against his chest. His heart raged beneath her touch, and he had a feeling she could tell.

"I love you." She stared at him for a moment, then she stretched up on her toes and pressed a kiss to his lips. Her lips were slick and cold from the rain, and he wanted to consume her. Wanted to pretend that words didn't matter. That there was nothing but this kiss.

For a moment, a heartbeat, he pretended that was true.

"I love you," she said again, when they parted. "But that doesn't mean I won't expect something from you. In fact, that would be pretty sorry love if I expected to come into your life and change nothing, mean nothing. I want you to love me back, Jonathan. I want you to open yourself up. I want you to let me in. I want you to be brave."

He grabbed hold of her arms, held her against his chest. He didn't give a damn who might see them. "You're telling me to be brave? What have you ever faced down that scared you? Tell me, Hayley."

"You," she said breathlessly.

He released his hold on her and took a step back, swearing violently. "All the more reason you should walk away, I expect."

"Do you know why you scare me, Jonathan? You make me want something I can't control. You make me want something I can't predict. There are no rules for this. There is no safety. Loving you... I have no guarantees. There is no neat map for how this might work out. It's not a math equation, where I can add doing the right things with saying the right things and make you change. You have to decide. You have to choose this.

You have to choose us. The rewards for being afraid, or being good, aren't worth as much as the reward for being brave. So I'm going to be brave.

"I love you. And I want you to love me back. I want you to take a chance—on me."

She was gazing at him, her eyes blazing with light and intensity. How long would it take for that light to dim? How long would it take for him to kill it? How long would it take for her to decide—like everyone else in his life—that he wasn't worth the effort?

It was inevitable. That was how it always ended.

"No," he said, the word scraping his throat raw as it escaped.

"No?" The devastation in her voice cut him like a knife.

"No. But hey, one more for your list," he said, hating himself with every syllable.

"What?"

"You got your kiss in the rain. I did a lot for you, checked off a lot of your boxes. Go find some other man to fill in the rest."

Then he turned and left her standing in the street.

And in front of God and everybody, Jonathan Bear walked away from Hayley Thompson, and left whatever remained of his heart behind with her.

CHAPTER THIRTEEN

THIS WAS HELL. Perhaps even literally. Hayley had wondered about hell a few times, growing up the daughter of a pastor. Now, she thought that if hell were simply living with a broken heart, with the rejection of the person you loved more than anything else echoing in your ears, it would be pretty effective eternal damnation.

She was lying on her couch, tears streaming down her face. She was miserable, and she didn't even want to do anything about it. She just wanted to sit in it.

Oh, she had been so cavalier about the pain that would come when Jonathan ended things. Back in the beginning, when she had been justifying losing her virginity to him, she had been free and easy about the possibility of heartbreak.

But she hadn't loved him then. So she really hadn't known.

Hadn't known that it would be like shards of glass digging into her chest every time she took a breath. Hadn't known that it was actual, physical pain. That her head would throb and her eyes would feel like sandpaper from all the crying.

That her body, and her soul, would feel like they had been twisted, wrung out and draped over a wire to dry in the brutal, unfeeling coastal air.

This was the experience he had talked about. The one that wasn't worth having.

She rolled onto her back, thinking over the past weeks with Jonathan. Going to his house, getting her first job away from the church. How nervous she had been. How fluttery she had felt around him.

Strangely, she felt her lips curve into a smile.

It was hard to reconcile the woman she was now with the girl who had first knocked on his door for that job interview.

She hadn't even realized what all that fluttering meant. What the tightening in her nipples, the pressure between her thighs had meant. She knew now. Desire. Need. Things she would associate with Jonathan for the rest of her life, no matter where she went, no matter who else she might be with.

He'd told her to find someone else.

Right now, the idea of being with another man made her cringe.

She wasn't ready to think about that. She was too raw. And she still wanted him. Only him.

Jonathan was more than an experience.

He had wrenched her open. Pulled her out of the safe space she'd spent so many years hiding in. He had shown her a love that was bigger than fear.

Unfortunately, because that love was so big, the desolation of it was crippling.

She sat up, scrubbing her arm over her eyes. She needed to figure out what she was going to do next.

Something had crystallized for her earlier today, during the encounter with Jonathan and her father. She didn't need to run away. She didn't need to leave town, or gain anonymity, in order to have what she wanted. To be who she wanted.

She didn't need to be the church secretary, didn't need to be perfect or hide what she was doing. She could still go to her father's church on Sunday, and go to dinner at her parents' house on Sunday evening.

She didn't have to abandon her home, her family, her faith. Sure, it might be uncomfortable to unite her family and her need to find herself, but if there was one thing loving Jonathan had taught her, it was that sometimes uncomfortable was worth it.

She wasn't going to let heartbreak stop her.

She thought back to how he had looked at her earlier today, those black eyes impassive as he told her he wouldn't love her back.

Part of her wanted to believe she was right about him. That he was afraid. That he was protecting himself.

Another part of her felt that was a little too hopeful. Maybe that gorgeous, experienced man simply couldn't love his recently-a-virgin assistant.

Except…she had been so certain, during a few small moments, that she had given something to him, too. Just like he had given so much to her.

For some reason, he was dedicated to the idea that nobody stayed. That people looked at him and saw the worst. She couldn't understand why he would find that comforting, and yet a part of him must.

It made her ache. Her heart wasn't broken only for her, but for him, too. For all the love he wouldn't allow himself to accept.

She shook her head. Later. Later she would feel sorry for him. Right now, she was going to wallow in her own pain.

Because at the end of the day, Jonathan had made the choice to turn away from her, to turn away from love.

Right now, she would feel sorry for herself. Then maybe she would plan a trip to Paris.

"Do you want to invite me in?"

Jonathan looked at his sister, standing on the porch, looking deceptively calm.

"Do I have a choice?"

Rebecca shook her head, her long dark hair swinging behind her like a curtain. "Not really. I didn't drive all the way out here to have this conversation with moths buzzing around me."

It was dark out, and just as Rebecca had said, there were bugs fluttering around the porch light near her face.

"Come in, then," he said, moving aside.

She blinked when she stepped over the threshold, a soft smile touching her lips. The scar tissue on the left side of her mouth pulled slightly. Scar tissue that had been given to her by the man she was going to marry. Oh, it had been an accident, and Jonathan knew it. But with all the pain and suffering the accident had caused Rebecca, intent had never much mattered to him.

"This is beautiful, Jonathan," she said, her dark eyes flickering to him. "I haven't been here since it was finished."

He shrugged. "Well, that was your choice."

"You don't like my fiancé. And you haven't made much of an effort to change that. I don't know what you expect from me."

"Appreciation, maybe, for all the years I spent taking care of you?" He wanted to cut his own balls off for saying that. Basically, right about now he wanted to escape his own skin. He was a bastard. Even he thought so.

He was sitting in his misery now, existing fully in the knowledge of the pain he had caused Hayley.

He should never have had that much power over her. He never should have touched her. This misery was the only possible way it could have turned out. His only real defense was that he hadn't imagined a woman like Hayley would ever fall in love with a man like him.

"Right. Because we've never had that discussion."

His sister's tone was dry, and he could tell she was pretty unimpressed with him. Well, fair enough. He was unimpressed with himself.

"I still don't understand why you love him, Rebecca. I really don't."

"What is love to you, Jonathan?"

An image of Hayley's face swam before his mind's eye. "What the hell kind of question is that?"

"A relevant one," she said. "I think. Particularly when we get down to why exactly I'm here. Congratulations. After spending most of your life avoiding being part of the rumor mill, you're officially hot small-town gossip."

"Am I?" He wasn't very surprised to hear that.

"Something about kissing the pastor's daughter on Main Street in the rain. And having a fight with her."

"That's accurate."

"What's going on?"

"What it looks like. I was sleeping with her. We had a fight. Now we're not sleeping together."

Rebecca tilted her head to the side. "I feel like I'm missing some information."

"Hayley was working for me—I assume you knew that."

"Vaguely," she said, her eyes glittering with curiosity.

"And I'm an asshole. So when I found out my assistant was a virgin, I figured I would help her with that." It was a lie, but one he was comfortable with. He was comfortable painting himself as the villain. Everybody would, anyway. So why not add his own embellishment to the tale.

"Right," Rebecca said, sarcasm dripping from her voice. "Because you're a known seducer of innocent women."

Jonathan turned away, running his hand over his hair. "I'm not the nicest guy, Rebecca. We all know that."

"I know *you* think that," Rebecca said. "And I know we've had our differences. But when I needed you, you were there for me. Always. Even when Gage broke my heart, and you couldn't understand why it mattered, why I wanted to be with him, in the end, you supported me. Always. Every day of my life. I don't even remember my father. I remember you. You taught me how to ride a bike, how to ride a horse. You fought for me, tirelessly. Worked for me. You don't think I don't know how tired you were? How much you put into making our home…a home? Bad men don't do that. Bad men hit their wives, hit their children. Abandon their daughters. Our fathers were bad men, Jonathan. But you never were."

Something about those words struck him square in the chest. Their fathers *were* bad men.

He had always known that.

But he had always believed somewhere deep down that he must be bad, too. Not because he thought being an abusive bastard was hereditary. But because if his father had beaten him, and his mother had left him, there must be something about him that was bad.

Something visible. Something that the whole town could see.

He thought back to all the kindness on Pastor John Thompson's face, kindness Jonathan certainly hadn't deserved from the old man when he was doing his absolute damnedest to start a fight in the middle of The Grind.

He had been so determined to have John confirm that Jonathan was bad. That he was wrong.

Because there was something freeing about the anger that belief created deep inside his soul.

It had been fuel. All his life that belief had been his fuel. Gave him something to fight against. Something to be angry about.

An excuse to never get close to anyone.

Because underneath all the anger was nothing but despair. Despair because his parents had left him, because they couldn't love him enough. Because he wasn't worth…anything.

His need for love had never gone away, but he'd shoved it down deep. Easier to do when you had convinced yourself you could never have it.

He looked at Rebecca and realized he had despaired over her, too. When she had chosen Gage. Jonathan had decided it was just one more person who loved him and didn't want to stay.

Yeah, it was much easier, much less painful to believe that he was bad. Because it let him keep his distance from the pain. Because it meant he didn't have to try.

"What do you think love is?" Rebecca asked again, more persistent this time.

He didn't have an answer. Not one with words. All he had were images, feelings. Watching Rebecca sleep after a particularly hard day. Praying child services wouldn't come by to check on her while he was at work, and find her alone and him negligent.

And Hayley. Her soft hands on his body, her sweet surrender. The trust it represented. The way she made him feel. Like he was on fire, burning up from the inside out. Like he could happily stay for the rest of his life in a one-room cabin, without any of the money or power he had acquired over the past few years, and be perfectly content.

The problem was, he couldn't make her stay with him.

This house, his company, those things were his. In a way that Hayley could never be. In a way that no one ever could be.

People were always able to leave.

He felt like a petulant child even having that thought. But he didn't know how the hell else he could feel secure. And he didn't think he could stand having another person walk away.

"I don't know," he said.

Rebecca shook her head, her expression sad. "That's a damn shame, Jonathan, because you show me love all the time. Whether you know what to call it or not, you've given it to me tirelessly over the years, and without you, without it, I don't know where I would be. You stayed with me when everybody else left."

"But who stayed with me?" he asked, feeling like an ass for even voicing that question. "You had to stay. I had to take care of you. But the minute you could go out on your own you did."

"Because that's what your love did for me, you idiot."

"Not very well. Because you were always worried I thought of you as a burden, weren't you? It almost ruined your relationship with Gage, if I recall correctly."

"Yes," she said, "but that wasn't about you. That was my baggage. And you did everything in your power to help me, even when you knew the result would be me going back to Gage. That's love, Jonathan." She shook her head. "I love you, too. I love you enough to want you to have your own life, one that doesn't revolve around taking care of me. That doesn't revolve around what happened to us in the past."

He looked around the room, at the house that meant so much to him. A symbol of security, of his ability to care for Rebecca, if her relationship went to hell. And he realized that creating this security for her somehow enabled him to deny his own weaknesses. His own fears.

This house had only ever been for him. A fortress to barricade himself in.

Wasn't that what Hayley had accused him of? Building himself a perfect fortress to hide in?

If everybody hated him, he didn't have to try. If there was something wrong with him, he never had to do what was right. If all he loved were things, he never had to risk loss.

They were lies. Lies he told himself because he was a coward.

And it had taken a virginal church secretary to uncover the truth.

She had stood in front of him and said she wanted love more than she wanted to be safe. And he had turned her down.

He was afraid. Had been all his life. But before this very moment, he would have rather cut out his own heart than admit it.

But now, standing with his sister looking at him like he was the saddest damn thing she'd ever seen, a hole opened in his chest. A hole Hayley had filled.

"But doesn't it scare you?" he asked, his voice rough. "What if he leaves?"

She reached out, putting her hand on his. "It would break my heart. But I would be okay. I would have you.

And I would…still be more whole than I was before I loved him. That's the thing about love. It doesn't make you weak, Jonathan, it makes you stronger. Opening yourself up, letting people in…that makes your life bigger. It makes your life richer. Maybe it's a cliché, but from where I'm standing you need to hear the cliché. You need to start believing it."

"I don't understand why she would want to be with me," Jonathan said. "She's…sweet. And she's never been hurt. I'm…well, I'm a mess. That's not what she deserves. She deserves to have a man who's in mint condition, like she is."

"But that's not how love works. If love made sense, if it was perfectly fair, then Gage West would not have been the man for me. He was the last man on earth I should have wanted, Jonathan. Nobody knows that more than me, and him. It took a miracle for me to let go of all my anger and love him. At the same time… I couldn't help myself.

"Love is strange that way. You fall into it whether you want to or not. Then the real fight is figuring out how to live it. How to become the person you need to be so you can hold on to that love. But I'm willing to bet you are the man she needs. Not some mint condition, new-in-the-box guy. But a strong man who has proved, time and time again, that no matter how hard life is, no matter how intensely the storm rages, he'll be there for you. And more than that, he'll throw his body over yours to protect you if it comes to that. That's what I see when I look at you, Jonathan. What's it going to take for you to see that in yourself?"

"I don't think I'm ever going to," he said slowly, imagining Hayley again, picturing her as she stared up at him on the street. Fury, hurt, love shining from her eyes. "But…if she sees it…"

"That's a start," Rebecca said. "As long as you don't let her get away. As long as you don't push her away."

"It's too late for that. She's probably not going to want to see me again. She's probably not going to want me back."

"Well, you won't know unless you ask." Rebecca took a deep breath. "The best thing about love is it has the capacity to forgive on a pretty incredible level. But if there's one thing you and I both know, it's that it's hard to forgive someone leaving. Don't make that the story. Go back. Ask for forgiveness. Change what needs to be changed. Mostly…love her. The rest kind of takes care of itself."

CHAPTER FOURTEEN

HAYLEY HAD JUST settled back onto her couch for more quality sitting and weeping when she heard a knock at her door.

She stood up, brushing potato chip crumbs off her pajamas and grimacing. Maybe it was Cassie, bringing up baked goods. The other woman had done that earlier; maybe now she was bringing more. Hayley could only hope.

She had a gaping wound in her chest that could be only temporarily soothed by butter.

Without bothering to fix her hair—which was on top of her head in a messy knot—she jerked the door open.

And there he was. Dark eyes glittering, gorgeous mouth pressed into a thin line. His dark hair tied back low on his neck, the way she was accustomed to seeing him during the day.

Her heart lurched up into her throat, trying to make a break for it.

She hadn't been expecting him, but she imagined expecting him wouldn't have helped. Jonathan Bear wasn't someone you could anticipate.

"What are you doing here?"

He looked around. "I came here to talk to you. Were you…expecting someone else?"

"Yes. A French male prostitute." He lifted his brows. "Well, you told me to find another man to tick my boxes."

"I think you mean a gigolo."

"I don't know what they're called," she said, exasperated.

The corner of his mouth twitched. "Well, I promise to be quick. I won't interrupt your sex date."

She stepped to the side, ignoring the way her whole body hurt as she did. "I don't have a sex date." She cleared her throat. "Just so you know."

"Somehow, I didn't think you did."

"You don't know me," she grumbled, turning away from him, pressing her hand to her chest to see if her heart was beating as hard and fast as she felt like it was.

It was.

"I do, Hayley. I know you pretty damn well. Maybe better than I know myself. And…I think you might know me better than I know myself, too." He sounded different. Sad. Tired.

She turned around to face him, and with his expression more fully illuminated by the light, she saw weariness written there. Exhaustion.

"For all the good it did me," she said, crossing her arms tightly in a bid to protect herself. Really, though, it was too late. There wasn't anything left to protect. He had shattered her irrevocably.

"Yeah, well. It did me a hell of a lot of good. At least, I hope it's going to. I hope I'm not too late."

"Too late for what? To stick the knife in again or…?"

"To tell you I love you," he said.

Everything froze inside her. Absolutely everything. The air in her lungs, her heart, the blood in her veins.

"You…you just said… Don't tease me, Jonathan. Don't play with me. I know I'm younger than you. I know that I'm innocent. But if you came back here to lie to me, to say what you think I need to hear so you can…keep having me in your bed, or whatever—"

Suddenly, she found herself being hauled forward into his arms, against his chest. "I do want you in my bed," he said, "make no mistake about that. But sex is just sex, Hayley, even when it's good. And what we have is good.

"But here's something you don't know, because you don't have experience with it. Sex isn't love. And it doesn't feel like this. I feel…like everything in me is broken and stronger at the same time, and I don't know how in the hell that can be true. And when you told me you loved me… I knew I could either let go of everything in the past or hold on to it harder to protect myself." He shook his head. "I protected myself."

"Yeah, well. What about protecting me?"

"I thought maybe I was protecting you, too. But it's all tangled up in this big lie that I've been telling myself for years. I told you I didn't love people, that I love things. But I said that only because I've had way too much experience with people I love leaving. A house can't walk away, Hayley. A mountain can't up and abandon you. But you could.

"One day, you could wake up and regret that you tied your future to me. When you could have done better… When you could have had a man who wasn't so damn broken." He cupped her cheek, bent down and kissed her lips. "What did I do to earn the love of someone like you? Someone so beautiful…so soft. You're everything I'm not, Hayley Thompson, and all the reasons I love you make perfect sense to me. But why do you love me? That's what I can't quite figure out."

Hayley looked into his eyes, so full of pain, so deeply wounded. She would have never thought a man like him would need reassurance from anyone, least of all a woman like her.

"I know I don't have a lot of experience, Jonathan. Well, any experience apart from you. I know that I haven't seen the whole world. I haven't even seen the whole state. But I've seen your heart. The kind of man you are. The change that knowing you, loving you, created in me. And I know…perfect love casts out all fear.

"I can't say I haven't been afraid these past couple of days. Afraid I couldn't be with you. That things might not work out with us. But when I stood on Main Street… I knew fear couldn't be allowed to win. It was your love that brought me to that conclusion. Your love was bigger than the fear inside me. I don't need experience to understand that. I don't need to travel the world or date other men for the sake of experience. I need you. Because whether or not you're perfect, you're perfect for me."

"*You're* perfect," he said, his voice rough. "So damned perfect. I want…to take you to Canada."

She blinked. "Well. That's not exactly an offer to run off to Vegas."

"You want to use your passport. Why wait? Let's go now. Your boss will let you off. I'm sure of it."

Something giddy bubbled up in her chest. Something wonderful. "Right now? Really?"

"Right the hell now."

"Yes," she said. "Yes, let's go to Canada."

"It's not the Eiffel Tower," he said, "but I will take you there someday. I promise you that."

"The only thing I need is you," she said. "The rest is negotiable."

His lips crashed down on hers, his kiss desperate and intense, saying the deep, poetic things she doubted her stoic cowboy would ever say out loud. But that was okay. The kiss said plenty all on its own.

EPILOGUE

JONATHAN HATED WEARING a suit. He'd never done it before, but he had come to a swift and decisive conclusion the moment he'd finished doing up his tie.

Hayley was standing in their bedroom, looking amused. The ring on her left hand glittered as bright as her eyes, and suddenly, it wasn't the tie that was strangling him. It was just her. The love on her beautiful face. The fact she loved him.

He still hadn't quite figured out why. Still wasn't sure he saw all the things in himself that Rebecca had spoken of that day, all the things Hayley talked about when she said she loved him.

But Hayley did love him. And that was a gift he cherished.

"You're not going to make me wear a suit when we do this, are you?" he asked.

"I might," she said. "You look really hot in a suit."

He wrapped his arm around her waist and pulled her to his chest. "You look hottest in nothing at all. Think we could compromise?"

"We've created enough scandal already without me showing up naked to my wedding. Anyway, I'm wearing white. I am a traditional girl, after all."

"Honey, you oughta wear red."

"Are you calling me a scarlet woman?"

He nodded. "Yes, and I think you proved your status earlier this morning."

She blushed. She still blushed, even after being with him for six months. Blushed in bed, when he whispered dirty things into her ear. He loved it.

He loved *her*.

He couldn't wait to be her husband, and that was something he hadn't imagined ever feeling. Looking forward to being a husband.

Of course, he was looking forward to the honeymoon even more. To staying in a little apartment in Paris with a view of the Eiffel Tower.

For him, trading in a view of the mountains for a view of the city didn't hold much appeal. But she wanted it. And the joy he got from giving Hayley what she wanted was the biggest thing in his world.

Waiting to surprise her with the trip was damn near killing him.

"You have to hurry," she said, pushing at his shoulder. "You're giving the bride away, after all."

Jonathan took a deep breath. Yeah, it was time. Time to give his sister to that Gage West, who would never deserve her, but who loved her, so Jonathan was willing to let it go. Willing to give them his blessing.

Actually, over the past few months he'd gotten kind of attached to the bastard who would be his brother-in-law. Something he'd thought would never be possible only a little while ago.

But love changed you. Rebecca had been right about that.

"All right," he said. "Let's go then."

Hayley kissed his cheek and took his hand, leading him out of the bedroom and down the stairs. The wedding guests were out on the back lawn, waiting for the event to start. When he and Hayley exited the house, they all turned to look.

He and Hayley still turned heads, and he had a feeling they always would.

Jonathan Bear had always been seen as a bad boy. In all the ways that phrase applied. The kind of boy no parent wanted their daughter to bring home to Sunday dinner. And yet the pastor's daughter had.

He'd definitely started out that way. But somehow, through some miracle, he'd earned the love of a good woman.

And because of her love, he was determined to be the best man he could possibly be.

* * * * *

Joshua Grayson looked out the window of his office and did
not feel the kind of calm he ought to feel.

He'd moved back to Copper Ridge six months ago from
Seattle, happily trading in a man-made, rectangular skyline
for the natural curve of the mountains.

But right now he doubted anything would decrease the
tension he was feeling from dealing with the fallout of his
father's ridiculous ad. Another attempt by the old man to
make Joshua live the life his father wanted him to.

The only kind of life his father considered successful: a
wife, children.

He couldn't understand why Joshua didn't want the same.

No. That kind of life was for another man, one with
another past and another future. It was not for Joshua. And
that was why he was going to teach his father a lesson.

He wasn't responsible for the ad in a national paper
asking for a wife, till death do them part. But an unsuitable,
temporary wife? Yes. That had been his ad.

He was going to win the game. Once and for all. And the woman he hoped would be his trump card was on her way.

The doorbell rang and he stood up behind his desk. She was here. And she was—he checked his watch—late.

A half smile curved his lips.

Perfect.

He took the stairs two at a time. He was impatient to meet his temporary bride. Impatient to get this plan started so it could end.

He strode across the entryway and jerked the door open. And froze.

The woman standing on his porch was small. And young, just as he'd expected, but… She wore no makeup, which made her look like a damned teenager. Her features were fine and pointed; her dark brown hair hung lank beneath a ragged beanie that looked like it was in the process of unraveling while it sat on her head.

He didn't bother to linger over the rest of the details—her threadbare sweater with too-long sleeves, her tragic skinny jeans—because he was stopped, immobilized really, by the tiny bundle in her arms.

A baby.

His prospective bride had come with a baby.

Well, hell.

Don't miss
CLAIM ME, COWBOY
by New York Times *bestselling author Maisey Yates,*
part of her **COPPER RIDGE** *series!*

Available April 2018 wherever
Harlequin® Desire books and ebooks are sold.

www.Harlequin.com

HDEXP0318

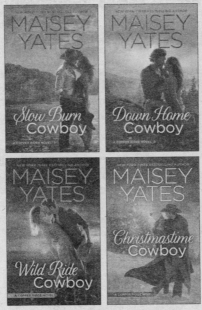

Get 2 Free Books,
Plus 2 Free Gifts—
just for trying the
Reader Service!

HARLEQUIN®
Romance